ALSO BY BUZZY JACKSON

The Inspirational Atheist:
Wise Words on the Wonder and Meaning of Life

Shaking the Family Tree:
Blue Bloods, Black Sheep, and Other Obsessions
of an Accidental Genealogist

A Bad Woman Feeling Good:
Blues and the Women Who Sing Them

TO DIE BEAUTIFUL

A Novel

Buzzy Jackson

DUTTON

DUTTON

An imprint of Penguin Random House LLC
penguinrandomhouse.com

LIBRARY OF CONGRESS CATALOGING-IN-PUBLICATION DATA

Names: Jackson, Buzzy, author.
Title: To die beautiful: a novel / Buzzy Jackson.
Description: New York: Dutton, [2023]
Identifiers: LCCN 2022020456 | ISBN 9780593187210 (hardcover) |
ISBN 9780593187227 (ebook)
Subjects: LCSH: Schaft, Hannie, 1920–1945—Fiction. |
World War, 1939–1945—Collaborationists—Netherlands—Fiction. |
World War, 1939–1945—Underground movements—Netherlands—Fiction. |
Netherlands—History—German occupation, 1940–1945. |
LCGFT: Historical fiction. | Novels.
Classification: LCC PS3610.A3454 T6 2023 | DDC 813/.6—dc23/eng/20220711
LC record available at https://lccn.loc.gov/2022020456

Printed in the United States of America
1st Printing

BOOK DESIGN BY KATY RIEGEL

I spent five years sitting next to her in class. She was very quiet, never joined in, and did not attend school parties. She never laughed and rarely smiled. But then, one time, somebody teased her. She reacted very fiercely. And that's when I realized: if you mess with this kitten, you better wear gloves.

—Cornelius Mol,
on his high school classmate Hannie Schaft

I have a lot of respect for pacifists. I don't mean people who just profess to love peace. I mean those who stand up for their beliefs, because the world is currently drunk on war.

—Hannie Schaft,
excerpted from her high school essay "People I Admire"

We would be starting a kind of secret army . . . and we were the only girls.

—Freddie Oversteegen,
on joining the Dutch Resistance at age fourteen with her sister, Truus

Contents

Historical Note

NAZI GERMANY INVADED the neutral Netherlands on 10 May 1940, destroying much of the historic city of Rotterdam in a blitzkrieg attack, and took power five days later. The fanatically antisemitic Austrian Arthur Seyss-Inquart, who had colluded with Adolf Hitler in the Anschluss and Kristallnacht in 1938, was then appointed Reichskommissar (Reich commissioner) of the Netherlands, setting in motion the terror to come.

Anne Frank is the most famous victim of the Dutch Holocaust. Her story—resisting, hiding, betrayal, murder—was not unusual. More Jews were killed in the Netherlands than in any other Nazi-occupied European country: an estimated 75 percent (approximately 102,000 individuals) did not survive the war. To explain these numbers, survivors and historians have argued that the flat, densely populated geography of the Netherlands made it a difficult place in which to hide; there were no vast forests or mountain ranges into which one might disappear. Another factor in the Dutch experience might have been the relatively slow implementation of anti-Jewish measures by the Nazis in the Netherlands, which delayed the development of the Resistance movement.

Yet the Netherlands was also the site of the remarkable February strike of 1941, the first and only mass protest by non-Jews against anti-semitic Nazi policies in Europe. Organized by the Dutch Communist Party, approximately three hundred thousand Dutch citizens mounted a huge nationwide general strike and demonstrations for three days, until it was violently put down by the Nazi occupiers and dozens of the movement's organizers were killed.

As the war went on, Dutch citizens engaged in forms of passive resistance such as displaying the national color, orange; reading contraband Resistance newspapers; and listening to Radio Oranje, the London-based radio programs of the exiled Dutch government. Among the general population of the Netherlands, approximately 5 percent are estimated to have openly collaborated with the Nazis. It is estimated that another 5 percent of the Dutch population participated in active resistance by sheltering Jews, spying on the Germans for the Allies, or taking up arms in direct confrontation with the Nazi occupiers. Of these armed resisters, only a few were women.

TO DIE BEAUTIFUL

Prologue

1945
Amstelveenseweg Prison, Amsterdam

YOU CAN WALK right past your fate your whole life without seeing it, but prisons are inconspicuous by design. The Amstelveenseweg prison occupies an entire city block, hewn out of slabs of pitted gray stone like something built for a pharaoh. I must have seen the building a thousand times on my way to the university. Yet none of this is familiar.

As I'm escorted into the central atrium, the air cools, the acoustics sharpen. Low whispers echo off soaring steel beams. If there are male captives here, I don't see them. Instead, women of all ages, from lanky teenagers to the hunched and elderly, are grouped by twos and threes in their cells, talking or praying, trying to sleep.

Heads snap up when I pass by, and I feel their eyes on me from behind. That's when the murmurs begin. The guards on either side of me tighten their grip, greedy fingers fanged around my upper arms.

"Mach," the guard says. Keep going.

We do, but the whispering slips past us like an incoming fog, rushing ahead into the hundreds of tiny, cold cells stacked four stories high. With each step I take, the sound grows stronger, thicker, louder.

The shuffle of women moving to the bars of their cells to watch. The clang of a shaken cell door, metal banging on metal. Something is growing. Somewhere high above me I hear clapping . . .

"Ruhe!" a guard above us says. Silence.

There is silence, for a moment. Then, across the atrium on another floor, two inspired souls let out a low whoop. The fog unfurls itself everywhere, swirling around us in the quietest of uproars, a floating, growing mist of righteousness. The sound of hope. Even here, in this place.

By the time I reach the end of the walkway, the women are greeting me by name.

Hannie, Hannie. Het meisje met het rode haar. Hannie Schaft.

The Girl with Red Hair. Hannie.

I don't acknowledge them.

When I pass the last cell, I pause to look inside. An older woman with deep-socketed eyes and long, uncombed hair rests on a cot, one knobby shoulder against the cell's cold wall for support. Her skin is ashen, and with her eyes closed she looks dead. They slowly open.

She sees me. I see her. Somehow, this corpse lifts her claw of a trembling hand. I've never met her, but I know her.

Too weak to stand, she raises one bony fist in salute.

"Verzet!" she whispers.

Resist.

I intend to.

Part One

OZO

1940–1943
Amsterdam

Chapter 1

Autumn 1940

I WASN'T ALWAYS AN only child.

Sitting on the chipped sink before me, the silver bird waits, frozen in flight, a silhouette like a bomber plane with two wings outstretched, tail swirling into a flirtatious spiral. A sparrow. I'd tried it on the last time I went to a music concert. Months ago.

It was Annie's pin, of course. Father gave it her after the real sparrow flew away. I was young, about four at the time, so Annie was nine. It had been after midnight, and I was asleep when Annie poked me in the arm.

"JOHANNA, LOOK." HOLDING a candle in one hand, she pointed with the other to the floor beside the bed we shared. There stood a small brown-and-gray bird, his head cocked to look at us as if listening to Annie's words. He peeped. I gasped and Annie threw her hand across me. "Shh!"

"Let him fly out the window," I said.

"I tried," she said. "But he flew right back in."

I didn't believe her. Peering over my sister's shoulder, I watched the ball of fluff bob and strut, his tiny claws a whisper on the floorboards. He finally fluttered up to the open window and flung himself outside. "See?" I said. "He's gone."

But half a second later the bird was back at the window, flapping against the glass in a zigzag panic before slipping inside, landing, then hopping to his chosen spot on the floor beside our bed. He peeped at us again.

"What do we do with him?" I asked.

"We keep him," Annie said. Annie always knew the answer.

We did keep him, for a while. When he finally flew away for good, Father gave Annie the silver bird pin, a hand-me-down from our oma. I was jealous, but it made sense: Annie was sparrowlike in her energy, her spark, her curiosity. They said Oma had been like that, too. A few months later, Father gave me my own pin: a small silver fox. It was brand-new.

"Mijn kleine vos," he said, "for you." My little fox.

"But I didn't find a fox," I said, confused. "Annie found a bird."

He laughed. "Your red hair, silly." He picked me up and buried his face in my curls.

It was the first time I understood that there was a difference between who I knew I was, on the inside, and who other people thought I must be.

JUST PIN THE damn thing on. I snatched the sparrow from the edge of the sink and poked its pin through the double-ply wool of my coat's lapel, instantly piercing my thumb on the other side. "Damn it."

"This is why they warn innocent young girls about the evil big city," said Nellie. "She's swearing like a pirate already." She and Eva tumbled through the door of the attic apartment we shared, laughing.

"Damn it, damn it." I'd tried to remove the brooch with my bleeding thumb and now the camel-colored wool was stained. I thrust it under the tap.

"Here, let me," said Eva, the mother of our group. The three of us had gone through school together in Haarlem, though we hadn't been close. They'd picked me because they knew me: the shy girl who did as much extra credit work as the teacher would give her; the girl who wore two sweaters on a spring day because her mother was sure she'd die of the common cold. I wasn't the type to cause trouble.

"My, where did this come from?" Nellie held up the pin, glinting in the low light. "It's pretty."

"My sister," I said, grabbing it back. "Thanks, I've got to get going, I'm late."

"Sorry," said Nellie.

"It's fine, I'm just late," I said, already out on the landing and headed down the narrow stairs. My cheeks flamed and my lashes were wet. Annie had been dead thirteen years now. Stupid sparrow.

I WAS AN expert at being nobody. I'd practiced it for years. So that evening I took my place in the university's grand ballroom in the spot I always felt safest: the back of the room. I made sure to take a glass of seltzer when it was offered to me, to have something to do with my hands. I sipped it while the room filled with university students, their conversations humming around me. The girls on the entertainment committee of the AVSV, the Amsterdam Female Student Association, flocked by the entrance with their bright dresses and musical voices. They welcomed everyone inside, especially the boys, whose arms and shoulders they touched as they talked. Sometimes they even hugged the boys and kissed them on the cheek. What did it feel like to be so relaxed with boys? Was I supposed to call them men? They seemed so boyish.

"'Scuse me," said one now, a male student backing into me as he searched for his companions.

"Excuse you," I agreed. Like baby giants, these young men, trampling on the world around them.

"Can I have a light?"

I flinched, annoyed. But it was a young woman about my age.

"Didn't mean to scare you," she said.

She was taller than me by several inches, which made her about five foot seven, but her presence was so grand she seemed even taller. Glossy brown-black hair fell to her bare shoulders in waves, the midnight darkness of her hair contrasting with the pale blue sky of her crinoline party dress. Her eyes were amber, with long, curled lashes and a surprisingly innocent gaze. Her lips were painted a tropical coral pink. She looked like a movie star. With my beige skirt and plain white blouse, I was surprised she'd even noticed me. She kept smiling. She blinked.

"Sorry," I said. "I don't have one." I really was sorry because I didn't want her to walk away yet. I'd tried smoking; it made me cough. But now I made a mental note to try again. It might make moments like this easier.

"What, a light?" she said. "Or a cigarette?"

"Either," I said, then corrected myself: "Neither."

She laughed, a chiming giggle that was friendly, not mean. "Philine! Over here." She waved at another dark-haired girl weaving her way through the crowd. This new girl, Philine, was a bit taller than me and slightly less of a spectacle than her friend. She was pretty, but in a more approachable way. Brown hair, brown eyes, a relaxed smile. Her dress looked as if it had been taken in and let out a few times at the hem, following the fashion. Mine had, too. Like her friend, Philine carried herself with a natural confidence. I could picture both of them on a movie screen. I, on the other hand, might be eligible to audition for the heroine's plain but intelligent friend. The sensible one.

"Why are you hiding back here, Sonja?" Philine asked her friend. "Trying to escape your suitors?"

"Something like that," Sonja said. "I thought members of the AVSV were supposed to look out for each other, but this one won't give me a light." She winked at me. My face flamed with embarrassment. I was twenty; I should have learned how to smoke by now.

Philine smiled at me. "I'm Philine. What's your name?"

"Hannie," I said, shocking myself. Everyone had always called me Johanna or Jo, but I had been contemplating giving myself a new identity when I started at the University of Amsterdam a year earlier. I hadn't actually tried it until now. The name seemed pretentious. Too bold. And I wasn't sure I'd really earned the right to think of myself as a different person.

"Hannie," she said, accepting my name without a blink. Like anyone would. Mother always said I thought too much.

Philine shook my hand. "And you've already met Princess Sonja." My eyes widened. "She's not a real princess," Philine said, smiling and still clasping my hand.

"Well, I am related to the Habsburgs on my mother's side," said Sonja with a hint of pride.

"I'll believe it when you marry a prince," said Philine. "What about you? Are you a princess? Or just a normal boring law student like us?"

I beamed back at them. They were so smart and pretty and bursting with energy, and I was desperate to keep talking to them. I'd hoped to make more friends at university than I had in high school, but I was making the same mistakes all over again, turning down invitations for coffee by claiming I had too much homework to do. I didn't have more than anybody else, but the thought of socializing with strangers made my palms sweat. They were damp now. I was only at this party because I'd made a vow earlier in the week to go and stay for at least thirty minutes. There were eight more to go.

"Just a boring law student," I said, feeling a bit more relaxed in the sunny presence of these two. How novel. "I'm from Haarlem."

"Lovely," said Philine.

"Never been," said Sonja.

"Sonja!" said Philine.

"What?"

"You've been to Paris and Rome, but you've never been to Haarlem? It's ten miles away."

"Well, Paris has the Louvre and Rome has the Colosseum. What does Haarlem have?"

"Sonja!" Philine slapped her on the hand.

"Sorry, sorry," Sonja said, turning to me. "I'm sure it's lovely. I'll go this weekend."

"No, you won't." Philine turned to me, too. "You can see why we call her Princess."

"Princess?" a deep voice interrupted our circle as a tall young blond man in a pressed navy suit approached us. "Sonja? Here you are. I've been looking for you."

Hair smoothly groomed, a confident smile, he was the kind of hand-some that made me nervous. Too good-looking. Too sure of himself. I avoided men like him because how would I ever speak to them? Fortu-nately, in Sonja's presence, Philine and I seemed to be invisible.

"Piet!" Sonja cried, draping her elegant arms around him in the same casual yet flirty hug the entertainment committee girls had perfected. She looked so natural. "How have you been?"

Piet's square jaw softened into a broad smile, relaxed and happy like a boy watching his birthday cake arrive. "I waited for you at the library yesterday," he said.

"Did you?" Sonja whispered something into his ear, and his eyes went wide with delight. I tried to imagine what one could say to get that effect but came up with nothing. She pulled herself away from his arms and introduced us. "Piet, you know Philine."

He nodded and took Philine's hand and kissed it with exaggerated formality. She curtsied, playing along.

"And this is our friend Hannah."

"Hannie," Philine corrected her.

"Hannie." Piet reached for my hand and I jerked it back, afraid he would kiss it, too. He looked abashed.

"Sorry," he said, checking to see if he'd offended Sonja.

"No, I am," I said, embarrassed and irritated at myself.

"What have you done to the poor girl?" Sonja said, teasing him. I knew it was all a joke, yet I felt a stab of gratification, watching her defend me. "Do you know, Piet, we were just about to leave," Sonja said. "But I'm so glad I saw you before we did." She kissed him on the cheek, leaving a perfect pink rosebud, and then grabbed one of Philine's hands and one of mine. "We have to get Hannie home," she said, pulling us toward the exit. "She's got a big day tomorrow. She's being honored by the queen."

Piet's confidence faded. "But the dance just started," he said.

"I know, but . . ." Sonja skipped faster, as if pulled by gravity toward the door against her will. "It's the queen." She blew him a kiss and dragged us past the AVSV girls ringing the doorway, who stared at her as she left, not entirely sorry to see this starlet go.

"Coats!" said Philine, turning and pulling us with her with a crack-the-whip effect. Sonja shrieked and I went sliding across the tiled floor to the coat check. We scurried out the door and to the courtyard and finally stopped, laughing at our silly adventure.

"Who was that?" Philine said.

Sonja rolled her eyes. "Pieter Hauer. I've been avoiding him for weeks."

"He seems nice," said Philine. "And good-looking."

Sonja looked at me. "What did you think?"

I tried to think of a clever thing to say about her suitor but failed. It was easier to just tell the truth. "I didn't like him much."

"Ha!" Sonja hugged me. "I knew you were a good one," she said. "Even if you won't give me a light."

"What's that?" Philine watched me fussing with my coat. I'd pinned Annie's brooch on top. "Pretty," she said, leaning in. "Is it a starling?"

"A sparrow," I said.

"Just like you," said Sonja with a generous smile, "sweet and plucky. See, this is what I was saying the other day," she said to Philine. "I'm so bored by these social mixers. We need to expand our circle. I was just saying that! And then Hannie appeared. Like a little sparrow."

I stood between them, mute with shock but encouraged. Sonja touched a lock of my hair, petting me. "I would die for hair like this."

"This?" I put my hand to my head and pulled a strand of my bright red hair straight. It bounced back into a curl when I let it go. My father's kleine vos—and my curse. Just ask any of the kids who teased me about the color growing up.

"Remember when you peroxided your hair?" said Philine to Sonja with a grimace.

"Ugh, cockroach brown. But this," Sonja said, rearranging one of my ringlets so it fell across one eye, "you have to be born with it. It's your glory."

I'd received more compliments in the past ten minutes than in the previous twenty years of my life, or at least it felt that way. I always blushed easily, and now my face was bright pink with embarrassment. And happiness.

"Let's go to your house and listen to records," Philine said to Sonja.

"Don't believe her," said Sonja, dropping her voice to a conspiratorial whisper. "We go to my house to tune in to Radio Oranje and drink wine."

Me, go with them, two glamorous big-city girls listening to Resistance radio from London? I thought Nellie and I were the only students who regularly tuned in for our exiled queen's nightly update. And drinking?

I wasn't sure how it happened, but these girls were interested in me. They didn't know I was a timid little fox who spent her nights alone, thinking and dreaming. They thought I was a sparrow, bold and "plucky." Best of all, to them I was simply Hannie.

And thanks to Sonja and Philine, all those things became true.

Chapter 2

Winter 1941

I MIGHT NEVER HAVE joined the Resistance if I hadn't gotten my period that Tuesday morning. Waking up, I saw a rusty wash of blood on my sheets.

I had my own nook of our tiny attic apartment, which was just one room cleverly arranged, with slanted ceilings like my childhood bedroom back in Haarlem. Nellie's and Eva's beds took up the two far corners of the room; mine was squeezed into an alcove by the fireplace. What Holland lacked in mountains, we made up for in tall, narrow buildings. We were constantly fashioning two or three rooms out of one, finding free space where, technically, none existed. As a country we prided ourselves on practical solutions, a small but tough nation of no-nonsense people who knew that the success of a tiny, crowded kingdom depended on good manners and respect for the rules.

"Morning," Nellie said, leaning over the cold-water sink to check her face in the mirror. Blond hair, blue eyes, a classic Dutch beauty, just like Eva. The kind I'd always wanted to be.

"Ugh," I said, "this stupid sanitary belt," twisting at the waist to fasten the thing back together with steel pins. Like most girls I knew, I used a belt my mother had made for me, and it was now falling apart without her here to repair it. I'd refused to learn to sew, a rare expression of rebellion for me. But I didn't want to get stuck mending things in my spare time, like my mother did.

"You can probably get a better one from the place where my aunt is volunteering," Nellie said. "They have the best stuff. Elastic belts, Kotex, all the modern things."

"They do?" I stood up and looked down at my bedsheets. Like a murder scene. "And they just let you have them?"

"I think so," she said. "They have piles of stuff." She gathered her coat and purse, preparing to leave.

I felt the shabby sanitary belt hanging from my hips underneath my ruined nightgown. "Can I get the address?"

ALTHOUGH I WAS still attending law school, nothing I was being taught about justice seemed to apply to the quickly changing world outside. I was born in 1920, two years after the War to End All Wars. Nobody imagined there would be a second one. And when Germany invaded, I wanted to fight or at least do something to help. But what could I do? The tiny Dutch military had disbanded after the invasion, and there were no female soldiers, anyway. Flee the country? I wouldn't abandon my home. I wanted to stay and do . . . something. I'd walked over to the office of the refugee alliance in search of a better sanitary belt and ended up volunteering twice a week.

The alliance was staffed by a few politically active older women around my mother's age, under the leadership of our formidable overseer, Nurse Dekker, who provided access to hospital medical supplies. These women had been volunteering on behalf of refugees—mostly Polish and German Jews fleeing the Nazis—since the early days of the Spanish Civil War. It wasn't dramatic, just folding linens and packing emergency parcels for needy families, but it was helpful. Something worth doing.

It also gave me another way to help my new friends Sonja and Philine.
Just a few weeks after I met them, all Jewish students, staff, and professors were expelled from public schools, including the University of Amsterdam. I made myself useful by attending classes in the morning and
repeating the lessons back to Sonja and Philine in the afternoon. I appeared at one of our study sessions with a whole box of the latest women's
sanitary products, extras for Sonja and Philine, and it was done. Nothing
cements female friendship like commiserating over bloodstains.

"Nurse Dekker said we're going to need twice as many care packages
now," I said as we walked through Sonja's neighborhood one afternoon.
It had been eight months since the German invasion and two months
since I'd first met the girls.

"They're getting their money's worth out of you," said Sonja. When
I'd started, the volunteer work had seemed quaint, sitting at long wooden
tables packing toiletries, shaving kits, and potted meat into neat bundles.
The kind of thing I'd done with my mother for church projects when I
was growing up. But there was a sense of urgency lately, and the pace of
work increased by the day.

"Where are they sending all those care packages?" asked Philine as
we navigated through the afternoon shoppers on the sidewalk.

"Westerbork, mostly," I said. Westerbork was a camp with barracks
and a train depot about a hundred miles northeast of Amsterdam, con-
structed before the war to house Jewish refugees already fleeing Germany. I'd heard rumors the Nazis were going to transform it into a site to
imprison Dutch Jews, but that seemed dramatic. You heard all kinds of
whispers about what might happen to Jews, to Gypsies, or to anyone
working on their behalf, but this was the Netherlands, home to Erasmus
and Spinoza and centuries of religious tolerance. I tried to dismiss any
worries. Just as I'd dismissed the possibility of a second world war.

"Why are these tables so crowded?" Sonja said. We'd planned to stop
for a coffee, but Sonja was right: every café we passed was packed with

people. We were used to seeing the streets flooded with German soldiers. The young ones in their peaked caps and short jackets were the friendliest, no doubt happy to get a posting in delightful, defenseless Amsterdam.

"Disgusting," said Philine in a low voice as we noticed a throng of soldiers across the street. They tossed brightly wrapped German candies to a group of schoolchildren. The kids screamed, thrilled and fearful as they snatched up the rare treats.

"So friendly in their hideous uniforms," said Sonja.

"Feldgrau," I spit the word out as if it left a bad taste in my mouth, which it did. Field gray. The basic color of most of the German troops, a nauseating greenish gray that had silently become part of the Amsterdam landscape, draped across their bodies, their trucks, their military checkpoints.

"It's barely a color," said Philine. "Like the sole of a shoe."

"The underside of a sofa," said Sonja.

"Or the linoleum they use in insane asylums," I said.

"Yes!" said Sonja, laughing.

"Hallo!" a soldier shouted, waving at Sonja.

"Ignore them," said Philine.

"Let's find somewhere to sit down," said Sonja, ever practiced at evading unwanted male attention. We rounded the corner, expecting to slip into one of several cafés in the square, and stopped cold. The small plaza had been taken over by a portable bandstand, a raised stage with a canvas roof under which a brass band of perhaps two dozen musicians sat in front of black music stands, each in uniform, holding his instrument. A conductor, also in uniform, tapped a baton to get the musicians' attention. A banner spread across the front of the stage read *Musikkorps der Ordnungspolizei*.

"The Orpo has a band?"

"Where do you learn this stuff?" asked Philine, still trying to decipher all the letters on the banner.

"The refugee alliance," I answered. The women there knew everything.

We lingered at the edge of the square, watching the musicians prepare. The band was crowded onto a small stage, but the rest of the plaza was only sparsely populated, with a group of German soldiers and commanders in flashy uniforms crowded near the front of the square and a few scattered groups of curious Dutch citizens, mostly teenagers and children, dispersed farther back. The square's many cafés had been cleared away.

So that's why the side streets were so full. The spectacle offended me to the marrow: the idea that the Germans could devote time and resources to something as useless as this police band, shipping all those instruments and music stands and even sheet music in trains from Berlin, forcing their poison culture on us even as they stole the country from beneath our feet. They could at least ship in some food. Shelves in the shops were already bare.

"At least they're a nicer color," said Sonja. The Orpo wore uniforms of a lighter, but still institutional, green-gray.

"Don't be fooled," I said. "They're still SS." It had taken only a few weeks after the initial invasion to learn the abbreviations for the absurdly complicated Nazi regiments. The Ordnungspolizei were the Orpo, the everyday cops; the dreaded Schutzstaffel were the SS, who filled a role somewhere between street police and back-alley thugs, and the Sicherheitsdienst des Reichsführers-SS were the SD, the intelligence service of the SS—the spies. It helped that I'd taken German in school. As I spoke, the conductor made a pronouncement in German, and the musicians began to play. The brassy blare of a military march filled the plaza with a defiantly upbeat oompah-pah. "Ugh," said Sonja, who preferred jazz on her phonograph at home.

"What else did you hear about Westerbork?" asked Philine in a lower voice, leaning into me to be heard over the music.

"Dekker said everything is being directed there now. The Germans showed up at her hospital and confiscated all the files on the patients, doctors, staff, everyone. They said they needed them to reorganize the relief efforts."

"Files?" asked Philine. "What files?"

"Just identification forms, I think. Name, address, where you work, et cetera. As if the Germans need their own system to replace ours." Nobody could beat the Dutch when it came to the orderly and efficient function of government; in the Netherlands, the civil service was more powerful than the army. "It's a gross invasion of privacy," I continued in my stage whisper to Philine, confident in my legal analysis, "one I'm sure is illegal under the 1929 Geneva Conventions."

"They're singling out the Jews," Philine said softly, staring down at the cobblestones. I could barely hear her.

"What?" I said. "No, they wanted all the files. Not just the Jewish ones." Sonja and Philine looked at me, incredulous. It took a second; then I felt the gulf of circumstance give way between us for the first time. I could see it in their faces: if the Germans ever wanted to segregate the hospital's staff and patients by religious or ethnic identification, the forms would make it simple to do so. That's how they'd started in Germany, before the war even began. I knew that. The shame of my stupidity made it difficult to look Philine and Sonja in the eye. "Oh," I said. From the stage, the song lifted in a crescendo and the mood of the German officials in the audience rose with it. We each fell quiet, staring blankly as the band played on.

When I'd first met Sonja and Philine a few months earlier, I had no idea they were anything but typical Dutch girls like myself. Which they were. Once I learned they were Jewish, it was like learning they were Catholic: it didn't matter. My mother was the pious daughter of a Protestant minister while my father was a secular socialist; that was never a problem for the two of them as a couple. Nobody I knew was particularly

religious, apart from attending church on the big holidays. I didn't con-
sciously know many Jews growing up in middle-class Haarlem, though
they surely existed. They were, no doubt, much like Philine and Sonja,
raised in nominally Jewish households but not especially observant.
Philine's and Sonja's families had been in the Netherlands for hundreds
of years, which was typical of most Dutch Jews. The very reason refugees
from fascism were drawn to the Netherlands was because we were known
as much for our religious tolerance as for our windmills and wooden
clogs.

When the Nazis invaded, they'd made a big show of how much they
loved us, too, their little Dutch brothers and sisters in the Tausendjäh-
riges Reich, the vision of the next thousand years of Nazi rule promised
by Adolf Hitler. The Germans didn't want to destroy the Netherlands,
they insisted; they wanted to save it. Embrace us. It was pure propaganda. But apart from blitzing the city of Rotterdam into dust on that
first day of invasion, they had generally left the Dutch people alone. Even
the Jews. The Germans were here, but they were not building ghettos or
bombing the countryside. It seemed as if things might proceed differently in the Netherlands from how they had in Germany and Austria. Yet
as each day passed, the sour tang of Nazism began to spread into every
corner of daily life. We weren't the Nazis' siblings, and they had no plans
to go easy on us.

I'd sat through innumerable arguments at home over the past decade
listening to my parents fret about the rise of Mussolini, Franco, and Hitler. Older, bolder Annie liked to be a part of those adult conversations. I
engaged by staying quiet and listening. As a ten-year-old, I often wished
they would change the subject to the things I imagined normal families
talked about, like the weather. Now I was grateful for those nightly debates; at least I had a sense of what we might be facing. My parents spoke
of defiance and the brave sacrifices of the partisans in Italy and Spain.
We all knew how those conflicts ended. Mussolini and Franco were still

in power, united now in Hitler's Axis. I was less naïve than some of my fellow twenty-year-olds, those whose families discussed the weather. But sneaking a glance at the girls who had quickly become my best friends, the first ones I'd had since Annie died, I knew I had much more to learn. We stood together at the corner of the plaza farthest from the band, listening as the music resolved itself in the final flourish and a tuba boomed. Sonja flinched. As horrible as the occupation was for me, it was a thousand times worse for Sonja and Philine. They were afraid of things I hadn't even considered.

The Germans in front clapped and shouted. The rest of the crowd stayed silent. Sonja surveyed the scene. "Things are getting worse," she whispered. I couldn't tell if she'd meant to say it out loud.

"Let's go," said Philine, taking Sonja's hand. We walked across the back of the square and turned down a smaller street, this one also absorbing the crowds of everyday people who would otherwise be in the plaza.

"I've been trying to talk to my father about leaving, but he's so stubborn," Philine said as we walked. "He says, 'As long as we follow the law, we won't get in trouble.' And since he's 'never broken a law in his life' . . ." She frowned.

"Ten years ago, my father persuaded my German aunts and uncles to come to Amsterdam for safety," Sonja said, shaking her head. "Now they don't know what to do. My parents and their friends talk about it, but so far, only the Baums have actually left. My mother said they were overreacting."

Philine and Sonja rarely spoke this frankly in front of me, though they must have been thinking about these questions constantly. Rising shame pinked my cheeks. I wanted them to be able to confide in me. Suddenly their trust seemed like the most important thing in the world.

"Where did they go?" I asked. "The Baums?"

"America," said Sonja. "Apparently they have cousins in . . . Detroit? Wherever that is."

The tone of our conversation changed. I had the feeling we were no longer stopping at a café. "Turn here," said Philine. We turned down a quieter street and all music died behind us, save the thump of a bass drum. "Detroit is where Henry Ford makes the cars," she said. Of course Philine knew. Thank God I'd never had to compete against her in high school, where I'd enjoyed my easy status at the head of the class.

"How did they get out?" I asked Sonja. Jews had been banned from leaving the country as soon as the Germans took over.

"As my father says, 'With money, everything is possible,'" said Philine. Then she looked at Sonja. "I only meant—"

"No, it's true," Sonja said with a shrug. "The Baums were wealthy. They sold everything they could, packed what they could carry, and got their money out of the bank—well, as much as they could get. Mother said the bank wouldn't let them take it all. She said Mrs. Baum left the country with at least one ring on every finger and toe, including her thumbs." She wiggled her fingers, each nail beautifully polished, for effect.

"Even if we had enough money to leave," said Philine, "my father refuses. 'I'm a French teacher,' he says. 'What will I do in America? Shine shoes?'" She rolled her eyes. "Everybody knows there are plenty of jobs in America."

Yes, that's what people said. People also said that on the day of the German invasion, dozens of Dutch Jews committed suicide, convinced death was coming. But afterward not much happened, and it seemed—to me, anyway—as if they had overreacted in the most horrifying way. Now I wondered. What about the other assumptions I'd made, the idea that this war would only last four years, like the Great War? It might go on forever. Nobody knew.

"Would you really leave?" I asked Philine.

"If I had to," she said. We were in front of her building. "You should come up," she said to both of us. I was relieved to still be included.

"I'm going," said Sonja.

"You should stay," said Philine.

"No," said Sonja, "I mean to America. I've already decided."

"To America?" I asked. "When?"

"Sometime," she said, following me up the stairs. "Not yet, but some-time. I'll go with or without my parents, but I'm not going to sit around and wait for . . ." She paused and lowered her voice in the close hallway. "If they're not ready when I am, I'll go on my own." She gave a quick nod at the end, as if to seal a promise to herself.

"No, Sonja," said Philine, twisting back around, her grip on the ban-ister white with worry, "it's not safe, you can't go alone."

Sonja rolled her eyes and laughed. "Look at the two of you, clucking like hens! You can relax, girls. I haven't booked my stateroom just yet."

I said nothing. I didn't think it was my place. Philine sighed. "Oh, Sonja," she said.

"Oh, what?" Sonja snapped, done with this dreary conversation. "Are we going in?"

"Nothing," said Philine. "Nothing."

Chapter 3

"A H, MA CHÉRIE."

Philine stood at the open door to her apartment, her father's soft voice floating through the hallway like a French ghost.

"Bonjour, Papa," she said. As she turned toward him, her expression rearranged itself from worry to its usual steady sweetness. "Sonja and Hannie are here."

I'd met Mr. Polak before. We walked into the sitting room, and there he was, as always, with a blanket over his knees and a book in his hands. He was in his early forties but had the look of someone who'd never been young, his hair silvered and his eyes perpetually asquint. It was a kind face, just like his daughter's. Philine's gentle father, the French teacher. Their bond was obvious, his love for her so tender. Like my bond with my father, also a teacher. But my father wasn't in the same kind of danger as Mr. Polak. I felt a lump in my throat. What was so bad, really, about shining shoes?

"I should be going," I said.

"But we haven't even studied yet," said Philine.

The Polaks' longtime maid, Marie, walked in with a steaming cup of tea and set it beside Mr. Polak. At least sixty years old, Marie was a

German refugee. Not a Jew, just an impoverished German citizen who'd left her homeland during the depression of the 1920s, coming to Amsterdam for work. She'd been with the Polak family for the past twenty years and was like a mother to Philine, whose own mother had died of a fever when she was just a baby. Though technically still an employee of the Polaks, Marie was starting to act as the public face of the family, doing all the shopping and interacting with strangers, since she was the only non-Jew in the household. She could shop in the better stores, where Jews were increasingly unwelcome. With her white hair in a bun and her spine curved from a lifetime of housework, she could have passed for Mr. Polak's mother. Not that having one gentile parent would have made a difference for Mr. Polak: according to the Nazis, a person was considered a Mischling—of mixed Jewish blood—even if they had just one Jewish grandparent.

Technically speaking, it was no longer legal for a gentile to work for Jews. But Marie went on, invisible the way only older women can be. "Will she ever leave, do you think?" I once asked Philine, who looked at me in horror. "Of course not," Philine said and then paused, searching for her reasoning. "She loves us," she explained. "And she has nowhere else to go."

"Merci, Marie," Mr. Polak said. Marie nodded and disappeared into the kitchen.

"Hannie," Mr. Polak said, "la petite dernière." The little last one. It was his nickname for me, trailing behind the two swans. A sympathetic smile. "Where are you off to on a cold evening like this? Home, I hope?" He was always fretting about the fact that I lived away from my family and ate bean soup most nights for dinner.

"A quick errand and then I'm going home, I promise."

"Watch your step out there." He pulled at the hem of the curtain beside him and looked out at the darkening streets. The sun set early this time of year, and its warmth disappeared with the light. Ever since the Luftwaffe had begun storming across the English Channel to bomb

Britain months earlier, the streetlights had been removed or shot out. We had all started learning to find our way in the shadows.

"I will," I said.

"Eh," he said, letting the curtain fall, "at least we don't have to worry about the Germans bombing us, n'est-ce pas?" He chuckled. "Perhaps the one benefit of having them as neighbors."

"I suppose," I said, disturbed by his determination to see anything hopeful about the situation. It must have been how Philine and Sonja felt when they talked to me.

"We're lucky to not be in London," he went on, gesturing to a newspaper on the table beside him. "They're blitzing churches now, can you imagine?" He looked thoughtful. "Rebbe de Hond says, 'The synagogue is our shelter and the tefillin are our antiaircraft guns,' eh?" He smiled weakly and sighed. "Well, it's awful what the British are enduring."

I didn't know how to respond. The tiny black tefillin boxes contained scrolls of the Torah inside . . . and nobody in the Polak family even attended synagogue, as far as I was aware. He was looking for hope wherever it appeared. I couldn't blame him for that. I did it myself all the time.

"I fear for our queen," Mr. Polak continued, patting the withered white carnation tucked into the buttonhole of his lapel. The favorite flower of Prince Bernhard, wearing a carnation had lately become an expression of loyalty to the Dutch royal family. Queen Wilhelmina, Prince Bernhard, and the rest of the family had fled to London at the beginning of the war, where they now operated a government in exile. We all listened to her rallying speeches on the Radio Oranje broadcasts, though it was forbidden to do so. "She can't be safe, in the midst of all this."

"Mmm," I said. I pictured the Orpo band we'd just seen in the plaza, the way the German troops walked through our city, claiming it for themselves. I could still see the looks on Sonja's and Philine's faces as we watched the band play. The apprehension. The disgust. "I'm sure the queen is worried about us, too," I said.

"Of course she is," he agreed. "But she has faith in us. On last night's broadcast she praised the 'courage of our resistance and the strength of our national character.'" Mr. Polak smiled, soothed by the queen's spectral presence.

I wasn't. It was something you said to a child, though I knew the queen had good intentions. I was interested, however, in her explicit mention of resistance. There had been a lot of talk of resistance in the early days of the war, but the word itself had quickly disappeared from the public conversation and was only spoken aloud by people like the queen, who was free to say anything she wanted from London. Yet somehow the vanishing of the word seemed like a portent of something powerful. Everything that might make a difference in this war was receding from view, from language to tools like guns and printing presses. But when the Germans outlawed home radio sets, resisters adapted. They stripped the sets down to jumbles of wire and metal and hid the disassembled parts under the floorboards, putting them back together solely to listen to the queen's nightly broadcast with a lookout by the front door, then hiding them again. The Resistance hadn't disappeared; it was just lying in wait, like the radios.

"That's good to hear," I said.

Mr. Polak put on his queen voice to quote her again: "'Those who want good will not be prevented from accomplishing it,' she said." He leaned back in his chair, content.

Had he not read the rest of the newspaper? Had he not seen the photos we had all seen, thousands of hard-helmeted German soldiers brandishing their shiny Imperial Eagle as they marched through the Arc de Triomphe? Sickening tourist snapshots of Adolf Hitler at the Eiffel Tower? Paris was only three hundred miles away. The Nazi-run newspapers that now flooded the city were full of updates on the continuing success of the Wehrmacht in Eastern Europe, too. Did he not realize those who wanted good were, in fact, being prevented from accomplishing it nearly everywhere? I swallowed my emotions with a wince. Each of us had to fight the war in our own way.

"Good night, Mr. Polak," I said, "it's so nice to see you."

"You're a good girl, Hannie," Mr. Polak said, as if reassuring himself. "À bientôt, mademoiselle." As I left the room, he began rearranging the wilting carnation on his lapel. Surely he realized it was becoming dangerous to wear those out in public. Marie, I hoped, would warn him.

"See you tomorrow?" Sonja kissed me on the cheek as I stood at the door to leave, Philine smiling beside her.

"My father loves you," said Philine.

I smiled. "Parents usually do." We hugged, and I ran down the stairs and back out to the darkening streets. So much had changed, I thought, since I'd met Sonja and Philine. I felt much more connected to the city, the people around me. After that night at the dance, I'd hoped to run into them again on campus but never expected them to include me in their friendship. Yet they had. They liked me. I suspected my presence also unlocked something between them. Most of the time, my presence kept them from rehashing the same grim dialogue with every passing week of the occupation. Instead of needling each other about the dreadful state of everything, they could focus on explaining things to me: the big city of Amsterdam, how to have confidence when talking to boys, what color sweaters looked best on redheads. Things I knew nothing about. Topics that kept us from dwelling on the obvious.

But today everything suddenly felt different. Things that had always been obvious to them were now, finally, becoming obvious to me.

THE COMMUTER TRAIN lurched to a stop on the west side of Amsterdam. Just across the tracks loomed the bricked peaks of the Westergas factory and the massive, cylindrical steel tanks that towered over the canal running through the working-class neighborhoods on this side of town. I disembarked onto the nearly empty platform, the air freezing and black in the evening gloom.

Nurse Dekker had asked me to drop off an envelope at a refugee safe house here on the outskirts of the city. "You seem like a sensible girl," she'd said that morning. "Can you do something for me?" She handed me an envelope and then a separate slip of paper with an address. "Just deliver this envelope to this address, yes? But keep the address to yourself."

I nodded. I did whatever she asked, always. Her brusque busyness reminded me of my mother, the quiet yet powerful force of gravity that held everything together in my childhood home. As with my mother, I rarely argued or even asked questions, something Nurse Dekker appreciated.

After stumbling through a few unfamiliar blocks of shabby buildings, I found the number and knocked on the door, convinced I was in the wrong place. A fortress of freezing red bricks five stories high, it was quiet and desolate on the pavement. Apartment 6 had no identifying name card; it looked as if someone had pried it out with a fingernail. But a cracked doorbell sat next to it, so I pushed the button.

"Ja?" A gruff voice emerged from above. I looked up. "Ja?" he said again. A wrinkled old man in a navy cap leaned out a window two floors above me.

"The alliance?" I said. I held up the envelope. I had assumed I was just delivering paperwork to another refugee assistance group. I wasn't so sure now. He gestured toward the door, and I pushed inside. The interior of the building was even darker than the starlit streets outside, the hallway lights either burned out or missing. I shuffled to the stairway and followed a slanted rectangle of light cast by an open door.

"Who sent you?" the man said, peeking through the slit in the doorway.

"Nurse Dekker."

He blinked. "Are you the new girl?"

"I don't know," I said. "I suppose." I glanced past his shoulder. "Is this the alliance?"

He shrugged. "I suppose." He put his hand out for the envelope. I handed it to him through the gap. He chuckled, three missing teeth in his grin. He cracked the door open slightly wider. Warmth and light came from inside the apartment, but also the stuffy fug of overcrowding, the scent of food, wood fires, and human bodies. Behind him I spotted two adults and three children huddled under a homemade quilt on a lumpy mattress on the floor. This was not the refugee alliance. These were the refugees.

"Thank Nurse Dekker for me," the man said. "And thank you, miss." Just before the door closed he gave me a wink. "Oranje zal overwinnen," he said. The door shut and the lock clicked into place before I could respond.

Orange will overcome.

I stood in darkness for a moment. The sound of voices whispered on the other side of the door, nothing that could be heard from the street. All those people in such a small room. Refugees. From Germany, from Poland? From here? The whole building reeked of sadness. And although I wasn't Jewish, or a refugee, I knew the terror of watching family disappear.

Annie.

I clung to the shadows of buildings as I walked back to the train station. I adored Annie. Everyone did. But she died of diphtheria at age twelve, when I was only seven. With her gone from our lives, my parents fell to pieces, each of us retreating into our own little islands of existence. My father's shelter was the Teachers' Union; my mother's was worry; mine was work. I had been a studious girl before Annie's death, but afterward I was possessed. Life became a scrolling slideshow of reading, writing, studying, and test taking. I kept my head down, waiting for something to change.

Not being Annie had defined my life up to the moment I met Sonja and Philine. Now I found myself being the kind of girl who found herself out on the edge of the city at night, knocking on the doors of strangers, exchanging secret passwords like some sort of swashbuckling spy: *Oranje zal overwinnen.* To Philine, to Sonja, even to Nurse Dekker now, I was Hannie.

"Ha!" I actually laughed out loud at myself for being so dense. Annie . . . Hannie. I'd never even noticed it before. Annie was still with me—within me, in fact. And I still had so much to learn from her.

I JOGGED THROUGH the cold November air until I got to the train station. It was empty except for a couple of German soldiers leaning against a pillar, smoking and talking. A swastika flag flew from the station flagpole as I picked up my bike and rode home as fast as I could, partly for warmth but mostly to distract myself from my thoughts. I parked my bike in the walkway between my building and the next, and when I did, I noticed a series of posters pasted up in the hours since I'd left home in the morning.

Six hung in a row, all with the same image. The Germans liked to hang them that way, repeating the message like a melody you hate yet gets stuck in your head. This poster showed a map of Europe with a surging wave of bright crimson blood flooding toward it from the Soviet Union, being held off by two flags, the swastika of the Third Reich and the double lightning bolts of the despicable SS.

Storm tegen het Bolsjewisme!

Storm against Bolshevism. The Nazis hated the Communists, of course. But this was code. I only knew this because Philine told me a few days earlier, after sighting another poster with a similar message. When the Nazis said *Bolsheviks*, it was usually code for Jews. The day's shame and confusion and sadness and dread began to churn into a hot, hard rock in the pit of my stomach. My breathing quickened as I stared at the bloody tidal wave meant to intimidate me into hating Sonja and Philine and sweet Mr. Polak. I glanced around my quiet street, and as if watching myself from some otherworldly vantage point, I grabbed the edge of the poster and ripped it down the middle, flinging its strips to the ground as I moved on to the next one and the next and the next, stomping the ribbons of red and black paper beneath my worn-down shoes.

Afterward I ran up my stairs with my heart hammering, a smile on my face for the first time all day. Perhaps Mr. Polak and Queen Wilhelmina were right, after all: those who want good will not be prevented from accomplishing it.

Chapter 4

Spring 1942

I'D INTENDED TO go to Sonja's house through the gardens of the Von-delpark, the vast park of meadows and ponds and walking paths in the center of the city. As I rolled up to its ornate iron gates, two German soldiers stood on duty. Beside them hung the now-familiar but still shocking painted sign, its dark, Gothic script silently screaming: *Voor Joden Verboden.*

Jews Forbidden.

The soldiers saw me looking at it. "You a Jew?" one of them asked. Nobody had ever asked before.

"What?" I said, fighting the tremor in my legs. I instantly knew that it was both a question and a threat. As I took a step backward, they leaned in to close the gap. "No!" I said in a sharp, high voice. I shoved my ID card toward them and they laughed at my panic. I scanned their young faces—what would happen if they didn't believe me?

"Go on, Mädchen," one said, giving the metal rack on the back of my bike a friendly push forward.

"Danke," I said, softened with relief. "Danke schön." The soldiers smiled and I did, too. I pedaled a few times before snapping back to reality.

I steered toward the center path leading to my favorite meadow, the trees parting just ahead. As I rode past, I gasped, and then remembered. The Germans were digging up the Vondelpark to make it impossible for foreign aircraft to use it as a landing strip. The field, formerly a carefully landscaped blanket of rolling lawn designed for picnics and toddling babies, had been plowed into deep ditch-like furrows stretching across the grass. The air smelled of soil and rocks, and all the flowers were gone.

Initially, Reichskommissar Arthur Seyss-Inquart assured the Dutch people by radio address that the Germans would rather arrive in our country "with the right hand raised in greeting, than with the mailed fist." I remembered hoping, as Mr. Polak had, that Seyss-Inquart might be more reasonable than Hitler. There was no Kristallnacht here, no construction of ghettos or mass graves on the outskirts of the city. The Reichskommissar was so sincere in his admiration for the Dutch national character, of the "ties of blood" that united our two countries, how could they happen here? They didn't. Not at first. Subtlety was Seyss-Inquart's weapon. In place of dramatic decrees, he issued piecemeal initiatives. The collecting of personnel files, for instance. The Dutch people were outraged and worried, but time passed and nothing seemed to come of it. When parks and libraries and public transportation were made off-limits for Jews over the previous year, the protests were huge, all over the country, by Jews and gentiles alike. But because the closures didn't actually interfere with the course of most people's daily routines, life went on.

Jews were, over time, forced to register their names with the authorities. Forced to register their valuables and art holdings. Required to move their money into Nazi banks. Had these all happened simultaneously, they might have provoked an uprising. Seyss-Inquart knew this— the general strike in Amsterdam in February 1941 flared up after Jews were removed from certain professions en masse. So he moved slowly, not wanting to arouse the temper of the Dutch people. And it had worked. Here I was, separated from Sonja and Philine. My two beautiful friends who just happened to be Jewish. Philine had once said, "I didn't know I was Jewish until Hitler told me." She knew, of course. But until the Germans invaded, it didn't matter. I kept riding. I'd spent my childhood eager to grow up, for my life to change. But not like this.

"Morning, Red."

Sergeant Becker, a Wehrmacht soldier, had been stationed at the end of Sonja's fancy street since sometime during the winter, six months ago now. Becker looked to be in his early thirties and was the laziest German soldier I'd ever met. Somehow he'd carved out the perfect assignment for himself, there on Sonja's corner, where he did nothing but smoke cigarettes, read paperbacks, and occasionally give orders to the few younger soldiers he supervised. He had reddish hair and freckles, which was how we started talking in the first place.

"Hello, Red," he'd said that first day. I ignored him. But he was always polite, and I had a feeling he'd instructed his soldiers not to harass me or Philine or Sonja, because they all kept quiet as we walked back and forth from Sonja's. Over time, Becker and I arrived at a pleasant detente. As I walked by, he hurriedly folded up his camp chair and stuffed his book inside the jacket of his uniform.

"Something happening?" I asked.

He raised an eyebrow. I remained stone-faced, as usual. I didn't want him to think we were friends.

"Don't know," he said. "But I just got reassigned to Dam Square."

"Is it a parade?" I asked. The Germans liked to polish their boots and their silver stars and clomp all over the cobblestones, performing their Heil Hitlers for hours on bright blue days like this, the sunshine bouncing off their uniforms. Why not Dam Square, in front of the Royal Palace? They even had their own photographers scurrying around to document the glory of discipline or whatever they thought they were celebrating. I tried to avoid Dam Square whenever possible; I still felt nauseated any-time I saw the swastika flapping atop the palace.

Becker shook his head. "I don't know," he said. "They don't tell us much." He shrugged, as if we were in this mess together.

We were not. I kept walking.

"The Frenk family in the white house with black trim," he said. "Your friends?"

I stopped and looked back. "Why?"

Our eyes met, but this time he didn't smile. He took one last drag off his cigarette and then flicked it into the canal. "Just asking," he said.

I walked on. A seed of dread buried itself in my chest. As I passed the tall houses lining the canal, I tried to guess which of them had already been "requisitioned" by the Germans. Nazi officers now lived in those buildings. Sonja's new neighbors.

A uniformed maid let me into the foyer of the Frenks' five-story home. When the door opened, the canal outside scattered light throughout the grand mansion. I'd only known houses like this from the old Hals and Rembrandt paintings from the Golden Age. Wide marble steps led up the five floors, and a hand-carved ebony banister ran alongside like a line of calligraphy, the most complicated staircase I'd ever seen. I went to Sonja's house all the time, but only ever ventured as high as her third-story bedroom. The rooms above were a mystery, inhabited by Sonja's German relatives who were waiting out the ongoing catastrophe on the fourth floor.

"Not that. I'll die of heat stroke." Sonja pushed away the mustard-colored cardigan as Philine leaned out of the doorway of the attached dressing room, a space bigger than the childhood bedroom I'd shared with my sister. Sunlight streamed in through tall windows.

I unbuttoned my drab old coat and flung it over the back of a green velvet chaise. "Sorry I'm late."

"We won't be long," Sonja said, pecking me on the cheek. "Just getting dressed."

"We will be long," said Philine, a hint of irritation threaded through her placid voice, "if she doesn't make up her mind soon."

"What about this?" Sonja asked, wrapping her shoulders with a flowery silk scarf.

"Nice," I said.

Philine shrugged. "Maybe."

I walked to the tall windows to look at the inner courtyard. Below was a neat grid of rectangular backyards, each one providing a small patch of greenery for the mansion in front of it. Here in the busiest part of the central city was a small refuge, hidden from the public but intimately known to all who lived in these private homes. More hidden spaces. As usual, the gardens below were empty.

"You ever talk to Becker?" I asked. "The soldier at the end of the street?"

"The sleepy one?" asked Sonja. "Sometimes. He's more polite than the rest."

"Never," said Philine, repulsed. "Why would I?"

I didn't know what to say. I had no real information for Sonja, so why scare her with Becker's vague hints? Rumors were already doing enough damage to our psyches.

"Just curious," I said.

Sonja turned to me. "Is this about the errands you've been doing for your nurse?" Her face lit up with hopefulness. I could see it made Philine nervous.

"I shouldn't talk about it," I said, trying to sound jaded and mysterious.

"Oh," said Sonja softly.

I waited for the inevitable teasing from Philine, but none came. The energy in the room had shifted, as if a storm had just moved in. For a long moment, none of us spoke.

"I brought some new study questions," I said. Lately I saw it as my job to keep us all focused on schoolwork. I'd gotten Philine enthused about my chosen area of law, international justice, but Sonja was less enthused. Sonja persevered to make her parents happy while she fantasized about a much more glamorous future for herself than being a lawyer. I imagined it as something from a Hollywood movie, with lots of slinky gowns, small dogs, and martini glasses everywhere. I wasn't sure if that's what she still imagined.

Sonja spoke up. "I can't study right now."

"I'm trying to get her outside for some fresh air," Philine said.

Sonja tried to summon her usual pep. "I just can't decide what to wear."

"It doesn't matter," Philine said. "We're only going out on the balcony." The days when we used to wander through the city streets in search of a café had been over for a while now. With most businesses requiring ID cards for service, Jews were excluded from much of public life because of the huge black *J* on their cards. The Frenks were fortunate to have their lovely private garden, but they rarely used it. The little green square in the middle of the block was pleasant enough, but it was like trying to relax in a prison, knowing the surrounding buildings were stocked with guards watching from the windows. It wasn't something we talked about; it was just something we all now knew.

"Hannie was late, anyway," said Sonja.

"Sorry," I said again. I said that word a lot these days.

Sonja threw another sweater to the floor and surveyed her open closet. "Maybe that striped blouse?"

"Enough, Sonja," said Philine. Her voice crackled with irritation.

"Everything all right?" I asked.

"Fine." Philine began folding the discarded items, rescuing them from the floor, bed, and nearby chair. Sonja, digging through a mahogany armoire, held up a different blouse, white with yellow flowers, and turned to the two of us. But before she could ask, Philine exploded.

"Not that. Come on." She glared at Sonja, who glared right back.

"Calm down, Philine," Sonja said.

Philine normally only commented on Sonja's wardrobe to compliment it. Now she took a deep breath, as if to launch into a speech, and then swallowed it, saying nothing.

"What," challenged Sonja. Like a dare.

Philine walked to the door to the hallway and reached behind it, pulling out a bright bolt of rough yellow cotton cloth, a color so ugly I couldn't imagine either of them wearing it. Then she unfolded it, and I saw its pattern. In the same angry black-letter script as the sign in the Vondelpark, one word repeated over and over: *Jood*.

Jew.

Philine selected a four-inch square of the cotton that she'd cut out of the sheet of fabric, isolating just one *Jood* encircled by a six-pointed Jewish star. She held it up to the lapel of an imaginary coat. "Those yellow flowers will hide the star."

"That's the point," said Sonja.

Philine spoke softly, her voice shaking with emotion. "You'll get in trouble."

"You really think they're going to have soldiers checking for stars on the streets?"

"Of course they will!" said Philine, her eyes white with incredulity. "Why do you think that redheaded soldier is always at the end of your street?"

"My father knows the leaders of the Jewish Council," said Sonja, "and they're the ones who decide who stays and goes. He gave them your family's name, too, Philine, to put on the list. It'll be OK."

"And you believe that?" Philine said.

"The Jewish Council has a plan," Sonja said. "They're some of the most important businessmen in the city, for goodness' sake."

We all knew about them. Leaders of the Jewish community who were negotiating with the Germans about future Jewish policies. But I found it hard to believe they could claim any real power in a state of occupation.

"Yes, the Jewish Council has a plan," said Philine, exasperated. "A plan to send all the Jews in Amsterdam to Westerbork." She spit the last word out as if warding off the evil eye.

"That's just temporary," Sonja said. "Anyway, it's probably nicer than here, with all the trash on the streets and sandbags everywhere."

"Sonja!" said Philine, astonished. "Westerbork is a labor camp."

"It's a transit camp, Father says."

"Where do you think they're in transit to? A nice trip to the seaside?"

Sonja had reached the end of her Father-supplied rebuttals. "Soon it'll be illegal to be Jewish at all," she said. Like a joke.

Philine looked at her incredulously. "Oh, Sonja. It already is."

We all sat in silence for a few long moments before Sonja spoke again.

"I don't want to go out," she said, dropping the blouse. She sat in the midst of a pile of flouncy things, all the colors of the rainbow, florals, houndstooth check, stripes, and polka dots, burying herself under her clothes like a swan fluffing its feathers, then tucking its head beneath its wing to sleep.

"You'll have to, sometime," Philine said, inspecting the bolt of yellow fabric again. "What's this?" An official-looking letter was stapled to the lower corner of the fabric. "Of course," she said with a bitter laugh.

"What?" I asked, desperate for any information.

"Instructions," said Philine, reading the memo off the swastika-embossed paper. "'Wash first to prevent discoloration or shrinkage.' Somebody took the time to include that." She held up the fabric and squinted at something printed in small type: "'Hergestellt in Deutsch-land,'" she read. "Made in Germany."

"It's stupid," said Sonja bitterly.

"No," said Philine. "Somebody actually wrote all these instructions, down to the last detail. This isn't some whim of the Dutch SS. This is part of a bigger plan. An organized, much bigger plan."

She looked up at Sonja, waiting for the expected protest. But Sonja was silent for once, her animated face now slack with what looked like fear. I longed to reassure them but had no idea what to say.

"I'll be right back," I whispered. I stepped out of Sonja's bedroom, closed the door behind me, and stood on the landing, trying to keep myself from bursting into tears. If they weren't crying, I wasn't going to either. I had nothing to contribute and no way to take on their burden. My stomach hurt. It seemed like I should pass on the warning Becker had given me, but what had he actually warned me of? Why make things worse? I lingered in the gleaming wood-paneled hallway and glanced up the stairs to where Sonja's older relatives resided. All I could see were closed doors. From somewhere on the fourth floor, I heard the soft, falling chords of a Victrola's Viennese waltz.

I LEFT SONJA's house soon after, none of us in the mood for conversation.

That's when I began to see them.

The yellow star badges. Those wearing them had faces set in stone, like the man who walked past me with a yellow star pinned to the shoulder of his double-breasted suit, his hat pulled down over his brow. The grim resolve on his face reminded me of the statues of Easter Island, eyes staring at nothing, impenetrable. I walked on through the bright sunlight, thinking of Sonja and Philine surrounded by garments as if drowning in the shallows, unsure how to save themselves. Then up ahead I saw him. Finally, a target for my rage.

"Becker!" I shouted, my fists tight. "Becker!"

He turned to look at me, and I saw it was not Becker at all, but another German soldier with auburn hair, who smiled. No one yelled at the soldiers unless they wanted to get arrested, so he was curious.

"Guten Tag, Fräulein," he said, his voice sweet. He and three fellow soldiers were standing in a ring, and in the middle was a young Jewish girl, a look of terror on her teenage face. There on the collar of her blouse was one of the yellow stars, fluttering at the edges like a poisoned corsage as the Huns circled.

"Get away from her," I said, walking directly toward them. I wasn't myself and this wasn't Becker, but I didn't care because the cumulative effect of the signs and Sonja and the yellow stars had blinded me with my own shame. "Leave her alone." My voice wobbled with fury. I didn't care.

The Becker look-alike laughed at me and so did his soldier friends, enough of a distraction for the girl to run, disappearing into a nearby crowd. That wasn't my plan, but I was relieved. I had no plan. I felt like a rabid dog chained to a post, wild and dangerous and frustrated. The soldiers saw it. Before I could reach them, they backed away in mock fear, holding up their hands in surrender. "Easy, easy," one of them said as they fell back, and I stormed past them, relieved. I marched onward, my head ringing, and a few steps later I heard one of them call out to me.

"Jew-lover!" he said.

A few people turned to look, but I kept going as if the comment had nothing to do with me. I walked without thinking of anything else, trying to forget the image of Philine holding up the yellow cloth, trying not to see the anonymous Jewish girl and the horror on her face. I walked until the sidewalk ended and my feet hit the steel tracks of the tramcars, their bells bringing me back to reality. Crowds of people streamed by, shoppers and students and German soldiers holding guns and children playing tag on the cobblestones.

And then I saw him. Becker. Standing a few yards away from me with a group of soldiers, hands on hips and leaning back to look up at the Royal Palace. I looked up, too.

From the center of the massive palace rose a giant cupola, a verdigris dome with a spike at the top and a ship to symbolize the glory days of the Netherlands' seventeenth century. This was the Amsterdam of the Frenks' home, the palace built by men in ruffled collars. Just below that was a gold clock and a carillon. The sound of those bells was familiar to all Amsterdammers, tolling the time on the half hour for as long as anyone alive could remember. But as I followed Becker's gaze, I saw men up near the clock, soldiers. They hung out of the balcony like spiders crawling over the face of the building.

"Becker," I said. He turned and saw me and gave me one of his ambivalent smiles.

"Hey, Red."

"What are they doing?" I imagined they were removing the clockface to melt it down for gold.

"Changing the time," he said. And as we watched, we saw the long gold wand of the minute hand sweep forward. I felt dizzy.

"Why?" I said.

Becker shrugged. "Seyss-Inquart sent the order," he said, pronouncing the name of our Nazi Reichskommissar with the same mocking faux-Austrian accent we all did. Even the soldiers seemed to despise Hitler's appointed commander and his slow, lisping voice.

"Seyss-Inquart?" I asked.

"They're moving it ahead, Fräulein," Becker said, turning to look at me. "We're on Berlin time now."

Chapter 5

Spring–Summer 1942

I FELT THE CLOCK'S presence everywhere, as if the Nazis controlled the weather, too. Everyone had to change their clocks to Berlin time if they wanted to synchronize with the train schedules. For a while I refused to change mine, and a small pearl of resentment began to grow in me, a hard new layer forming each time I recalibrated my schedule with Berlin.

How does evil spread? Like a disease, from one human to another? Or the way the new anti-Jewish measures sifted down into the private lives of Dutchmen, like dust in a closed room, mote by invisible mote, until one day we turned the key in the lock and found ourselves trapped, then looked back at our little room and discovered it so entombed in filth it was not fit to live in anymore? The imposition of Berlin time awakened me to a new truth: we were not awaiting a tragedy; we were living it. Each time I looked at the alarm by my bedside and took the extra step of adjusting the clock, I felt that bitter pearl grow. Now, when I walked through the city, yellow stars screamed at me from street corners: *Do something.*

———

SIX THIRTY: TIME to go. The sun was already warming the bricks of the buildings as I studied my reflection in the mirror, splashing water on my sleepy face. Hair brushed, pale yellow blouse and blue wool skirt. Just a normal Dutch college girl, twenty-one years old, nothing remarkable except the red hair. "No one's going to mistake me for a Dutch peasant," Philine had joked once, and as a fellow non-blonde, I understood. I checked my hair again. No one was going to mistake me for a Jew, but they still might notice my red hair. I grabbed a hat. I was eager to get to the Zuiderbad swimming pool during the morning rush of ladies taking their daily exercise. The more crowded, the better. I got to the door and heard my mother's voice: *Don't go out without a coat. You'll catch a chill.* I reached for the coat, then stopped myself. When I first moved away, I'd taken the train home to Haarlem several times a week, just to see them. Now I visited perhaps twice a month. I left the coat hanging. I didn't need it. I shut the door quietly behind me and jogged down the stairs.

For the past two years, I thought I'd done as much as I could to help Jewish refugees, to support Sonja and Philine.

But that wasn't really true.

I was beginning to notice a new pattern of behavior. Two people make eye contact. One of them is wearing a yellow star. The other notices the star, then drops their gaze to the ground and keeps walking. Whether it's because they're embarrassed or ashamed or disgusted, it doesn't matter, because the result is the same: they stop looking at Jews. Which means they stop seeing them. And when you stop seeing something, it no longer exists.

It wasn't just the strangers, though. I was doing it, too.

That was why I had to go to the swimming pool.

My bike was tangled with all the others against the front stoop of my apartment building. I leaned into a turn around the corner and nearly collided with a policeman who hopped aside to avoid a crash. "Pardon," I said, but didn't brake. He tipped his hat to me. My hands and fingers tingled, like they always did when I was scared, and I wiggled them on the handlebars to shake it off.

On every block that morning, men and women, girls and boys, were getting on bikes, boarding trams, walking through the gray cobbled streets to work and market and school. Bells rang from drawbridges as they lifted like wings, allowing freighter boats through the canals. Amsterdammers thronged at the edge of the water waiting to cross, orderly yet tense. Learning to live under occupation was learning to live outside of time, never daring to plan too far ahead.

I skidded to a stop at the edge of the crowd, catching my breath.

"Stay in your place, miss," a flower seller scolded, scuffing my bike tire with his worn boot. I scanned the moving crowd for a gap into which I might slip and finally plunged forward in a clash of ringing bicycle bells and angry exclamations.

"Sorry, sorry!" I said again, my voice high and shaking. Bells on bicycles jingled, a flower vendor furled a spray of yellow daffodils in newspaper, and two Luftwaffe fighter planes screamed across the sky toward the English Channel on a daylight sortie, the rumble of their mighty engines vibrating in my bones, and I almost stopped being scared of what I was about to do.

The fortress of the Rijksmuseum. It loomed across the plaza with towers like castle turrets. Seeing them brought a wave of unexpected relief: no swastikas flying, at least not yet. And there, just across from the museum, I saw what I was looking for: the massive redbrick building housing the Zuiderbad swimming pool. Amsterdam had quite a few public swimming pools, though few were so ornate.

I'd imagined this part a thousand times. I rode across the street, each detail just as I knew it would be: the high peaked roof, the tall white-framed windows, the curved portico at the entrance with its green tiles and blue painted waves. It looked like it always did, apart from the sign on the door: *Voor Joden Verboden*. No Jews allowed.

I needed a place to park my bike that would be easy to find again, but the outer walls of the building were three deep in bicycles. In a way, that was good: it was busy. I leaned mine against the rest, took a deep breath, reminded myself to be calm.

As if I did this all the time.

I'd never done this before.

I arranged my expression into one of bland boredom and walked into the entry hall. An old man took my ticket, his thick white hair swept back from his lined face as if he were facing into a storm. He looked me over, from my navy blue hat to my black lace-up shoes, and gave me a chummy wink.

"Goedemorgen," he rasped. Good morning.

I smiled and kept walking.

Inside the walls were tiled in green and yellow, summery colors of lightness and life. It looked the same in here as the one time I visited before the war to go for a swim with Nellie and Eva. The giant central pool shimmered bright blue, with diving boards at one end and tall, high windows all around designed to catch the meager winter light. Sound bounced off the tiled surfaces and metal roof, and although it was a quiet crowd, the place hummed with the low din of conversations and splashing water.

The paper ticket wilted in my clenched fist, and I stretched my fingers, wiping my hands on my skirt as I headed for the women's changing room. There were a few different ways to do this—I'd considered them all. I'd decided to go with the simplest plan. I heard Annie's voice: *Quicker is better.* Had she actually said that? Maybe.

"Goedemorgen," a white-haired woman said as we slid past each other in the entrance, and I nodded. No need for anyone to hear my voice unless they had to.

Inside the changing room three other women busied themselves with dressing and undressing, smoothing their skirts or tucking their clothing away in the warren of cubicles lining both walls. I set my bag on a bench where I could see the others and pulled my own bathing suit out. I stalled, picking nonexistent lint from the fabric. Looking to my left, I saw a brown-haired woman place her folded clothes on a shelf, then quickly tuck a small purse into the center of the stack of clothes, hidden like a mouse in its hole. She walked away and out to the pool.

I'd worried how I'd stall for time, waiting for the right opportunity, but that wasn't the problem. Now it was nerves. My hands. They trembled, pinpricks of anxiety running through my arms. I crossed my arms and hugged myself tightly to calm the shaking. As I looked down, I saw a ribbon that had fallen from some little girl's hair and lay on the floor, its white-and-yellow pattern like a crushed flower. Like a yellow star.

I breathed deep.

I stepped a few inches closer to the woman's cubicle. The two other women were now standing in front of the mirror, combing their hair and readying to leave, chatting with each other about meaningless things: the chill in the air, the chill in the pool. Every word rang like an omen to my ears, but of course they were oblivious to my thoughts. They scooped up their belongings and walked to the exit, still chatting.

I'd taken two quick steps to the folded clothes in the cubicle when I heard the echo of clicking footsteps behind me. I froze. But it wasn't the brown-haired woman come to collect a forgotten item. Just another swimmer using the changing room. I lowered my shoulders and calmed myself, stretching my arms as if performing some kind of preswimming calisthenics.

The woman disappeared into a bathroom stall.

I dipped my hand into the center of the folded clothes and plucked out the purse in one clean movement. As if I'd been picking pockets for ages. Footsteps again: another swimmer coming in. I had hoped to grab more than one ID on this visit, but it was too busy to risk it.

I passed the incoming woman without making eye contact, looking down to fasten the clasp on my satchel. The stolen purse was inside. I took one look back: the clothes appeared undisturbed. I walked out of the changing room and past the pool and realized I was scanning the water for the woman I'd just robbed. I regretted having to take her entire purse. All the bobbing heads in the pool looked the same, so I silently apologized to them all. My heel slipped on a puddle, and I slowed my step even though I wanted to sprint out of the building.

The ticket-taker was the only person who gave me a second look.

"Leaving so soon, Rosie?"

"Water's too cold for me." I smiled as I said it, like it was our private joke. Surprising, since I'd never been good at flirting. The metal handle on the front door was warm with steam as I pushed into the cold outside. He said something as I left, but I didn't pause to listen. I walked to my bicycle and hopped on, standing on the pedals as I rode in the direction of the crowds swarming in front of the Rijksmuseum and then on the path cutting past what remained of the great green lawn of the Museumplein. This used to be a nice place to have a picnic. Now it was all dirt and sand, the grass bulldozed to install a wall of one-story concrete bunkers. From the other side of the dull gray wall, I heard men's voices. The Germans now held military exercises here.

The air was fresh and dry compared to the humid Zuiderbad, and I gulped it in. With each push of the pedal, I was farther from the scene of the crime and closer to success. Steering into the flow of cyclists, I scanned each face with feral intensity: this man's black glasses, this woman's red enamel brooch, it all jumped out at me, animated and alive. I shouldered into the slipstream of bicycle traffic and exhaled at last. Just another workday and I was just a small part of the mass of local folks making our way to business and school, anonymous and un-remarkable.

"Hey!" An elbow stabbed me from the side as a harried delivery boy and his bike nearly knocked me over. For a moment, I thought I'd been followed and they'd caught me, and a bolt of terror ran through me like a lightning strike. The swift river of bicyclists pulled me on. Then I was in the park, floating past the huge elms and the pretty little ponds, small wooden bridges curving over them like something from a fairy tale. The glen widened into a broad lawn rutted with German ditches dug to dis-courage any planes landing. The birds still sang, though, high in the branches of the towering elms. Up ahead, the column of moving cyclists split into two as they maneuvered around a trash bin.

A trash bin. Everyday objects seemed to take on new meaning, and normal things looked brand-new. They hadn't changed, but I had. It was not yet nine o'clock in the morning, and I'd already committed a crime. Top of my high school class, honors law student, silent observer in every classroom, bumbling bicyclist, reluctant redhead. Now a thief. Today a trash bin was a place to dump evidence. Everything in your world can change.

I tilted to the right and found a gap in the column of cyclists, cut across them, and skidded onto the grass. I hopped off and laid the bike down in a grove of smaller trees newly fledged with pale, bushy leaves, perfect for concealing a criminal. In the coolness of the shade, I tore open my bag and pulled out the small cloth purse. Unsnapping its flap with shaking fingers, I stupidly spilled its contents on the damp, dirty ground.

"Idiot," I said to myself, scrambling to recover everything.

"Can I help you, miss?"

It was a policeman, tall and lanky as a crane. Dots of cocoa-colored mud constellated the lower half of the navy blue pants at my eye level. I looked up. His eyebrows were raised and head cocked, assessing me in the dirt just like the birds in the polders, the marshlands outside Haarlem, long necks angling curiously, seeking a better view of fish in the muddy water below. He bent his long body in half, and before I could grab it, he scooped up the contents of the stolen purse: a few coins, scraps of paper, and then the thing itself. The ID.

He held it up in the practiced way policemen did by now, their duties distilled to one foundational task: sorting people into categories. He looked at the photograph. Then he looked down at me.

"This is you?"

I hadn't even seen the card yet. But the woman I stole it from didn't look much like me. That wasn't the point. She had to look at least a little bit like Sonja or Philine.

So, was this me?

No.

The cop cleared his throat, waiting.

"Officer," I said, eyes wide as if I were just as surprised. My thoughts flew and whirred like thrown paper and suddenly stopped on a childhood memory of my sister Annie hanging halfway out our second-story bedroom window, about to sneak away for the night. I was terrified, not only for Annie but for myself. What would I tell our parents if they asked? "Say anything," Annie whispered with the wisdom of experience, an eleven-year-old bespectacled rebel. "If you can't answer the question, just answer a different question." And she'd been right.

I bit my lip and began to speak. My voice didn't even shake. "Officer, I got pushed off my bike and everything scattered."

He frowned at my bike laid out on the grass, still pinching the ID between his fingers, its stamp-sized photograph a blur of a dark-haired visage. For the woman at the pool, replacing the ID would be an annoyance. For Sonja or Philine, having a fake ID might mean extra food, access to medical care, or even her life.

The policeman kept his eyes locked on mine, his face expressionless, and then looked over his shoulder at the people riding by on the path a few feet away. I waited for him to speak. A small muscle in his jaw flexed and relaxed. His muddy blue uniform was the same one from before the war. It was impossible to know where his loyalties lay. Had he sworn allegiance to the Nazi Party, too? Or was he just an honest Dutchman with a family to support, trying to keep his job? I didn't trust appearances.

As I knelt rigidly on the muddy ground, the dampness of the grass soaked through my stockings. A perfume of rotted oak leaves rose around me, the rich humus of the half-frozen earth. The policeman turned back to me, his eyes squinting, the card small in the span of his huge hand.

I hadn't told Philine and Sonja what I was doing. They would have told me to stop. Nobody knew I was here. I swallowed, my mouth dry. My fingers curled around the little purse as if it were enchanted, a fairytale talisman. But this wasn't a fairy tale. Magic wouldn't save me.

I took a deep breath, looked up at the policeman, and smiled.

"Officer," I said, my voice soft as a petal. "May I have my ID?"

Chapter 6

A RIPPLE OF EMOTIONS slid across the policeman's long face. He reminded me of my father, a tall man with the quiet presence of a mountain.

"Sta op," he said, stretching out his hand. Get up.

I tried to breathe, but my chest felt clamped in iron. He reached his long arm to help me out of the grass, and instead of running, I put my hand in his. I followed his command. Maybe because he reminded me of my father.

He pulled me up to standing, then let go of my hand. But he'd placed something in it.

The ID: he'd given it back to me.

"Take care, miss," he said. And then, in a whisper: "Oranje zal overwinnen."

Orange will overcome. The motto of the Resistance, scrawled on walls around the city before it was scrubbed off by the Germans: *OZO*. Did he think I was in the Resistance? Was he?

But these were questions one could never ask.

"Your ID, miss." He returned the contents to me and I tucked them back inside the purse.

"Bedankt." Thank you.

"Good day, miss."

He touched his fingertips to his cap and walked off, stalking through the crowd on heron legs, nothing to distinguish him from any other cop on the street.

I LEARNED SEVERAL lessons that morning: Never look over your shoulder to see if someone's watching. And do nothing to indicate that something significant will happen, is happening, or has happened between the two of you.

The act itself is the acknowledgment.

I CLEANED OFF my skirt and my muddy hands. My body shook and I felt light-headed, my shirt collar plastered to the back of my neck with sweat. The sounds of conversations glided by on bikes from the other side of the bushes like broadcasts from a new world, and the dazzling blue of the sky, black of the branches, and green of the grass made my eyes water. My thumping heart, my champagne-bubble head. I felt strange, different.

I wheeled my bike out from behind the trees. A little boy in brown corduroy pants stared at me. When his mother saw me, she yanked him away. If I looked the way I felt, I couldn't blame her. I could feel the ID burning through the leather of the satchel against my back, pulsing with righteous energy. It was my first taste of the power of contraband. I'd ridden through the park hundreds of times before the war, but now, with this stolen object in my bag, the familiar felt new. As if the air had a fresh flavor, each lungful flowing deeply through me, from my lips to my fast-pumping feet on the pedals. I rode with the boundless vigor of an outlaw, guiltless and tough.

It was Nurse Dekker who had subtly encouraged my foray into

pickpocketing. She'd once demonstrated how to lift a coin purse from a jacket pocket by walking through the office and stealing one from a volunteer right in front of me. She slipped it out and back in while we chatted about something banal, and the girl was never the wiser. Of course Dekker claimed it was a joke. But it was training.

"Watch it," an older man scolded as I sped in front of him.

I didn't look back. I didn't say sorry.

BETWEEN THE THREE of us girls, we agreed the photo on the ID looked closest to Sonja. I'd expected to feel terrible about not finding one for Philine, but I didn't. Because now I knew I could steal another one. A few days later, crushed in the middle of a crowd attempting to board a tramcar, I looked down and saw the rounded leather corner of a man's wallet poking out of his jacket. It felt like an invitation. Later that day, I stopped by Nurse Dekker's office, dropping the wallet on her desk. She raised an eyebrow.

"There's a couple IDs in there," I said. "One for his work, one for some organization he belongs to." A double score.

"Can you get more?" No congratulations, no surprise, but the Mona Lisa smile on her face let me know she was impressed. I nodded.

And so I became a serious pickpocket, jostling against people on the street and walking away with their wallets, casually nabbing a lady's purse from her bicycle basket as she looked the other way. Twenty-two years of being a polite young lady had trained me well for the job because the way I looked and carried myself was so unthreatening. Just another tactless youth bumping into pedestrians during the evening rush home. I stole so many IDs in the months that followed that I began to think of it as just another skill to add to a postwar résumé, like speaking a bit of Spanish or doing advanced algebra. I felt useful at last.

There were other things I did after that first stolen ID:

Stopped mailing refugee care packages abroad and began
    distributing them to the Jews of Amsterdam, who needed them
    badly. Jews were suddenly allowed to shop only between three
    and five o'clock, the grocery shelves low on basic supplies like
    food and medicine.

Overheard Philine and Sonja discussing Jewish friends who had
    suddenly disappeared.

Delivered food and baby clothing to a refugee family of five living in
    a horse stable on the eastern edge of the city, hiding until they
    could find some way to get across the English Channel.

Offered the wrong information when German soldiers, lost in the
    city, asked me for directions. Anything to make their job a tiny
    bit more difficult.

Watched as the deportations started. "To Westerbork," the SS
    explained, "just temporarily." The trains left every Tuesday.
    Nobody came back.

Thought it could not get any worse.

Chapter 7

Early 1943

B Y NOW, WE were used to the yellow stars. I say "we," but of course it was different for Sonja and Philine. Even once I'd stolen the IDs, each had to make the decision every day about whether to go out with the fake ID and no yellow star, or to wear the yellow star and carry her real ID. It was a risk either way. A Jew who got caught using a fake ID could be arrested on sight and deported to Westerbork, presumably before being shipped to a so-called labor camp: Sobibor and Auschwitz were among the names I heard. I knew nothing about them, the names themselves becoming weapons of Nazi terror. To go out dutifully wearing a yellow star was to invite harassment from German soldiers, and talking back to them was a form of resistance. Not all women, Jewish or otherwise, felt safe doing even that, so duos and trios of Jewish girls walked together for safety. "There are so many stars around my cousin's neighborhood now," said Sonja, "they're starting to call it Hollywood."

Philine uttered a grunt of disgust. "People on the street smile at me sometimes and whisper to 'stay strong,'" Philine told me, grateful for gestures like these from everyday Dutchmen, which she received daily. "It was raining the other day and a tram conductor stopped and practically demanded that I get in, out of the weather," Sonja said. She hesitated; Jews were no longer allowed on the citywide tram system. "'Nonsense!' he shouted, and his face turned bright red with frustration as the other passengers stared. 'Take off that silly thing,' a woman near the front of the car said. She meant the star. I just stood there," she recounted, her voice thick with emotion. "I couldn't take it off, I was worried a soldier might be watching. And now we had created a scene. I know they meant well, but I shook my head, thanked the driver, and ran off in the rain." I was relieved she had. Better to get cold and wet than arrested.

Philine and Sonja eventually solved the problem of whether to wear the star or use the ID with the obvious solution: they stopped going out. They'd leave home for necessary trips to the grocery or the baker. Sonja got a filling from a Jewish dentist whose practice had moved into his kitchen, where he received only Jewish clients. And Philine spent much of her time at Sonja's. The Polaks' neighborhood had been officially designated as Jewish, with Jewish families from other parts of the city forced to "resettle" there. The mood was tense, and so were the soldiers stationed outside. It was better to avoid it.

And yet. Despite all the Nazi propaganda shoved in our faces, we also knew the Soviets had crushed them in Stalingrad and elsewhere in the Soviet Union. The German newspapers available all over town never mentioned these defeats, of course, but the tenor of their propaganda was changing. *TOTALER KRIEG*, read the headline after a recent speech by the despicable Nazi minister of propaganda, Joseph Goebbels. TOTAL WAR. It was meant to inspire the German people and terrify the rest of us, and it did. I couldn't imagine a war more "total" than the one we were already experiencing.

I was heading toward the refugee alliance. Although we were friends, Nellie and Eva had their own social circle, and I no longer confided in them about my fears for Sonja and Philine. My roommates watched me race around Amsterdam doing errands for the alliance, and they'd never intruded or asked too many questions. They'd been good friends, always offering me a serving of their dinners and helping me carry packages up the stairs. Nellie and Eva were sweet, but they couldn't help me. I needed Nurse Dekker and the distraction of work.

The humble, barely furnished office of the alliance always cheered me; at least someone was doing something useful in this city. And Nurse Dekker's stern, steady presence reassured me that there were still people in this country who hadn't lost their moral bearings. It was mid-morning when I arrived; the office would be at its busiest. I pushed through the front doors and stopped. The first thing I noticed was the silence. The usual cast of volunteers was missing. Then I looked around. A catastrophe. The beautifully organized shelves of supplies that Dekker and we volunteers had diligently commandeered, from medical instruments to emergency blankets to the boxes of rubber baby-bottle nipples, looked as if they'd been ravaged by wild animals. The spotless tile floor was streaked with dirt and the harsh black streaks of boot soles. Only Lottie, one of Nurse Dekker's assistants, was there. She started talking as soon as she saw me.

"They stormed in last night and took everything, Hannie," she said. "Just box after box of supplies, everything." Lottie's normally pink face was ashen as she slumped on the floor, sorting the remaining scattered items into boxes.

"Where's Dekker?" I asked.

"Hannie. Come in." Dekker sat in the chair behind a massive oak desk like a captain on a tanker ship navigating an angry ocean of paperwork strewn across the room. Private medical files, daily memoranda, all the evidence of our hard work laid to waste at her feet. She sat with her muscular arms resting on her chair, face set in disgust. Like all emergency aid volunteers, the refugee alliance was officially neutral. Of course, so was the Netherlands itself.

"I don't understand."

"They came for the files," Dekker said. "But when they saw the supplies, they took those, too."

"Can I help?" I asked.

She shook her head. "I've sent everyone home except Lottie. You should go home, too."

A burst of anger zipped through me. "But we have to get back to work," I said.

"This office is now defunct, Hannie," she said, a simple matter of fact, "and I've been conveniently reassigned to a hospital in The Hague." She shook her head, bemused by the transparently strategic timing. It was an easy way to get rid of her here, where she was doing important work, and send her to a different city where she presumably had fewer troublesome Resistance contacts. "You've been so helpful, Hannie. Your family is in Haarlem, no? Go there. Wait for things to calm down."

"Calm down?" I could only imagine further escalation.

"We're in a new phase. The work you've been doing for me"—she lowered her voice so Lottie couldn't hear—"has been very helpful." She stood up and, for the first time since we'd met, embraced me like a mother would, holding me against the warmth of her broad chest. I smelled the starch and the bleach of her white uniform and the slightly sour scent of sweat. She was always so composed, I never imagined her sweating at all.

"I'm not going back to Haarlem," I said. "I have to finish school." Hearing it out loud, it sounded foolish, the worries of a child. But I'd never considered doing anything else, even before the war. And now? As much as I loved them, hiding in my parents' house wouldn't solve anything.

Dekker nodded. She had never tried to talk me into anything, and she didn't now. "Well, then. I have something for you. Come." She stood up and I followed her into the back storeroom. It had been stripped of most of its boxes of emergency supplies and jars of cotton swabs, but a few items were still scattered across the shelves. Dekker picked up a small cardboard box and handed it to me. I looked at the label stamped on the top: *CELLULOSE BANDAGES.*

"This?" I had no medical training, as she knew.

"I'm sorry to say . . ." She searched for the words. "The soldiers stole everything we had, even the sanitary pads and belts, if you can believe it. But we still have a few of these, and they're better than those old cotton rags, eh?" She smiled darkly. "Women are the real experts in blood. Go on, take it, Hannie, a thank-you from me."

As she said it, her stare lingered, communicating something I couldn't quite follow. I was still blindsided by the destruction of this formerly sacred space. "Off you go," she said, walking me to the front door. When we got there, she pulled a slip of paper from the breast pocket of her white uniform and slid it through a slit in the top of the box. "If you ever need to reach me."

"OK," I replied, bewildered.

"Hannie, look at me." Dekker held me by the shoulders to make her point. "You're good at this. You're a hard worker. You're tough and you're a lot more cunning than that freckled face would appear."

I was tough? I blushed, honored.

"Who knows how long this war will last?" Dekker said. "How much worse will it get? I have no idea. No one does. But as long as it lasts, you can keep helping, Hannie. There's always something to be done."

"Yes," I said, not sure what I was agreeing to. I felt a lump building in the back of my throat but refused to give in to it here, in front of her. Nothing that was supposed to happen in my life had happened yet. I needed more time.

"You know how to get in touch, eh?" She tapped the top of the box again.

"What will they do with the files?" I asked. Some of the alliance volunteers had been Jewish. The thought of their private information—names, addresses, emergency contacts—in the hands of the Nazis made me feel ill.

She smiled. "Nothing. I burned all the files a few weeks ago."

"Nurse Dekker!" I laughed.

She shrugged. "God called me to be of service, Hannie. He does not mind what form His service takes."

Dekker took me in her arms and pressed me against her bosom again. She looked me up and down tenderly, like my mother did on the first day of school, making sure all my buttons were buttoned. "Be good, Hannie," she said, her eyes sparkling with emotion. "Goed zijn, goed doen."

Be good, do good.

I nodded and left the refugee alliance for the last time. As I walked away, I had a deep, sickening feeling that I would never see Nurse Dekker again.

ON THE STREET in Amsterdam on a bright day, you could forget for a moment about the horror. The golden sunshine, the sparkling canals, the blue sky, the faces of children—these things were still beautiful. That's what I told myself as I walked to my bike. It's what I told myself as I crammed the box of bandages into my basket so they wouldn't fall out, and what I was thinking when I crashed, basket-first, into the back of a car moving so slowly down the street that I'd thought it was parked. My clunky old bicycle shuddered, clanging against the cobblestones, but the driver of the car didn't seem to notice. Damn these things—the car, the bike, the basket, this war. All of it. I picked my bike up and kicked the fender back into place, then rode around the car. Or what used to be a car. It moved, jerking forward, then stopping, then straining forward again because it had no engine. The old black sedan was being pulled by a wheezing draft horse attached to it with an ancient plow harness, the owner walking alongside with a switch as if plodding through a field. The interior of the vehicle was crammed with clothing, cooking pans, and other household items, rolling slowly on tireless metal rims down the street. The cavity where the engine block had once been now held a wooden crate filled with jagged pieces of scrap metal. Was the old man selling or buying? Probably both. And this old automobile was now his home and his farm wagon. I knew I was staring; I smiled in apology as I passed the man, but he never so much as glanced at me. Both he and the horse were harnessed to the plow, focused on the next footstep, the next minute, the next meal. The bell on my handlebars rang as I rode over a bump, and the horse whinnied. A welcome sound. Most of the pets of Amsterdam, from canaries to house cats to dogs, had disappeared by now. People were hungry.

Still trying to comprehend the horse-drawn car, I started to see a new city all around me. Occupied Amsterdam. A city in filth, in dust. A lone soldier in Wehrmacht green stood in front of a brick wall painting wide slashes of dull gray paint across a rough, bright red series of Allied *V* and *VERZET* graffiti that had been slapped across the night before by someone in the Resistance. *V* for victory. *V* for verzet: resist. It vanished as I rode by. Looking up, I saw that the wall only extended a few feet above the soldier's head before crumbling into crushed bricks. The entire side of the apartment building was half demolished, the remnants of the second floor cracked open to reveal a life-sized dollhouse, the green wallpaper of a sitting room exposed to the elements and streaked with rain damage, ghostly emerald rectangles where paintings used to hang. When Jews were taken away to Westerbork or to prison or . . . who knew where, their homes were scoured clean. The German soldiers collected the most valuable items and those easiest to carry: jewelry, silverware, art. After the Germans came the neighbors, some trying to save the possessions of their former friends, others simply looking for anything useful, from food to soap to wooden furniture they could burn for heat. This particular building had already been picked over; you could tell because no soldiers were guarding it. There was nothing left to protect. Philine had told me about buildings like this in her neighborhood, but seeing one for myself was a shock. I'd waited my whole life to move to Amsterdam, the proud, cosmopolitan city of history and art, of philosophers and adventurers. A city built in a golden age. What the war—no, the Nazis—had done to it was perverted. And I'd closed my eyes to it for too long. It was time to talk to Sonja and Philine.

"She's not here, miss." The Frenks' maid looked nervous. So was everyone these days when they heard a knock on the door.

"Did they go to Philine's?"

She shook her head.

"But where . . . ?"

She saw my fear and reached out to reassure me, her hand landing gently on my arm. "Miss Sonja and Miss Philine went out for a social call," she said. "Mrs. Frenk did ask her to leave the address." She showed me a piece of paper with Sonja's loopy handwriting. I didn't recognize the address.

"Near Wertheim Park," she said, frowning, "in the Plantage."

I hadn't been to the Plantage neighborhood in months. It was a lush, pretty district in the central city, near the zoo and the botanical gardens and other pleasant attractions that were no longer in operation. And the Hollandsche Schouwburg, the Dutch Theater. Or—as I now recalled, the renamed Joodse Schouwburg, the Jewish Theater. I'd read in the Resistance newspaper *De Waarheid* that the Germans had turned the building into some kind of Jewish cultural center. Like most places reserved for the Jews, the area was heavy with German soldiers and checkpoints, discouraging uninvited visitors. Certainly no Jews were eager to visit, whatever the Nazis said about preserving their culture. So why on earth would Sonja go there?

"They went alone?" I asked.

"Miss Sonja said she was visiting a friend. A Madame . . ." She nibbled her lip, trying to recall the name. "Rajah?"

"Ceija!" I said, relieved. Slightly. Sonja had been talking about her for weeks. Madame Ceija, a Gypsy woman who could read the future. So Sonja claimed. She'd begged us to go see her, yearning for a vision beyond the grim horizon of the occupation. I hadn't realized quite how desperate she was.

"Thank you," I said, turning back down the steps.

"Don't you need the address?" she asked, holding the paper aloft.

"I got it," I said. The maid gave me a funny look, but Nurse Dekker had taught me to memorize them.

Chapter 8

ALTHOUGH IT WAS a short ride there, not more than fifteen minutes, the difference between Philine's neighborhood and the Plantage was stark. Vanished was the formerly verdant little island of botanical gardens and lush public parks. As soon as I crossed the bridge, the barometric pressure seemed to drop; a heaviness permeated the air as clumps of soldiers clustered at every street corner eyeing me and the few other passersby with suspicion, their eyes lingering on the left shoulder of my coat in search of a yellow star. From a block away I recognized the familiar arched doorways of the grand Italianate theater. A few old posters for an orchestra concert—by and for Jews only—still hung in the box office windows. A few German soldiers stood out front. I swung my bike in a detour, taking the long way to the address around the opposite side of the block from the theater.

Madame Ceija lived on the fourth floor of a tall apartment building that appeared relatively untouched by the occupation so far, its limestone facade still smooth and white and the welcoming front stoop neatly swept. I let myself inside and waited outside the elevator for a minute, listening to it clanking laboriously somewhere above me. I decided to take the stairs. At each landing, a long narrow window allowed light in;

from the interior courtyard beyond, I could hear people outside, but I didn't stop to observe, taking the stairs two at a time in search of my friends. I flung open the door to the fourth floor, panting.

"Hannie!" Sonja's bright voice sung out from the end of the hallway and she clapped her hands. "How did you find us?"

Philine hugged me, too. Tightly. I knew she got nervous being out on the streets for long these days.

"Have you seen her yet?" I asked, hoping they were ready to go home.

"She's getting prepared for us," said Sonja, walking me down to Madame Ceija's apartment. It was a plain wooden door like all the other ones, except Madame Ceija's had a small totem, a glass trinket that looked like an eye, tacked to the upper corner of her doorway.

"Wards off evil," said Philine. "Supposedly."

"We should leave," I said. "We need to talk." The evil eye only confirmed my own suspicions about the general state of safety.

"It's still legal to walk around the city, Hannie. My God." Sonja frowned.

I stomped my foot and Madame Ceija's door rattled in its frame. "There was a raid at the alliance office," I hissed, wishing I could scream. The girls stared at me, mouths open in shock.

"Are you all right?" asked Philine.

"I'm fine," I said. "Just listen to me."

"Were you there?" asked Sonja.

"I wasn't there when it happened, and they didn't arrest anybody," I said, the words tumbling out as I tried to explain, "but . . ." I looked beseechingly at them, Philine's expression fretful, Sonja's defiant. "I have an idea," I whispered.

Madame Ceija's apartment door opened a crack and all three of us turned. A whiff of incense floated into the hallway. She was not the Brothers Grimm witch I'd imagined. Madame Ceija's skin was the color of strong tea, her eyes a striking hazel, graced with delicate wrinkles around her eyes and mouth from a lifetime of deep emotion. Sonja began to introduce us, but Madame Ceija raised one elegant hand that traveled gracefully despite the weight of heavy brass and silver jewelry adorning her fingers and wrists, and pointed at me. "You. With the red hair." Her accent seemed to come from somewhere to the east. "Come."

"Me?" I asked, taking a step back.

Sonja whirled around and grabbed me by the shoulders. "We can talk afterward, I promise. This will be fun. We need some fun, Hannie." Her cheeks were flushed with excitement; we were finally out of the house, doing what she wanted to do, and she looked as excited as a bird freed from its cage. My heart broke.

"OK," I said. We would talk after.

Sonja beamed and pushed me forward. Madame Ceija regarded Philine and Sonja with polite indifference. "You, wait. Out here."

I gave them one last look. "Don't go anywhere," I said as the door closed behind me.

An indigo velvet curtain draped across the doorway to the sitting room, which was lit by glowing tasseled lamps. A perfumed haze of incense, candle wax, and cigarette smoke wobbled in the air, and the floor was covered in a collage of multicolored fraying Oriental rugs. Madame Ceija positioned herself at a small table draped with a pink silk shawl for a tablecloth. The shuddering slump of a candle dripped into a puddle on a porcelain tea saucer to her right, and next to it sat what I assumed were tarot cards and a large, exotic seashell filled with the butts of a dozen hand-rolled cigarettes, rolling papers, and loose tobacco. It didn't look like any seashell I'd ever seen.

"I—" But Madame Ceija raised her hand to stop me. I folded my arms and leaned back in the bentwood chair. Fine. Let's see what she came up with. When it came to spiritual matters, I tended to be even more of a skeptic than the eternally levelheaded Philine. "Will this take long?" I asked.

"You did not want to come."

I regretted being rude, but I also got the impression Madame Ceija wasn't easily offended. "This wasn't my idea," I admitted.

Madame nodded. Instead of reaching for the tarot deck, she picked up a feather-thin rolling paper and a pinch of tobacco and began to form a cigarette. "Tell me your name," she said.

I cleared my throat. "Hannie."

She flattened the paper and sprinkled a narrow line of tobacco leaves down the middle, the tips of her fingers stained from years of this same ritual. "Your real name."

"Ha!" I laughed, despite myself, and saw the edge of her mouth curl into the ghost of a smile. "My parents named me Johanna," I said. "Jo." I hadn't called myself that since I met Sonja and Philine.

All her attention was directed at the spindly cigarette in front of her. She rolled it between her fingers, smoothed it, then licked it shut. When she was done, she set the cigarette aside and looked up.

"So," she said. "There was a death?"

"Pardon me?"

Madame Ceija tilted her head, as if implying I were the one causing confusion.

"I don't know—"

"Of course," she said. "And that death was too much. For everyone." Her words were soft and almost musical. "But now what? It's been many years." She picked up the cigarette, still unlit, and rolled it between her knobby fingers. She looked into my eyes, then set the cigarette down on the pink silk cloth. "Death is real. We all die. You, as much as anyone, know this."

It was sixteen years ago, but the lesson still felt fresh. Death was not an abstract concept. It could come anytime, to anyone, whether they deserved it or not. Even to someone as full of life as my big sister. Death left nothing behind. Only absence. Madame Ceija's deep-set eyes peered into mine, and for the first time in years, I felt fresh pain from that loss, the balm of time's passage wiped away by her simple acknowledgment. My shoulders bowed with the weight of grief.

"Yes," I said. "I know."

Madame Ceija nodded, as if she didn't quite believe me. "But that was her death. I'm speaking of yours."

"Mine?" Although the room was cool, my cotton blouse clung to my perspiring back. Madame Ceija leaned down and produced a delicate handmade glass ornamented with gold filigree and filled with what looked to be wine. I hesitated. I wasn't sure I should drink anything she offered. But I was thirsty and wanted to get this over with. I took the glass and downed it in a gulp. The wine was syrupy, and its sweetness plucked at something in my brain. In my heart. "Madame Ceija I . . ." I began, not knowing quite what I wanted to say. I closed my eyes, and the taut cords of my neck slackened. I rarely drank alcohol.

"I have nothing more to tell you, my little rose," Madame Ceija said. Her face was soft, her eyes kind. She smiled. "Except this: you will also die."

My chest tightened and I instinctively gulped down a deep breath.

"But not today. And not soon," she said casually, as if informing me I'd just missed my neighborhood tram. "Today, little one, you are alive."

I smiled.

"Something is funny?"

"It's just . . . I thought you were going to tell me about my future husband. Children."

She narrowed her eyes. "Is that what you wanted to hear?"

"No," I said. "Not at all. I just . . ." From where I sat, I had a view of the block's interior courtyard, and once again I heard voices coming from down below. I squinted, trying to get a better view. "What's going on down there?"

Madame Ceija's face darkened. But she pulled back the curtain to give me a better look.

Below us, the empty space in the middle of the block was divided into quadrants. Three of the four featured the usual array of small gardens, clotheslines, the domestic features of a crowded city, a humbler but similar tableau to the one behind Sonja's house. But in the fourth quadrant something else was unfolding.

The space was gray and devoid of greenery or decoration of any kind, just a cement square filled with people—adult men and women—huddled together in small groups and talking, some arguing, others barely moving, leaning against the walls where they could. It was overcrowded. Tension hovered in the air like electricity.

"Is that behind the . . ." I saw the peaked white roof of the building. "The theater?" I asked.

She nodded, staring down at the crowd with me. A few people looked up at the windows of the apartments, but I doubted they could see in.

"They're changing the name again," she said, watching with me. "Some soldiers delivered the signs a few days ago but they haven't put them up yet: *Overslagpunt*. They're not pretending it's a theater anymore."

Overslagpunt: shipping depot.

"They're Jews," I said, looking at the people below.

She nodded.

"They're being deported?" I asked stupidly. The words felt sticky in my throat.

"So it would seem," she said.

We looked down at the open-air prison like children watching ants trapped in a jar, tracking them as they milled about in the confines of the small space, clearly nervous yet trying to remain calm. The theater had been a stage not only for musicians but also for the proud citizens of

Amsterdam, who attended in their finest gowns and topcoats, bejeweled women and men wearing shiny shoes. Now the people below wore layers of unmatched clothing to stay warm in the shaded courtyard, their bare heads covered only by matted hair, faces dull with anxiety.

"Can't we do anything?" I asked, scanning the interior of the buildings for fire escapes or anything else one could use for a ladder to go down and reach them. Or for them to climb up to us. But the interior walls had been scoured bare, and, I realized, anyone dropping a rope down would be doing so in full view of scores of office and apartment windows and the invisible omnipresence of dozens of not-so-neighborly strangers who might earn a reward for describing what they saw. The imprisoned people below collected there like the last drops of water at the bottom of an abandoned well.

"They've been moving Jews in and out of here for months," Madame Ceija said. "There are hundreds more inside the theater; they take turns going inside and out." She gestured toward the hundreds of other windows surrounding the courtyard. "The neighbors here drop things down sometimes," she said. "But only at night when guards can't see. Otherwise . . ." I finally noticed the guards. They stood in small groups at the corners of the concrete square, guns slung across their shoulders and hips. "They arrest anyone who tries to intervene." I followed her gaze to a window across the courtyard, its glass smashed into jagged teeth, the apartment behind it presumably emptied.

Maybe it was the wine. Maybe it was the people milling about in the purgatory below. Or the ravaged office of the refugee alliance, the horse-drawn automobile, the expression on the maid's face, the worried and hopeful voices of my friends in the hallway. Death. Death was terrifying. Too much. And real.

I leaned on the table for support as I clasped her papery hand in my own. "They have to get out."

She raised an eyebrow. "They're trapped," she said, prepared to admit that even her talents, whatever they were, could not help the people held below.

"Not them," I whispered. I pointed to the front door of her apartment, beyond which stood my friends.

Madame Ceija's expression changed. "They are your . . . sisters?"

"Yes," I said, "like sisters. Friends." Staring into her amber eyes, I felt an understanding pass between us.

"How old are you, Johanna?"

"Twenty-two."

She smiled. "You were born into troubled times," she said. "There is only one thing you can do."

"What?" I whispered, hoping there were a spell she could cast or a magical amulet. In this moment, I was willing to put my faith in anything.

She leaned forward and placed the cigarette she'd rolled in the center of my palm, closing my fingers around it. "Be brave."

We stared at each other for another moment; then she leaned back and nodded toward the door. "Tell them to come in."

PHILINE AND SONJA sat on the floor of the hallway outside. "So?" Sonja asked, jumping to her feet. "What did she say? Will he be tall or wealthy or—"

"Hold on," Philine said. She leaned toward me. "Hannie, have you been drinking?"

"She gave me some wine," I said, avoiding the first question. "You should go in."

"You weren't with her for very long," said Sonja. "She did tell you your fortune, didn't she?"

"Just go," I said. "Both of you. Together."

Sonja's eyebrows furrowed. "What did she tell you?"

Madame Ceija appeared in the doorway with an expression so serene it even reassured me for a moment. "Beautiful girls," she said, smiling and beckoning them with her bejeweled arms. Sonja looked back at me, still curious, but they dutifully walked inside. I slid against the wall to the floor, trying to slow down my breathing. Whether Madame Ceija could foretell the future, I wasn't sure. But I knew her advice was sound. It was no different, really, from that of Nurse Dekker: Be good. Do good.

Be brave.

"HANNIE." I HEARD the door click shut. I'd been pacing the hallway, and now, after an excruciating five minutes, Philine and Sonja were stepping outside Madame Ceija's apartment, their faces pale.

"What did she—?" I began to ask, but Philine raised her hand to silence me.

Sonja's face was blotchy, eyes wet with tears. "Dr. Bern," she said, her lips trembling. "I saw him down there." She crushed her face into a handkerchief, sobbing, muffling her cries. "He's supposed to be in Leiden." Her voice broke again.

"The family doctor," Philine told me in a low voice, "he disappeared a week ago; the Gestapo said he was needed at a hospital in Leiden, but . . ."

"He's here," I said. She nodded. I'd heard rumors about the different ways the SS was rounding up Jews, from emptying entire apartment buildings en masse, to arresting young Jewish men right off the sidewalk, to politely requesting the presence of individuals for various kinds of temporary assistance to the Reich. It all added to the sense that, if you were Jewish, you could simply vanish at any time. The scene in the theater courtyard was, finally, evidence that even the worst of the rumors were true.

"Madame Ceija said they were all going to Westerbork," said Philine. She looked into my face for confirmation. I nodded and her hand went to her heart instinctively, as if to shield it. She shook her head.

"Oh, Philine," I said, "Sonja." The three of us stood together, holding each other. Sonja rested her head on my shoulder as her body twitched with soft sobs. We heard the shuffle of footsteps from the other side of a neighboring apartment's door.

"It's time to go," said Philine, turning toward the stairs.

Yes, finally. I silently thanked Madame Ceija. It was time.

Chapter 9

WE WALKED OUT of Madame Ceija's apartment building into a darker world. I could tell by their silence that Philine and Sonja understood, like I did, that this city where they and their families were born was no longer their home. They held each other's hands, keeping their eyes down until we were over the bridge and away from the Plantage neighborhood and the Jewish Theater. I wasn't in as much danger as they were, not technically, but one read in the papers every day about "Jew-lovers" getting arrested and deported to labor camps for the smallest gesture.

"Come on," I said, pushing my bike by the handlebars and veering off the main thoroughfare to a side street, "this way." Although it was late afternoon, well before the eight p.m. curfew, it felt safer to keep a low profile. We knew the propaganda those Wehrmacht soldiers had been sold before the occupation: throngs of beautiful blond girls in curved white bonnets and wooden clogs throwing tulips at the German army's feet. But that hadn't happened. We hadn't welcomed them as brothers. We had folded inward like flowers at dusk, hiding our faces from the trespassing shadow. We Dutch had been a disappointment to our occupiers, and a growing presence of German surveillance was the consequence.

We walked as quickly as we could without drawing attention to ourselves. Shop windows shrieked at us from the dozens of swastika-stamped signs now required in every store: *JEWS FORBIDDEN, JEWS ALLOWED BETWEEN 15:00–17:00 ONLY.* One shop had moved its cash register and counter up to the front door so it could accommodate Jews without allowing them inside, an attempt to continue serving their Jewish customers without violating any laws. Of course, the law could change tomorrow.

A few minutes later, we emerged onto Sonja's street, where I saw Becker smoking at his usual post. Except it wasn't Becker. This soldier was taller, with brown hair, just another anonymous soldier pacing and bored. He hadn't yet looked our way. I skidded to a stop and thrust my bike at Philine. "Take it," I hissed. She looked at me and frowned. "Take it!" I insisted, and she grabbed the bike from me, still confused. But I couldn't explain. I was acting on instinct. My papers were good; perhaps if Philine had a bike they wouldn't question her. Sonja, I hoped, could get by on her looks and charm. If it came to that.

"Guten Tag," I said to the soldier as we approached, hoping to earn the benefit of the doubt by greeting him in his native tongue. He looked up and smiled. Then frowned. Three girls, one bike.

"Guten Tag," he replied, his eyes scanning across the three of us.

I normally tried to fill these interactions with German soldiers by chattering away about the weather, but now I stayed quiet. Afraid of what I might say after seeing the horror of the theater.

"Zigarette?" The soldier stepped forward with a rare pack of the Wehrmacht ration cigarettes and shook a few out. Generous. Suspicious. I was just about to decline when Philine reached out and accepted one. "Bedankt," she said, in Dutch. Thank you. The soldier smiled. Maybe he was a good one. I didn't care. I didn't trust him. Philine was smart—and brave—to take him up on it. Anything to avoid a conflict with a soldier. Sonja took one, too.

"I'm fine," I said, finding the hand-rolled cigarette Madame Ceija had given me, safe in my coat pocket. I fished it out and held it in the air, waiting my turn for a light. With matches scarce, we lit our cigarettes off the burning end of another's. I watched as first Philine, then Sonja leaned forward just inches from the smooth face of the young German, sharing his fire with an intimacy that unnerved me. I noticed Sonja's hands trembling as she held the cigarette. As soon as hers glowed red, I pushed in to relieve her, hoping my own hands were steadier. As I raised Madame Ceija's cigarette up to the glowing red ember of his, I froze. Madame Ceija had written something on the cigarette. As I stepped close to his face, I read the letters there, in faint blue ink: *OZO*.

OZO? "Oranje zal overwinnen," the policeman in the park had said, the one who let me steal that first ID. Orange will overcome. The battle cry of the Resistance, this time from Madame Ceija.

It was awkward and obvious, but there was no time for subtlety as I pinched my fingers around the middle of the cigarette, obscuring the letters as I inhaled, bringing me even closer to the soldier's face. He grinned at his own magnanimity and I relaxed.

"Bedankt," Philine said and kept pushing the bike. She dropped it with a crash at the bottom of the Frenks' stoop, and we darted inside, panting as we flew up the stairs to Sonja's bedroom. Sonja and Philine finished their German cigarettes next to the open window. I stubbed mine out immediately and tore it into pieces before tossing it out, just to make sure. I was shocked by Madame Ceija's boldness, just as I'd been surprised by the sympathetic policeman. Gratified, inspired, but alarmed. Why did they think I was someone who could be trusted with their confidence? Was Madame Ceija part of the Resistance? Did she think I was?

Objectively speaking, nothing had changed since we'd all woken up and begun the day. No new mandates had been passed down from Reichskommissar Seyss-Inquart; no gray-jacketed SS officers had arrived at the door with their terrifying paperwork. But we'd seen what we'd seen. Sitting there in Sonja's bedroom, an oasis of beauty in which we'd always felt protected from the forces of ugliness beyond, we were scared. I could see it in my friends' faces, the lines of worry at the corners of Philine's deep brown eyes, the way Sonja chewed at her bottom lip.

Sonja poured us each a glass of water from the carafe she kept next to her bed, and we drained our glasses as if we were athletes just finishing a race. Philine picked at the hem of her skirt, deep in thought. In worry.

"You've heard," I began, trying to calibrate my voice so it shook less, "about onderduikers, right?"

Philine gasped softly, her eyes still on her dress. Sonja turned to look at us.

"No," she said. "I can't."

"Sonja . . ." said Philine. When she looked up, her eyes were sparkling with tears.

"No," Sonja said again. "I told you, I'm going to America. I won't live in a cage."

"That's not what I'm talking about." *Onderduikers*—we'd all heard the word. Under-divers, a euphemism for what the Jews had to do to survive: dive under, in order to hide. The Netherlands was the same size as Switzerland, but we had only flat land and water. So Jews were hiding underground, in basements, barns, closets, stables . . . At the refugee alliance, I'd heard a story of an entire Jewish family who'd evacuated to a farm to live inside a haystack. I wasn't sure how that was even possible.

"There are people who want to help," I said, thinking of Nurse Dekker. "They'll find you a place to stay—a home, with a family."

"No," Sonja said, her face reddening. "We can't leave now. The Germans are losing in Russia, aren't they? My aunt said so at dinner last night. Things might be changing for the better soon."

"If those are questions," Philine said quietly, shaking her head, "the answer is no. It's not getting better, Sonja. It's getting worse. You saw the theater."

"But . . ." said Sonja, turning to the window again. I realized I was watching a conversation that had taken place dozens of times before, without me present. "How can you live with strangers in a basement? And never go outside, never breathe?" She was near tears. "Just imagine it, Philine."

Philine got to her feet, angry now. "You know about what they're saying about Poland, Lithuania? Jews shot in the street? My God, Sonja," she said with a softer voice now, "you saw it today."

"It's different here," muttered Sonja, her voice breaking.

"Is that why Dr. Bern is locked up at the theater?" asked Philine in a gentle but firm voice. "Because it's 'different here'?"

Sonja was quiet. Her chest rose and fell as she tried to calm her breathing.

"I'll help you," I said, the words spilling from my lips, surprising as unexpected tears.

They both turned toward me, as if they'd forgotten I was there, looking at me with a mixture of love and pity. My heart hammered against my ribs. I hadn't planned on saying it—I had nothing to offer them—but I had to do something.

"You're sweet, Hannie," Sonja said.

"I mean it," I said. "I have a few contacts now and . . . they'll know what to do." My only contact was Nurse Dekker. But she was the kind of person who might be sheltering an onderduiker. Or at least know how to find one. Surely she had contacts in the Resistance, though she never said as much aloud.

"Sonja?" The sound of her mother's voice floated up from somewhere downstairs. Both girls' eyes widened, and they looked at each other.

"My parents swore they'd never go into hiding," whispered Sonja, her voice crumbling to a sob. "And . . . and I'm not ready to go to America yet. I haven't made arrangements."

Philine nodded and put her arm around Sonja's shaking shoulders. "It's too late."

Hearing the words, Sonja melted into Philine and wept. "I know," she cried as she gulped for air. "I know . . . but even if I went with you, what about my family?" Philine and I exchanged a glance: Sonja wasn't fighting us anymore. It felt like a victory as well as a defeat.

"They know people on the Jewish Council," said Philine, stroking Sonja's hair, "like you said."

"Yes." Sonja's breathing began to slow. "Yes," she said again, persuading herself. "It's probably safer to split up, anyway. We can't all hide together." We nodded, watching her. "They'll get out, somehow," she said, her voice vaporous. "They'll find a way." She closed her eyes, and a shiver ran through her body. Philine held her tighter and looked up at me searchingly.

"Hannie?" Philine said. Sonja looked up at me, too. The enormity of what I'd just promised began to seep into my mind like fear.

"Stay here," I said. "I'll be back soon."

I RODE MY bike straight to the refugee alliance "Nurse Dekker? It's Hannie."

Lottie was gone. The main room was empty, still strewn with papers from the raid. I walked to the back and barged into her office, urgency obliterating my usual sense of propriety. "Nurse Dekker?"

Nurse Dekker was gone, too. The room was empty except for her naked desk and rows of barren shelving. Had Dekker been arrested? Detained? Had she already moved on to The Hague? I stood in the echoing space, lost. Most likely she'd just gone home. But I had no idea where she lived, and if I asked around for Dekker now, it would only put her in danger. Just being in the building felt foolish, like walking into a trap. I jogged back outside the building, my senses twitching. At a loss, I rode back to Sonja's to check on them. Philine came downstairs and met me in the foyer.

"I'm going to stay here tonight," she told me in a quiet voice. She often stayed over at Sonja's, now that the curfew was in place. "I'm going to try to talk sense into her. Tomorrow I'll be back at my father's. Meet me there in the afternoon?"

"Of course," I said. "I'll see you then."

We hugged. I hated letting go of her, and my hand lingered on hers, giving it a squeeze. I turned to go.

"Wait, Hannie," said Philine, catching me before I closed the door. "What did Nurse Dekker say?"

I held my breath. Her face was still pale but hopeful, her eyes wide.

"She's working on it," I said. "I'll know more tomorrow."

"Thank you, Hannie," said Philine, her voice cracking. "And please, thank Nurse Dekker, too."

"I will," I said, lying. "I'll see you tomorrow."

I hoped that much, at least, was true.

Chapter 10

LATE IN THE night, Nellie and Eva came back to our apartment. Their whispers filtered into my half-consciousness, obscure and mysterious. Conspiratorial. In my dream, they were plotting against Sonja and Philine. They were going to prevent me, somehow, from helping my friends. I jolted awake with my heart pounding. Worry had found me, even in my dreams.

"Hannie?" Nellie looked over. She and Eva sat on Eva's bed, drinking tea.

"Sorry," I said. "Just a dream."

"You have a fever?" she asked.

The damp cotton nightgown stuck to my chest, and I pulled it away, breathing deeply. "No, I just got overheated," I said. If anything, I felt chilled.

"You left this box on the stairs," Eva said, handing it to me.

It was the cardboard box from Nurse Dekker; I'd left it outside when wrestling with the key to the door. Careless of me to leave it out in the hallway where it could be stolen in an instant. We blamed most petty crime on the German soldiers, but I wouldn't have faulted any of my neighbors in the building for nabbing the bandages for themselves. I shoved the box under my bed. "Thanks," I said to Nellie, embarrassed.

Around three in the morning, I woke up again and heard only the soft rustling of the girls in their beds. It still amazed me that the city could be so quiet in the midst of war. I stared at a corner of the window glass where a feathering crack drew in the freezing night air and a thousand tiny frost crystals were beginning to grow. Half an hour passed as I watched the frost flowers blossom and spread, like the chill that had settled in the minds of my countrymen over the past three years. The streets of the cities were filled with well-behaving people attempting to walk gracefully alongside the constant threat of violence, men with guns around every corner. Over time, the aggression had turned inward, against ourselves. Every day I held a thousand silent conversations with myself, arguments about the right and wrong ways to go about life under occupation, the better and worse strategies for coping with the growing normalcy of Nazi rule. There was no military front in the Netherlands, and so the minds of the people became the front. That's where we were fighting the war.

I sat up in bed for the second time that night.

The box.

As quietly as I could, I pulled the cardboard box out and brought it up to my bed, trying not to wake Nellie or Eva. I moved the box into the patch of moonlight on my sheets so I could see it more clearly. The gift had struck me as odd, even in the moment. Nurse Dekker was always thoughtful, but setting aside an intact box of bandages in the midst of the chaos that morning was unusual, even for her. I slipped the tips of my fingers underneath the cardboard flaps and pulled them apart as slowly and quietly as I could, feeling the woven texture of the tight rolls of soft cotton bandages underneath. Then I touched something different. Smooth.

I pulled it out—a small scrap of white paper—and held it up in the moonlight.

Jan
Hals Tabak & Sigaren
Lange Begijnestraat 9
Haarlem

This was not Nurse Dekker's address. It was a shop address in my hometown. And who was Jan? I looked in the box again, searching for more. The neat rolls of bandages sat like little loaves of bread packed into even rows. Except for one bandage, misshapen, in the corner. I pulled it out. It was an actual Kotex pad. Maybe the last one? I flipped it over, inspecting it in the moonlight. Everything looked normal. Then I prodded it, and my finger slid through an invisible slit in the packaging and I turned it over.

There, on the cushioned surface of the pad, someone had scrawled three letters.

OZO.

I caught my breath and Nellie muttered something in her sleep. I stared at the Kotex pad as if it were a religious icon, glowing with power.

Nellie's bedsprings squeaked again with her movements, and without a second thought I tiptoed to the fireplace. Stoking the last few embers, I set the pad and the note alight in a bright burst of flame that blossomed and died, disappearing to ash in the grate. I knew exactly where the tobacco shop was.

I'd always thought of myself as a remarkably unremarkable Dutch girl. Quiet. Obedient. A bit clever, perhaps. I was good at being dutiful. Until recently, that meant finishing my homework and brushing my teeth every day. Now, for the first time, duty meant something deeper. Somebody had to make sure Sonja and Philine didn't end up in the courtyard of the theater, and there was no one else to do it. It had to be me.

I DOZED UNTIL the early light and then heard Nellie and Eva stirring. Opening my eyes, I saw Eva slipping out the front door. Nellie looked anxious.

"What's wrong?" I asked.

"Hannie." She sat with her knees pressed tightly together, picking at the wool of her sweater with fingers that had been nibbled to the quick. Her face was tight with worry. "You haven't heard?"

"Heard what?" I swung my legs over the bed and pushed the box further underneath with my bare heels.

"There are rumors at the university, Hannie," Nellie said.

"What? What rumors?" My stomach twisted. I half-expected the Wehrmacht soldier with the cigarettes to jump out of a closet at any moment. My mouth went dry. Nellie looked out the window as if she might hear more gossip wafting up from the street. "Some say the Nazis are shutting down all the schools, others that there will be SS officers in all the classrooms. I don't know. Eva is going with her boyfriend to the university to see."

"Is it safe?" I asked. Even as I did, Nellie was pulling on clothes as if she couldn't bear the suspense any longer and had to find out for herself.

"I don't know," she said. "Come with me."

We started riding the ten minutes to the University of Amsterdam. We could tell there was something wrong even before we reached the campus. Clusters of students were talking to each other, leaning into small circles reading a piece of paper, looking over their shoulders. Some of the girls were crying. Some of the boys were shouting. We coasted our bicycles to glide to a slow stop at the edge of the great lawn. A few students stood on the law school steps, their young faces stricken and confused. Everywhere around them, from the doorway to the sidewalks, was covered with a motley carpet of cream-colored flyers, some ground into the grass, some balled into projectiles, some pristine and untouched. At the top of each one was the spidery stamp of a swastika. I turned to Nellie, but she already had one. I leaned over her shoulder.

I, a student of the University of Amsterdam of the Netherlands and the German Reich, swear loyalty to the Reich's constitution and pledge:

That I, as a courageous German citizen, will always protect the German Reich and its legal institutions,

To be faithful and obedient to the leader of the German Reich and people, Adolf Hitler,

To uphold my loyalty to the Reich upon graduation by swearing allegiance to the Wehrmacht, so I may be of service to the Reich and the Nazi Party in war and in peace.

That if I do not make this pledge of loyalty, I will be removed from the university immediately and barred from further education or employment within the Reich.

Always attentive to such details, the Nazis had left a designated space for the student signature.

I laughed. Funereal laughter, the terrible, truthful reaction one has when faced with a horror beyond absurd. I laughed because it was now so obvious. We were on Berlin time, and now we were to become Germans, too. "So, we have to join the Nazi Party to stay in school?"

Nellie shook her head, amazed. "It's crazy," she said, turning the paper over to make sure there was nothing else on it. There wasn't. This was it. A loyalty oath. Now, after two national strikes, thousands of gallons of paint thrown at their recruitment posters, and a Resistance movement that felt as if it was gaining power, the Germans had finally figured it out:

we didn't like them. Demanding we pretend to—with a declaration of loyalty—was their logical response.

"I guess that's it," Nellie said, shaking her head. "De kogel is door de kerk."

It was something people had said after the Great War: the bullet is through the church. We were past the point of no return. When a war first begins, most people still share some sense of basic decency, tacitly agreeing about what's off-limits and what's not. But then people get desperate. Eventually they attack the very things they swore to protect: women, children, holy places. I pictured a Wehrmacht soldier spraying thousands of rounds of ammunition into the vast cavern of the St. Bavo Church. It was easy to imagine.

"I think you're right," I said. *De kogel is door de kerk.*

Students milled around the edges of the campus, but nobody was entering the buildings. There was no sign of administrators or professors, just German soldiers holding their guns and watching us.

"Well, I'm not signing this," Nellie said. She tossed her flyer to the grass. Unassuming, modest Nellie. I'd never thought of her as a rebel, but she knew what was right.

"Me either," I agreed.

Neither of us said the next thing. We didn't have to.

Riding my bike out of central Amsterdam, I passed sandbags lining the front of the corner café where a small riot had broken out a week earlier, and rough pine boards covered the broken window. The circular kiosks that previously had featured posters for the Amsterdam symphony orchestra were now plastered in the repeating patterns of Nazi propaganda: young blond men and women smiling and looking skyward and fly-eyed, ratlike "Jews" leering and plotting and scaring children. Across the canal, parallel to me, I saw a long Wehrmacht truck with drab canvas covering its rear cargo, parked in front of a house. German soldiers with rifles pushed two people, a man and a woman, into the back of the truck.

Were they Jews? Resisters? Troublemakers of some other kind? I rode on. Raids and arrests like this one were happening everywhere now. *We should have taken these steps earlier.* It ran through my head over and over as I passed boarded-up shops and hollowed-out buildings. *They need to get out of here.* I pedaled faster. By the time I got to Philine's apartment, I had rehearsed my lines a dozen times. *It's time to go.*

"It's Hannie," I shouted as I approached the Polaks' apartment door, hoping to allay the fear of an unexpected knock.

The door opened, and Marie, the German housekeeper, welcomed me inside. "Everything all right?" I was still panting from the ride.

"Fine," I said. I looked past her, but nobody was in the sitting room, so I started down the hall. "Is Philine here?" I asked, glancing back. Marie's eyes were red. I'd never seen her emotional at all. "Marie?" I stopped.

She dabbed at her eyes with a handkerchief. "They're at the end of the hall," she said. The last door led into what I assumed was Mr. Polak's bedroom. I'd never been inside. I knocked. "Philine?" I said. "It's Hannie." Softer now.

I heard a low murmuring and then the door opened. It was Mr. Polak. "Et voilà, la petite dernière," he said with his usual sweet smile. "Come in." He didn't look well. His already thin face was now gaunt and greenish white, his eyebrows too large for his face. His deep brown eyes were dark with worry.

"Hannie," said Philine, embracing me tightly. She had been crying, too. Her body vibrated with emotion as we held each other. Then, unexpectedly, somebody else was hugging us both.

"Sonja?" I said, but she buried her face in my back and said nothing. Eventually Mr. Polak untangled us gently, keeping hold of his daughter's hand.

"We're ready, Hannie," said Sonja, looking at Philine. "Just the two of us." She pointed to a bulging suitcase on the floor. "Philine said I should just take one." I stiffened at the sight of it. Sonja had actually packed a suitcase. I could only guess how painful it must have been for Sonja to leave behind her parents, the aunts and uncles on the fourth floor, all her beautiful things, her entire life. Next to it I saw another suitcase: Philine's.

"De kogel is door de kerk."

"Yes, I'm afraid so," agreed Mr. Polak. I wasn't even aware I'd said it out loud.

"Oh, Mr. Polak," I said, choking on the emotion rising from my heart to my throat, but he patted my hand firmly, like a good teacher, reassuring.

"No time to dwell on it," he said in a kind voice. We were all trying to maintain our composure. "Thank you for coming, Hannie." He looked in my eyes, and for the first time I saw a tremulous flicker of fear there. "Philine says you have a . . . plan?" I was nearly knocked over by a wave of nausea and I must have gasped a little. "Hannie?" he asked, concerned. They all looked pained, ashamed of having to ask this of me, or of anybody.

I steadied myself with one hand on the dresser. There was an old photograph tucked into the mirror hanging above it: Mr. and Mrs. Polak; a little boy, Philine's brother; and what must have been baby Philine in the woman's arms. I'd never seen her mother before, but she looked just like Philine. She was gone, of course, and Philine's brother was gone, too. Now I was taking Philine. Soon it would just be Mr. Polak, alone. I wondered about Marie: Would she really stay on as the housekeeper? Would she be permitted to? Philine's father tenderly plucked a stray thread from the shoulder of his daughter's blue sweater. His hand trembled, and he quickly placed it back in his pocket. How much longer would Mr. Polak even be here? In this apartment? In this city? There were no answers. As I followed my questions to their logical conclusion, I felt my knees bow and I coughed, my throat dry as sand—and then I looked at Philine and Sonja and Mr. Polak, who stood silently observing my every movement and expression. They had all the same questions I did, and they were looking to me for the answers. Only a few seconds from dissolving into hysteria, I wanted to drop to the carpet and wail . . . but I couldn't let them down. I took a deep breath.

"Yes, I do," I said, to give myself courage. I knew my voice was wobbling, but I ignored it. "I have a plan." It had all been slightly abstract, my ideas about the loyalty oath and the soldier with the cigarette and Madame Ceija, the Jews in the courtyard, and the slip of paper Nurse Dekker left me in the box. *OZO*, and only a vague notion about how all these things fit together. But I knew one thing. "They're coming with me to Haarlem, to a safe place to stay for a while," I said, steadying my voice with each new word.

"Haarlem?" said Sonja, who had still never been there. Philine looked surprised, too. No doubt they'd assumed we'd look for a hiding place somewhere in Amsterdam. As Philine and Sonja stared at me, I felt the weight of this decision for the first time. My best friends, these two beautiful, smart, educated, loving, kind, funny people, were entrusting their lives to me. Mr. Polak asked me thousands of silent questions with his eyes, none of which I could answer except with smiles and tears. He squeezed my hand so hard it hurt.

"I have a contact there," I said. Sonja's eyes lit up. She seemed a little like herself again.

"Who?" she asked.

"Shh!" Philine said. "Not out loud, Hannie." We glanced around, although we were alone. Philine was right. We had to be careful.

"We're ready," she whispered. "Sonja already said her goodbyes."

"Let's go, then," I said. It was midday, the least suspicious time of day. "Make sure you've removed all the stars," I said, touching my own shirt collar to demonstrate, "and only fake IDs from now on. Don't even bring your real ones with you."

"What about your schooling?" said Mr. Polak to me as we walked toward the front door. Always the French teacher.

"I quit," I said.

The girls gasped. "Hannie?" said Philine, as if she thought I might be joking. I fished a copy of the loyalty oath out of my pocket and handed it to the three of them, watching as they read.

"I'll go back after the war," I said with a nonchalance I didn't really believe. I could feel my career evaporating minute by minute, like a wisp of smoke, and it hurt. But it was nothing compared to what Sonja and Philine were facing. "I'll go wait in the front room," I said, giving Mr. Polak a hug and a kiss on the cheek, which he accepted with softly closed eyes, as if praying.

"Take good care of them, Hannie." Tears began to spill down his sunken cheeks, but his voice never wavered. "Perhaps I'll come visit you in Haarlem sometime. We can take a walk in that beautiful park, the Haarlemmerhout. I went there with Philine's mother once."

"Yes." I nodded, knowing it wouldn't happen. "I'd love that."

"All right, then," he said. "Thank you, Hannie."

I nodded awkwardly, unable to accept his thanks. I wasn't sure I was worthy of it. "Please take care of yourself, Mr. Polak."

"We all have to do our part, eh?" he said. "I'm grateful to be here, in my home, where I still have the opportunity to make whatever efforts one can. I couldn't survive in a closet anyway"—he laughed, or tried to—"but you girls have each other and you'll be happy together. And I'll be here, fighting for you girls out there while you're fighting for me over here. Fighting against fate, n'est-ca pas? It's a worthy goal." His voice was even in tone, but tears rolled down the wrinkles of his cheeks and onto his collar, damp with love. He opened his arms, and both Sonja and Philine folded themselves into his embrace, the three of them huddled in grief. This was, I realized, the second harrowing farewell Sonja had endured today, and her eyes were raw and red with the sorrow of it. I stepped backward toward the hallway to give them privacy. Sonja hugged Mr. Polak, and he whispered something in her ear. She nodded, sobbing, and he gave her one last embrace. As Sonja walked to the doorway, Philine turned to her father.

"Write to me," he said, as if she were just leaving for a summer holiday, "and remind me what book that was you told me to read." Philine's arms were draped around her father's neck, her body convulsing with racking sobs, and he placed his hand at the small of his daughter's back to help her remain standing. "I'll let you know what's happening here and Marie will send you a note, too. And when you finish knitting those mittens, you can send them to me, yes?" Philine couldn't speak; she just cried into his shoulder. Her father patted her hair, smoothing it with the palm of his wrinkled hand. Then Marie was at her side, and they embraced like mother and daughter, silently sobbing.

"Go on, now," he said finally, pushing his precious daughter to arm's length so he could see her face one last time. Sonja and I stood transfixed. She and Philine might never see their families again. Then Sonja spoke up.

"My mother said something when we left," she said, her voice tremulous. She wasn't one for speeches but couldn't seem to help herself. "A person—a human being—is not just what we see here, but it's also our souls." She sniffed back tears, trying to recall her mother's exact parting words. "The soul, or the memory of the people we love, it never leaves us. Suffering ends, pain ends, even life ends. But love doesn't." She burst into tears and we all surrounded her. "She said that if we have the memory of someone we love, then we are the mazldik." Sonja smiled at me and translated: "The lucky ones." It was the first time I'd heard her speak Yiddish. She wiped her face with Mr. Polak's handkerchief and then handed it back, shaking her head. "I don't have any tears left," she said with an exhausted sigh.

"Go with Hannie, girls," Mr. Polak said, guiding her gently in my direction. "I would give you advice, but . . ." He paused and then said with a sense of awe, "None of us have traveled down this road before, eh?" He looked at me. "Perhaps I should be asking you."

Me? I knew nothing, had no experience. But I held out my hands to Sonja and Philine because it was the only thing I could do. I reeled with memories of how they had invited me into their world, how loving and generous they had been to me. Maybe God, if He was really up there, knew it would take two hearts to replace Annie. Sonja looped her arm through mine, and Philine stood suspended in space between me and her father, each one of us holding a hand.

"I love you," Mr. Polak said. "More than anything. You know that."

As we stood in the open doorway of Philine's apartment, suddenly the door across the hall opened. "Hallo!" A husband and wife about Mr. Polak's age greeted us with a neighborly wave, their friendly expressions fading when they saw ours.

"Mr. and Mrs. Barend," Mr. Polak said in a bright tone, pasting a smile on his face and turning to his daughter. "Now, remember, when you girls come back tomorrow, make sure to bring that book you borrowed." Unblinking, we all nodded. The two neighbors nodded with nervous smiles and hurried to the stairwell. They knew better than to be curious.

Mr. Polak turned back to his daughter, and with one slender finger he tipped her chin up to look in her eyes. "We'll see each other soon," he said. "Je t'aime. À bientôt." With his back to the neighbors, rivers of tears now streamed down his cheeks. Marie stood behind him silently, staring at the worn carpet beneath her feet, unable to meet our gaze.

Philine nodded to them both, her chin wobbling. "À bientôt," she whispered, her voice quaking with grief. "Je t'aime." Marie handed over a small suitcase. I carried it for her as we descended the stairs slowly, afraid to imagine the future.

On the way to the Centraal train station, we passed the University of Amsterdam, its broad green lawns now empty. The girls stared. Soldiers stood in small groups in the street, but all was quiet. None of us spoke.

Coming out of the apartment, Philine and Sonja were new people. No yellow stars on their clothing, false gentile identification papers in their wallets. We bought our tickets to Haarlem in silence and boarded the next train. Finding seats together and stowing their two little suitcases, we each turned to the windows, speechless. I could only imagine what was going through their minds. Leaving home, even as I was headed back to my own. In that moment, I had a powerful sense of running toward something instead of running away. The Nazis hadn't kicked me out of school; I quit.

I'd always been someone who stuck things out. But as I discovered that day, there is power in quitting. You only have to do it once to learn the lesson forever. Quitters are dangerous because quitters know a secret: it is always possible to start over.

Part Two

The
RVV

1943–1944
Haarlem

Chapter 11

Spring 1943

I T WAS NIGHTTIME. Better if nobody saw Sonja and Philine at all. The
Germans had turned off all the streetlights at the beginning of the war
to make bombing more difficult for the British, so at night the streets
were dark as the woods. We walked through Haarlem wordlessly. What
was there to say?

I found myself nervous to see my childhood home through the eyes of
Sonja and Philine. I'd described it to them the way I'd always perceived
it myself: "A little yellow-brick house, two stories, with two bedrooms
upstairs, a kitchen garden out back, and a park across the street with a big
grassy lawn." All this was still true. But as we approached on foot in darkness, it looked different. Shabbier. Less a beacon of hope than a drab out-
post. I couldn't imagine anything as exciting as onderduikers hiding in
dull little Van Dortstraat 60.

"That's it right up there," I said. "Four houses in from the end." I tried
to make out their expressions. When Amsterdammers thought of Haarlem, they thought of the soaring St. Bavo Church in the city's central
square, with its organ played by Handel and Mozart and the Golden Age
painter Frans Hals buried in the crypt. It was an old city, and I wondered

if the girls had envisioned the Schaft home as a traditional Dutch gable-roofed cottage with a dairy cow out back, not this bourgeois block of yellow-brick homes with their tidy flower boxes. It all looked so small and common to me now.

"There's the park," said Philine. I glanced over and for the first time realized the central feature of the little park was not a little fishing pond, as you'd find in Amsterdam's majestic Vondelpark, but an ancient windmill—an actual thatch-roofed windmill—that looked like the pastoral backdrop to a Pieter Brueghel painting. We were a long way from the elegance of central Amsterdam.

"It's nice," said Sonja. She always had excellent manners.

"We should get inside," I said. "My mother must be waiting."

Of course she was waiting. I'd asked Nellie and Eva, themselves traveling back to Haarlem, to let my parents know about the loyalty oath and my plans to move back. Only me. It was cowardly but time-efficient. Now they would be waiting for my return, desperate to know my plans for the future. I was desperate to know my plans for the future, too.

"I can't wait to meet your mother," Sonja said. Now we'd seen the windmill, she was probably picturing a red-cheeked matron in braids and wooden clogs to open the door. Actually, the only thing wrong with that picture was the clogs.

"She'll love you," I said. I hadn't told them that my mother and father didn't know Sonja and Philine were coming. The girls had enough to worry about.

"Did you get your red hair from her?" asked Philine.

We were almost at the door.

"I'm the only redhead in the family," I said. "Though my father said something about an ancient Viking ancestor . . ."

"That's your wild side," said Sonja.

Philine nodded. "She has the heart of a berserker."

I laughed, relieved they were still able to find humor in the present situation. Whether or not they were serious, I took it as a compliment. Especially as I was about to be treated like a fragile figurine. From the moment Annie got sick when we were children, my mother took up worrying about the family's health—my father's and particularly mine. And not just my health, but anything that might possibly be perceived as dangerous. Boating, skating, or just crossing the street, these were all causes for worry.

I stood on the stoop, and the girls waited behind me. I raised my hand and paused. If you have to knock, is it still your home? Then the door opened.

"Johanna!" my father pulled me into his body, crushing me against his oak tree of a chest, and I felt like I was six years old again, a tiny thing in a giant world. I pulled back and saw my mother behind him, eyes crinkled in a mix of love and anxiety. With her, it was always both.

"Jo," she said, opening her arms to me. As I turned to hug her, her gaze caught on Philine and Sonja standing behind me in the shadows, and her mouth tightened into a prim line. She grasped my hand, putting off the hug for now. "You brought friends," she said.

"Yes, let's go inside," I said brightly, attempting to set the mood.

"Come in," said my father, holding open the door for the three of us.

My mother took two steps back and reached for the hem of her housecoat in a gesture I knew by heart: fingers burrowing into the thin cotton, twisting and pleating the fabric, wringing her hands with fear. We stood in the closet-like space of our entryway, my shoulders rubbing against Sonja's and hers against Philine's.

"It's a pleasure to meet you, Mr. and Mrs. Schaft," they said over each other, sweetly and gratefully.

"Pieter, please," my father said, bending down the way he had to because of his height, like an ancient tree bowing to the wind. They nodded, smiled. He was a calming presence.

"I told you about Philine and Sonja, my friends from university?

They're also studying law." I picked up Philine's suitcase in one hand and Sonja's in the other and turned toward the stairs. "Or were, anyway. Come on," I said, looking at the girls.

"Where are you going?" my mother asked. Her eyes were wide, panicked. She knew. For the thousandth time, I questioned my strategy. I knew the situation would put my mother into a state of panic, her natural Christian charity wrestling with a very real fear of arrest, deportation, and death. Better to just show up.

"Oh. Philine and Sonja are going to stay here for a little while." I turned to the girls, who smiled nervously. "Come on, I'll show you the bedroom. It's not fancy, but for now it'll do."

Philine glanced back at my parents, her face pale. "Thank you," she said. Sonja said the same in a whisper, and they followed me up the narrow stairway. When I got to the top, I paused and looked back. My mother turned to my father, her face ashen. She opened her mouth, said nothing. Then closed it again. My father put a hand on her shoulder and she brushed it off. They disappeared into the living room.

"You didn't ask them first?" asked Philine, her eyes wide.

"I knew they would say yes," I said, "so it doesn't matter." This was partly true. I had a feeling they would agree to letting the girls stay at least for a few days until I made contact with the Resistance and found something more permanent. I could tell the girls were unhappy, but nothing else mattered except getting them hidden.

"Watch your head," I said as Philine bumped into the steeply pitched ceiling of my attic bedroom. She put her hand to her forehead but didn't complain. She and Sonja were silent, staring at their new home. Could I picture Philine and Sonja sitting on the double bed together, passing their time sewing and reading and helping my mother with the cooking? Maybe. I knew Philine, at least, could cook. There was probably something Sonja could do. Embroidery, perhaps. Would this really work?

It had to. And I hadn't asked my parents' blessing because it was not the kind of favor one could ask of someone else; it was too much.

The double bed, which I once shared with Annie, took up nearly the entire room even though it was pushed into the corner to save space. There was one spindly bureau with four drawers for clothing and a trunk at the foot of the bed, along with a row of hooks on the wall by the door to hang things. A folding wooden chair leaned against the wall; once unfolded, it would take up most of the free floor area remaining. A single window looked out onto the back garden. Not that anyone would be looking out of it. I made a note to cover the glass with a dark cloth tomorrow to keep nosy neighbors from peeking in. If they were to help my mother, they'd have to do it hidden up here. I tried to picture Philine and Sonja cheerfully darning socks to pass the time but couldn't quite convince myself. The vision abruptly dissolved into something more realistic: two thin, anxious girls huddled together in a shrouded room, worrying.

"Hannie," Sonja said. Philine laid her hand on Sonja's wrist.

"Hmm?" I said.

Sonja looked at Philine as if seeking permission to speak. Philine was quiet.

"It's just . . . where will we all sleep?" Sonja said.

"You two will sleep in the bed and I'll bring up a cot. My father has one in the shed."

"You didn't ask your parents?" Sonja whispered.

"It's fine," I said. "They understand."

Sonja appeared to be on the brink of tears.

"I'll be right back," I said.

I galloped down the stairs, swinging around the baluster as if behaving like a carefree child would take us all back to an easier time. "Where do we keep the extra blankets?" I asked, bursting into the living room. My parents stood by the little woodstove, staring at the flames through

the open door. My father turned and smiled, but my mother kept her
back to me.

"Your friends," he said.

"Yes, sorry!" I laughed, as if it were a shared joke. "It all happened in
the past few days and I didn't have time to talk to you—after everything
with the loyalty oath, things got so busy. Nellie told you about the oath?"
My father nodded as my words tumbled out like marbles from a jar. "It
seemed obvious they should come to Haarlem, to be with us. I know you
haven't been to Amsterdam in a while, but you wouldn't believe how
much it's changed. Philine's neighborhood is barricaded with these huge
barbed-wire fences too high to climb over, it's disgusting. And the cur-
fews are getting worse and the restrictions on shopping—"

"What are you talking about?" he said.

"She's Jewish?" my mother whispered, verifying something she already knew. She looked as if she might faint, her face was so white. "It's
just . . . it's just, I didn't see a yellow star," she said finally. "They have to
wear a star, don't they? The Jews, I mean?" Her voice shook.

A part of me wanted to scream. But now I took a deep breath. She was
right to be scared. I was putting them both at risk. Hugely.

"They do," I said calmly, though also keeping my voice low for safety.
"But I got Sonja and Philine fake IDs so they can take off the stars. It's
safer."

"How?" my father asked. "Got them where?"

"I stole them."

"What?" My father's jaw fell ajar.

"The people I got them from can get replacements. They're not in any
danger. But Philine and Sonja are."

"The people you 'got them' from?"

"They asked you to do this?" my mother said. "Those girls?"

"God, no." I laughed and saw my mother flinch as I took the Lord's name in vain. "Sonja and Philine discouraged me. But there's a whole group of . . ." I stopped myself. "Lots of people are doing things like this. Helping. Like we are."

"We?" said my father.

"Onderduikers," my mother whispered, as if the word itself was dangerous. It was.

"That's right," I said. "If we can't get them out of the country, then we can find them a place to hide."

"Don't they have families of their own?" she said.

"Aafje . . ." my father said softly, calling her by her name to get her attention.

"I have a right to ask." Her voice grew louder. "We have a right to know these things, Piet. This is our home. Will the rest of their families be joining them here, or . . . ?"

"Philine's father refuses to leave his apartment in Amsterdam; he's convinced this will all end soon. But he's wrong," I whispered. "Sonja's family is still trying to decide what to do. But time is running out and I'm afraid they don't realize . . ."

My father took me and my mother by the arms and walked us into the kitchen for privacy. My gaze landed on the shelves where we kept our dishes. Over the past three years, as a daily-use dish got chipped or cracked, my mother had relented and begun to serve off the nicer china she used to reserve for Christmas and Easter. It had been their fanciest wedding present. Now the fine china was mixed in with all the rest.

"We don't have enough bowls for them," she said, pointing to the shelves. "They say Jews eat on separate dishes for different days . . . and they eat special food, don't they? We can barely feed ourselves these days with nothing to buy at the market."

"They're not religious, Mother. They don't need anything special. They eat the same things we do."

My mother stood with her hand at her lips, as if afraid of what she might say next. "It's just . . ." She started to speak, then stopped. Then started again, compelled by some wild emotion that made her voice quaver. "What if one of them dies in our house? What would we do with the body?"

"Aafje!" my father shouted without shouting. He looked at her as if trying to place a name to a stranger.

"Oh, I've shocked you?" she said, her face twisted with fear. "What about the thief?" She pointed at me.

"Now, wait," he said.

"No." She fixed her gaze on me. "Let me ask something else: What about the extra laundry on the line? Mrs. Snel next door knows more about the runner beans in my garden than I do; that's how much time she spends looking at my backyard. You think she's not going to notice two new sets of clothes? And how do we feed five adults with ration cards for three?" She waited, furious. "Well? These are ugly questions, I know, but your father and I have a responsibility."

"That's exactly what I'm saying," I said. "We have a responsibility."

She shook her head as if amazed by my incomprehension. "A responsibility to protect our children—our child," she said, then turned toward my father and began to cry, burying her blond head in his rough wool vest the same way I had when I walked in. Her body quaked with sobs.

"Go upstairs," my father said to me. Not angry, exactly. Grave.

I stalked out of the room, my spine stiff with self-righteousness. But as soon as I reached the stairs, I was flattened by a wave of emotion, like a toddler caught in a swell at the edge of the beach. I made it halfway up the stairs, suspended between my family and my friends, when I heard an extraordinary sound rising from the kitchen: the suppressed wail of my mother's sorrow and fear. A sound I hadn't heard since Annie died. She gasped for breath, my father soothing her. They moved to the living room by the fire, and I heard their low murmuring, soft as doves. I peeked through the railings and watched as my father caught a stray golden curl and tucked it behind my mother's ear.

They'd known each other only a few months before they got married, over thirty years ago. What I knew of their lives before children was pieced together from years of family gatherings and overheard conversations because they rarely talked about themselves. She was the daughter of a Christian minister, a good girl, pious and pretty. My father was worldly in comparison. Full of philosophical ideas and political convictions with his talk of the means of production and the coming revolution of man. Yet over the years, he turned out to be even quieter than she. In the beginning, this troubled my mother, she once told me, wondering what he was thinking, wondering if he was happy or sad. But over time, she'd come to appreciate the quiet. She said it gave her space to think.

"Aafje," my father whispered, kissing her small fist. I stayed on the stairs to listen.

"We should consult Father Josephus," she whispered.

My father took her face in his hands and stared into it, full of love. "Nobody can know," he whispered, a small tremor in his voice. They looked in each other's eyes for several long moments as tears rolled down my mother's pink cheeks.

"Did you see?" she said finally, her voice rough from the crying. She cleared her throat. "Did you see what they were carrying?"

My father shook his head.

"Just one suitcase, Piet. Each girl had just one."

He nodded.

"Imagine all your belongings, everything, in one small suitcase."

My father was silent, staring at the orange glow of the fire as if it were a crystal ball. They watched together, not speaking. Finally my mother wiped her eyes with the hem of her apron and smoothed it over her lap.

"I suppose it's for the best," she said. "Since the bedroom is so small."

She rose from her chair and walked to the oak chest by the sofa. It, too, had been a wedding gift from her parents, who hoped she would have a large family, three or four children, maybe more. The carved lid of the chest creaked under its own weight as she lifted it on its brass hinges and took two of her hand-knitted blankets out, handing them to my father.

"It may not be winter anymore, but it's still cold," my mother said. She peered around the arched doorway and looked at me on the stairs. She'd been aware of me the whole time. "Take these to the girls," she said with a gentle, tired smile.

I shot to my feet. Standing, I found that, just like my mother, I needed to smooth my skirt and wipe my cheeks. Somehow they had gotten all wet.

Chapter 12

"Is it still cold out?" Sonja asked, watching me get dressed. She and Philine sat scrunched together in bed, holding their teacups in both hands against their chests like tiny furnaces, the vapor rising like smoke. They hadn't been outside in two days.

"Good luck," said Philine, as if I were going on a job interview. Which, in a sense, I was.

"Bring some magazines back, would you?" Sonja called after me. "Or sweets?" They were making a huge effort to seem cheerful, despite the situation. I knew they felt a sense of relief at having made the decision to leave Amsterdam at last. We were all aware the novelty would wear off at some point, but it seemed bad for morale to bring it up.

"Keep your wits about you," said Philine. "That's what my father always says."

"I'll try." I imagined Mr. Polak standing in his apartment doorway and then banished the thought. "See you later on," I said, leaving them with a casual wave, trying to forget the fact that I had no idea how long they would have to stay in that tiny room. Months? Years? They must have been wondering the same thing.

Hals Tabak was on a narrow but busy little side street not far from Haarlem's Grote Market square at the center of town. It was the kind of street that, before the war, thronged with people on a typical Saturday, when Haarlemers would be out buying all the usual sundries, some necessary, some not, from a variety of establishments: a hardware store, a bakery, a newsstand, a butcher, a cheese shop, a toy store, a smoke shop. That's where I was to wait for my Resistance contact. This Jan person.

Three years into the war, the downtown shopping district was quieter now. At least half the stores were closed, and the others were operating on ration cards. Lines of weary citizens threaded out the shop doors and meandered down the sidewalks, where grandmas and fathers and the oldest daughter in the house took their spots against the papered-over windows of the toy store and the men's haberdashery, both closed for ages now. The people in the lines were quiet, bored, acclimated to the daily routine of waiting for the things they used to take for granted, often receiving items they didn't even want. It's not as if there were a choice between rye bread and dinner rolls at the bakery anymore; now there was just one basic loaf of something they called bread, though we all suspected it was mostly sawdust. As soon as you attempted to slice it, the whole thing crumbled into sandy, tasteless clumps that stuck to the roof of the mouth. We hated it. The people barely looked at me as I walked my bike past them. Nothing was interesting now.

The tabak was closed and, judging by its dust-covered windows, had been for some time. Peering through the haze, I saw glass cabinets and ceramic canisters and a heavy brass cash register ready to serve, if only someone would stock the place with goods and someone else had money to buy them. The scale hung perfectly balanced in the air with nothing in either of its tarnished brass pans.

I stopped by the front door of the shop and waited. I tried to affect boredom, jutting out one hip and pulling a cigarette from my satchel. I decided against smoking it, since I smoked so rarely it usually made me cough. I kicked at the cobblestones, scuffing my shoe, then reminded myself to stop doing that. I hadn't gotten a new pair of shoes in five years.

A few people walked past me or joined one of the queues along the street. Dekker's instructions had said to carry an envelope with the Red Cross symbol visible so this Jan person would be able to spot me. I had no idea what he might look like. Or if Jan was even his real name.

The familiarity of the tabak put me at ease slightly. Even through a locked door, the place smelled comfortingly like my father, pipe tobacco and cigarettes. All smoke shops smelled the same. I spent lots of time in them as a girl, waiting for my father to buy his tobacco, look at a pipe or two, chat in a manly way with the proprietor, who always gave me a few pieces of licorice to keep me happy. My mouth watered at the memory.

At the end of the block, I spotted a man walking alone. He had the stooped shoulders of a youngish man grown old before his time, a worrier. Perhaps thirty-five, he was skinny but strong-looking, like a boat handler from the docks. As he walked, he glanced up every few seconds to take note of who and what he was passing.

I knew he was the one. Not wanting to stare at him, I calmly gazed the other way, as if looking for a friend.

As I did, I noticed a cluster of three teenage girls, not too much younger than me, giggling and blushing, the only cheerful sight on the street. The girls stood in front of a man who looked to be in his twenties. Blue-eyed and broad-shouldered, he was about average height but seemed bigger, the energy of his smile and laughter drawing the girls. I got nervous around men like that. They walked through the world like they owned it, because they did. Too loud, too brash. Too confident. Fortunately for me, I was invisible to his kind.

I looked back to my target. He was still walking with purpose directly toward me, but he hadn't made eye contact yet. Instead, he looked at the cobblestones, one foot in front of the other. I tried to be patient. A bouquet of girlish laughter rang out to my right. Blond Man had made a joke and the girls were delighted, their cheeks pink and shiny. I tried to ignore the distraction.

"Well, thanks anyway," the Blond Man said loudly, and the girls fluttered again. He looked up then, right at me, his blue eyes clear and keen. And then there was the jaw, the hint of stubble on his ruddy cheeks, the way he stood with the kind of proud yet relaxed bearing of a young warrior who enjoys his strength, self-conscious and yet completely natural. I looked away, mortified by the flush in my own cheeks.

To my left, the stooped man drew closer. I cleared my throat to get his attention, but he didn't seem to hear. I cleared it again. He continued walking, pulling his coat closer around his body and muttering something through pursed lips. At this point, I was standing directly in his path; there was no way he could miss me. Yet still he muttered, not looking up, trailing his fingertip along the bricks and glass windows of the shops he passed by. Probably a strategy. He'd learned how to be aware of everything in his surroundings even as he appeared to be lost in his own world. These resisters were so good.

"Hey!" a voice called out to my right, and then, in a whirlwind, the Blond Man was lunging toward me—me?—snatching me by the arm and yanking me away from the window of the tabak as the stooped man plowed forward like a ship in the open ocean, oblivious to whatever might be in its path. The Blond Man pulled me toward the street, and my purse went flying, and I gasped, shocked, as the stooped man hurried past me, past the Blond Man, past the three giggling girls, who were lingering. The stooped man walked on down the block, never having noticed me at all. The Blond Man's rough hand still held my wrist, but gently.

"Torpedo juice," he said.

"What?" I asked.

"That pure grain alcohol folks are resorting to. It's a shame to see 'em so far gone, eh?" He shook his hair as he watched the alcoholic shuffle off, then smiled at me. He held my wrist. He looked into my eyes. "You dropped this," he said, stepping into the street to collect my satchel.

Down the block, the drunk man turned the corner and disappeared. I glanced the other way, looking for his replacement, the person I was supposed to meet. A couple of women across the street stared at me, curious at the little burst of excitement I'd caused. Perhaps the name was meant to throw me off; it was reasonable to think one of them might know Nurse Dekker.

"Thanks," I said. I tried not to look at him again. I knew my cheeks were still glowing. And I had, possibly, already messed this whole thing up. I took a deep breath and calmed a welling sob. No crying.

The Blond Man was still standing there. "Pleasure," he said.

I fussed with my purse, stalling.

"Spare one?"

I was still holding the unlit cigarette between my fingers, but in the commotion I'd crushed it and it sagged to the side, broken.

"Here," I said, pulling out the last intact cigarette from my purse. He thanked me, put it to his lips, and cupped a Zippo at the end of it, drawing one satisfying lungful, then held it out toward me.

"Here," he echoed me, handing me the straight cigarette and taking the bent one from my other hand. He rolled it between his palms, licked its paper seam, and the cigarette was good as new. He lit it and smiled. "That's better." He blew perfect smoke rings into the air above our heads.

"I gave you the good one," he said. "The least you could do is smoke it." The ash at the end of my cigarette trembled under its own weight. I took a self-conscious inhale and immediately started coughing. He laughed.

"You all right, sweetheart?"

My eyes watered, and my face was bright red. "Actually," I said, taking a tiny puff of the cigarette the next time as I sniffed and held my head high, "I gave you the cigarette. Remember?"

"Ha!" He laughed, and everyone who heard it looked over at us because the sound of his laughter was so loud and so free. Even the three
girls, who were almost out of sight, turned to look. I sighed. It was over.
Whatever chance I'd had to make a connection with the Resistance today, it was over. I'd drawn so much attention to myself, no one would
approach me now. The two women across the street were no longer looking my way. It was his fault. The Blond Man. I inhaled again, deeper this
time, eager to feel the evil burn of it at the back of my throat. I'd have to
find a new way to make contact.

"Where'd you get these?" he asked, admiring the Belgian cigarettes.

"A friend," I said. Sonja was the only one of us who could afford cigarettes. The Frenk family maid procured them on the black market, and
she'd brought two boxes with her to Haarlem.

"Very nice," he said. "I haven't had one of these for ages."

I looked around for my bike.

"You're leaving?" He jerked his blond curls toward the tabak behind
us. "Aren't you waiting for this place to open?"

"Well, it's closed," I said. Nonchalant, I hoped. What I really wanted
was to get the hell out of there.

"You're in luck, then." He stepped around me, pulled a huge ring of
keys from a lanyard attached to his belt, and unlocked the tabak's front
door and walked in, inciting a small tornado of sunlit dust in the tomb-
like space. "Come in," he said, holding the door.

"This is your place?"

"Kind of. I mean, I got the keys."

"Then why'd you ask me for a cigarette?"

He shrugged. "I never turn down a free smoke." He looked around at
the bare shelves. "And anyway, they're out."

"Thanks," I said, not sure what I was thanking him for, just eager to
leave. I took a step backward toward the street. Whoever this Blond Man
was, I didn't want to be stuck in an abandoned smoke shop with him.

He stuck out his hand. "Jan Bonekamp."

Jan? I took his hand and he nearly crushed mine. "How do you do. I'm Hannie Sch—"

"First name's fine."

"But you . . . ?"

"I'm too dumb to remember the rules," he said, knocking his knuckles against the side of his head with an audible thump. "Not like you college girls."

I was already on my way out the door, but the heel of my shoe caught the edge of the first step and I almost fell over. Steadying myself against the doorjamb, I looked him up and down. He laughed, and then did the same to me.

"Excuse me," I said.

"What?"

"Are you . . ." I tried to pull myself together. "I mean, you're not . . ."

"A friend of Bettine's? Yes."

Now I was truly confused, and my expression must have betrayed it.

"Bettine Dekker?" he said. "Tall, kinda scary? Favorite color's white?" As my brain processed the information, he kept talking. "War hero. You know that? Dekker is a legend."

I nodded. I'd never, ever considered calling Nurse Dekker by her first name. Bettine, of all things.

"Anyway, we found each other," he said, taking my elbow and walking me back inside. "Gotta be careful about these meetings." He narrowed his eyes and peered around like a cartoon spy and then looked back at me and said in a stage whisper, "That's how we do it in the . . . you-know-what."

The Resistance? I stood in the center of the empty shop while a clammy sensation slowly rose from my feet to my ankles to my knees like a rising puddle. I'd walked into a trap. There was no way this joker was the real thing. I moved backward toward the street as slowly as possible, sliding my feet through the carpet of dust on the hardwood floor.

"What did I say?" Jan looked at me with raw curiosity.

"I'm in the wrong place," I said with a smile. "My mistake."

"Ha!" His too-loud laugh again. "You know her as Nurse Dekker. I know her as Bettine, and if she says we can trust you, I'll take her word for it." He glanced over his shoulder. "Unfortunately, she's not around to convince you." I frowned. Dekker might have been arrested and that's how this strange man got her information? Or maybe Jan really was my Resistance contact, only much more handsome and unruly than I expected?

Or maybe he was just a collaborating policeman. "How do I know you're not a cop?" I asked.

"Fuck the cops," he said, so offhandedly it was clearly not the first time he'd said it recently. I flinched. "Most of those snakes couldn't wait to pledge their allegiance to Herr Hitler as soon as the occupation began. I'm not a cop." His easy tone was now edged with steel. "How do I know you're not a cop?"

"Me?" I almost laughed. "Do I look like a cop to you?"

"No," he said. "Far too pretty. And besides, the police won't hire red-heads. Too . . ." He mimed a spiral at the side of his head: *Crazy.*

My mouth fell open, but nothing came out. I was both appalled and flattered.

"Look," he said, unbuttoning his jacket and spreading it wide. "I'm not carrying a gun. Are you?"

I rolled my eyes and turned to walk out. I couldn't think straight. But he caught me by the wrist and pulled me against him, my back against his chest, his arm encircling my body while his other hand firmly but respectfully patted my ribs and waist.

"You really think I'm carrying a gun?"

He removed his hands and gently spun me around to face him. "Not anymore," he said, smiling. "Bettine has lots of contacts, and she could have sent you anywhere, but she sent you to me. You trust her, yes?"

"I suppose," I said, unsure where this was leading.

"Well," said Jan, serious now, "I trust her, too. And I'm willing to train you if you're willing to try."

"Train me?" I imagined the volunteers sitting around tables at the refugee alliance, stuffing envelopes and packing emergency supplies. "I've already been trained," I said.

Jan shook his head. "Not if you don't have a gun."

Chapter 13

I RETURNED HOME THAT evening to a chorus of questions from Philine and Sonja about where I'd been all day. "I shouldn't talk about it," I said apologetically, no idea how to handle the situation.

"We're the only ones you can talk to," argued Sonja, who was gamely trying her hand at something new: knitting. "We're just stuck up here all day—who would we even tell?"

"I know, but . . ." I never stopped imagining horrifying scenarios: What if the Gestapo burst in tomorrow and interrogated us all?

"It's safer for her not to talk to anybody," said Philine. Sonja rolled her eyes but eased up. Fortunately, my parents asked me nothing. They'd hugged me tightly as soon as I returned home, held me at arm's length and looked me up and down as if to check for damage, and kept their mouths closed. I recognized the look in their eyes; it was similar to the one Mr. Polak had given Philine when they said goodbye: a gaze filled with too many emotions to put into words. I ate dinner that night in the upstairs bedroom with the girls, spreading a tablecloth across the bed and making an indoor picnic. We kept our conversation focused on good things, like how nice it was not to study for final exams. The evening was pleasant. I only got sad once I was settled onto my little cot and the house went quiet and the room was dark. Seeing the shape of their two bodies sleeping in my childhood bed was like watching an old movie: my sister and me, years ago, warmed by each other. Remembering Annie gave me courage.

THE NEXT DAY I walked into the Grote Market around three thirty in the afternoon and strolled past the long lines of weary citizens. If there was something worse than pure boredom, it was boredom steeped in paranoia, fury, and fear. I took my place at the end of the line. But I wasn't planning on picking up the leeks my mother asked for. I was waiting for Jan Bonekamp.

"First asparagus of the season, mevrouw?" A farmer standing next to a hand-pushed wagon was moving slowly down the line, selling produce to whoever still had cash.

"No, thank you," I said.

"What'll this get me?" asked a man behind me. He brushed against my shoulder as he tossed a few coins in the farmer's hand. "Keep the change."

"Dank u, meneer," the farmer said, grateful for just a few of the wartime zinc pennies. Nobody said "keep the change" anymore. I turned, expecting to see a Nazi officer, but it wasn't a German in a uniform. It was Jan Bonekamp. The Blond Man.

"You're early," I said. He kept his shoulder pressed against mine, as if he were my husband joining me to buy dinner for later that night. The farmer smiled at us, the young couple.

"So are you," said Jan.

"This is where we agreed to meet," I said.

"Sure." Jan smiled. "But not everybody who says they're going to show up does." He accepted the small bunch of asparagus from the farmer. "Thanks." Then he grabbed my hand in his and led me through the throngs of the market stalls and people and onto the crowded street without looking back. He wore a flat cap and a navy jacket and gently muscled through the crowds as I bobbed in his wake. We got to the other side of the street and his bike.

"Get on."

"What?"

"Get on the back," he said, gesturing to a homemade rack.

"I brought my own bike," I said.

"It's better if we go together. Come on."

I hesitated for a moment. I'd already made the decision to meet him today. Now it was time to follow through. No more second-guessing. Jan looked around, then tapped an old woman on the shoulder. She was standing in line outside a bakery. She turned, suspicious.

"Solidariteit, mevrouw," he said, touching his cap. Solidarity, madam. He tucked the asparagus into her empty shopping bag and turned back to me. Her face blossomed into a wrinkled smile.

"Coming?" he asked me.

Whatever doubt I'd felt melted away. Questioning my own decisions was an instinct, but maybe instincts weren't always correct. It had never before occurred to me that one could simply decide not to doubt. It was thrilling! I climbed onto the sturdy rack on the back of his bicycle, setting my hands on his shoulders for stability.

"Put your hands around my waist," he said.

"I think this should work," I said pertly. It was unnerving enough touching him like this.

He reached up and grabbed my left hand and placed it around his midsection. "You'll fall off if you don't."

Blushing, I complied, and he started pedaling. He was right. Jan rode so fast and made so many sharp turns I almost fell off anyway, and I had to lean into him to make sure I didn't. Each time we rounded a corner, I felt the muscles in his back and stomach tighten and stretch. His warmth traveled through his jacket and mine. It would have been easier to rest my cheek against his shoulder blades, although I couldn't bring myself to do it.

If this was the Resistance, I should have quit school years ago.

"Where are we going?" I shouted over his shoulder.

"Haarlemmerhout," he said.

THE HAARLEMMERHOUT—THE HAARLEM Wood—existed before the city did, a landscape that would have been familiar to the Romans when it was part of their empire. I used to go there for family picnics when Annie was still alive. She and I would run to explore as soon as our mother had picked a good spot for the blanket—"not too far!" because the Haarlemmerhout was no ordinary city park. Once you moved off the gravel paths, the forest was untended and untamed, no walking paths or fountains or children's playgrounds, making it a magnet for caravans of Gypsies and "the rougher sort." Or so my mother said.

"Napoléon marched his troops through here," I said as I tromped through the bushes and over tree roots after Jan. "My father taught us how to spot the soldiers' initials still carved into the trees." I pointed.

"Imperialist whore," he said.

"Pardon me?"

"Napoléon," he said, kicking at the scurf of dead leaves beneath his boots.

I had no idea how to make conversation with this man. I grunted, tripping over a rock, and tried to make it sound like a graceful sigh.

"You all right back there?" He glanced over his shoulder, the start of a smile on his lips.

"Fine," I said. My nails were digging crescents into my palms.

"Here we are." He stopped at an unremarkable spot next to a thicket of alders where we were well hidden from sight and would hear anyone approaching. "Bettine thought you were ready for more serious training. Are you?"

Dekker's faith in me was greater than my own. I had no idea what "serious training" meant, but I surprised myself by wanting it. Especially if Nurse Dekker believed I was ready.

"I am," I said, wondering what came next. Learning the code words? Memorizing secret addresses? I knew I could do that, at least. "Where are the others?"

"Others?" Jan raised an eyebrow.

"We're not meeting anybody here for training?" In my head, I'd envisioned a half dozen scrappy folks assembling to learn our new guerrilla skills. I'd been eager to meet them.

A smile crept across Jan's expressive mouth. "Yeah, sure . . . there's fifty more men on the other side of these bushes." He laughed. "It's just you and me today, sweetheart. How many of us did you think there were?"

"Sorry," I replied, embarrassed. Although I felt as if I were the last person to join the Resistance this far into the war, of course I wasn't. If everybody was in the Resistance . . . well, things would be very different by now.

"Don't be sorry," he said. "It's good you're here. Now, time for some target practice." He reached into his jacket pocket and tried to hand me a small black gun. I froze in place. "What are you doing?" he asked.

"I've never . . ." I felt so stupid. But it also seemed dumb to just pretend I'd ever held a gun before, or ever even touched one.

"Go on, it won't bite." He was teasing me. I snatched it from him.

"Nope," he said, and smacked my hand down toward the ground. "First lesson: don't point the gun at your instructor."

"Oh!" Embarrassed, I retracted my finger from the trigger and kept the muzzle pointed at the dirt. All my unearned confidence vanished, and I held the grip by my fingertips, as if I were being asked to hold a lizard that might crawl up my arm at any moment. This was a real gun. I'd seen plenty of them, from pistols to rifles to baroque things with bayonets in marching formations, since the Germans arrived, but they'd all been in their hands. Holding one myself was an entirely different thing, simultaneously thrilling and disturbing. I'd never pictured myself holding one, much less using it. "We're starting with this?" I asked.

"What else?" he said cheerfully. "There are other things to learn, but this one takes the longest. I assume you already know how to do the other stuff—deliveries, pickpocketing, surveillance? So Bettine says."

"She does?" I asked, shocked and relieved. "Are you in touch with her now?" I asked, trying to sound casual when in truth I'd been afraid to imagine what happened to Dekker since I'd seen her.

Jan peered at me, trying to understand what I was really asking. "Don't worry about Bettine; she knows how to take care of herself," he said. "And she's fine. At least, she was a couple days ago."

"OK." I nodded. I knew he was right. Not that Dekker was not in danger, for we all were. But that I shouldn't worry about her. I had enough to worry about already.

Jan continued the lesson. "Sabotage is a huge part of Resistance work," he said, repositioning me in front of the target. "Freddie is particularly good at that type of thing: setting explosives, derailing trains, even little things like siphoning petrol from Nazi vehicles. It's important work, and you'll be doing some of that, too, probably." Derailing trains? I said nothing, just nodded. "But you may as well get comfortable with shooting now, eh?"

"Sure," I said, hoping my voice didn't sound as wobbly as it felt.

"Go ahead, wrap your hands around the grip," he said, watching me handle the gun awkwardly. "It's not loaded." He retracted the cartridge so I could see for myself: no bullets.

"How old is this thing?" There were dozens of scratches on the barrel and grip. It was a well-used gun.

"If you want a shiny new Mauser, you'll have to join the Wehrmacht for that, Professor."

"I was just asking."

"I'm just telling." He took the gun back and looked it over himself. "It's a nice little FN Browning 1922 we got off a Nazi cop in Heemstede last week." He handed it back to me. "It's perfect. Small but powerful. Like you."

I knew I was blushing.

"Go on," he said. "It's not gonna hurt you."

The gun was colder and heavier than I expected, like something dead. I turned it over. The matte-black steel was nicked, blunt-nosed and brutal-looking. How did one get a gun "off a cop"? I didn't pursue it. "What's this for?" I asked. A little metal loop hung off the end of the grip.

"House keys. You'll never lose them again."

"Really?"

"No," he said. "It's a lanyard loop. For soldiers out in the field. They can attach it to their wrist so they don't lose it in the mud or the scramble. We'll take that off yours, though. You don't need it and it'll be noisy when you're sneaking around in the night." He rattled my hand, and the metal loop jingled against the gun like a bell on a carriage horse. I felt a flush of pleasure and couldn't tell if it came from imagining the activity or the fact that he seemed to think I'd be capable of it.

"Remind me when we get back to the apartment," he said, walking deeper into the woods. "I'll take it off for you."

I presumed I was to follow him, so I did. It was the first I'd heard of an apartment. But it was silly to be worried about something as banal as safety at this point. There was no safe way to join the armed Resistance. How could there be?

We were deeper into the Haarlem Wood than I'd ever ventured before. It was approaching dusk and the ensuing curfew. "Are you sure we're all right out here?" I whispered. Jan didn't seem to hear me, so I tried again. "Is it OK to be here this late?"

He laughed and kept tramping through the brush, brandishing something in the air above his head. His pistol. "Who's gonna stop us?"

Right. Guns were used to intimidate people. And we had guns.

"Safety is a form of false consciousness," Jan continued, ever the patriotic comrade, not bothering to whisper. "But you can't be irresponsible. We're hidden pretty good deep in here. The Krauts on the night watch are too lazy to hike in, they just hang around the edges smoking cigarettes. And even if they did . . ." I heard the tap of his fingernail against the metal of the pistol, and I thought I saw him grinning in the darkness. "This is the only real safety." Jan twirled his pistol around his index finger like an American cowboy before slipping it back into its holster.

We came into a small clearing where the moonlight came down like an overhead lamp. "First thing: inspect and clear it." Jan held up his gun and did something to make it click. I pulled my own slide back. That sounded right.

"What did you say?" I asked. "'Clear it'?"

He moved my hand and the gun into a pale patch of moonlight so we could both see. "What we did before," he said. "You've pulled it open to inspect it. What do you see in there?"

"Nothing."

"Good. That's the information we're looking for: Is my gun loaded or not?"

"It's not."

"Right. It's clear."

"Clear," I repeated, ever the student. "Is yours loaded?"

He looked insulted. "Why carry an unloaded gun." It wasn't a question. "Let's fix yours. Yours is unloaded—no magazine in the gun, no round in the chamber." He pointed to the spot where a bullet would go. "Now we load it."

"I know how to do it," I said. I had no idea. But I was anxious to prove myself. And I'd seen it done a thousand times in the movies. He handed me six rounds. I immediately dropped two into the brambles below. "Damn it." I crouched down, feeling around on the forest floor, where every small thing felt like a bullet.

"Step two: don't drop the ammunition."

"Sorry. I'm an idiot."

He handed me a few more rounds. "Forget it. You're learning."

I glowed on the inside and felt the taut muscles in my neck and shoulders relax at last. I was out here in the forest, actually training for Resistance work. I was learning. And that was something I knew I was good at.

"Now. Stand like me, legs wide. Stable. Good. Lean forward a bit, not back." He stepped behind me and held up his right arm straight alongside mine so we were both pointing at an imaginary target in front of us. "That's it. Nice and straight, strong. Look how I'm holding my gun. See the way it fits right in there between my thumb and index finger?" I nodded, aligning my outstretched arm with his. They bumped.

He pulled the gun out of my palm and then slowly slid it back in. "It should feel good," he said. "It should feel like it belongs there." His mouth was at my neck now, his breath brushing warm against my ear as he leaned down to whisper. I shivered. Surely he noticed, but he stayed quiet. Our bodies swayed together gently, like the trees.

"Good," he said, his voice slightly lowered. "Now take your shot. Get ready for the kickback. But don't be afraid of it." He stepped back to watch.

I squinted into the blackness of the night forest. "What am I aiming at?" Ahead was just a blur of tree trunks and bushes that got darker the deeper I looked.

"Nothing. This is just to get the feel of it. But who knows? You might get lucky and hit a lost Kraut. Now go."

I tried to focus on the tiny bump of the sight at the end of the barrel, but I couldn't really see it in the gloom. Oh, well. I took a deep breath, held it, and fired.

BLAM.

The power of the discharge rattled through my straightened arm and into my body, and for a moment I thought I'd somehow shot myself. There was no pain, though. And no sound. But soon a high-pitched ringing emerged from somewhere deep in the center of my head and started to get louder. I turned, and Jan grabbed my arm, pushing it toward the ground. I couldn't hear what he was saying, but he seemed to be smiling, so I finally exhaled.

"What?" I said.

He put his finger to his lips: apparently, I was yelling.

Jan leaned toward my ear and spoke directly into it: "I said, 'Don't point the gun at anything—or anyone—you're not ready to shoot dead.'"

"Oh." I looked down. The gun was now pointing at my foot. My arm was so tense, it was easier to move the foot.

"So, how'd that feel?" he asked.

"Loud." My ears were still ringing, but my hearing was coming back. "The impact of it wasn't as bad as I expected," I added, shaking out my arms. "But it's so loud, won't somebody hear us?"

He shrugged. "Probably. But the night is full of gunshots now."

He had a point. The nights lately were a weird mix of silence, thanks to the curfew, and odd blasts and shouts, thanks to whatever criminal activity the Nazis were up to. At the moment, though, all was quiet. No sign of soldiers running through the forest to find us. Perhaps they were even running away.

"Hannie?" he asked, his voice soft. At the sound of it, my heart started banging inside my chest like a blacksmith at an anvil, and I hoped it only seemed that loud because of the ongoing din in my ears. "Yes?" I said, remembering not to yell.

"There's five more bullets to try."

"Of course. Right." I planted my feet wide again. It felt reckless to aim a gun at oblivion. Then again, all our lives had become reckless, ever since the war began. I just hadn't faced it until now. "I'm not going to hit anyone, am I?"

"If you were gonna hit someone, you either did it on the first shot or scared them away. Now go ahead."

I fired off the rounds quickly this time, now that I knew what to expect. The power was thrilling, and the sound and the recoil lessened for me with each bullet I fired. As for accuracy, I had no idea. But I allowed myself to feel proud anyway. Jan and I stood next to each other, firing into the night for a while. I found the act of shooting hypnotic, the process of focusing and controlling my breathing a welcome change from worrying about Sonja, Philine, my parents, the war, this Jan Bonekamp person who was somehow now in my life. The harsh blasts made everything else quiet. I also felt a strange, unearned sense of power that was nevertheless gratifying.

"How do you like it?" Jan said after many more rounds of the same.

"Shooting?" I asked.

He nodded.

Was I enjoying shooting a gun? Yes, I was. More than expected. Maybe a little too much. "It's OK."

"Come on, it's fun. Admit it, Professor."

"What do you have against professors?" I asked. It came out sharper than I'd intended.

He shrugged. "I never got along with schoolteachers."

I believed him; when I was in school, the boisterous boys like Jan Bonekamp were always being sent out of class. I caught myself aching to know more about his private life, but I couldn't ask him for details that might endanger his own friends and family, whoever they were. In his sturdy twill pants and jacket, he appeared to be a laborer, but that could mean anything: dockworker, carpenter, plumber. Whatever he did, it had prepared him better for Resistance work than being an ambitious law student. Yet we had something in common, the urge to resist, and suddenly I was grateful again.

"It's a scary kind of fun," I admitted. He smiled. "But we don't even know if I hit anything."

"You did. You will. I could tell from the minute you squeezed the trigger. Calm. Steady. Not jumpy or nervous. That's what it really takes. Of course you have an advantage."

"Oh, really?" I steeled myself for a joke about professors.

"Women are better with guns than men."

"Come on," I said.

"It's a fact," Jan said, sitting down now on a fallen tree and wiping the oil off his gun. "In my experience, women do better at staying calm in an armed situation. Bettine Dekker, for instance."

That was easy enough. I'd never seen Nurse Dekker flustered. The thought of her with a gun made me smile.

"Hands tired?" he asked.

"A bit."

"You might be squeezing the grip too hard—it's a beginner's mistake—but otherwise you're, uh . . ."

He lit a cigarette.

I waited. He continued smoking. Slowly.

"Yes?" I prodded him, longing for his approval, despite myself.

"You're a goddamn natural."

A natural! Thrilled, I sat down beside him, and he took my gun from me and wiped it down, too.

"So how much practice does it take before you can . . ." I wasn't sure how to talk about Resistance work yet. "Before you can use it for real?"

"You could go out tonight," he said, slipping the gun into the pocket of my coat and patting it.

"No," I said. "Really."

"I'm serious," he replied, looking me straight in the eyes. I blushed, aware of our thighs touching through the fabric of our clothes. "It just depends on your mood. And whether you can get close enough to your target."

Was he joking? And then, with no preamble, Jan said, "So, where are you staying tonight?"

"Home," I blurted out. "I mean, I was supposed to be home already. My mother will be worried, but . . ."

"But?"

It only dawned on me as I told him. Normally the nine p.m. curfew the Nazis imposed loomed over my consciousness like a thunderhead, threatening all my plans for the day. But once I'd wrapped my hands around Jan's waist on that bike ride, I'd handed my safety off to him. "I can't go now," I said. "It's too late."

I hated sounding like a lost kitten. But if I got caught, they'd either arrest me or escort me home, straight to Sonja and Philine's hiding place, and I couldn't afford either.

"Where do you live?" Jan asked.

"On the north side of town: Van Dortstraat."

"I'll take you," he said.

"What about the curfew?"

He stood up and extended his hand, pulling me to my feet. "That's no problem. We do most of our work at night."

WE FINALLY REACHED the edge of the park, and Jan pulled his bike out of the bushes where he'd stashed it earlier. He nodded toward a clump of three German soldiers huddled together a block and a half away, smoking. Putting his finger to his lips, he led me along the stone wall at the edge of the park where the moon cast a shadow from the trees. We walked in this darkness away from the soldiers and then scurried across to a dark, quiet residential street.

Moments later, I was sitting on the back of Jan's bike again as he leaned over the handlebars like the valiant figurehead at the prow of a ship, the two of us streaking through alleyways, under bridges, and down side streets I'd never explored in all my years of living in Haarlem, making a wide loop to get to my neighborhood. We stuck to industrial areas and middle-class neighborhoods where there was little German presence. His hips rose and fell with each stroke of the pedal. The night air was damp against my cheeks, my hair whipping into tangles behind me.

At first, I was scared, alert for the sound of shouting in German or the screech of car tires following us. But soon I felt free. Free of worry, free of fear, free of my own constant self-consciousness. Just this: in motion in the darkness in the middle of the night, with him. Jan Bonekamp. I'd never been in a position to meet anyone like him—not at university and certainly not before that. He was all forward motion, no looking back. Every time he said something that offended me somehow, he immediately turned it around, charming me. But the way he regarded me felt respectful and real. He saw Hannie, the woman who'd shown up to join the Resistance. Maybe this was what being the new Hannie felt like: freedom.

"A left up here?" he said.

I leaned closer and pointed. "About halfway down."

He pulled to a stop right up against the edge of the house in the shadow of the eaves. Our little street was empty and silent, like the set of a play when the play is over. He stood to steady the bike and turned to me, twinkles of perspiration clinging to his hairline, his cheeks flushed. He looked happy.

"See? It's easy to avoid curfew," he said. "And now Mother can rest." He nodded toward the kitchen window, where the dimmest outline of candlelight glowed around the edges of the blackout curtain. There was no doubt she was waiting up.

"Thanks." I reached into my coat pocket and handed him the gun.

"There you go again," he said, shaking his head and pushing the barrel down toward the ground.

"It's empty," I said.

"It's 'clear,'" he corrected me. "But you've got to stop pointing guns at me." Then he stuffed it back into my pocket. "You keep it, Professor."

My heart dropped at the nickname, but at least he was smiling. "OK," I said.

"You've got a knack. But don't shoot anyone yet, all right? Except the Krauts. Shoot all the Krauts you want."

"Sure," I said, unsure if he was joking. Probably not.

He walked me to the kitchen door, one hand at the small of my back. Neither of us had yet uttered the word *Resistance* out loud, I realized. He hadn't told me anything about who he worked with or what they did. "You did very well for your first day," he said at the door.

"As far as we know," I said. "Some of those bullets might still be airborne."

He chuckled. "Oh, I'm sure you took out at least one squirrel back there. A born sniper. You did great. I'll introduce you to the rest of the crew soon. You're not the only girl working with us, you know."

"No?" I was surprised to hear it.

"You'll meet 'em soon enough. Good night, Hannie."

"Good night, Jan."

He turned away and then took a step back. "Hey. Hannie."

Something about the way he said my name. Happiness poured through me like honey through hot tea. "Yes?"

"Give these to your mother."

He took my hand and placed a tidy packet of folded newspaper on my palm. I peeked inside. Three perfectly white cubes of sugar.

"Tell her I'm sorry for getting you home so late." He shook his head and sighed. "War is hard on mothers."

Chapter 14

I GAVE THE SUGAR cubes to Philine and Sonja. I knew if my mother saw them, she'd just worry about how I got them. Although she had waited up for me that night, she never confronted me about my whereabouts. I didn't take that for granted. She loved me, and it was tough on her. But a luxury like sugar cubes was a sign I'd accessed a whole new level of danger.

"Oh, my God," said Sonja when I gave her one the next morning. She looked up from her breakfast tray with the wide eyes of a little girl, admiring the lump of sweetness as if it were a diamond. Philine held hers to the tip of her tongue, savoring the taste. "When this war is over, I'm eating sugar with every meal," she said. "Sugar on my fish, sugar on my potatoes."

"Me, too." Sonja plopped her sugar cube into her cup of tea and stirred.

"You're just going to have it all, right now?" Philine said.

"If I portion it out, it won't taste as sweet."

"Hmm." I could see Philine turning the quandary over and over in her mind. Finally she took a butter knife and shaved a crumble of crystals onto her saucer, then tipped that into her tea, then carefully wrapped the remaining cube in paper. She took a sip of tea and smiled at me. "So did you steal it, Hannie?" She was proud of me.

"No, it was a gift."

"What's his name?" prodded Sonja.

I sighed.

"So, he's handsome," she said.

"Just a boy I met," I said. "A man."

"What's his name?" asked Philine.

"Jan," I said. It was common enough to share with them.

"This gift is so kind," Sonja said. "He sounds sweet."

"Not exactly sweet," I said, "more . . ."

"Sour?" said Philine.

"Spicy?" said Sonja.

I could still feel the intensity of Jan's shooting instructions as he hissed them in my ear, both harsh and intimate. "Bittersweet," I said.

The girls' eyes widened in fascination. "What does he look like?" asked Sonja.

"Well . . ." I said, trying to maintain control of the conversation. I needed to practice discretion. But when I thought of him, I felt the warmth of his strong back against my chest, on the bike, and the cords of muscle in his forearms. It made me flustered just thinking about it. "He's blond," I said.

"You don't even like blonds," countered Philine.

"That's not true," I said.

"I agree with Hannie," said Sonja. "She's equally mean to all the boys, including the blond ones. And they love it."

"I am not," I said. Was I?

"You can't talk about it, can you?" asked Philine.

"No."

Sonja sighed. "Hannie, look at us. We're stranded here in this room— no complaints, we're very grateful—but nothing interesting happens

here. Give us something to gossip about, please. And when I say 'gossip,'
I mean Philine and I will just talk to each other because we never get to
talk to anybody else. Your secrets have never been safer."

I smiled. She and Philine were, of course, my greatest secret. Every
decision I made, I asked myself if it would endanger them. But they had a
job as well: staying sane in a dark little room. If I could make their job
easier, I should. We were in this together. "He is kind of handsome,"
I said.

Sonja squealed. "Yes! What else?"

"He's tall," I said. "You remember Erik Timmermans from the study
group? He looks sort of like that."

Sonja raised a perfect eyebrow. "Erik Timmermans . . . he was good-
looking. Bit of a brute."

"Not a brute," I said. "Just muscular."

"Oh," said Philine. "And how close did you come to those muscles?"

"Well, I had to hold on to him on the back of his bike." Now I was
blushing.

For the first time in days, Sonja glowed.

"So?" said Philine. "What's he like?"

It was difficult to describe Jan without also describing my feelings
about him. And I wasn't capable of talking about those sensibly. "He's
cranky," I said. "He makes a lot of jokes, although I usually don't know
when he's joking and when he's not. He's never relaxed, and he's always moving, in a hurry. He teases me a lot. But he was a good teacher.
Patient."

"What did he teach you?" asked Philine, rapt. I was going to have to
get better at this.

"Self-defense."

They frowned.

"You know, just in case."

There was a lull in our conversation. Sonja dragged her finger across the bottom of her teacup to collect the last grains of sweetness there. The golden moment of girlish giddiness was already over.

"So, do you like it?" said Philine, finally. "The work?"

"I love it," I said. I didn't even have to think.

I WAITED FOR Jan at the tabak again a few days later, as instructed. I showed up early and so did he. It was late morning and a cloudless spring day.

"Morning, Professor," he said. "Got something special for you."

"Are we meeting the others?" I asked. "The other girls?" I'd been aching to know more about them, and I knew Philine and Sonja would want to hear.

"Not today," he said, then looked me up and down. He whispered, "Did you bring it?"

I patted my purse, which held my gun.

"Good girl." He smiled.

The day was gorgeous, warm and blue. Two young mothers walked by, pulling wagons filled with children and the morning's food rations. The toddlers played with each other and laughed in their wagons; their mothers walked silently, their wan faces tense and tight. They reminded me of Sonja and Philine.

"Got someone else I want you to meet," he said, leaning into my ear to whisper, "a real-live Nazi."

"What?"

"Shh," he said, "trust me." He led me around to the alley behind the tabak, where it was dark and cool. No Nazis around that I could see. "Not yet, just relax," he said.

"OK." I had to trust him now.

"Let's have it," he said, looking at my purse. I handed the gun over. "Loaded?"

"No point in carrying an unloaded gun," I said.

Jan fiddled with the pistol and handed it back. "Well done." He smiled. "You feel ready?"

"I haven't had much practice."

"That's OK. We don't need you to be a sniper."

I nodded, mystified. I had no idea what he was talking about.

"What we do, we do at close range," Jan said in a low voice. "You don't have to be a perfect shot at ten meters . . . but at one? You have to be willing to get right up next to the bastard and follow through. Then you don't worry about hitting the target. Think you can do that?"

I doubted it. And was he actually talking about shooting a Nazi? Today?

"Yes," I lied. It seemed like the only thing to do.

"Good. Let's go."

"Right now?"

"That's right. And put that thing in your pocket," he said.

I nodded and tried to ignore the jellylike feeling in my knees. Two bikes, not ours, leaned against the garbage bins. Like more and more bicycles these days, they had no rubber tires on their wheels, just curved wood attached to the metal rims, in the new, handmade wartime style. Rubber was reserved by the Germans now for military use. "Take one of these," said Jan. We wheeled the bikes down the alley, the wood rattling against the stones. It wasn't particularly stealthy, in my opinion. I still didn't know what we were doing. Maybe he'd try to make me shoot a real squirrel—though most of them had by now been hunted for food.

"There's an SS bastard who always comes by here around the same time," Jan said just above the clatter of our wooden tires. "We'll follow him on our bikes, and when we get close enough, you shoot him. Got it?"

He didn't appear to be joking as he kept moving, waiting for me at the end of the alley and looking up and down the little street. I stopped next to him and found I had nothing to say. So I nodded. He nodded back, dug a cigarette out of his jacket, and cupped his hands to strike a match. He passed me the lit cigarette and I took it gratefully. My fingers were shaking. If he noticed, he didn't say. We stood at the mouth of the alley, passing the cigarette back and forth for what felt like an hour but was probably five or six minutes. Then, at the far end of the main street, the sound of tires splashing through water. It was a man on a bike, riding in our direction.

"Don't stare," Jan whispered.

I looked at the ground and pulled on the cigarette, desperate to calm myself. I could smoke without coughing now. I pictured the parakeet Mrs. Snel used to keep in the front window of her house on our block, the way it jumped around its cage, fluttery and frantic. That was my heart. Jan glanced at me, and I wondered if he could actually hear the sound of it.

The squeal of the man's rusty bike pedals got louder as he approached, rasping metal on metal with every stroke. I tried to keep an eye on him without looking at him, a difficult thing to do. My thoughts sped past, too fast to track each one. I heard the man getting nearer and nearer.

Then, just as he passed us, Jan grabbed me by the waist and pulled me against him, his hips against my stomach, arms encircling my body. I gasped. "Shut up and act like a couple," he hissed. He wasn't really kissing me, just pressing his mouth near mine. I got a glimpse of glossy oxblood shoes and blue wool pants as the man pedaled by.

"It's him," Jan whispered, pushing away from me and swinging his leg over his bike. "Not in uniform, but that's normal for these fucking Huns. Undercover."

I wiped a hand across my mouth, frozen in place.

"He's taking a left turn up there by the newsstand." Jan started riding away and then swiveled back to look at me.

"Coming?"

I looked back down the street one last time: Was it possible this was all just some kind of test? If so, I had no strategy. I could follow Jan now, or I could go home and never come back. For a moment, I considered it. There was plenty to do at home, as my mother kept reminding me. I could help out with the cooking and cleaning for Philine and Sonja. Perhaps I could do some other kind of Resistance work, something less crazy than riding around the city with a loaded gun. My mother was always saying they needed volunteers down at the church, and I knew it was true. As I thought all these things, Jan disappeared around the corner and I was alone.

I could turn around now. Stay home, where it was safe. In my house where we were hiding two Jewish girls whose presence could get us all arrested anyway.

Nowhere was safe.

I hopped on my bike and followed Jan.

MY WOODEN TIRES scraped and slid on the paving bricks as I turned onto the busy downtown street. It was crowded with people standing in lines at shops with their ration cards, overflowing the sidewalks and pooling onto the streets. This was prime shopping time. Fortunately, the lack of gasoline meant few cars were taking up the streets anymore, aside from German vehicles. I saw the man ahead, with Jan trailing a few lengths behind. I never would have guessed he was a Nazi by the look of him. But I assumed Jan had inside information.

The Nazi took a sharp turn right, nearly toppling his bike, and disappeared. Maybe he knew he was being followed? Jan kept after him. I kept after Jan, who disappeared, too. Who was going to . . . do what to this undercover member of the SS, exactly? I didn't know.

I rode around the corner, skidding, wooden tires splintering against the stones beneath, and I turned in behind them to a dead-end alley strewn with empty metal drums, sacks of garbage, and a greasy sheen to the bricks. Down at the dead end was the German, just turning to face us. Jan looked up at the sound of my arrival, my brakes screeching, tires clattering, echoes bouncing off the buildings.

"Get him," Jan said. I was standing just behind him. He glared at me. "Now."

Jan's blue eyes found mine and held me there, asking me the only question that mattered: Was I going to do this? It wasn't a question you answer. You just do. Somehow my gun was my hand; somehow I'd left my bicycle behind. I heard it crash to the ground. Somehow I was just a few feet from the Nazi, my arms straight, eyes fixed on the largest possible target: his chest. He was raising his hand—in defense? In surrender? Too late. Humming with fear, I funneled every atom of it into the tip of my index finger and pulled the trigger. Tight. Deadly. I closed my eyes. The gun clicked.

Click.

Click.

My mouth went dry. The bird in my chest flapped wildly, desperate to escape. I glanced back at Jan, then back at the Nazi, who was still standing tall. Had I shot him?

I couldn't tell.

The Nazi took a step toward me. And another one.

Nope.

I pulled the trigger again, harder.

Click.

Click.

No bullets.

The Nazi smiled and flipped his chestnut hair away from his half-lidded eyes like he'd never been more relaxed. "You can lower the gun now," he said. In Dutch. So I did the only thing I could. I cocked my arm and then bashed the steel barrel of my gun against the side of the Nazi's head. His eyes went white, and his hand flew up to stop the impact, deflecting it and sending the gun flying out of my hand and into the debris at our feet. Damn it. Hands were on my shoulders, my waist, my arms, pulling me backward—there must have been more of them hiding here. No. No. No.

It was a trap.

"Easy, easy!" the Nazi shouted and held his hands up in surrender, a strangely tender look on his handsome face. I struggled to free my arms from the grip of whoever was holding me, but it was no use. "Relax, Hannie," the Nazi said.

How did he know my name?

"I'm Hendrik," he said.

Hendrik, Fritz, what's the difference? My arms were still pinned by the others. Would I be shot here, or sent to Westerbork first?

Then I realized how he knew my name. I angled my neck: Where was Jan?

He was the one holding me back.

New thoughts ripped through my brain. Jan was a collaborator. He'd sold me out to the Germans in a matter of days. Very efficient. Was Dekker in on this, too?

Not possible.

Anything was possible.

My thoughts boiled, a froth of rage and fear. It was a dead end, all right. I had walked—rather, ridden a bike—right into this mess all on my own.

Idiot.

"Get your hands off me," I said, writhing in his grip.

"You did well," Jan said from behind, and I flailed my arms helplessly, enraged.

"Very well, I'd say," the Nazi said. In Dutch again. He and Jan both laughed.

I was nauseated by my own stupidity. I should have known. As if a Resistance group would welcome a college girl with no experience. Sonja said I was paranoid, but apparently I hadn't been paranoid enough. Would these two get paid for turning me in—eight guilders? That's what cops got for ratting out Jews, anyway. I wanted to spit on the men, but my mouth was dry as sand, and of course Jan was much stronger than I was.

The Nazi reached his hand out again as if I were eager to shake it. A glamorous devil with wet, lashy eyes and shiny white teeth. Poised, relaxed, completely at ease. Jan let go of me and stood beside him, equally calm. I had nowhere to run. The Nazi gently touched my arm. I flicked it away. Bitterness rose at the back of my throat and I thought I might faint.

"So you're the redhead." His hazel eyes never left mine. "Forgive me," he said. "I'm Hendrik Oostdijk. Commander of the Haarlem Raad Van Verzet. You can call me Hendrik." He looked me up and down.

I pressed my back against the grimy brick wall, my thoughts blurred and furious. Raad Van Verzet?

Raad Van Verzet. Council of Resistance.

I wanted to slap Hendrik across his handsome face, but I didn't have the strength. Instead, I bent over and vomited on his shoes.

Chapter 15

YOU DID VERY well." Hendrik smiled and dabbed at his shoelaces with a clean white handkerchief. "Are you all right?"

My mouth tasted like acid, and I was damp with sweat. "I'm fine," I said. I stood, shivering from the roots of my hair to the soles of my feet, trying to extract myself from the horror of the last few minutes. The man on the bike, the people in the street, this dingy little dead-end delivery alley and the jungle of boxes and junk all around. The way he'd looked at me over his shoulder from the end of the alley, seductive, as if waiting for me—because he was waiting for me—the ugly crash of my bike against the bricks, the weight of the pistol in my hands. Then it all slowed down and I could see the wet of his eyes, the tip of his pink tongue as he licked the corner of his mouth. And then I'd done it. Pulled the trigger. Tried to kill him. A stranger to me. Because Jan Bonekamp, whoever he really was, told me to.

"Everyone must go through this," Hendrik said with a gentle smile. He held his soiled handkerchief pinched between two fingers as if considering refolding it, then tossed it onto the trash heap instead. "It's the only way."

Jan lit a cigarette and handed it to me. "It was a test," he explained, shrugging an apology. "Sorry, but those are the rules."

A test. And I'd . . . passed it? The whine of fear in the back of my mind slowed slightly, but I was still bewildered.

"May I offer you a drink?" said Hendrik. "Don't say no. There are no small victories in wartime." He pulled a silver flask from his inside jacket pocket with a little grin. If he were a cat, he would have purred. He produced a second pristine handkerchief and offered it to me. "It's all right, darling. You're OK. We're all friends now." Jan looked proud of me. I took the handkerchief from Hendrik, its ironed corners stiff, crisp. I hadn't seen starch in so long. When I brought the handkerchief to my face, I smelled the world before the war: clean laundry, light starch, a hot iron. It was as if Hendrik had stepped out of a time machine from somewhere food was still abundant and people had time for things like shining shoes.

"Sind Sie wirklich nicht Deutsch?"—You're not really German?—I asked in German as one last, admittedly pathetic, attempt at confirmation.

Hendrik laughed. "Ich bin ein Holländer, darling. Promise."

Jan pulled a couple of battered crates up and offered me the least filthy one.

"If we went to a bar," Hendrik said, "we'd have to buy their watered-down swill. But this, comrades, is the real stuff." He passed me the flask. "Unfortunately, it's not real whiskey; in fact, it's from Belgium. But it'll do the job. À votre santé." Hendrik handed me the flask. "Cheers."

The fumes alone made me cough. I took a tentative sip and welcomed the burn as it went down my throat. It distracted me from thinking about all the other things. The three of us sat together quietly, facing the street, watching the people pass by, their lives normal, or as normal as life under occupation could be. My own sense of time was recalibrating. I was no longer registering every detail around me with the breakneck terror of a few minutes earlier. Within a few minutes, Jan's cigarette and Hendrik's whiskey had sanded the edges of my splintered thoughts. "We're all friends now," he'd said.

"You make a convincing German," I told Hendrik.

"I've spent far too much time observing them and learning their habits, but yes, it does pay off in situations like this. Cigarette?"

"Please." I'd never smoked so many cigarettes in one day. Or one week. He rolled one for me, licked it closed, and lit it. When I inhaled, I felt a great veil of anxiety floating off and away from me like a dandelion puff on the breeze. I planned on smoking more often.

"Feeling better?" Jan asked.

I nodded.

"We should get going," said Hendrik. "Come on."

We walked our bikes out of the alley. I was amazed when we emerged and no one took a second look at us. I'd just tried to kill a man back there. It was, by far, the worst thing I'd ever attempted to do in my life. Nobody noticed or cared. The cage of my chest softened a little bit, expanding with relief.

"I studied in Heidelberg for a year," Hendrik said as we walked down the sidewalk. "You speak it well. Any other languages?"

"I studied Latin and French," I said. "But I can speak German pretty well and a little Italian, too. I learned all the Swiss languages, just in case." There was a pause and I realized I'd lost them. "I was planning to move to Geneva."

"Geneva?" asked Jan, wrinkling his brow. "What the hell for?" He made the place sound like the Black Hole of Calcutta. For me, it was the noble birthplace of the Red Cross and the humanity of the Geneva Conventions.

"It's where the League of Nations is," I said.

Jan burst into laughter. "Ha! I bet you were a fun kid."

Hendrik ignored him. "League of Nations?"

I was embarrassed, but then I remembered I'd just thrown up on his shoes and, in contrast, my childhood dream of becoming a lawyer for the League of Nations seemed unremarkable. "It's why I was going to law school."

Hendrik thought for a moment. We'd turned onto a side street and could now speak more freely. "How did a nice law student from Haarlem end up in an alley holding a"—he nodded at my pocket where the gun was—"at my head?" Jan laughed and Hendrik gestured toward him. "Accompanied by this devil, no less."

I tried to think up something clever, but failed. "I'm not sure either."

We all laughed at that. "She was sent to us by Dekker," Jan added. "So . . ." They exchanged a meaningful look. "Bettine says she's OK."

"You should have said that at the beginning," Hendrik looked impressed. "So, Hannie, how do you feel now?"

How did I feel? The bird in my chest was huddled in the corner of its cage, shaking. But I was also a little in awe of myself.

"I feel . . ." I said, ". . . like it was the right thing to do."

"Good girl." Jan clapped me on the shoulder like a good comrade.

"It was," agreed Hendrik.

"Is that how you really do it?" I asked, keeping my voice at a whisper. "When it's a real Nazi? Just ride up to one of them and . . ." I pantomimed shooting a gun.

"Why do you think we carry them?" said Jan. So blasé.

The sun shone on the three of us, there in the middle of Haarlem, chatting and existing in a wholly different reality from everyone else around us. It was emotionally liberating to not be pretending anymore. Pretending not to feel beaten down by the occupation, pretending not to be filled with rage each time I left the house. A week before I was crossing the street to avoid German soldiers. Now I would be searching them out. Nazis were no longer just my enemies; they were potential targets.

By squeezing that trigger, I'd earned my spot in this secret society. All those civilians walking by? They were in a war. But we were in the Resistance.

"Hold up now," Hendrik said as we approached a busier corner in the central business district. "Let's wait here for a minute." We leaned our bikes against a wall and turned to face the intersection. It was lunchtime and the streets were crowded. People streamed by, old women carrying cloth-covered baskets, children zipping through the throngs chasing each other, men in suits, and the rumble of heavy Wehrmacht trucks and soldiers from corner to corner. "So, Jan. What do you see?"

"That man reading the paper across the street," Jan said, "the one sitting on the folding chair, smoking."

Hendrik nodded.

I looked. Nothing memorable or threatening about him, as far as I could tell. Just a middle-aged man enjoying the sunshine.

"He's a guard," Jan said. "OZO." We were speaking in low voices, standing back from the flow of pedestrians. "A lookout. If the Kraut wagons show up down the street, he'll go through the secret door to warn the guys in the basement to run."

I searched for the secret door, but the wall behind him appeared to be solid brick.

"It's under his chair," Hendrik said. "A hatch in the sidewalk." The borders of the square of sidewalk beneath him were rough-edged, set in place without mortar. The whole slab could probably be lifted and removed. But you would never suspect it.

"What's in the basement?" I whispered. I pictured Jewish families huddled underground or maybe an armory of stolen weapons.

"A printing press," said Hendrik. "That's where *Trouw* comes from."

I knew the Resistance newspaper: *Loyalty*. I'd delivered it for Nurse Dekker, but I never knew where they printed it. Now, standing across the street from its secret headquarters, I was even more impressed with the shrewdness of the Resistance. I hadn't realized underground newspapers were actually printed underground.

"It's the riskiest job there is," said Hendrik. "The printing presses are so big and heavy, once they're installed, they can't be easily moved. Stationary targets. Not like us."

"Like you?" I asked.

"Our group moves all the time. If you stay in one place too long, the neighbors start to talk."

I thought of Mrs. Snel, next door to my parents. She was just the kind of prying neighbor who could cause problems for them. Acid rose in the back of my throat as I pictured the little yellow-brick house and my mother, father, Sonja, and Philine crammed inside. Stationary targets. Why was I the only one with a gun? Suddenly I wanted to rush back there, just in case.

"Come on," said Hendrik. "We should keep walking."

I couldn't leave now. And nothing had actually happened back at my house, I reminded myself. That was just my imagination.

"I'll take you to the apartment tomorrow," Jan said, walking alongside me. "Our current headquarters. Show you around."

I nodded. Walking always calmed me. As they toured me through the city for the next hour, pointing out all the secrets hiding in plain sight, from trapdoors to Resistance graffiti, Hendrik and Jan explained the principles of Resistance work.

"The first thing to remember is that there is no action too small," Hendrik said, clearly enjoying himself. "Jan is not particularly fond of this one—he prefers the big actions—but believe me, the little things make a difference, too. Take any opportunity, no matter how minor, to chip away at the resources and morale of the enemy."

Jan walked a few paces ahead of us before stopping in front of the tall wooden doors of the post office. He made eye contact with Hendrik, who followed his gaze. "Well done, Jan," he said, and kept us walking along.

"What?" I asked, baffled.

Jan strolled up beside me and laid his palm out flat, showing me a tangled ball of fine wire. "Jam it into the locks of useful buildings. Makes it hard for them to lock up the place at night and it means some miserable Kraut's gotta get peeled off guard duty to deal with it." We kept walking, and he dropped the wire into my hand. He smiled. "Doesn't have to be wire either. Wood chips, wax, even a lady's hairpin can do it." He gave me a wink.

We passed a fountain, around which German soldiers were being marched in circles. From here, in between Hendrik and Jan, the soldiers didn't seem as intimidating. In fact, they looked miserable and pathetic. My mood improved.

"No action is too insignificant," Hendrik continued, and I was eager to hear more. "Next is surprise. Aside from our local knowledge, it's the greatest weapon we have. The key to this aspect is controlling information."

"What he's trying to say is 'don't talk to anybody,'" said Jan. "No gossiping."

"I don't gossip," I said, scoffing.

"Of course not," said Hendrik. "But don't. In any case, planning is what takes up most of our time."

Jan groaned. "Endless planning."

"We don't have an army of thousands, so we have to be better than they are," Hendrik said. "We have to plan carefully, thinking of everything. Not just the action itself, but the escape route and contingency plans if something goes wrong." This was something he and Jan had debated before.

Jan needled him. "But, like you said, surprise is our greatest strength. What if there's no time to plan?"

Hendrik sighed. "Improvisation is important, yes. But it's best when deployed within a well-planned operation." He walked us onto a bridge spanning the Spaarne River, where a few other groups of locals were gathered, watching the water flow by. We found a spot at the railing near the crest of the bridge; a young family kindly shifted over so I could squeeze in.

"If you look only at the river," said Hendrik, "you can pretend there is no war." Ducks paddled in circles, staying near the bank to avoid the little sloeps, the dinghies that delivered smaller goods around the city and to the bigger ships in the Noordzeekanaal, the waterway connecting Amsterdam to Haarlem, and Haarlem to the North Sea. I closed my eyes and felt the warm sun on my upturned face. I was getting better at appreciating small moments of grace. The three of us enjoyed the peaceful hiatus for a few minutes, then moved on. Jan and Hendrik did most of their talking on the move, for discretion.

"You haven't mentioned one of the most important things yet," said Jan. "Never carry incriminating documents on you. If you're delivering papers, that's different. That's an operation. I'm talking about everyday stuff."

"What about a fake ID?" I asked.

"We'll make sure you get a good one. Then it's OK. But nothing else—no lists, no names, no addresses. And nothing from the RVV."

"Of course not," I said.

"In fact," said Hendrik, "the RVV shouldn't even have any documents around. If we need to write something down, fine. Then we burn it. Right away." He shot a meaningful look at Jan. "You need to meet Truus and Freddie," he then said to me. "The Oversteegens. May I ask how old you are?"

"Twenty-two," I said.

"They're a few years younger," said Hendrik. "They'll be back in town soon."

"Oh," I said, trying not to ask too many questions, yet desperate for more information.

"Just lying low for a little bit," said Jan. "They've been busy."

"So, you were a law student, Hannie?" asked Hendrik.

I nodded. "What do you do?" I asked, looking between them.

"Do?" Jan asked. Hendrik sighed. Every so often a moment of tension would flare between the two men, set off by some signal I couldn't read. Hendrik walked on my left, suave and well pressed. Elegant. To my right was Jan, untrimmed locks of blond hair constantly falling into his eyes, a reddish Viking stubble covering his jaw, and hands so rough they looked dirty even though I was fairly sure they were clean. These were two men who never would have been colleagues during peacetime.

"I meant for work," I said. "Or school."

"School?" Jan spit on the cobblestones. "Haven't seen the inside of a classroom since I was in short pants," he said. "Never saw the point."

"Work, then."

"Hoogovens, on the shop floor like my father before me," he said, chest swelling.

So, Jan was a trade unionist. An ironworker at the Hoogovens factory in IJmuiden and, like my father, a Communist. They were behind most of the major Resistance actions, from the nationwide strikes to the string of recent shipping sabotage attempts. I was sympathetic, of course, given my family's political leanings, but we had never been party members.

"You, too?" I asked Hendrik.

"Hoogovens?" He brushed an invisible speck off his lapel. "No. A bit of this, bit of that . . ." He smiled again. Hendrik was probably a lawyer. Or a teacher. Something smart, refined. He could have been an actor with his looks. He already seemed a bit like an older brother.

"They teach you about the coming revolution at university, Hannie?" Jan said. When he uttered the word *revolution*, a passerby gawked at us, then looked away.

"I've heard of it," I said, wary of wherever he was headed. I didn't want to argue politics with Jan.

"Nationalism," Bonekamp said. "That's the real enemy. When the revolution comes, we'll erase national boundaries from all the maps and restore the earth to the people. All the people. The workers."

"My God, Bonekamp," said Hendrik with a good-natured laugh, "are you running for party secretary?"

"Yeah," Jan said, "it's tough to find a good boss, you know?"

Hendrik winked at me. "Don't mind him."

We all stopped at the edge of a small bricked plaza while Jan lit his cigarette, cupping his hands against the breeze. There had once been a small park in the middle, but now, instead of a circle of grass and some shade trees, there was just a ring of dust and a few stumps. Firewood had been scarce over the winter.

Jan dragged on his cigarette as if he were about to breathe fire. "What makes me special, sweetheart, is that I don't give a damn." He smiled. "When it comes to taking down fascists, I'll do it. No questions, no argument. It's why Hendrik needs me. I don't give a damn more than anyone you've ever met."

Hendrik laughed. "I can't argue with that."

"See all those?" Jan said, pointing to the iron lampposts lining the square. "By the end of this, there'll be a Kraut hanging from every flagpole and post in the country." He beamed, imagining it.

"Yes, well . . ." Hendrik frowned. "That brings us to the most important thing to know about this kind of work," he said, his voice soft and slow. "The Germans are, as you're well aware, absolutely ruthless. So we must be, too." He lowered his voice even more, though there was nobody nearby. "Informants. Spies. Double agents." He looked me in the eyes, as serious as I'd yet seen him. "If you turn on us, we will turn on you. Ruthlessly. If we get proof of guilt, we terminate that person immediately." He buttoned and smoothed his blazer. "Then we leave that traitor in a public place with a note explaining their crime. Treason," he said, to make his point.

Jan closed his eyes, as if praying. I nodded and kept my mouth shut.

"Sadly, comrades, I must bid farewell for now," Hendrik said, as we rounded a corner. He said *comrades* as if it were in quotation marks, a gentle jab at Jan, then turned to me, taking my hand in his. "Thanks for your work today. You did well, Hannie. And in case I haven't said it yet: I'm pleased to welcome you to the RVV." He shook my hand. No signature forms, no ceremonies. The act itself was the acknowledgment.

"Thank you," I said.

"Don't thank me," Hendrik said gravely. "I'm not responsible for your success, your failure, or your safety. You are. But we are all of us fellow soldiers in this struggle. And we help each other as much as we can."

"Yes, sir," I said. He laughed that off, too. "Wait," I said. I dug into the pocket my mother had sewn onto my skirt. "Can you find a good use for this?"

Jan snatched the ID card out of my hand. "This looks real."

"It is real," I said. "I just stole it a few minutes ago." Both men turned to stare at me. It had been so easy to lift the ID from the grocery basket of the young wife standing next to me on the bridge.

"Well, well, Hannie!" said Hendrik, plucking the card from Jan. "We can certainly put it to use. Very well done, indeed."

"Thanks," I said, blushing. It was good to not feel like a complete novice, for once.

"I have something in mind for you when Truus gets back," said Hendrik.

"Sure," I said. "With her brother, too?"

"Pardon?" Hendrik asked.

"Freddie?" I said.

They both laughed. "The Oversteegens are sisters," said Hendrik. "Truus is about your age, and Freddie is still a teenager."

"Oh!" I said, reshuffling my vision of the siblings. Heroic sisters. I'd wanted that for me and Annie, long ago. My heart beat faster, the little bird fluttering again in its cage. "It will be nice to meet them," I said, excited at the thought of meeting the Oversteegen girls.

"Wonderful," Hendrik said, taking my hand and kissing it. "Just bring your little friend," he said, glancing to my purse, where I'd stashed my gun, "and you'll be fine. See you soon." He jumped on his bike mid-stride and rode off.

"Flashy fucker," Jan said.

"He seems so professional," I said, watching Hendrik disappear down the street.

"There's a beast hiding under that suit, believe me. Only shows itself occasionally, but it's there." He handed me a cigarette. "You were pretty scary yourself, earlier. I thought we might have to find a replacement for Hendrik."

Earlier, when I'd tried to murder Hendrik. The test already seemed so long ago, experienced by a different person. "Don't remind me," I said.

"It's true. For a second, I worried I'd left a round in the chamber. You'd have blown his head to Denmark, no question." He winked at me. "You sure you've never done this before?"

"Well, I was just doing what you told me to." I paused. "Though I may have closed my eyes right at the end."

Jan laughed. "They weren't closed once you started pistol-whipping him. You pulled yourself together pretty quickly, too. Afterward, I mean."

"That's kind of you," I said, "but I did throw up."

He shrugged. "It happens. The important thing is to keep yourself from thinking too much while it's happening. Just concentrate on what comes next, do it, then leave. Plenty of time to think later."

The moments after pulling the trigger in Hendrik's face were a jumble of jarring images, my brain trying to process something I'd never imagined myself doing. Taking the life of a fellow human being. My trigger finger tingled at the thought.

"You're still thinking about it," he said.

"So?"

"Put it out of your mind. Nothing happened."

"Nothing happened?" I asked.

"Nothing happened."

"Hmm," I said. "And then what?"

"If nothing happened, there's nothing to think about." He sucked so hard on his cigarette his cheeks hollowed into their sockets. "Staring at the ceiling, alone in the dark?" He shook his head. "Not if I can fucking help it."

"What about learning from mistakes?" I asked.

"Ha," he laughed mirthlessly. "If you're still learning from your mistakes, it means you're still alive. Which means whatever mistakes you made didn't matter." He looked around the plaza. "We should keep walking."

I agreed, mostly because standing close to him made me self-conscious. The afternoon sun blazed down on his bare head and face, turning his skin to a golden caramel. My skin just went pink and speckled.

"So what's next?" I said.

"Attagirl." He led me down a street that opened onto one of the industrial canals where no young families or flower sellers came. He offered his hand to help me step onto a crumbling cement block to look at the view. He touched me, and I trembled and rubbed my arm, pretending I had an itch. We stared out at the gray snub-nosed transport boats the Germans had parked in the water, all lined up together. On the bow of each one, a swastika.

We watched dozens of uniformed grunts swabbing the decks, the oldest among them perhaps twenty-five. "What do you see when you look out there, Hannie?" he asked.

"Boats?" I said. "Soldiers?"

"Not me," he said, a smile creeping across his face. "I see our next targets."

"Them?" I asked, looking to the boats, shocked. "Now?"

"Not them and not now." Jan laughed. His smile faded, and his eyes narrowed like a lion tracking prey. Keeping his pistol in his jacket pocket, he took hold of the grip and pantomimed shooting a trio of German soldiers on the next pier, one-two-three. "Dead Nazi, dead Nazi, dead Nazi," he hissed. "When I look around these days, dead Nazis are all I see."

Chapter 16

Late Summer 1943

I HAD TO WAIT through most of the summer to meet Truus and Freddie, who had to go underground after a successful but dangerous operation that remained a mystery to me. The warm weeks went by, and I wasn't asked to do anything exciting, apart from my ongoing pickpocketing. I spent most of my time at RVV headquarters, which was currently located in a shabby apartment building near the Haarlemmerhout.

The two-bedroom RVV apartment was wild in its chaos. The main sitting room was so randomly furnished with desk chairs and tables obviously stolen from an office building, it seemed more of a warehouse than a home, functioning simultaneously as a barracks, an office, and a gunsmithing shop. The stuffy air reeked of coffee, ink, old socks, and dirty plates. Sometimes that summer, when I was alone and bored, I considered taking a broom and a mop to the place and cleaning it up, but I stopped myself. I didn't want to set a precedent. What I wanted was to chase down another Nazi—a real one this time.

I stayed at the RVV apartment most of the time, loath to face my parents and the girls when I was in this state of mind. I knew they'd ask questions. Where had I been? What was I doing? When would I be home?

I didn't want to lie to them; I just wanted to work. I told myself it was better to stay away from the house, where I'd only crowd the place and get in the way. But it was also true that Sonja and Philine could have used the company, and it might have been good for my parents to get a daily reminder that I was still alive. It wasn't fair, but I turned my focus to the Resistance. For them, I told myself. But it was also for me.

JAN TOOK ME for target practice whenever I asked. He loved guns, so we did a lot of that, most of it in the depths of the woods. But most of that summer was devoted to intelligence operations by Hendrik and Jan, who had connections to the national Resistance network. One phrase dominated the conversation: *Aktion Silbertanne*. In German, it meant Operation Silver Fir.

Resistance informants, who ranged from sympathetic Dutch cops to prison inmates, told us about it. Aktion Silbertanne was the coming assault, an operation that Commander Hanns Albin Rauter, the Austrian head of the Netherlands SS, was aiming directly at active resisters all over the country. For every Nazi or Nazi collaborator killed by the Resistance, Silbertanne would execute three of ours. These murders would be carried out by specially trained Einsatzgruppen: paramilitary death squads. The squads would not be in uniform, but instead dressed as citizens and posing as resisters themselves. Wearing plain clothes. Speaking Dutch. Killing with Allied weapons. Aktion Silbertanne was to be a theater of death, with costumed Nazis performing a lie for the citizen spectators, a play about a Dutch Resistance in chaos, attacking itself from within. If the charade succeeded, it might make the Dutch people suspicious of the Resistance and of each other. In a country already ground down by three and half years of occupation, it was difficult to hold on to hope. Aktion Silbertanne was designed to shatter the few fragments of optimism that yet remained.

———

"NOTHING EXTRAVAGANT," HENDRIK told us one afternoon at the apartment. "We keep up our normal day-to-day operations, delivering ration cards, IDs, newspapers, weapons, but no one-on-one attacks for a little while."

"How long?" asked Jan.

"Until things settle."

Jan shook his head. "I say we up our attacks, not pull back. They're just going to keep doing it. Makes no sense to wait them out."

Jan, Hendrik, and I sat together at the beat-up wooden table in the dining room, drinking plain boiled water and pretending it was tea. Still no sign of the Oversteegen sisters. There were other members of the cell, too, but Hendrik explained that not everybody in the Resistance needed to know everybody else. It was safer like that.

Hendrik sighed. "This isn't a retreat, Jan. It's a strategic repositioning. I expect all of us to carry that through, whatever our personal feelings about it. For the security of the Resistance as a whole."

"Whatever you say, sir." It was a form of address Jan only used sarcastically.

"Wonderful," said Hendrik. He cleared his throat. "That said, plans are still in place for the power station."

Jan looked up, surprised. I'd heard Hendrik talking about it earlier in the week, a big job, bombing a critical power station in nearby IJmuiden, Jan's hometown. It had taken months to plan and, I now realized, I'd been included in those plans the entire time.

"Freddie did the surveillance, and it's ready to go, so we may as well strike."

"That's more like it," said Jan, sitting up in his rickety wooden chair. "Am I doing this solo, or . . . ?"

Hendrik frowned. "You can't do it, Jan. You're too recognizable in that area."

"Come on," he said. "At night? We won't be seen."

"Truus will do it, and you can help her prepare the package," Hendrik said.

"But I know it better than anyone."

"Then you can draw us a detailed map. That would be extremely helpful, Jan."

"Fucking nonsense." Jan stood up and stomped out to the backyard.

Hendrik shook his head. "He's a terrific soldier, which makes him bad at sitting things out."

"So will the Oversteegens do it?" I asked.

Hendrik smiled. "Yes," he said, "with your help."

"Of course," I said, trying to remain calm.

"All right, then. Truus, Freddie, and Hannie. Just the girls." He drained his teacup. "You can learn a lot from those two." Hendrik rummaged in his jacket pocket, and I leaned forward, eager to learn whatever else he had to show me. He pulled out a penknife, flipping its silver blade out with one hand, and I jerked back. "Easy, easy!" He laughed, holding it up so I could see how harmless it was, and then picked up a piece of mail from the table, slipping the thin blade into the corner of the envelope: "This deadly weapon is used for opening letters." He patted my hand sweetly. "Even the revolution requires paperwork."

THE NEXT TWO days were a welter of delirium and dread. I ran the plan through my mind constantly, testing my memory. If this bombing plot succeeded, it would take out power to what was rumored to be a U-boat defense station in IJmuiden, along with the electricity that powered the regional rail system. It would be bad for Nazi morale. That thrilled me.

I was equally excited to meet the Oversteegen sisters. Besides Nurse Dekker, they were the only other women I knew of working for the armed Resistance. And the way Jan and Hendrik spoke of them, I was already awed and intimidated. All this made it easier to forget the terror of working with homemade explosives; Jan told me you could tell a Resistance bomb handler by their singed eyebrows and fingerless hands.

JAN OPENED THE door for me Thursday afternoon at the RVV apartment. No smile, just a brisk nod. "Hannie," he said.

"Where is everyone?" I'd expected to see the Oversteegen sisters.

"Truus had to leave early," he said, walking into the living room. "She'll be waiting for you to bring the package. Hendrik was supposed to tell you."

"Oh," I said.

Jan was still irritated. "Let me give you something, though." He walked to the sideboard, squatted down, and rummaged inside the cabinet, crammed with miscellaneous junk: metal wires, scraps of paper, pieces of tin. He drew out a wrapped package about the size of a kitten. "Here we go," he said, standing up with the bomb. "Truus is starting around eleven thirty in Velsen-Noord, in the power station's rail yard."

"All right," I said, vaguely imagining what a power station rail yard looked like. I'd never had occasion to tour one before, much less detonate a bomb there.

"I should really be the one doing this," Jan said, muttering to himself.

"Pardon?"

"Festung IJmuiden," he said. Fortress IJmuiden was a key station along Hitler's international Atlantikwall, Germany's attempt to fortify the entire northwestern coast of Europe and Scandinavia, from France to Finland, against Allied attack. They'd displaced thousands of residents along the Dutch coastline to create an empty no-man's-land around important military and industrial operations. IJmuiden was one of the most important sites for the Nazi war effort, strategically located at the meeting of the North Sea and the canal that led to the rest of Europe. The cliffs of England were only a hundred miles across the Channel. With its established military bunkers and the presence of the Hoogovens steel factory and neighboring power station, Festung IJmuiden was a Nazi stronghold.

"Can I see the map?"

Jan handed it to me, a simple but legible overview of the coastal area. He'd marked two big towers in the power station yard. "This is a much more significant target than we usually get," Jan said, forgetting his resentment for a moment. "Losing power to this place will be a nice blow to the German military effort, even if it's just for a few weeks. You ready?"

"I think so," I said. I folded the map and tucked it into my bra. That earned a smile from Jan.

"Better get going," he said. "It's the second switching tower at the power plant. Look for Truus. Meet her at the tower and she'll explain the rest." I took in the sparse details and memorized them. I was embarrassed to ask him to repeat it, and I knew I couldn't write it down. Jan handed the package to me. It was heavier than I expected. He grinned as he watched me frozen in place. "Relax. It won't go off until you set it."

I'd done a number of transports, both for Dekker in Amsterdam and also in Haarlem over the past few months, delivering concealed guns and boxes of ammunition and who knew what else, hidden in fruit baskets on the back of my bike. I'd even pushed a rocket launcher hidden in a baby carriage, but they were all dead objects. A bomb was the bullet, the target, and the explosion in one. It scared me.

"Why didn't Truus take this with her?" I asked like a coward.

"Because it wasn't ready yet, Professor. I had to fix a part."

The idea that Jan, who had little to no bomb-making experience as far as I knew, was in charge of the device made the hair on my arms stand up. "Where do I put it?" I asked.

"In your bag is fine. I wrapped it up."

I slid the package into my leather satchel, making sure it rested on a soft sweater underneath. I didn't even know how to be careful around it. My fingertips grazed the cool grip of the gun in my jacket. "Should I . . ."

"What?" Jan said.

"Nothing." Of course I should bring my gun. I should bring anything that might help. I had to come prepared.

"Give 'em hell," he said. As he closed the door behind me, he blew me a kiss.

I TOOK A few quick peeks up and down the street before I set out, wondering, as always, about what the neighbors thought was going on in the RVV apartment. Just a group of young volunteers, Hendrik had told them when the RVV first moved in, mentioning something about the Red Cross. The neighbors rarely met our gaze. But in truth, nobody met a stranger's gaze anymore.

I pedaled away past the edge of the Haarlemmerhout, past the weary farmers in town from the country, hawking mealy parsnips and potatoes with a thousand eyes. What we used to throw to pigs we now felt lucky to haggle for, spending more effort paring away the spoiled parts of vegetables than we did cooking and eating them. I cinched my jacket tighter around my waist. It was becoming easier to tell who was collaborating and who wasn't, just by the curve of their cheeks, the fit of their clothing. Anyone who appeared overfed was suspect. But a ruddy vigor seemed to be an indelible aspect of a few people's makeup. Like Jan, whose broad shoulders always appeared to be straining the seams of his canvas work jackets. I brushed the image away and kept pedaling.

———————

I STOPPED A little distance from the power station just to get a look at it. And also to catch my breath. The power station was just the kind of huge, anonymous industrial site I'd never really thought about or even noticed before the war. This place supplied electricity to nearby towns and cities but also, I now saw, to the electrified train lines transporting valuable Dutch steel to the Nazi U-boat operations elsewhere. There wasn't much to observe, just scattered high-windowed buildings and elaborate arrangements of electrical wires strewn around the property. Guards, but not many. I saw a few of them clustered together in a drab-green clump, smoking. It was a boring job.

I peered around for Truus, realizing I had no idea what she looked like. I'd spent so much time imagining the Oversteegen sisters that I'd never asked for a detailed description. Fortunately, she would no doubt be the only other woman at the Nazi power plant in the middle of the night. I looked for the two switching towers and saw those, just as Jan said. But which one was the first and which the second? It had sounded so simple back at the apartment. I left my bike hidden in the bushes and crept up to the southwest fence near one of the towers. Then I heard something.

Two pebbles clicking against each other.

The creaking of a piece of wood under the weight of something.

The high-pitched spray of glass shattering on the ground.

I jumped, flattening myself against the chain-link fence with a rattling crash, the loudest sound of all. I squeezed my eyes shut like a child hoping the monster would be gone when I opened them.

I opened them.

A cat jumped down from a stack of boxes and landed next to my feet, then stretched its orange-and-white neck against my ankle, purring and looking for a scratch.

Good Lord.

I reached down to pet it, but in typical cat fashion, it swerved away from my kindness and swished its tail as it disappeared between my legs. When I turned to look at it, I saw it walk through the fence behind me and into the rail yard of the power station.

Through the fence.

I crouched to the dirt. The chain links had been snipped by someone, and if I pushed on it a little, a gap opened up just big enough for me to squeeze myself through. The cat watched from a few feet away, licking its paws. I pushed through. I brought the wrapped bomb in after me, and the paper caught on the metal link of the fence and ripped, audibly. I scanned the rail yard, looking for guards. They still had lights at night here, so it was bright and the shadows were harsh. Only the cat noticed.

But then, in the shadow of the closest tower, I thought I saw her. A person who looked to be about my size, maybe a little taller, sat against the brick wall just ahead, balanced on her haunches and wearing work boots and a man's flat cap. She was probably in disguise. Nobody had suggested that to me. I squinted. It could be a man. I sat stuck in place, running the possibilities in my head. If it was an undercover Einsatzgruppen soldier, I was doomed. I looked right and left. I squinted at the figure again. Then I ran.

The person turned toward me as my footsteps scattered the gravel. I could see a bit better now. A bulky canvas sack sat to the figure's side, one hand clenched around it, the other hand holding a gun. Face still in shadow, they nodded at me, beckoned me closer, and flattened their hand to the ground: *Stay low.* The gun wasn't pointed at me, so I kept going.

"Hey," she said.

It was a woman's voice.

"I didn't think you'd get here in time," she whispered. Relief softened her features.

"Truus?" I said.

She nodded. "Just stay out of sight. It may seem quiet here, but they're watching."

Looking around, I saw no one. The smoking soldiers had wandered off somewhere, and the only sound was the mysterious thunder of machinery from inside the factory like an ongoing earthquake. I didn't know how fearful I should be, or of what, exactly. Nothing in my cloistered little life had prepared me for this, another one of those moments when I wondered how I'd ended up in the situation at all.

Truus nodded toward a concrete bunker near the steel fence at the far edge of the yard. "There's at least one guard inside there."

We waited.

We stared at the bunker.

We stared at the cat.

The cat licked its paws.

Nothing happened.

Minutes passed. My feet began to tingle and go numb beneath me.

"Truus."

"What."

She was peering around the corner of the building, not looking at me.

"I don't . . ." I wasn't sure what it was I wanted to say.

"You don't what?"

"I don't know the plan."

Truus wound herself back around to face me. "Then how did you get here?"

"Jan told me where to meet you, but . . .

She sank to a squat. "That was the first plan. Before it changed."

"Is Freddie here?"

She shook her head. "Fucking Jan." Truus chewed the inside of her lower lip for a moment, thinking. "Doesn't matter. You're here now."

A clang from across the yard, a metal fence crashing against itself. We both froze and then waited. Nothing.

"Right," she said at last. "You have the package?"

I shoved it toward her, and her eyes widened as she took it with both hands. "Jesus, woman, be careful," she hissed. "You have to handle a bomb like a baby. Gentle. You'll get us killed."

"Sorry," I said, embarrassed. She ignored the apology.

"See that rail line? That's the one we're hitting. We were supposed to have two of these," she said, nodding toward the package, "but it looks like Jan fucked that up, too. So we're only doing one." She was thinking, reconsidering. "We'll have to get it as close to the factory as possible, to do the most damage," she said. She seemed to be talking to herself, but then she looked at me. "Did he show you how to attach it to the rails?"

I shook my head.

"OK." Her finger caught on the torn paper. She swore while she kept unwrapping it, and the sound was deafening in the quiet night. The cat looked our way. "This is a fucking disaster," she whispered. "It's supposed to be wrapped in a blanket. This thing is . . ." She took one more peek around the wall and ripped the paper off with a quick, noisy tug. The cat cocked its head and flicked its tail. I was coated in cold sweat.

Nothing happened.

We both exhaled.

"Let's just do it," she said. "I'll run over and attach it to the rail while you cover me. You watch, I'll attach. OK?"

I nodded, pulling my gun from my pocket. She saw it. "Just try not to kill me," she said, her face serious. "But if you have to, shoot anyway."

I didn't know how to respond, so I said nothing. She reminded me of Jan. The same confidence. The same no-nonsense attitude. She didn't seem to like me quite as much as Jan did, unfortunately.

"It's not important you hit anybody," Truus said, trying to teach me the basics of suppressive fire in the few seconds we had left. "Just spray bullets at them," she said, miming herself sweeping a machine gun in front of her. I had a pistol with eight rounds inside. She pointed at her head. "You don't have to kill anyone. It's a psychological thing. OK? Just keep them pinned down and scared of the bullets."

"OK," I said, comprehending only a fraction of what she'd just said. We knelt at the edge of the tower. No one was around. I had just enough time for one of my periodic pangs of doubt: *Am I really doing this?*

I was.

"Is it strange that there's no guards?" I said.

"No," Truus said. "Because these assholes are terrible at their jobs." She swiveled her head left and right. "All right, I'm going. If you see anything move, don't think about it, just shoot. Not at me. Then run and I'll follow you. Got it?"

I nodded.

Then she was off, a lithe blur streaking across the empty dirt yard, the package under her coat throwing her gait off slightly. She was magnificent. So brave. I scanned for movement. The cat leapt away from her, and my finger quivered on my trigger. I came close to making that cat my first casualty. But I managed to stop myself and heard a comforting click as the hammer slid back into place.

Truus threw herself down flat, in between the rails, and it actually did camouflage her a little bit, if only because you'd never think anybody would hide in such an exposed place. The bomb was made up of two small objects plus a bunch of wires, and I saw her push them up at the rail and secure them with some kind of shiny strap. Her hands were right in front of her face as she twisted a series of wires together and laid them down, then placed two small flat discs on top of the rail. The detonators, I assumed. They were noticeable, but only if you were looking for them. No one seemed to be.

My hands were damp around the grip of the gun as I scanned the yard for guards. Nothing. Truus tapped the rail to secure something, a tinny ring. No one but me and the cat noticed. Then her eyes were peering over the rail and straight at me: *All clear?*

I made a visual sweep one more time and nodded back: *All clear.* She scurried out of position and raced toward me, sliding into our slice of shadow with a gasp of relief.

"It's done," she said. "Now we just have to get out of here before the train arrives."

"When's that?"

She checked her watch. Too big for her narrow wrist, it was a German military watch, I realized. Stolen off a soldier she'd killed, probably. "Ten minutes. I was going to wait for the later train, but since you got here early . . . It'll be a little close, but we should do it. We should go. Now."

"There's a gap in the fence where I came in," I said.

"Good. I'll follow you."

The tiniest hint of her approval filled me with unearned confidence. "Let's go," I said.

I ran to the fence, curled back the free section, and was on the outside all in one go. I jumped to a crouch and turned around, looking for Truus. But she wasn't there. I stared harder. She was still back at the tower, unmoving.

And then I saw him. His stride was casual, easy, but he was still a soldier with a long gun slung over his shoulder and he was walking in my direction. Relaxed, though. He hadn't seen me yet. I whipped my head around and saw the huge wooden spool again. I could hide behind that, if I could get there.

I looked back at Truus, but the shadows were so dark I couldn't see her expression. I pointed toward where I planned to go but had no idea if she understood. I rose almost to standing to prepare.

But Truus was moving, too. I saw her reach for something, her small hand darting out into the light momentarily; then I heard it: WHACK. She'd thrown a rock.

The soldier spun on his heel, following the sound, and I ran in the opposite direction toward the spool and collapsed behind it, panting. Quietly, I hoped.

Three guards now materialized from behind the factory and ran to the rock, poking it with their gun muzzles. They snooped around the area a little bit, nudging at the stacks of industrial materials nearby. One tapped his rifle against a box of rusty springs, and our old friend the cat jumped out, snarling. The soldier jumped back.

"Eine Katze!" another soldier shouted, and they laughed and pointed at the soldier, scared by a little kitty. He spit in the general direction of the animal, and the soldiers returned to the other side of the factory, still laughing. Some excitement in their dull night.

Thank you, Truus. I angled my head around the spool and swallowed hard. The other soldiers left. But not this one; he was staring right at me. At the spool, anyway. I heard him unlock the metal gate, and his footsteps got closer as he walked toward me. There was nothing else to do.

I stood up.

"Wer ist da?" he said, his thin voice cracking. "Who's there?"

"Sorry, sorry! I just got a little lost." I spoke German to make sure he understood. Half the time they didn't even notice the difference. I smiled at him, with his watery eyes and nervous voice. I shivered theatrically and shoved my hands deep into the pockets of my wool overcoat, burying my gun with it.

"Papiere." He steadily advanced on me until he had to stop or his rifle would have poked me in the cheek. "Papers," he said again. He seemed scared.

I handed him my fake ID, and he inspected it, holding it up to the light to read. He handed it back, looking me over, skeptical. "You shouldn't be here. It's past curfew."

That wasn't the only reason I shouldn't be there, as we both knew.

"I know, I know," I said, stalling. I yearned to check on Truus but couldn't risk him following my gaze. "I dropped something around here this morning when I was walking and I just . . ." I let my voice trail off. And then I began to cry. Well, I pretended to.

"Wait, no," the soldier said, flustered, "don't do that." The sight at the tip of his rifle barrel dipped down and away from me, but he stayed fixed in place, flustered. "What did you lose? Miss?" I continued crying. He looked around for backup. There was none. "You shouldn't be here," he said again. "You could be arrested."

"Don't arrest me!" I sobbed, my face still buried in my hands as I smeared my mascara down my cheeks with my fingers and a little spit. I looked up, blinking, and his eyes went wide at the sight of a hysterical female. "Please."

When women cry, men get scared. I filed that one away.

"Just get what you're looking for and go," he said. "What is it, jewelry? Money?"

"I might have dropped it over there," I said, looking away from the factory and back toward the houses and my hidden bicycle beyond. "Can I go look?"

"Yes, yes, just go," he said, looking over his shoulder. He pointed with his rifle. "Go."

I ran toward my bike as he watched, his rifle trained on me with every step. When I got there, I bent down and ran my hands over the dirt, cursing the poverty that left the streets scoured of all the discarded bits of junk we used to take for granted before the war. We saved everything now, every bent spoon and candy wrapper. I snatched a skinny twig and held it aloft, hoping he wouldn't investigate further.

"Found it!" I said.

He started toward me and my heart sank. *Don't. Please don't come any closer.* I felt for my gun again and then we both heard it: WHACK.

Truus was throwing stones again.

One of the other soldiers jogged back out to the yard, and my soldier's face went white, as if he knew he'd screwed up. "Just go!" he hissed at me.

I ran to my bike, not looking back. I jumped on, rode around the corner of an abandoned house, and then stopped, listening. The sound of his footsteps disappeared, jogging in the direction of the factory and almost masked by the low chug of something else. I waited a few more minutes and tried to slow my panicked breathing, then tiptoed to the corner and looked toward the towers. The chugging sound was loud now: here came the freight train. Squinting, I tried to spot Truus from this distance, but it was too dark and too far.

A hand on my shoulder.

"Let's go." Truus had come around the building behind me and was already turning down the street, where she ducked into an alley, pulled out a bike, and started pedaling in the direction of Haarlem. I turned to get mine and then everything stopped.

Everything was bright.

Everything was crashingly loud.

Everything was quiet.

Then everything was chaos.

I'd fallen to the ground in the blast and my hip ached, but I was fine. The factory was not. The yard behind me was now a cloud of smoke, flames, and dust billowing up and out and raging. Windows were shattered, and workers and soldiers poured out of the factory like ants from a picnic basket, swarming and blind. There in the middle of the yard, the train was bunched on its buckled tracks, some of the cars overturned completely and others shoved against each other like toys, the coal inside spilling onto the siding in sooty black dunes.

We'd done that. Truus and I. The heat of the explosion warmed my face and forced me to squint. I pedaled in the direction Truus had gone, my chest swelling with pride, and I laughed out loud with a cracking voice, my vision blurred with joyful tears.

Chapter 17

Autumn 1943

"YOU'RE GOING TO get a reputation." Jan squeezed the trigger and the gun went off. It was late afternoon, a week after the bombing, and Jan had suggested he and I do some shooting practice before an upcoming job. I was eager to see Truus after IJmuiden, but she and Freddie had disappeared the next day. Hendrik mentioned that the Oversteegen family belonged to a much broader Resistance network, of which the RVV was only one small part. As far as I could tell, the two sisters never stopped working.

I reloaded and waited him out.

"People are talking about IJmuiden," he said, "about what you pulled off at the factory. They stayed up celebrating all night, just to watch it burn." He sounded happy for me. Proud.

"Truus did it," I said. In my mind, I could see her hiding between the railroad tracks and marveled again. "I just helped out."

"I have plenty of sources in those parts," he said, "and one of them told me she could have sworn she saw a beautiful redheaded girl fly by her window on a squeaky bike that night." He grinned with satisfaction. It showed off his dimples. "So of course I requested you for my next assignment."

He aimed, fired. He bit his lower lip when he squeezed the trigger. I made two mental notes: to try to be less conspicuous when fleeing the scene and to find some grease for my creaking bike pedals.

"They think you two are wonderful. Which you are, of course." He cleared his throat. "For girls."

"Shut up," I said, punching him in the shoulder. "What am I aiming at here?" We were deep in the woods again, in a close clearing.

Jan pointed to a copse of cedars a little way off. "Try to hit one of the three tall ones: Fritz, Karl, or Adolf."

Impossible. The tree trunks were thin and spindly and difficult to aim at. And they were much too far away. But I took aim and fired a series of shots in a row, as Jan was encouraging me to do. Every round whizzed past the trees, which stayed standing, motionless in the still evening air.

"Sorry," I said, embarrassed. But Jan didn't mind.

"Don't rush through it," he said.

"'Dress me slowly, for I am in a hurry.'"

Jan's eyes narrowed, intrigued. "Go on."

"It's just an old saying," I said, laughing, "from your favorite old whore."

"What?" His eyes bulged.

"Napoléon."

He rolled his eyes and I pulled the trigger. The sound of flapping bird wings announced yet another miss. "Damn it," I said.

"Dress more slowly, Hannie," he teased. "And don't worry about it," he said. "Just keep practicing. I'll be doing the shooting Friday. You're my backup." He smiled. "That is, if you want to be."

The unwritten rule of assignments was that they were always optional. "The pay's not good enough," Hendrik explained. This was a joke: there was no pay; we were all volunteers. But the truth was, nobody ever turned down a job. If anything, we were eager for more. I knew I was.

"Of course," I said, sounding more confident than I felt. "What is it?"

"A real prize." He practically licked his lips. "Freddie staked this one out and got some solid intelligence on the comings and goings of a bunch of big shot Nazis. Friday night we're targeting one of them: Corporal Ernst Kohl, sent here from Poland to oversee the Aktion Silbertanne plans. Apparently he's some kind of expert in murdering resisters. We'll get him Friday."

Jan explained that he and I would get dressed up as if going on a date. Then we would make our way to a bar that had become a kind of club-house for the officers. "We won't go in, it's too risky," he said. "Not enough exits. But we stand outside and wait for him." He grinned. "You'll be good at this."

I wasn't quite as confident. "Won't it look suspicious if we're just standing around outside?"

"Well . . ." Jan said. He walked closer. "I have an idea." He seemed shy, for once, which flustered me. And I was flustered around him to begin with.

"There's an alley right next to the bar," he said. "We can hide out there while we wait. And if anyone sees us in there . . ." He shrugged.

I was confused. "What?"

"Well." I could smell him now. Fresh sweat, tobacco, something mas-culine. I inhaled it like a drug. "If anyone does see us, we could just pre-tend we're a couple."

"A couple?" I said. "How does that make us less suspicious?"

"I thought . . ." His face was right in front of mine now. "If someone walked by, we'd just be . . ." His gaze drifted between my eyes and my mouth. "Kissing."

"Oh," I said. We stood inches away from each other, so close I could feel the heat of his body through the air.

"But not if you don't want to," he said.

I licked my lips. He did, too. We hovered there like two magnets trying to resist an elemental attraction, then he leaned into me and kissed me hard, his hands gripping me as if afraid to let me go.

I'd kissed a boy before. Once. It was the first party of my college career, a roomful of bewildered strangers pretending to have fun. Somehow I ended up on the dance floor yoked to a boy named Tom who, just as the song ended, kissed me on the mouth and then drew back as if he'd surprised himself. "I always wanted to do that," he said. I just stood there dumbstruck and embarrassed. "Sorry," he said, then ran away. After that, I never wanted to do it again. I felt as if I'd been slapped in the mouth with a dead herring.

Jan's kiss was not like that.

When Jan kissed me, I wanted to pull him in closer. *Oh.* Kissing wasn't just something to do; it was something to feel. We kissed and kissed and finally pulled ourselves apart.

Jan laughed. "Well, then."

"What?"

"Nothing," he said. He tucked a lock of my hair behind my ear. "That was nice. That's all."

"It was nice," I said. Then we kissed again. And a few times more. "For practice," I said. "For Friday night."

"Friday night," he said. We kissed again and then heard a rustling in the trees. We both looked, saw nothing.

"It's getting dark out here," he said. "We should probably get going."

"It's not that dark." I didn't want to go anywhere. I never wanted to stop kissing him. I was starting to think I might finally be feeling what everyone else felt . . . maybe love, maybe not, how was I supposed to know? It was addictive.

"Then let's get a little more practice in while we can," he said. "For Friday night."

"OK," I said. He took out his gun and I realized he meant target practice.

"Try those three trees again," Jan said, pointing to the cedars he'd named.

"It's pointless," I said.

"Just try." His tone of voice, post-kiss, was softer now.

If I couldn't kiss him, I at least wanted to impress him. I planted my legs apart, narrowed my sight down the barrel, and fired. The big cedar on the far right shuddered and dropped a flurry of leaves.

"Adolf! Well done." Jan clapped me on the back and then let his hand rest there.

"I'm not sure I really hit it," I said. "I think I just clipped a branch."

"Have a little faith in yourself, woman."

I laughed. "Fine, I hit it."

"Bet you five cigarettes you missed," he said.

I threw a stick at him. "Go away."

He laughed, and I started walking toward the trees.

"So?" he called after me.

"I'll take your bet," I said, not looking back, "but I'm not going to take your word for it. I'll check."

He laughed. "I'll be waiting for my smokes."

I continued tromping through the underbrush and thought about the touch of his hand. The feel of his kiss. My skin tingled everywhere. I got to the cedars and inspected Adolf for bullet holes, but in among the trees, it was even more difficult to see anything. I ran my hand over the papery bark searching for a wound. Nothing. Then, looking up, I saw a branch snapped in half, hanging down like a loose tooth. Just as I thought. Then I spotted the next tree, a huge oak behind it. I stepped deeper into the forest. If I hit that oak, or any one of these others, I might still win this bet.

It was tough going. I was now in the heart of the woods and there were no paths. Just deep coolness and quiet. I picked my way over moss-covered logs and pulled my sleeves over my hands to push away the brambles. I took another step toward the big oak, and my foot landed on something slimy. I lost my balance and, afraid to reach for the thorny bushes, fell to the ground with my arms over my face for protection.

The ground wasn't wet, though. At least, not as wet as what I'd just stepped on. I pushed myself up and cleared away the forest litter. Mushrooms? Thick green moss, maybe. A dead fish, but that made no sense.

Reading the ground with my fingertips like a blind person, my hand jerked back on instinct before I could register the thing itself. So pale it seemed to glow.

A human hand.

"Jan!" I screamed. "Jan!" I spasmed to my feet and stumbled away, falling backward onto a stump and staying there, my thoughts blurring.

"Hannie?" Jan crashed through the forest.

"I'm here," I said.

"What is it?" he said, scrambling over a boulder to reach me.

"I shot someone."

"What?"

"Over there, on the ground." I pointed. "A hand. There's a woman's hand." I could still see it in my mind. Outstretched, palm up, the fingers curved inward like any hand at rest. The nails were painted coral pink. Jan took a few steps, then stopped.

"Hannie, come here."

I wanted to run in the opposite direction. Instead, I pushed myself up and returned to where the hand, and the body attached to it, rested. Jan had cleared some debris that had fallen on her, and now she lay like a snow angel on the forest floor. Luminous in the dusky light, she wore only a torn satin camisole in peach, the color of her skin, and frumpy but practical white panties, the waistband snapped and fabric ripped down the middle to expose her. Jan had left the branches over her there. Her face was covered in dirt, and her long brown hair disappeared into the leaf litter and soil. I didn't see a gunshot wound. But I didn't want to look closer. I could barely understand what I was looking at.

"She's been here . . . a week, at least." He touched the point of her elbow with the toe of his boot and the arm rolled to the side.

"Don't."

"They're only stiff for the first day or so."

"Ugh." I turned and walked a few steps farther away, trying to erase my mind. "Oh, God, Jan."

"It's OK."

"No." I stood, pointing at the ground. "It's another one."

Jan ran over. "Jesus. A couple."

The man lay next to a log, his body nearly wedged underneath. He wore only white cotton briefs and black socks, a hole in the right big toe. His head was turned toward us. Just a normal-looking man, perhaps thirty-five or forty years old, like the woman.

"See if you can find any of their belongings," Jan said, stalking the ground between the two bodies like a bloodhound, "a purse or a briefcase. They look like"—he glanced back and forth between the two of them—"professional types, maybe. Bourgeoisie."

"This isn't a May Day rally," I said. He could be so pitiless.

"You know what I mean. They haven't been living rough."

"She does have nail polish," I conceded.

He looked up at me as if surprised by my detective work. "Exactly."

We looked for their belongings for ages, finding nothing, until it got too dark to see the ground.

"Hannie, we should go." Jan lit a cigarette, and it was the only point of light in the darkness. He handed the cigarette to me.

"Thanks," I said. I sighed. Were they Dutch? She was, probably. Was he a Nazi? Maybe. Maybe not. I didn't know whom to hate.

"Well, I guess you lost the bet."

"Shut up." My voice was hoarse. I was trying not to cry.

"Hey," Jan said, lifting my chin to meet his gaze. "They were probably just..."

"What? A suicide pact?"

"Suicide pact?" he said. "My God, woman. Where do you get these ideas?"

"Well, maybe they were Jewish and it was just too hard to go on."

"And maybe they were Jewish and the Krauts took them out here, beat the guy to death, had their way with the girl, then made sure they were both dead with a quick bash to the back of the head. I haven't found any bullet holes."

"Ugh, Jan." I pushed myself away from him. "Please."

"Sorry," he said, and he did sound remorseful this time. He watched my face, concerned. "I'm sorry, Hannie. Come here." He tugged me toward him, then held me in his arms. I felt the warmth of him through his wool sweater and listened to the beat of his heart.

"It's OK," he said. "You've probably never seen a dead body before."

"I have," I said.

"The bombing the other night?"

I paused. I hadn't devoted much thought to that at all. "No, my sister."

"Oh, Jesus. I'm sorry."

"It was a long time ago," I said. "Before the war."

"So you're not bothered by this." He stroked my hair.

"I just don't think about it," I said, parroting his advice.

"Uh-huh," he said. "And how do you do that?"

"I just put it out of my mind," I said, taking a deep breath.

And then I burst into tears. I smashed my face into his sweater to mask the sound of my choking sobs. I wasn't sad, exactly. It was more confusing than that. I let the crying take over and wept into him, and somehow he absorbed the feelings. With my eyes closed, I could still see the woman on the ground. Her face, shoulders, legs, were bruised.

"It's not easy," Jan said, still holding me. "But it does get easier."

"Is that right, though?" I whispered. "Should it? Those people who died at the factory . . ."

"Listen," he said, taking my chin in his hand and tilting my head up to look at him. "I'm so sorry about the death of your sister. But another Nazi gone is a good thing, Hannie. A very good thing. How many lives do you think you saved there, hmm? You took out a goddamn power station: that's lives they won't touch now." He kissed my hair. "And the best part is, it reminds these bastards they're not winning. Cocksucking goddamn Krauts."

I laughed and wiped my tears. He pulled a handkerchief out of his pocket. "Not as fine as Hendrik's, but it's clean. Mostly."

"Thanks." I sat for a minute, composing myself. "How long have you been doing this?" I asked.

"Me?" said Jan. "I've been at this game a long time. There were plenty of fascists here before the Germans arrived. I've been arrested."

"You have?"

"It was right at the beginning of the war and I was working on the line at Hoogovens," Jan said. "Agitating, distributing underground newspapers and such. Next thing you know, this troop of Gestapo assholes— now we call them the SD—marches into the factory with a list of names and Bonekamp was one of them. There was nowhere to run, so I got taken into the police station in IJmuiden along with a couple dozen other troublemakers."

I couldn't see much, but occasionally the light from our cigarettes illuminated his face, smiling now as he was transported back to the night in question.

"They throw us in cells, right?" he said. "Disgusting, filthy. And I'm in there for what seems like twenty-four hours. Other guys got taken out and never came back. Finally they dragged me into an interrogation room with these two Nazi pricks. It's two village idiots from Austria. By this point, it was three in the morning: the loser shift.

"That was lucky for me. They get me in there, handcuffed because otherwise I could easily take them, and start going through their paperwork. It's the Krauts' favorite thing: lists of fucking names. They go on and on and finally they start talking to me.

"'Bonekamp?' one says.

"I consider lying, but I know they pulled my personnel file when they left the factory. They love that shit. So I say yeah.

"'Jaap Bonekamp?' the other says, holding up the paperwork to show the other idiot. Something's wrong. They're starting to sweat.

"'Fuck no,' I say. 'Jan Bonekamp.' They got the wrong file. There's a half dozen Bonekamps in those files, but they don't know that." He laughed. "Jaap's my cousin.

"They're scared, I can tell. Sweating and yelling at each other and shaking the papers in each other's faces. They're Krauts, so it sounds like barking dogs. I can tell I'm getting under their skin. So I yell at them again.

"'Get me the fuck out of here!' I shout. 'This is an illegal arrest, I can't wait to talk to your boss about the two losers who can't even read a goddamn list of names right. A list of names! Get these things off me!' And I start yanking the cuffs against the back of the chair, making a racket. The two goons looked at each other, checked the papers one last time, then had me escorted out of the station."

I was awed. "Really?"

"Yeah. But it wasn't over." He was so handsome when he was animated like this.

"They followed you?" I asked.

"Sort of. As soon as I got out to the street, I ran as fast as I could to my parents' house—I was still living there at the time—and my dad says I better hide, just in case they figure out their mistake. Then my little brother runs in the house and says there's Gestapo coming down the street. My mother pulls me into the kitchen and points to a low cupboard next to the sink. 'Get in there,' she says.

"I don't understand, but I go over and then I see that they've made the cupboard a sort of secret entrance to the crawl space under the kitchen floor. I squeeze myself in there—it was close—and crawl to a spot where I can lie flat under the floor."

Jan was holding my hand when he started the story. His grip was getting tighter and tighter.

"About five seconds later, there's a classic Gestapo knock at our front door: the two polite knocks and then just march the fuck in. I hear my parents arguing with them, my little brother shouting. I was proud of them. They stood up for themselves. But when the guys wanted to search the place, there was nothing they could do. So for the next forty-five minutes, they tear the house apart, shelves crashing to the floor, furniture flipped over. Just to be pricks.

"And the whole time I'm just lying there, still as a fucking stone. Every so often, one of them would walk over me and the dirt from their boots dropped down into my eyes and mouth. I didn't budge."

"So what did you do . . . ?" I asked.

"Just fucking swallowed it. Disgusting, but who cares! After a while, they got bored and they left. We waited a while, then I crawled back out, and we had a party back at the house. It was a good night."

"They never came back for you?"

"I went underground for a couple months, visited my aunt and uncle in The Hague. That's where I met Hendrik. When I joined the Resistance."

"I can't picture the RVV without you," I said, and it was true. He had a special energy about him that made you feel safe, like he was willing to do things others wouldn't do. Even if he was, possibly, exaggerating the story he'd just told me. I didn't care. He was on the right side.

"I chose the RVV because it has a reputation for violence," he said.

"Don't they all?"

"Nah. Some cells just print newspapers, you know? Or smuggle things in and out of the country. No, armed resistance, that's what I wanted." He took one drag of the cigarette and then handed it to me.

"I didn't realize I was joining the most violent Resistance group."

"Bettine didn't mention it?" he said, smiling at the thought of her. "Well, she knew. And she knew you'd fit right in."

"Here," he said, and tossed me the lighter. It was a silver cigarette lighter. "For you." It was heavy in my hand, one side smooth and the other lumpy. I flipped open the cap to light the flame and saw the design on the side.

"Ugh," I said. "The Iron Cross."

Jan laughed. "Yeah, well. I got it off a Kraut."

"You should keep it, then."

"Nah, I got a bunch. Here, give it back for a minute."

I tossed it back. He unsheathed a sharp little dagger from his waistband, and with a few twists of the blade, the Iron Cross popped off and fell in the dirt. He held the lighter up like a glass of champagne. "Down with Hitler," he said.

"All the way down," I said. "Thank you."

Jan smiled and pounded his heart with his fist. "How about one for Bettine Dekker," he said, "for sending me such a crazy redhead to train." He shook his head as if in exasperation, and I leaned in to punch him— but he caught my fist in his hand. Then he brought it up to his mouth and kissed it. We paused. And then I put my other hand around his neck and pulled myself all the way up and sat on his lap and kissed him on the lips again.

He leaned back against the huge oak tree behind us and looked me in the eyes. "Hannie," he said.

I wanted him. So much.

"Shut up," I said, and pushed him against the tree and kissed him again.

"Hannie?" a voice called.

It was Truus.

Chapter 18

I JUMPED TO MY feet before she could spot me. I'd never been caught kissing anyone before. It was embarrassing. Especially in front of Truus. Especially with Jan.

"Truus?" I walked toward her voice.

"Wait," she said. "Stop. Don't come over here."

She was at the woman's body.

"No, don't," she said. "It's bad."

"I already saw it," I said.

The trees shook behind me and Jan appeared. "Truus," he said.

She glared at him like Medusa.

"There's another body, too," I said. "A man. It's over there."

"Same condition?" she said.

I nodded. I'd hoped we'd have a chance to talk about the job at IJmuiden before launching into another operation. We barely knew each other, but we now had a bond. I felt it, anyway.

"How did you find us?"

"I come here to shoot," she said. "When did you find them?" she asked Jan.

"I found the bodies," I said. A flicker of approval passed over her face. "We've been trying to identify them."

"And?" She asked. "Find anything?"

"Neither of them have ID," I said. "I thought maybe they were Jewish. There were a lot of Jewish suicides at the beginning of the war."

"Yes," she said. She looked down at the body. "But this happened recently. What about you?" she said to Jan.

"Germans did it. Just an unlucky couple in the wrong place at the wrong time. Could be a jealous boyfriend."

"Find anything else?" she asked.

"Well, her fingernails are, um, painted," Jan said. "They're polished. So that tells me these are just a couple of rich folks who bumped into the wrong people."

"What do you know about nail polish?" asked Truus.

"What, you want to know if he's circumcised, too?" Jan said.

"Well, is he?"

Jan glared at her. "We were just finishing up." He worked his jaw the way he did when he was irritated. Truus had ruined the moment. "I'm out of ammunition, Hannie. Let's go."

"What about these two?" asked Truus.

"What about them?"

The dead woman's corpse lay on the forest floor between us.

"We can't just leave them here," I said.

"Sure we can," said Jan. "For all we know, they could be German spies."

"It's all right, Jan, you go along," said Truus. "We'll take care of this."

He knew she was patronizing him and he hated it. He looked to me with those blue eyes and his face softened a little.

"It's OK," I said to Jan. "We'll talk in the morning." As much as I wanted Jan to lead me out of the forest and away from this crime, it felt wrong to simply leave the bodies where they lay. Maybe they weren't German spies.

Jan was confused, but too annoyed to discuss it further. "Fine. See you later." Jan gave me a look before he left, one last chance to join him.

"I'll see you soon," I said. He crashed away through the woods. Then it was quiet again.

"Show me the other one," Truus said. "The man."

I walked her over. She did most of the same things Jan did, inspecting the body for wounds, personal effects, the condition of the corpse. Then she did something else.

"Help me pull him out," she said, squatting beside his torso where it was pushed under the log.

My stomach flipped in on itself at the prospect. "He's kind of . . . decomposed."

"It's important." She stared, testing me.

"OK," I said. I took a gulp of fresh air and then held my breath as I reached down to pull him out by the boot. Working together, we freed the left half of his corpse from where it had been half buried under the log. Somehow he seemed even more dead than the downed tree, his white skin glowing like marble. Truus walked around, looking at him. She knelt down and lifted his left arm and seemed to poke around his armpit, then set it back down and rummaged in her pocket for a rattling box of wooden matches.

"Pull up his arm," she told me.

Acid crawled up the back of my throat. The man's skin, especially on the left side, was mottled and sticky-looking, like dough. I didn't want to touch it.

Truus looked up at me. "Hannie. I'm serious."

"OK," I said, unwilling to risk her thinking less of me. I encircled his left wrist with both hands and pulled upward, horrified that the arm would detach itself from the rest of the body. Thankfully, it was more solid than I expected. But oh, God, the stench. Truus held the guttering match so close to the man's armpit I worried she'd burn him. Then I disgusted myself with the realization that it wouldn't matter if she did.

"Look at this," she said.

I forced myself to look at the pale patch of skin illuminated there and saw something written on the underside of his upper arm.

"What does that look like to you?" Truus said.

"It's a letter, maybe?" I said. "*V*, I think?" I made the *V* symbol with my fingers, the way Churchill and all the Allied troops did in photos. "Maybe he's a resister. *V* for victory."

"He's not," she said. "Look at that."

I leaned in.

"You're looking at it upside down, Hannie."

A thin horizontal line joined the two sides of the letter.

"It's an *A*."

"Yeah."

"You can lower it."

I tried to drop his hand as quickly as possible without desecrating the dead. We rubbed our hands in the dirt and leaves on the ground in an attempt to clean them. "Probably the name of his sweetheart," I said, wishing I could plunge my hands into a pot of boiling water. "Annabelle. Alice."

"No," said Truus. "He was SS."

"What?"

"They all get a blood type tattoo."

"Oh," I said. "So, he's blood type A?"

"Yeah. Or it could be an *A* for Adolf," said Truus. "Ha-ha."

Neither of us laughed.

". . . and I'm *O*. For Oversteegen." She raised her fist. Truus and Freddie's parents had divorced when the girls were little. Hendrik had told me their mother renamed them with her maiden name.

"That's good detective work, Truus."

She shrugged. "You're the one who noticed the nail polish."

I turned to her. She laughed. "As if Jan Bonekamp would notice something like that."

She knew all about Jan. And she still liked me. I thought my heart might explode. Could I really have them both?

"So the guy was SS," Truus said. "But who was she?"

We walked back to the girl and stood over her.

"You expect to find a dead woman's body. But a man? A member of the SS? A couple?"

The woman's face was turned away from us, which made it a fraction less upsetting.

"Men can walk home alone at night." She looked in the direction Jan disappeared. "Women have to carry guns. And not just during wartime." She considered the body again. "If it was just the girl, alone, I'd say she got used by some soldiers."

"Yes," I said with a shiver. It was easy to imagine. Our streets were overrun with young German men frustrated that they couldn't always get a date with a Dutch girl. It was an unnerving feeling when you passed by a group of soldiers in that mood. They hated us, but they wanted us, too. I had often doubled my travel time, circumventing entire neighborhoods, just to avoid such interactions.

Truus led us back to the clearing to form a plan. She gave me a cigarette, and we tore into them, sucking down the smoke to burn out the smell of death. "So were you practicing shooting in the dark?" she asked.

"Well, we would have left earlier if we hadn't found them."

"Ah," Truus said. "Jan telling you war stories?" A flat laugh.

"Sort of," I said.

"He tell you how many men he's killed?"

"No," I said.

"Huh," said Truus. "I know he keeps a list." She bent a branch back on itself so I could follow her through to the clearing.

"You don't like him."

Truus laughed. "Jan's a very good fighter, and he's brave. It's just sometimes I expect him to come back to the apartment with actual scalps. For him, it's a game. The list is his scorecard."

"Well, in the story he told me tonight, he didn't kill anyone."

"Let me guess, he hid under the kitchen floor?"

"Well, yes."

"It's a good story," she said. "Might even be true." We both laughed.

"I think Jan told it to me to give me courage," I said.

"Could be. And it's a story with a happy ending, and there aren't many of those these days." She offered me another cigarette. "So, did it?"

"It gave me hope, I suppose."

"Hope?" She made the word itself sound skeptical.

"That even if you're captured, it's not necessarily the end."

"Hmm." She pondered it. "They caught Jaap, you know. Jan's cousin, the one they were looking for. They eventually found him and sent him off on a train to the Silesian coal mines. No one's heard from him since. Did he tell you that?"

"No," I said. We were quiet for a moment. Truus sat on one of the stumps in the clearing and I did, too. The little open space was lit with moonlight, and I was grateful for anything to push the darkness of the past hour away. "He was just trying to explain how he joined the RVV," I said.

"Mmm," mumbled Truus. She lit a fresh cigarette off the end of her dying one. "That's the thing about war stories," she said, blowing the smoke out the side of her mouth, away from me. "They never really end. Unless the person telling the story dies. Then, that's the end." She was speaking more softly now. I stayed quiet, hoping she would go on.

"If Jan ends that story where he did, it's a funny story. If you end it where I did, it's a tragedy. So which is it?" I began to formulate a response, but she spoke again. "It's both. It's neither. And anyway the story's not over yet, right? We still don't know the ending. Well, I suppose we know Jaap's ending."

"The ending?" I said like a dunce.

"When I die and stop telling my version of the story, and Jan dies and stops telling his. Then we'll know how it ended."

"How do you know Jaap's ending?" I asked.

She kicked at the dirt at our feet. "Nobody who gets put on a train ever comes back, Hannie. Everybody knows that."

I hadn't been willing to make such a bold statement before I joined the Resistance. I'd always been the girl who could come up with a scrap of good news when the outlook was bleak. There were fewer scraps now.

Truus paused, turning something over in her mind. "I asked you what stories he told you because I want you to know . . ." She hesitated, then sighed. "I've been doing this a long time. And so has Jan. But we do it differently." She looked at me in the black night air, her eyes glinting in the red ember of the cigarette. "You know?"

"Yeah," I said. I didn't know and I wanted her to go on.

"The way Jan talks about this war, you'd think he was the only one trying to do anything about it. It's not all arrogance, it's just the way he sees things. He's at the center of the saga, and the whole thing is about him. The Saga of Jan." Truus raised her cigarette like a tiny Viking torch.

"Can I have another cigarette?"

She laughed and handed one to me. "What we do, we do as a last resort. Because there's nothing else to be done. Do you understand what I'm saying?"

"I think so," I said. I didn't.

"We keep doing this, fighting these bastards, because it's the only thing we can do. Maybe that's what these two were doing," she said, gesturing toward the dead bodies we'd found. "Who knows?"

"The Nazi?" I said.

She shrugged. "One thing I've learned, doing this, is that you might think you know something for sure. But you don't."

I smoked my cigarette and tried to think of something to say. She didn't seem upset, really. Just mystified. Philosophical. She reminded me of Philine. With the self-confidence of Sonja. And the competence of a decorated military hero.

"Hey, Jan said that folks around IJmuiden think we're 'wonderful,'" I said with what I hoped sounded like a self-deprecating laugh. She said nothing.

I cleared my throat and waited for her to speak. I glanced over at her. Truus exhaled slowly. Like a boxer steadying himself in the corner of the ring. Then she started to talk.

"My mother started doing this work years before the war started. It's what split my parents apart. My father needed more attention than she could give him. She told him that from her perspective, he needed less attention. So he left. My mother went on with her work.

"She sheltered refugees for years. People escaping Germany, Poland. Mostly Jews but also some Gypsies, even some German boys trying to escape military service. So when the occupation happened, Hendrik showed up on my mother's houseboat to talk about the Resistance. She told him she had too many to feed as it was. Then he saw me and Freddie standing behind her. He introduced himself, and then asked her permission to recruit us. I was sixteen, Freddie was fourteen." I thought I saw a smile. "Freddie and I were excited," Truus said, "and I think Mother was just happy to have us out of her hair."

I could barely imagine the freedom of their childhood. The wildness. "All of this is new to me," I said. "The guns, everything."

"That part was new to me, too," Truus said. "I never used a gun before the war." She stared up at the stars. "I'd never been in a war. And everything is different in a war. No matter how much experience you have."

"Do you ever take a break?" I asked. "From all this?"

"Not really," she said, "though there's plenty of slow days, as you know." She sighed. "Of course I have considered quitting."

"Quit . . . the Resistance?" I couldn't imagine it myself, now that I was in it. And certainly not Truus. Never.

"Yeah," she said.

"Why?" I asked. I'd heard a few incredible stories about Truus and Freddie but didn't know how much of it was true. Birds shuffled in the trees, rustling leaves. The night air was warm. Peaceful. I waited for her to keep talking.

"We should do something with these bodies," Truus said.

"You don't want to talk about it?" I asked, feeling bold.

"Maybe that's the real difference between me and Jan," Truus said with a chuckle. "I never want to talk about the war—"

"And it's the only thing he wants to talk about," I said.

"So?" she said, rising to her feet. She held her hand out and pulled me up beside her. As much as I wanted to never think about the dead bodies again, I knew we had to do something.

"We should either turn them over to the authorities . . ." I looked at Truus, realizing how stupid my idea was as I said it. "Or bury them."

Truus nodded. "Yes. We have to bury them."

We walked to the woman's body and stood over it.

"I still think she could be Jewish," I said.

"Yeah," said Truus. "Me, too."

The ground beneath the top layer of leaves was cold, wet clay. With no tools but our hands, we began to dig.

Chapter 19

MY LIFE BECAME split down the middle: the excitement and occasional terror of Resistance work, and the relative safety and accompanying sadness of my family home. I slept at both places but increasingly was spending more time at the RVV. I was always the rookie at the apartment, scrambling after the others and constantly pretending I knew what I was doing. Yet life at home was fraught, too. As soon as I saw the yellow bricks of my childhood home, whatever progress I'd made in convincing myself I was a tough soldier of the Resistance began to dissolve like my mother's krakelingen cookies when you dipped them in tea. Like they used to, anyway.

It didn't help that I couldn't talk about anything I did. If I'd been able to tell Sonja and Philine some of the wilder details of my work—they'd have been amazed anyone would trust me with a bomb—I might have been able to make the two halves of my new life whole. But I couldn't. The moment I shot at Hendrik, I knew I could never tell them anything. For one thing, they wouldn't believe me. And if they did, it would only make them feel worse about being locked inside twenty-four hours a day. Then they would worry. And Sonja and Philine had enough to worry about. Not to mention my parents. But everyone worried anyway.

"Mijn kleine vos," my father said when I walked in the door a few days after Truus and I buried the bodies. The morning light filled the entryway with warmth. My little fox. He smoothed my hair from my forehead. "What henhouse have you been terrorizing today?" he asked. He didn't know I was carrying a gun.

"Look at you," my mother said. She walked over and took my skirt in her hands, the one I'd worn target shooting. A light blue cotton one she'd sewn for me the previous year out of fabric she'd found at the church rummage sale. She rubbed the material between her fingers where the fabric was darkly streaked with gun oil. I must have wiped my hands on it.

"Don't tell us anything; we don't want to know." He put his hand on my mother's shoulder to keep her from asking, too. The presence of Philine and Sonja in our home meant all five of us were effectively members of the Resistance now. I was sure they told themselves a story about my work that they could live with. That I was just doing paperwork, nothing too dangerous. Because if they knew what I was really up to, they wouldn't joke about it. My parents were not just generous. They were courageous. Just a few days after Sonja and Philine arrived, my father pulled me aside to tell me to stop searching for a more permanent hiding place for the girls. "They're as safe here as anywhere," he'd said, giving me a solemn look that communicated the depth of that commitment. Now I kissed them each on the cheek.

"Give that skirt to our guests, they're excellent laundresses," my father said.

"They're not servants," I said.

"They'll be happy to have something to do," said my mother.

My father looked somber. "Seeing you will cheer them. Go up and see, little fox."

———

I KNOCKED SOFTLY as I cracked open the bedroom door. Philine was sitting in the sole chair in the corner, crocheting, and her face brightened when she saw me.

"Hannie!" she said in a whisper, rising to hug me.

Sonja remained motionless on the bed, legs stretched out and one arm over her eyes as if sunbathing on a blazing day at the beach. But it was dark in the room. Dark and warm, the air heavy. My first instinct was to throw open the window and let in the fresh summer breeze, but we couldn't do that; we couldn't even pull aside the dark blue curtains in case a passing neighbor looked in. No wonder Sonja was still asleep at eleven o'clock in the morning. There was simply nothing to do.

"How are you?" I whispered to Philine, and she shrugged.

"Fine."

I raised an eyebrow and nodded toward Sonja.

Philine shook her head. "Not too well."

"Is she sick?"

Philine shook her head. "She hasn't been herself lately. She's been . . . like this."

I sat down next to Sonja and placed a hand on her shoulder. "Sonja?" I asked. "Can I get you anything?"

A faint groan. Without lifting her arm from her eyes, she said, "An airplane ticket to New York City would be lovely."

"I'll look into that."

Sonja didn't move.

Philine tried to change the conversation. "Any news, Hannie?"

There was nothing interesting I could safely share with them. The war was getting in between me and my best friends, even here in hiding. I sighed and reminded myself to stick to the obvious topics. "They say the

Germans are losing their courage after the defeats in Russia and North Africa," I said.

"Really?" said Philine, skeptical. "Who says?"

"*Het Parool* and *De Waarheid*," I said. *The Password* and *The Truth.*

"Of course the Resistance papers are going to say that," said Philine. She was also in a darker mood than usual.

"Well, that's what some say."

"Good," said Sonja from the bed. "Because if this war goes into next summer, I don't think I'll make it."

"That's months from now," said Philine. "It has to be over by then." I could tell she hadn't really thought it through before saying it. She searched my expression. "Right? Like you said, the Germans are losing."

"Yes, well . . ." I wanted to say something to cheer them up, but I didn't share Philine's optimism. "I don't have any secret information," I said. "But they have had some big losses, it's true."

"That's it?" Sonja said. "That's the best you can do?"

"It's been three years," Philine said to no one.

"So?" said Sonja.

"So I'm just saying. It can't go on much longer."

"What do you think?" said Sonja, looking at me. "How long will it last?"

It was something we usually avoided talking about, but Sonja no longer cared about these little social conventions.

"Well . . . Philine's right," I said. "I mean, it can't last forever. Nothing does."

Sonja snorted. "It already has."

"Sonja!" Philine said. "What the Schafts have risked—"

"I'm sorry," said Sonja in a softer voice. "Everyone's been wonderful. But I can't stay locked up in here forever. I mean it. I'm not spending 1944 in this tiny bedroom." She looked at me. "No offense."

It had only been a few months. But I didn't want to argue with her.

"It will end," a voice said. We all turned to see my mother, her cheeks pink with the exertion of the unending housework: sweeping, mopping, peeling, paring, whisking, washing, wringing, making something out of nothing, all day, every day. Her hands were as rosy as her cheeks, chapped from the cold water of the laundry. "Before you know it, all this will be over," she said, looking around the room crammed with the flotsam of three young women's lives, silk scarves dripping from the small spotty mirror and stockings drying on the back of a chair. "That's how these things go," she said. "You think it will never end and then—boom—it's done. That's how it went the last time. In the Great War."

She smiled, but it was as weak as the substitute coffee we all pretended to enjoy now. This war that some were now, depressingly, calling the Second World War. They were having a worse time of it than those of us who were young. They'd gotten through the Great War the way everyone did, by making promises to themselves that it would never happen again. They were once hopeful.

"Come on, now," my mother said, reasserting order. I watched as she rearranged her face from sorrow to a sort of calm resolve. "Out of bed, girls, and tidy up, it's almost time for lunch." She would bring their plates up to the bedroom on trays because they couldn't risk being seen by the neighbors through the kitchen window.

"I'll help you," I said.

She turned when we got downstairs. "You go," she said. "You have your own work to do."

I was shocked. It was the first time she hadn't needled me for neglecting my family obligations: pressing the sheets, blueing the whites, pulling the turnips. Real work.

"What is it, Mama?"

"There was a razzia here in Grote Market square," she said. "Rounding up young men—Jews, some Gypsies—in front of God and the cathedral, can you even . . . ?" Her face flamed with disgust. "It's not . . ." She took a deep breath and smoothed all her edges on the exhalation. "It's not right." My father stood in the doorway, watching her.

My mother was so blond and blue-eyed and fair she was almost translucent. Her face was ivory, the feathery wisps of curlicues and cowlicks where the wrinkles in her pale forehead met the meadowy edge of her hairline were white, silver, platinum. I saw an old woman. Old before her time, but old nevertheless. She was fifty-three years old.

She brushed a lock of my hair away from my cheek. "Be—" she started to say.

"Be kind, be considerate, be courageous," my father said, walking forward and completing the inevitable sentence. It was what she had always said to Annie and me before we left for school in the morning.

"Be careful," she said. "I'm including that now."

"I will."

She rose on tiptoe and kissed me on the forehead. I was only an inch or so taller than she. Her familiar motherly perfume entered my body and filled me with the solid, centered feeling of home. I hadn't felt that way in years.

"You're enjoying the work, aren't you?" she said.

My sensible mother had never really understood how to joke around, how to tease, but now I saw mischief in her uncertain smile. The wood floor creaked as we talked, a big sound in the little foyer, and I realized what an uncomfortable space this was, not just because it was cramped and cluttered with hanging coats and shoes on the floor and the usual jumble of incoming miscellaneous things that crowded the dainty mahogany table, inherited from some grandmother, pushed against the wall, but also because it was the room where all the greetings and goodbyes happened, and these were hard for my mother. With us, it was always either too much or too little; if I walked in with arms wide for a hug, she shrank backward, but if I entered with a quick kiss, she'd look hurt, as if I'd rebuffed her somehow. My mother had a tendency to say the most important things to me just as I was leaving, with no time to discuss or reply. It was one of my pet peeves, but now something I did, too. We approached our goodbyes with a subconscious fear of what we might say. But in this moment she was smiling.

"Yes," I said. "I am."

My father smiled. "Still reading Gandhi?"

"Papa," I said. I'd had long debates with my father over the dinner table about whether Gandhi's protests and hunger strikes could ever overthrow a real army. I always defended Gandhi.

"Don't tease her, Pieter," my mother said, but then she laughed. She'd had to sit through the debates, too.

"I still read Gandhi," I said, which was true. Jan teased me about it. I still admired Gandhi's courage and his commitment to his cause. I'd just changed my mind about whether his nonviolent strategy would work here, against the Nazis. I didn't say this to my father. He already suspected.

"Just wondering," he said with a smile. Then he kissed me on the head.

There are moments in life when you can feel yourself growing up. Aafje and Pieter Schaft stood before me, and for the first time I was able to see them for who they really were. They were my parents, but they were more than that: teachers, caretakers, churchgoers, law-abiders, labor activists, children of their parents just as I was. And resisters. I kissed them both on the cheeks.

"I should say goodbye to the girls," I said.

My mother shook her head. "It's hard for them when you leave. Just go."

That stung, but I knew she was right. "OK."

She retied the long cotton straps of her apron, an unmistakable signal that it was time to return to her housework. "Don't worry too much about those two. I'll keep them busy." I almost hugged her, but that would have disturbed our farewell ritual; the emotional portion of the interaction was now over.

"Now go on," she said, opening the door a few inches to let me squeeze through, the way we did now. "We'll be fine. We've got you out there protecting us, don't we?" She gave me a wink. It felt like the Bronze Cross of bravery.

Chapter 20

WE FOUND THE bodies on a Monday night. After a few days at home, I returned to the RVV apartment.

"Hannie." Truus nodded and smiled as I came in, then peered out to see if I'd come alone.

"Everything OK?" I asked.

"Mmm," said Truus vaguely, "nobody's heard from Jan since that night in the woods. Have you?"

"I have," said Hendrik, walking into the main room at the RVV apartment. "Just saw him with Brasser." Jan Brasser was another RVV commander, Hendrik's counterpart in nearby Zaandam.

"Is he planning on showing up Friday?" asked Truus. I sat down at the dining table where we'd cleared a few square inches of tabletop among the chaos of underground newspapers, cigarette butts, and dirty teacups so we could play cards. I'd told her what Jan had shared with me about the upcoming elimination of Kohl.

"If he feels like it," said a young girl sitting to Truus's right. She was a skinny, cute teenage girl with blond braids and a heart-shaped face. Could this be . . . ?

"Hannie, this is Freddie," said Truus, barely looking up from her playing cards. "Freddie, Hannie."

Freddie leaned across the table and shook my hand with the vigor of a traveling salesman. "Nice to meet you," she said. Despite the vigor of her handshake, she looked at me shyly, like a girl. I knew she was seventeen, yet she seemed at once younger and older than that, both a sweet schoolgirl and a hardened soldier.

"Nice to meet you," I said, returning the smile and the grip.

"Come on, come on," said Truus in her older-sister voice, "we were in the middle of the game. Here, Hannie." She slid the first five cards from the top of the deck to me without shuffling. "See what kind of hand you got."

Freddie threw down a ten of hearts. "I'm using this as a five."

There were only forty-six cards, so almost everything was wild. We gave each other a lot of leeway. Truus called the game Resistance. "It's good for your training," she said, "because you have to constantly convince yourself you have a chance at winning." In the game of Resistance, the winner was only obvious at the moment the game ended.

"I'll allow it," I said. We allowed everything in Resistance.

"You'll make a great judge someday," said Hendrik.

"Yes," said Truus. "She's very judgmental."

I kicked her under the table. Because we were friends now.

"She's also violent." Truus kicked me back. "Ow."

My heart ballooned with happiness.

"Ow!" said Truus again, now irritated. This time it was Freddie who kicked her.

Freddie laughed and looked across the table at me. "Don't let her fool you, Hannie, she's not as tough as she pretends to be." Truus rolled her eyes. I felt a tightness in my chest and had to swallow a surge of emotion. I missed having a sister.

"I want to talk to you about Friday," said Hendrik, who was watching us play.

"Officer Kohl?" I asked.

Truus stared at her cards. She waited to hear more.

"I know this was supposed to be your and Jan's mission. But he won't be available. I thought Truus might step in."

"Friday night?" said Truus. "Tomorrow?"

"That's right. Tomorrow night." He looked at me. "If you and Jan already worked out a plan, perhaps you could adapt it for Truus."

I glanced at the Oversteegen sisters. Truus was taller and sturdier than Freddie, but they shared the same serene, half-lidded eyes and high cheekbones that gave them the poise of Siamese cats. I could almost see their long tails twitching as they listened to us, taking everything in.

"Adapt it?" I repeated. Hmm. Jan's plan had involved pretending he and I were a romantic couple, with him kissing me in an alleyway while he waited for Kohl to walk by; then he'd jump out and shoot Kohl while I played lookout. I'd been looking forward to the kissing part. But partnering with Truus on another big assignment was alluring in a different way. The most difficult part would be getting close enough to Kohl to kill him. If we shot at him from across the street, there was a good chance he'd only be injured, and his screaming would cause a commotion on the quiet street. Across the table, Truus had a hint of a smile on her face. She was already planning.

"WE'LL DRAW A lot of attention if we just wait around this corner all night," Truus said. We were scouting the scene. "What if someone tries to talk to us out here, just when Kohl is coming out?"

"Maybe we could get Hendrik to come with us to pose as our brother?" I said, knowing it was a stupid idea. Why not just bring an army?

"You wouldn't need me there, if Hendrik came," said Truus.

"What we need is for the man to hang around just until Kohl walks out. Then he needs to disappear so Kohl will come over," I said. It sounded too complicated. The best plans were simple.

"What if one of us pretends to be a man?" Truus said. "Then, when Kohl shows up, off goes the disguise and it's just two women." She took a few steps down the alley to scout it out. "Or they could just run and hide down here. That's possible."

"So who plays who?" I asked.

Truus laughed. "You'd look ridiculous as a man," she said.

"I would not," I said. But I was relieved. I had no idea how to pretend to be a man. Plus, Truus was taller than I. "But fine. I'll be the woman."

"You mean the femme fatale," Truus said.

"You know what I mean," I said.

THE NEXT DAY we walked the various escape routes one last time, making sure we knew them by heart when it was the middle of the night and dark. All the streetlights were out. This tended to be an advantage for us—we knew the city better than the Germans.

"You realize what it means to play the woman in this," Truus said, speaking in the almost-silent whisper we used when we discussed plans out on the street. We made sure we walked quickly while we did.

"What?" I said.

"You'll have to do it." She glanced over at me. "You'll be the one with Kohl."

I knew. "But you can back me up, right?"

"Yes," said Truus. "But I'll be down the alley."

"Oh." My pace slowed. Truus pulled me off the sidewalk, out of the flow of pedestrians. "It's a good plan," she whispered. "But, Hannie, now is the time to decide if you're ready to do this." She smiled. "If you don't want to, it's fine. It really is. This isn't for everybody."

I paused for a second. Tonight would be different from the power station rail yard. Tonight I would have to shoot a man face-to-face. It didn't seem real. I wished I could discuss it with Philine and Sonja . . . Sonja, last seen lying on my bed, barely moving. Losing hope with each passing day.

"I can do it," I said.

"All right then," she said. She patted me on the shoulder. "Once we begin, the nerves and the doubts will disappear. Waiting is the difficult part. Until then, just try to ignore them. Don't let those thoughts take over, just focus on yourself, your actions. Reduce yourself to zero. You really only have one thing to think about: getting it done. So focus on that."

"OK," I said, trying to imagine what she meant. Like an understudy who's learned all the lines and suddenly has to take the stage for closing night, I was trained for this, but I was also in a state of nervous disbelief.

"Good," Truus said. "I'll see you tonight at nine." We pushed our bikes into the sunlight. "I'm going to take a nap and you should, too," she said. "And if you can't sleep . . . do some target practice."

SONJA WAS SITTING up when I came home that afternoon, looking more herself. She flipped through a copy of the Resistance newspaper *Het Parool*. I watched her scan the paper for any names of people arrested or killed. We all understood it was an incomplete list.

"What about the cute one you told us about?" said Philine.

"Yes," said Sonja. "The Blond Man."

I didn't want to talk about Jan. I hadn't seen him since the night we found the bodies. Maybe he was embarrassed about the interaction with Truus? Jan was hard to read and I had no way of contacting him. I'd just have to wait for him to show up again. I folded a dress and placed a pair of fancy heels in my valise.

"Aren't most Resisters Communists?" Philine asked, watching me. "I thought they liked their women in overalls and work boots."

"He's handsome," I said, throwing them a bone. "But I can't say much more, except no, Philine, there's no dress code. That I know of."

"I knew it!" Sonja said, bouncing on the bed. "She's in love."

"Sonja," Philine said, rolling her eyes. Then she looked at me. "Are you?"

"Have you ever known me to fall in love?" I said.

"No," said Sonja. "But there's always a first time."

My heart stuttered when she said it. I knew I'd start blushing if I thought about it too much. "You know I can't talk about it," I said, trying to seem professional. I put a pair of earrings and a purse into my bag and closed it up. "I won't be here tonight, but probably tomorrow. Do you need anything from outside?" I asked from the doorway.

"Yes," Sonja said, wiping the cheap newsprint off her fingertips with a handkerchief engraved with the family monogram. "Everything."

THE NEXT FEW hours were long. I rode my bike back to the RVV apartment and shut myself in the only bedroom that had a mirror and tried to get myself ready for the night. Truus peeked in.

"Wear something pretty," she said, "and, you know..." She waved her hands awkwardly around her head. "Do something to your hair." She held up a man's flat cap. "I'm wearing this."

I laughed. Prettifying myself was the only area in which I had more experience than Truus, though in comparison to Sonja, Philine, and almost any other young woman my age, I was still a novice. I experimented with different ways of doing my hair, pinning the front up, then all of it up, then all of it down. I decided to doll up in my favorite light blue dress, belted wool coat, and patent leather dancing shoes. The last time I had worn any of it was to a birthday party a year and a half ago, when the dress had stuck to my modest curves like a bandage. Now it draped from my hips like a flapper dress. Even my fancy bra was loose, so I left it in the drawer. I checked myself in the mirror. I looked older, more sophisticated. With my hands on my jutting hip bones and the barest outline of nipple against the soft blue fabric, I felt like a grown woman.

I thought of one more thing. I took out the little toiletry case I'd brought from home and dug through it, hoping it was still there: it was. Leaning right up against the glass, I drew a careful coat of Spellbound, a deep brick red, across my lips, then blotted it with a handkerchief. The more dramatically feminine I appeared, the more Truus would look like a man.

"WELL, WELL," HENDRIK said. He looked me up and down. "You look lovely, Hannie."

"Thanks." I touched the silver locket at my throat. "This is my mother's," I said, nervous.

"It's beautiful," said Hendrik.

I patted my pockets, making sure I'd brought everything I'd need.

"Ammunition?" Hendrik asked.

"Got it."

"Weapon?"

"Got it." I pointed at a glass sitting in front of Hendrik on the table. "Can I have some of that?"

"By all means."

It was some kind of awful grain alcohol. I gulped it like water. "That's good," I said as the warm rush of alcohol loosened my shoulders and nerves.

"Well, it's good for your morale," said Hendrik.

"Have you heard from Jan?" I asked, the alcohol loosening my tongue.

"Not since yesterday. Have you?"

"No," I said. "I was just wondering."

"You'll be fine," Hendrik said. "Truus knows what she's doing."

"I know, I know," I said. If anything, I felt better doing the job with Truus. She was more likely to stick to the plan. I gathered my things to go. I wanted to walk around for a little while before meeting Truus, to calm my nerves. Walking always helped.

"So . . ." I said to Hendrik. I'd noticed no one made a big deal of good-byes in the RVV. "See you later."

"See you on the other side."

Chapter 21

I**T WAS ALMOST** midnight when I reached the meeting point. A favorite hangout for the Gestapo, the bar held private parties for the SS past curfew. Truus had already been waiting in the alley for twenty minutes, arriving early. I reached for the steel pistol, heavy and cold, slipping my hand inside my purse in what was becoming a nervous tic.

"Stop playing with that," Truus said. "And fix your hair."

It sounded harsh, but she wasn't angry. She was scared. And she'd lowered her voice, trying to sound like a man to match the man's overcoat and wool cap into which she'd tucked her own curls. Petite little Truus, passing herself off as a man. She pulled the cap lower to cover more of her face. It was dark in the alley. We needed the shadows to complete the illusion.

I tamed a strand of hair that had escaped from my tortoiseshell barrette and tucked it back into place.

It was a dangerous night. But then again, I told myself, it was dangerous because of us.

———

IN THE ALLEY, I took a deep breath. Truus put a finger to her lips. I was three years older than Truus, but she was the veteran here. I smiled at her. She winked.

It was quiet again.

A moment later, just around the edge of the building, the door to the bar opened and a glaring rectangle of light, cigarette smoke, laughter, and music splashed onto the empty street. We'd walked by a few times yesterday and today, but only Truus had gone inside. When she came out, she confirmed it: we would approach Kohl outside. The tiny tavern with only one exit was a trap.

Truus peeked around the corner to see as a cluster of four noisy German soldiers clutched each other's shoulders, creating one huge boozy beast, laughing as they lurched off the curb and almost fell.

Truus shook her head: not Kohl.

The soldiers staggered in our direction, and Truus pressed herself up against me as we'd practiced, pressing her cold cheek against mine, wrapping her arms around my neck: just another young couple sneaking a kiss in the dark. One soldier whistled in our direction, but the others were too distracted by their own hilarity to bother with us. They stumbled away and their rough voices faded. The little street returned to stillness. I used to walk down this street a decade ago to go to piano lessons, I realized.

Truus and I pulled apart and exhaled. We looked in each other's eyes, communicating without speaking because we'd gone over it fifty times— no, a hundred: *Be patient.* This would only work if Kohl came out of the club alone.

"Kohl's no different than the grunts," she muttered, watching the soldiers disappear. "He thinks he's on an armed vacation."

A lot of Germans saw the Netherlands that way, happy to visit a not-too-foreign land filled with blondes and Heineken. I stood up straight and fussed with my hair again, tightening the belt on my coat. As I reached into my purse, Truus glared, but I pulled out a cigarette. Two cigarettes. I flipped open my silver lighter and she leaned in, her freckled features rosy in the flame. In the distance the faint tinkling of a canal-boat bell floated in the frosty air. The metallic click when I snapped the clasp of my purse echoed off the cold stone walls. Truus flinched.

"Relax," I whispered. She glared. Not that I was relaxed. But it made me feel more relaxed to pretend.

The door to the bar opened again: the bright shaft of light, the noise of the drinkers inside again puncturing the cold silence of the narrow street. I leaned out to look and shuddered to a stop.

There he was, just as we'd imagined. At least half a foot taller than either of us, ducking down to exit through the old wooden doorframe, the sweep of his leather greatcoat making him look even bigger. A monstrous raven released from a small cage, flapping and flaunting its wings. The door banged shut behind him.

He was alone. Truus nodded. "Pak die rotzak!" she hissed.

Get the bastard.

KOHL TUGGED HIS visored SD officer's cap onto his head using both hands to center it and then swayed on his feet, taking in a sharp gulp of icy night air. The silver symbols of rank arrayed on his uniform sparkled in the dim light. I felt as if I could smell him from where I stood, a dank perfume of sweat, leather, and alcohol filling my senses. He was real.

Truus melted back into the shadows, and I stood alone, one shoulder pressed against the brick wall of the building. As if I were bored. But I was electrified. I could hear the flat slap of the water against the canal bank, see every point of starlight in the sky. I was sure I'd never feel bored again. With no outside lights, the flare of the cherry at the end of my cigarette was the brightest thing around. It glowed like a firefly in the November chill: red, warm, and out of place. I touched the toe of my shoe at the edge of the alleyway, toying with the gravel there. Pulling a drag off the cigarette, I exhaled a mix of smoke and the white fog of winter breath, a small puff of cloud materializing in the night.

Kohl saw it out of the corner of his eye, and his head turned, smooth and quick, body following. He scanned me up and down as if evaluating a racehorse and calculating the odds. I was just a girl. A pretty girl with red lipstick. Alone.

My eyes met his. My heart hammered. I held his gaze just a few more seconds . . . then looked away and down, bashful. Then I looked back again. He was still staring. He stopped fastening the silver buttons of his long leather coat, fingers resting on the seams. Suddenly he wasn't so cold. I smiled—just a hint of one.

He took a step toward me, his black boot catching on a cobblestone, and he stumbled like the drunken soldiers before him. A good sign. The corner of his wide, full-lipped mouth turned up, lips wet with his last drink or maybe with appetite. I had to acknowledge he was handsome despite the metallic tang of contempt in the back of my throat. A tall, square-jawed, broad-shouldered Nazi officer—the Aryan ideal. I recognized the delicate silver-leaf insignia on the collar of his stiff uniform from the images Truus told me to look for.

Get the bastard.

"Guten Abend, Fräulein?" He asked as if it were a question. And maybe it was. Good evening, miss? He wouldn't speak Dutch, of course. No point in learning the language of the country they've occupied when soon it would all be part of a single German Reich.

I spoke fairly fluent German. But not that night. Truus and I had changed that part of the plan. I didn't want to get wrapped up in a long conversation when we both knew he was only interested in one thing, and it wasn't talking.

"Goedenavond," I said. Good evening. In Dutch. My voice was soft and low. This wasn't about words, anyway. He was definitely drunk, but his gaze was steady. His eyes never left mine.

I crossed one foot behind the other and then again, backing slowly into the shelter of the alley. He cocked his head like a puppy, then took a quick glance over each shoulder. No one around. He walked toward me, his steps surer now.

"Sind Sie alleine hier, Fräulein?" The words slid into each other, slippery with whiskey. You're here all alone, miss? As he spoke, he walked, his strides long, confident. By the time he got to *Fräulein*, he was only inches away from me.

Do not move.

Every muscle in my body begged for release: *Run.* Instead, I smiled, took one last pull on my cigarette, and tossed it onto the stones below. Instantly his heavy black boot crushed it, grinding it out. As a flirtatious gesture, it was on the brutal side.

He smiled. He patted the outside of his leather coat, then frowned. "Es tut mir leid, aber ich habe keine mehr." He's out of cigarettes. "Ich hole mehr drinnen . . . und vielleicht ein wenig Whiskey?" he offered, and his face brightened to the idea: he would go inside and get more—and a little whiskey, too.

No. That wasn't the plan.

"Wait." I reached out and touched his hand. His skin burned under my cold fingers. I gripped his hand harder, to stop my trembling. Beneath my fingertips, I felt the blood coursing through the blue veins on the back of his hand, the fine hairs there.

"Don't," I whispered. My purse was still tucked under my arm. "Ik heb meer." I have more.

He smiled and nodded and rummaged in his pocket for a lighter. He was excited. He'd left the bar alone only to find a girl outside waiting for him? Lucky night. But he was having trouble finding the lighter in those deep pockets, and he looked down: Where was it?

My hand was already inside my purse, but my fingers were clumsy and cold. I was breathing so fast I thought I might faint. The borders of my vision began to feather and blur into a tunnel. I pushed myself against him, and the sour male aroma I'd sensed earlier now embraced me in a fog.

"Mein Liebling," he murmured under his breath, and I flinched.

I blinked and snapped into focus, the image of Philine and Sonja in my own childhood bed. Hand on the cold metal grip, finger on the trigger. No safety. In one motion the pistol was out and jammed hard against his broad chest, just as practiced. I looked up and into his gray eyes, the color of tarnished silver. His front teeth white and shining. He didn't understand.

"Was ist das?" he said, pale brows furrowed but still smiling. As if it were a game.

It wasn't.

I squeezed the trigger, my arms shivering with the kickback, and I stumbled backward, away from him as if he'd shot me. My head throbbed.

He was still standing.

His expression was unchanged, his pale blue eyes locked on mine. Finally he lowered his head and looked down at his coat. It was too dark to see much, so his hands flattened against his chest seeking answers, flopping like fish around a drain as his broad shoulders slumped and caved inward. Something was wrong.

"Again!" growled Truus from against the wall, behind me.

I took one step closer, and he clutched me to his chest as if following through on his original idea: Wasn't he supposed to hold the girl, kiss the girl? Wasn't that what this was? But then his legs folded beneath him like a sagging jack-in-the-box, and he dragged me to the ground, his hands snatching at my shoulders, my neck. A drowning man grasping for anything that floats. I fell against him, desperate to push away but aware that, as Jan always told me, everything was an opportunity if you were still alive to take it. And he had trained me for this. I thrust the barrel of the little gun into Kohl's ribs like a bayonet and pulled the trigger once more. This time I was braced for impact. Against him.

He gasped, mumbled, and then pitched backward, the crown of his closely shorn head slamming to the stonework with a vicious crack. The shiny black hat spun away toward the street, its bright silver eagle flashing in the dim light as if trying to escape on its own. It circled to rest visor-down in the slush. Truus darted out to scoop it up and skimmed it toward the dark end of the alley. "Help me!" she hissed.

We grabbed Kohl by the collar and dragged his body away from the open street. Nerves humming, eardrums buzzing, I could barely hear Truus's voice over the noise in my head. But I knew what to do. We grasped the wide leather lapels of his coat, and together we hauled him across the cobblestones. He would be discovered, and we wanted him to be. To send a message. But it was better if he wasn't discovered right away. We dropped him at the dead end of the alley with a thud. As if we were moving furniture.

"Come on," she said, reaching for my hand and heading for the street and our escape route. I stumbled after her, then ripped my hand away and turned back.

"What—" Truus started to say, then stopped. I sprinted back to Kohl and braced myself above him with one dainty dancing shoe positioned on each side of his neck, arms locked and pointed straight down. I aimed the pistol at his head and saw his gray eyes, now rolled back like lost marbles, and I moved the barrel there. Just like Jan told me to: right through the eye if you can; then you know for sure. I fired and his head jerked and I was sprayed by a cloud of pink mist and the troubled scent of burning flesh and hair. Got the bastard.

My feet moved then, but I couldn't feel them; my chest heaved with rasping breath, but I didn't care. Truus gripped my hand harder as we ran down the middle of the empty streets, slipping on frosty cobblestones as we slid around corners. "Hurry," she kept saying. Her voice was a leash pulling me forward, across a great chasm, and then I reached it and joined her on the other side.

Chapter 22

"MAMA," I SAID.

My mother cracked open the door and pulled me inside the house. It wasn't much warmer there than on the December streets outside. I hadn't visited since before the Kohl job almost a week earlier. My mother's face was grave. As if she knew what I'd done.

"What is it?" I said.

She held out a scrap of paper.

"From Sonja," she said.

It was written on a page ripped from a movie magazine, across an advertisement for shampoo that offered just enough white space for a short message:

Dear Mr. and Mrs. Schaft and my darlings Philine and Hannie,

Thank you more than I can ever say for all you've done for me. You've risked so much, and I am so grateful for your kindness. But if I'm going to disappear, I'd rather go when I'm out in the world instead of staying here waiting in a box. (Sorry.)

I promise to be careful. Don't worry about me, I'm going to Amer-
ica! I know someone who can take me to Switzerland first, so I'll try to
write you from there. I hope to see you . . .
Love,
Sonja

"When did you get this?" I asked, searching for more information on
the back, but it was just another glossy advertisement.

"A few days ago," she said. "We didn't know how to reach you."

My breathing quickened. "Where's Philine?"

My mother looked up and I took the stairs two at a time and flung
open the bedroom door. There was Philine, sitting where Sonja once sat,
in bed with the quilts pulled up over her knees, reading. She looked up
and burst into tears when she saw me.

"Oh, Hannie," she said as I ran to her and hugged her tight. "I begged
her not to go."

"I know," I said. Sonja had been threatening to leave since the day we
first arrived. It had been nine months. For Sonja it might as well have
been nine years.

"She was going crazy," said Philine, wiping her eyes. "The uncertainty
was so hard for her."

I knew Philine was talking about herself, too.

"I tried to remind her how much better we had it here than so many
others who are hiding in pantries or haystacks, and she knew it was true,
but it wasn't enough." Philine's voice broke into a tattered sigh.

We'd all heard the stories by now. Jews hiding in basement crawl
spaces, allowed to stretch their legs and use the toilet only late at night,
when it was safest. There was a rumor that a family on a farm somewhere
in northwest Holland was hiding dozens of Jews in drainage ditches and
grain silos. And one late night after much drinking Hendrik had broken

down in tears when he told me the story of a Jewish boy from Amsterdam, perhaps seven years old, who'd been hiding in a deserted room alone after the rest of his family was taken away, scavenging food from neighbors. "I never learned his name," said Hendrik, "because, after ten months alone, he simply stopped speaking." Too many stories.

"I know," I said, holding her. "I know."

"It's terrible, not being able to do anything about it," she said. "Just sitting here, doing nothing to help."

"You're not doing nothing," I said. "You're helping my parents, and by being here, you're helping me. How could we ever get along without you, Philine?" She hugged me harder.

"I think what you're doing here is the bravest thing a person can do," I said. I believed it. "It's much more difficult to stay still while the world goes to hell all around you. At least if I panic, I can run outside and scream." I'd thought about it so often, the freedoms I still enjoyed while the girls stayed locked inside, unable to simply take a walk in the sunshine to clear their minds. "What you're all doing here is so important."

"I know, your parents are wonderful," said Philine, miserable.

"Not just them!" I held her hands in mine, trying to make her believe me. "You leaving your father and Marie, Sonja leaving her family . . . you're doing the most of any of us." Philine shrank back and looked at me with a raised eyebrow, as if I were teasing her. "I'm serious," I said. "It's important that you . . ." I struggled to explain it.

"Stay alive?" she said with a snort of disgust. "That's our job?"

"Yes, damn it." A whiff of Jan Bonekamp's righteousness surged through me as I tried to make her see. "What do the Krauts want? For you to disappear. So that's your job: don't. You stick it out, you stay safe, you do not give them what they want. It's our job—me and my parents— to help you do that. That's what we're all doing, in our different ways." I stared into her soft amber eyes, so intelligent, so sad. "Your job is probably the hardest. Just staying still in the midst of it all."

She smiled. "It is hard. But I'm grateful. Sonja was—is—too."

"I know," I said. I paused before asking the next question. I feared the answer. Sonja had received word a week or so earlier that her family was still safe in Amsterdam, but nobody knew how much wasn't being communicated, for safety reasons. We didn't know about Philine's. "Have you heard from your father?"

We all worried about Mr. Polak. A few weeks earlier, a letter had been smuggled from him to Philine. He said he was fine, still in their apartment in Amsterdam. Philine had thrown the letter down in disgust. "He never tells me the truth," she said, "because he can't see it himself." She sounded more fearful than angry. "He still thinks if he breaks the law by hiding, he'll be arrested. But he'll be arrested anyway if he stays where he is." I agreed with her. We'd already discussed it many times.

Now Philine shook her head. "I haven't heard from him since that last letter," she said.

This worried me. In the past few months, at least one of the Jewish neighborhoods in Amsterdam had been completely "cleared" of residents. The Germans helped themselves to whatever furniture, silver, and other valuable items they could find, leaving the remnants to be picked over by neighbors. In the Resistance, we knew more of this was coming. But I was desperate to make Philine feel better, so I tried to think of something reassuring to say.

"I'm going to look for Sonja," I said. "If she did get arrested, maybe she's still nearby."

"What if they sent her to . . ." Philine began, her voice wobbling. She didn't finish the sentence, but I was thinking it, too: *Westerbork.*

"I'll find her, Philine. I have help."

"OK," she said, despondent. She grasped both my hands in hers, which were shaking. "But, Hannie," she said, begging me, "whatever you're doing, please be careful. I can't lose you, too."

"I'm going to find her, and we'll both come back here safe and sound. Promise."

"No," Philine said, her face pale. "Don't say that."

As I BICYCLED back to the RVV apartment that afternoon, I tried to formulate a plan. I was devastated but not surprised. Imprisoned in that room with no idea how long she'd be stuck there? I might have done the same as Sonja. I hoped Truus or Hendrik would have some suggestions on where to look. I let myself into the apartment, and there, for the first time in two weeks, was Jan.

"What's wrong?" he said as soon as he saw me. I didn't smile. I couldn't. I thought about asking him where he'd been, but it seemed unimportant now. "I got this letter," I said, handing it to him. "From my friend Sonja, the one who . . ."

"I know who Sonja is," he said. It moved me. She was alive in someone else's thoughts, too. Jan took the letter and read it, flipped it over to search for more details, then handed it back. "We'll find her," he said. He pulled me against him, holding me tight. "Don't worry, we'll find her."

And there he was again, the Jan Bonekamp I adored. Strong, confident, fearless. I stood on my tiptoes and gave him a grateful kiss on the lips. "Thank you, Jan." I no longer cared why he'd been gone so long. He kissed me back softly.

"It'll be OK, Hannie," he whispered tenderly. "I'll have someone check at Westerbork."

"What?" I grabbed hold of the back of a wooden chair to steady myself. I didn't want to believe Sonja might be there. "Westerbork?" I repeated, as if I'd misheard him. I hoped I had. Jan looked away. He didn't have to say it.

Westerbork was where all the Dutch Jews ended up, eventually. The people I'd seen in the courtyard of the theater months ago? They were in Westerbork now. There was a train station inside the camp, and people said it departed every Tuesday for Poland, to the work camp called Auschwitz. It left Westerbork with a full train of Dutch Jews. But when it returned, it was always empty—as Truus said, nobody returned from the trains. Neither did we know what happened in Auschwitz—nobody ever sent a letter back. When people left Westerbork, they simply disappeared. I'd seen a few smuggled photographs of what was purportedly a Nazi work camp somewhere in eastern Germany, a grainy, blurry, terrifying image of almost nothing: a couple of low buildings and what must have been prisoners following each other in a line. They looked like wisps of former people, stick figures stalking by, one by one.

No, not Sonja. It was all wrong. Sonja should be sipping hot chocolate in a genteel drawing room in Zurich by now or marveling at the lights of New York City's Times Square. She couldn't be in one of those places. I couldn't imagine it. I felt myself gasping for breath.

"Hannie?" Jan asked. "You're breathing too fast. Slow down." I heard myself panting. I was stuck to the spot with fear. *Not Sonja. Not Sonja.* "Come on." Jan held his arm tight around my waist, supporting me.

"I shouldn't have brought her to Haarlem," I whispered, my stomach turning on itself as I recalled all the persuasion it had taken to get her here. So many confident stories I'd told about how much safer she and Philine would be, about how this would all soon be over. My mind felt like the ocean, wild, deep, and roaring, roaring, roaring. "I should have let her stay home."

"Hannie." Jan's voice was louder now. "Hannie, listen to me. We'll find her. I know some people to talk to . . . we'll find her."

"I'll help," I said, straightening myself up and taking a few deep breaths. "I know her best, I'll be able to find her. To recognize her."

Jan shook his head. "This isn't a job for you. You have work to do here.

Like that Kohl job." He gave me a little nudge of respect. "We need more of that. Especially now."

"I can't, Jan."

He furrowed his brows, on the edge of anger. "Yes, you goddamn can, Hannie. You think girls show up at the tabak every day who are willing to do what you and Truus did? We need you."

"Freddie can do it," I said, miserable.

"Verdomme." Jan sighed, frustrated. "You want to tell Truus you're not helping her anymore?"

God, no. "No, I . . ."

"You just need a minute. That's fine."

I nodded. Eventually my breathing slowed. I sat down in the rickety chair and sighed.

"You OK?" he asked me.

I nodded.

"That's my girl." He lit the burner on the stove and filled the teakettle. "Now. Tell me everything I should know about where Sonja might be." I started talking. Within the hour he had made me a cup of tea and written down every scrap of information I could come up with about Sonja's life and potential whereabouts. "I'll find her," he said before leaving that afternoon. "Go home. Go be with your family."

I WOKE AROUND dawn in one of the twin beds at the RVV. I hadn't gone home. The prospect of facing Philine and my parents with nothing to tell them was too grim to imagine, so I'd stayed at the apartment all night, alone, taking turns racking my memory for names or places, anything that might give me a clue as to where Sonja could be. "I know someone who can take me . . ." she'd written. Who? Neither I nor Philine had any idea.

A thin golden band of light crept across the bedroom ceiling as the dawn arrived. Following it to the other wall, I expected to see an empty bed. But there he was, Jan Bonekamp, asleep and still in his overcoat, the collar pulled up to his ears in the chilly room. He'd returned. Sliding out from under my warm covers, I unlaced his boots, placed them on the floor, and tucked a second scratchy wool blanket over him. A hand reached out for me from underneath it. "Come here," he said.

I paused. A shiver passed through me. I lifted the blanket and sat down on the bed, and he pulled me against him, curling me into him like I was nestling into a shell.

"Jan," I said. "What happened last night? Did you find anything?" The previous twenty-four hours felt like a dream. A nightmare.

He took a deep breath, his eyes still closed. "Not yet, but we have people looking." He turned his head to mine and kissed my forehead softly. "We'll find her." He went on breathing, possibly awake and possibly falling back asleep; he had probably been out all night.

"Thank you," I whispered into his chest. He squeezed me a little tighter. His breath on the nape of my neck tickled. Behind my ear, his breath on my collarbone, and then his lips on my skin, kissing my neck and shoulders. An unfamiliar boldness made me arch back to turn and kiss him, and he pulled me closer and kept kissing. I reached back and felt his hips locked against mine, with one hand around my waist and the other on my breast, and I pressed myself against him harder. It wasn't boldness that was turning this tender moment into something bigger, tidal in its swells. It was a sensation I'd felt yet never succumbed to before. Now I gave in. I turned off the problem-solving half of my mind, the sorrow, the violence, and the unknown. Better to be here with Jan, no matter what else had happened or would happen in the future. I surrendered to the comfort of being closer to another person than I'd ever been before. Becoming part of each other. I closed my eyes and heard his voice. "We'll find her." I let him lead me.

Chapter 23

Summer 1944

WEEKS PASSED, THEN a month, and I made myself stop hoping for news of Sonja. Then a letter arrived. It was postmarked in Belgium. Scrawled in her curvy penmanship across the back of an old grocery receipt, it read:

Dear ones—
    Am in Belgium, almost to Liège.
    Will write more once in Switz.
Love—Sonja

Philine watched as I read the note. "It's good news," I said, turning the paper over and over in an attempt to drag more clues out of it, just as Philine had probably done. She smiled weakly, in solidarity. We had to believe it was good news.

More weeks passed. We didn't hear from Sonja.

I DISTRACTED MYSELF with more and more Resistance work. After the Kohl job, I assumed Truus and I would just keep doing more of the same, but the hit had been almost too successful. News of the assassination of a high-ranking SS officer spread like a fire through the Nazis' Dutch administration, or so the Resistance whisper network said. As a result, Truus and I had to keep a slightly lower profile for a while. "Watch out for the Girl with Red Hair," Jan teased me, echoing the gossip. "She lures you in with her smile and then POW!" He pointed an imaginary gun and blasted away. I rolled my eyes, but I enjoyed it. Hendrik actually suggested I wear a disguise or a wig to hide my hair color. That seemed a bit dramatic to me. Soon I was missing the thrill of the dangerous work, but Hendrik insisted we busy ourselves with the less exciting but "equally important" work of dropping piles of underground newspapers off in public areas for citizens to accidentally find the next morning and delivering forged ration cards to the homes of onderduikers. It did not feel equally important. It felt pointless. Just a way to keep busy. Which was, I realized, how Sonja had felt locked up in my bedroom. A month passed, then two, but no more letters arrived.

"Maybe it got intercepted somewhere," Philine suggested one evening. "It's easy for mail to get lost."

"Could be," I said. It was possible. But neither of us believed it. Jan assured me he had all his contacts alerted for any trace of Sonja, but otherwise I was as helpless as Philine when it came to looking for her. Like an onderduiker myself, I had to get used to waiting.

By now, Aktion Silbertanne was in full effect. Recently the Nazis had pulled twenty-five random men out of a crowd in downtown Amsterdam and executed them on the spot in front of hundreds of horrified onlookers. Then some Nazi Kommandant got up on an apple box, Sieg-Heiled, and read a statement explaining how that was the legally justified consequence of the sabotaging of a German fuel depot two days earlier. That was only the beginning. The anti-Resistance operations had begun. "We have to keep up the pressure," Hendrik kept saying. Nobody argued. We knew the Germans would keep killing us whether we fought back or not.

Jan asked me to help him bomb a movie theater in downtown Haarlem, where the Germans went to see their propaganda films. This involved my bringing a homemade bomb about the size of a puppy into the Rembrandt Theater, placing it in a dark corner, then leaving. But the bomb didn't go off; it just fizzled and the fire alarm started and we all ran out in the street. Jan wasn't angry, which was a relief, but I was furious with myself. Disappointed. Nothing was going the way it should. We were making no progress.

More weeks passed with no word from Sonja.

Jan seemed to invent reasons for us to spend time together, whether it was shooting practice or taking me on a bike tour of the towns beyond Haarlem, closer to where he was from. He was trying to cheer me up, or at least distract me. It did help. More weeks passed and spring came. But Sonja? Not even a rumor. I tried not to let myself imagine what had happened to her or, even worse, what was happening to her right that moment. I tried never to think about her dead. When I visited Philine once a week or so, she and I talked of other things, though there was nothing else to talk about. My parents stopped asking me about her. Jan didn't have to ask. We were spending so much time together, he'd know if I heard anything.

I WAS LYING on the balding velvet couch in the RVV living room reading a pamphlet the Allies had dropped by the thousands a few days earlier. The illustration showed how to build a secret room (unsaid: when you need to hide someone), how to navigate by the stars (unsaid: when you're fleeing the Germans at night), and how to carry an "unconscious or injured person" (unsaid: they're dead). Useful things. Jan burst in.

"There you are," he said. He looked at me as if I were insane for lying around reading when I could have been doing something else. "Come on, let's go."

"Well, hello." I'd seen him the day before and hadn't expected him again until the following week. He disappeared for days at a time, and since he never offered an explanation, I'd learned not to ask.

"Remember Pieter Faber?" Jan said. "The Fascist Baker of Heemstede?" As if it were the title of a Brothers Grimm fairy tale. I did. Heemstede was a town twenty minutes north of us, a lush collection of mansions belonging to families whose fortunes were made in the cities of Haarlem and Amsterdam. Some of them were summer homes, a concept I'd only become aware of once I met Sonja. "I got his home address," Jan said. "Let's go."

Faber was a powerful Dutch collaborator, a prominent businessman who had been agitating against democracy for years. This I had learned over the past several months from Hendrik and Jan, who kept a running list of potential targets. Some were notorious Jew-hunters everyone knew by name; others were more anonymous souls whose lower public profiles often made them easier to track down. The monstrous plan to rid the Netherlands of Jews was not just the pet project of Reichskommissar Seyss-Inquart or our old friend Kohl. It was a vast bureaucracy of strategy and project goals carried out by thousands across the country, from the highest members of the Gestapo to the lowliest functionaries of small village councils. There were plenty of villains for us to pursue. If it wasn't the top man in charge, that was OK. The peons who kept the gears greased were equally deserving of our retribution. All of us in the RVV agreed.

The Fascist Baker of Heemstede, for example, had two adult sons who also worked for the SS. The whole Faber family ratted on its neighbors for profit and got special favors from their Nazi overlords, like decent-quality flour, so that the Faber Bakkerij could remain one of the only bakeries still in business. The Fabers had been obnoxious since before the war, as vocal members of the fascist Dutch NSB party. They were longtime Nazis-in-waiting.

"What do you plan to do once you get there?" I asked.

Jan grinned. "That depends." He wore a long shirt that almost covered the bulge of his pistol tucked into the waistband of his pants. He probably had another one in his pocket. Jan was known for being brave, theatrical, and worryingly daring. He preferred to do his jobs in public spaces filled with light and witnesses; he said it doubled the impact of our work if people saw it with their own eyes. Some of his biggest hits were assassinations he'd perpetrated simply because the opportunity presented itself, with no advance planning at all. We were different in most ways, and this was just one more example. Like Truus, I preferred to rehearse a big job over and over before doing it, even if the rehearsal was just in my mind. But after doing so little for the past few weeks, my taste for caution had dissolved.

"All right," I said. I had planned on seeing Philine later in the day, but I was dreading it. She was so pale and quiet these days, a fading flower in a darkened room. I always left feeling worse, not better, and it was, I suspected, the same for her. The Faber job was an excuse not to go. Jan grabbed my coat for me and led me out the front door. "This way."

We walked to the curb, where a faded black Peugeot was parked, then he leaned down and opened the passenger door. "Ladies first," he said.

"What is this?" I said, unmoving.

"Never seen a car before? Get in."

"Whose is it?"

He made a frustrated sound. "Just get in the car, woman."

That made me laugh, so I got in. The inside of the car smelled like hot dust. I dragged my finger through the downy fuzz on the dashboard and left a black stripe behind. Jan got into the driver's seat and fiddled with something near the steering wheel; then the engine rumbled to a roar, thin gray smoke seeping out from under the hood. Jan veered into the middle of the street, corrected himself, and we were off.

I didn't spend a lot of time in cars, but I knew enough to understand the Peugeot was in very poor shape. Coils of steel springs corkscrewed their way out of the seat cushions, and tufts of horsehair stuffing came with them. Every lump of gravel we rolled over rattled the frame of the car. Each stop-and-go became a raucous event, and it was often too noisy inside to talk. But once we reached the outskirts of Haarlem and picked up speed alongside the dairy farms and tulip fields, the clatter settled into a smoother, oceanic drone, and it was finally possible to ask.

"Where'd the car come from, Jan?"

"I stole it," he said, as if the answer were obvious. "I kept seeing it parked on a side street near the post office and it never moved. I figured it was abandoned."

Plausible. Even wealthy people were generally unable to pay the high cost of gasoline now. "Where'd you get the gas?" I asked.

"Stole it, too," he said, nodding toward the back seat. A clunky metal gas can sat on the floor behind the driver's seat, painted in Wehrmacht green with the obligatory swastika splatted on top.

"You shouldn't be driving around with that," I said.

He looked surprised. "You worried, Professor?"

"It's risky," I said. And stupid. It would have been easy to transfer the gasoline to a less conspicuous container. I enjoyed Jan's bravado most of the time, but this was insane. If we got stopped at a German checkpoint, something that was more likely than not, since so few civilians were out driving their cars around the countryside these days, we could probably explain the car. But the Nazi gas can?

Jan pulled his little tin flask from his coat pocket, took a swig, smacked his lips, then handed it to me. I'd adapted to the RVV approach to cigarettes and alcohol right away: whatever time of day they appeared, we partook, knowing the day would come when they'd stop appearing at all. Every inhale and sip was a little win.

"You make it tough on a guy," Jan said.

"Pardon?"

He shook his head, marveling. "Most girls, just showing up with some smuggled whiskey would make them happy. You wouldn't be impressed if I arrived with a U-boat."

I laughed, mortified. What was he talking about? I spent most of my time around Jan trying not to look like an idiot. "Impress me?" I asked.

"Come on, Hannie," he said, sounding almost irritated.

I stared at him, astonished.

"If you have a boyfriend, it's OK. You can tell me." He kept his eyes on the road.

"No!" I said.

"What, never?" Jan glanced over to see if I was kidding.

"None of your business," I said, unnerved by the line of questioning. That first night together after Sonja disappeared had not been our last. Although we acted like friendly comrades around the others, whenever we were in private, we found ourselves drawn to each other for a hug, then a kiss, then more. It was sporadic, only happening when we were alone on target practice or late at night in the RVV apartment, but it was ongoing and, for me, an almost magical escape from the otherwise brutal nature of everything else. When I kissed Jan, it was the one time everything else left my mind. So of course I didn't have a boyfriend. I was naïve enough to believe that, if I did, it was him. Obviously, I didn't say this.

"Have you ever been in love?" he said.

"Jan."

"Come on. We bombed a theater together." He laughed.

"Tried to," I said.

"Tried to," he agreed. "So?"

We'd done more significant things together in the dark than fail to bomb a movie theater, in my opinion. I kept that to myself. "No," I said. "I don't think so. Not if it means the other person loves you back."

Jan kept his eyes on the road ahead. We hadn't seen a car for miles; it was like driving on the moon. It seemed like we had the whole world— all the vast green flatness of irrigated fields, anyway—to ourselves alone. "You are a strange one, Hannie Schaft." He shook his head. "Are you really not aware of it?" he asked, looking over at me. "The effect you've had on all of us?"

"Stop," I said, shaking my head. He was trying to change the subject now.

"That's what's so funny about you," he said. "You're smart, but you miss the most obvious things."

"What obvious things?"

"The way you do this work," he said, "as if you were born to it. Even Truus respects you, and she doesn't like anyone except Freddie."

"That's not true," I said, overwhelmed. Was he serious?

"It's all true."

Suddenly overheated, I rolled the window all the way down and stuck my head out, the gust blasting my cheeks. Was Jan teasing me? Or was this his way of having a deep conversation? I had no idea. The wind brought tears to my eyes. I squinted, then saw it. Something coming up on the road ahead of us.

"Hey," I said. "There's something—"

"Yep," he said. He stared ahead and I followed his gaze. A German checkpoint.

"Just stay calm," he said, "and let me talk." He glanced at me. "Gun?"

I patted my purse beside me on the car seat. He slowed the car as we approached, the Peugeot rattling and juddering to a stop as if the circus had just arrived in town.

Jan thrust his handsome blond head out the window and smiled at the German soldier, so young he looked like he hadn't started shaving yet. The soldier shifted his clunky Sten to ready position and stood in the middle of the road, sandbags on either side and irrigation canals beyond that. There was nowhere for us to go except in reverse. But a soldier stood there now, too.

Behind the teenage soldier was a Wehrmacht flatbed truck with a canvas awning over the back, parked in the middle of the road. Two more soldiers strolled up from that direction. This had to be the most boring post in the Netherlands. The soldiers looked pleased to have a diversion.

"Stop," said the soldier. We had already stopped. He approached the car and peered in at me, then Jan. "Destination?"

"Heemstede," Jan said. I winced. Why tell them that when there were a dozen other towns farther on we could be headed toward? Why share a single shred of the truth with these jackals?

The soldier nodded, inspecting the car. He walked past Jan's door and peered into the back seat. The gas can. He stopped. His forehead wrinkled. "What's this?" he asked Jan.

Jan swiveled around as if he had no idea there was anything in the back at all. As if that were convincing. "Oh, the gasoline?" he said, turning back around, still relaxed and happy.

"Ja. The gasoline. Property of Wehrmacht, as you can see for yourself."

"Right," said Jan. "That's hers." He pointed at me. Then he turned to look at me in a way that just barely convinced me to go along with whatever he had in mind. Barely. He turned back to the soldier. "Yeah, her father is the mayor. Of Heemstede. So he sent her out to get some gas and here we are."

The soldier looked past Jan to me, appraising me.

Do what Sonja would do. Or Annie.

I sat up straight and smoothed my skirt over my knees. "Hello," I said, and gave the soldiers one of Sonja's dainty, waggling-finger waves.

"Your father is the mayor of Heemstede?" said the soldier.

"That's right," I said. "He's expecting us back already . . ."

"OK," said the soldier. The two others behind him walked up.

"What's the problem?" said the dark-haired one to the young soldier.

"No problem," he said. "They're just going to Heemstede." During this exchange, the second soldier walked around the car and discovered the gas can, too.

"You saw this?" he said.

The young soldier's face went red. "Ja, ja," he said, nodding. "But it's OK, I got to the bottom of it."

"Oh, yeah?" The two soldiers were now standing just behind me. "So?"

"Her father's the mayor," explained the young soldier. "She was just getting gas for him. The mayor of Heemstede."

His colleagues looked skeptical. They pointed at Jan. "So who's this?" asked the dark-haired one.

"Her driver," said Jan with a bright smile. All three soldiers stared at him. They didn't like him.

"In this piece of shit?" the soldier said, kicking the rear wheel well of the Peugeot, and the loose hubcap clanked.

"We had a Mercedes," I said, "but it was requisitioned." They'd know who requisitioned it.

The two soldiers conferred with each other in low voices, each trying to convince the other. Finally the dark-haired one spoke up. "What's the mayor of Heemstede's name, then, soldier?"

Jan swallowed hard, but I was already sliding my fake ID across the seat to Jan hidden under my palm. Without moving his head, he lowered his eyes and looked back up again. His arm rested in the open window of the car door, and he lightly tapped on the metal, just enough to get the young soldier's attention. The soldier looked at him.

"Elderkamp," Jan murmured.

"Elderkamp," the young soldier said.

The two soldiers rapped on the outside of my door. "Papers."

"Just a minute," I said, setting my purse down so Jan could slide the

ID back underneath it. I dragged the purse back and produced the ID alone. I pushed the purse, the gun still inside, under my thigh.

The two soldiers looked at me, then the ID, then me again. Across the car, the young soldier's collar was damp with sweat. The dark-haired soldier leaned down. "Give my regards to Mayor Elderkamp," he said, touching his cap and winking at me.

"I will," I said brightly. "Thank you!"

The dark-haired soldier pounded the top of the car twice, and we drove on, around the Wehrmacht truck and toward Heemstede. I laid my head on the back of the seat and exhaled, relieved and furious and thrilled.

"Ha!" Jan said, looking over his shoulder at the soldier disappearing behind us, then over at me. "That's what I mean, Hannie. All that back there. You were great."

"I wouldn't have had to be except you brought a piece of stolen Nazi property on your escapade," I said. "Mayor Elderkamp?" I shook my head. "What's the mayor's real name?" I asked.

"Who knows?" he said, grinning. With his eyes still on the road, he leaned over and elbowed me in the ribs. "You have to admit, it made our day more interesting."

"This is a date?"

"Our day," Jan said with an innocent smile. "You said 'date.'"

"It's not a date," I said.

"No, it's not," he agreed.

"Because . . ." I stalled.

"Because the mayor's daughter would never be allowed to date her chauffeur."

"Right," I said. "Then again, my father is pretty understanding. And he likes you."

"Oh, he loves me. Parents always do."

I wondered about that. I had a feeling my parents would find Jan a bit too brash and boisterous for their tastes. They were modest, mild people. Like I used to be. I lit my own cigarette and then did one for Jan and handed it to him.

"Did you roll this?"

I nodded. He smiled.

We were leaving the farmlands now and entering the woodsy suburb of Heemstede with its tidy sidewalks and colorful flower beds. Jan seemed to know where he was going. We drove through the residential neighborhoods, and I felt like I was in a different world. As we rattled through the tree-lined streets past the expansive, broad-gabled homes tucked into the landscape, I realized the Dutch families who used to live there—gentile? Jew? no way to know—were gone now, replaced by the Nazi elite. You could tell by the official black Mercedes parked in the driveways. Inside, the new German residents were presumably eating off their stolen chinaware, sitting on their sofas, and sleeping in their beds. Just like in the Frenk house in Amsterdam.

"My father the mayor must really love the Nazis," I said as we passed a mansion with a shiny limousine parked outside.

"He's not a great mayor," Jan said. "Sorry." He looked at his watch and slowed the car, scanning the street ahead. "That checkpoint held us up. Faber should be coming out anytime now." He looked at me. "It's pretty simple. You get out first, walk up to him at his mailbox, shoot him right there, and then I follow up from behind. We get back in the car and keep driving."

I followed his line of sight. Faber lived on Jan Tooropkade, his home one of dozens of whitewashed houses with dark gabled roofs and white stucco walls, all facing the cobblestone street. It was a residential area, so there were no newspaper hawkers or honking delivery trucks to mask the sound of gunshots, just people talking as they walked alongside the water, bicycle bells jingling here and there, and the creaking wood beams of a traditional thatched-roof windmill turning in the breeze. Just beyond the street was a grassy embankment and the Zuider Buiten Spaarne canal beyond. The waterway, which would have been thronging with business in the years before the war, was now quiet, most people's boats hidden by their owners or confiscated. The gentle sounds of the surroundings would have to be enough to distract from the shots and whatever sounds Faber made, though I doubted they would. And that was assuming we hit him. Assuming I went through with this.

Jan reached for my hand. "Ready?"

I closed my eyes. An hour ago, I was safely on the sofa at the RVV. Since then, I'd been an accomplice to a stolen car, a stolen Nazi gas can; I'd assumed a false identity in front of Wehrmacht soldiers, and now we were supposed to assassinate the Fascist Baker of Heemstede. I blinked my eyes open. Then I thought back to the satisfaction of taking out Kohl. It erased all the other thoughts and feelings. "Ready."

"You sure?" Jan looked nervous, but I was beyond that now. "What's that?"

I was tying a light scarf under my chin. "Hendrik said I needed a disguise," I said.

"The Girl with Red Hair?" Jan smiled.

"So they say," I said, annoyed and trying to conceal the rest of my hair with the scarf.

"Maybe I should do it, and you can drive."

"I'll do it," I said. I didn't know how to drive.

Jan's tone changed from sweet to sour. "There's Faber."

I saw him, too. The front door of the house was now ajar, and Pieter Faber was standing in the slice of sunlight in the doorway. He was short and overstuffed, like a Dutch Mussolini.

"See the postman down the street?" Jan said. "As soon as he drops the mail in the box, Faber will waddle out there to get it. That's when we do it. He'll be distracted."

"Will he have a gun?" I asked.

"He's one of the most hated bastards in Holland, so I assume so." Jan licked his lips. "Fucking traitor."

"He's walking." We watched him slowly step outside his house and look both ways before proceeding. "He's nervous," I said.

"He should be." Jan started the car. It clanked and rattled, but Jan Tooropkade was a wide street and the passing of other cars made us less conspicuous.

"I'm going to approach slowly, trailing the postman," Jan said. "As soon as he leaves and Faber has his mail, you walk right up to him."

"OK."

Faber was halfway down his footpath now, timing his arrival at the mailbox to coincide with the mail delivery. He wore an old brown sweater his wife had probably knitted him. This was nothing like seeing Kohl for the first time, with his black leather and barroom breath. The closer we got to Faber, the more I imagined I could smell freshly baked cookies and bread. He appeared so benign, but he was the one in disguise.

The postman approached him with a wave, part of their daily routine. Faber took several letters from him, and the postman started to proceed down the street. I'd already opened the car door; I held it closed but un-latched, ready to spring out. We rolled a few inches closer to Faber's walkway, and I took a deep breath.

"Stop." Jan threw his arm across me to stop me from jumping. My foot was already on the pavement. "Look," he said.

I'd been totally focused on the mailbox, waiting for the postman to clear the area. But as Jan held me back, I saw a boy, maybe ten years old, running down the sidewalk behind us and toward Faber. As we watched from the car, the neighbor's son handed Faber one more letter, delivered to the wrong house. Faber patted the boy on the head. The friendly neigh-borhood baker.

"My God." My heart was hammering; children had never been part of the situation before. I looked at Jan. "That was close."

He nodded. "Now, go."

The arm that was holding me down now pushed me out of the car. Surprised, I leapt out and Faber noticed my flamboyant entrance, turning to look at me with surprise. The boy, thankfully, had run home. I recovered myself and in five quick footsteps ran up to Faber with a big smile on my face to keep his defenses lowered. "Mr. Faber," I said. "You're Pieter Faber, aren't you?" Still beaming.

"Ja, ja," he said, smiling back, a glimmer of curiosity in his eye.

"Where's Sonja?" I heard myself hiss. It was unplanned, but she was the reason behind everything I was doing. My pistol was already in hand, and I pushed its muzzle straight into Faber's bulging gut. He didn't know whether to hug me or push me away. I squeezed the cool trigger of my pistol and felt the whump of the impact in his body and in mine, too, as I kept the gun pressed into him to act as a natural silencer. Faber's mouth opened like a goldfish blowing bubbles, and my wrist was warm with his blood. He blinked rapidly and let out a gasping groan.

"Come on!" said Jan, and I saw him, now out of the car and standing right behind Faber. I jumped away as Faber turned to the sound of Jan's voice. "Fucking Kraut," he said in the same calm voice he'd used on the soldier in the plaza, staring him in the face; then he shot Faber in the middle of that old brown sweater. A jet of red gore spurted out Faber's back as the round passed all the way through. Somewhere behind us a woman on the street screamed. "Get in the car!" said Jan as we ran. I reached for the door handle with my right hand, but it was slippery with blood. While I fumbled, Jan leaned over and opened it, the car already starting to move. "Get in," he said, grabbing my arm. We roared off in the rattling car while behind us a small crowd began to gather around the body of Pieter Faber, lying motionless in the grass.

"I think he's dead," I said, staring out the back window of the car as we drove out of sight. Nobody followed us, though a few people pointed helplessly. No sirens yet.

"He's dead," said Jan. "He was dead with the first shot, he just didn't know it yet."

"That little boy," I said.

"Jesus, that kid." Jan shook his head.

"I didn't even see him," I said. "If you hadn't stopped me—"

"It's fine, Hannie. You were great." He drove through the quiet neighborhood at a normal speed but when we got to the edge of town began to speed up. We had gone maybe two miles when Jan wrenched the steering wheel to the right, and we squealed around a corner onto a dusty farm road. He made another sharp turn and turned off the engine, parking the car behind a sagging barn. The car clicked and hissed as it cooled. "Come on," he said. I followed him out of the car and into the barn. "You can have the black one." He pointed to the two identical old bicycles leaning up against a horse stall. "It's nicer."

"Thanks." Both bikes were equally broken-down. "Are we riding home?"

"It'll be a little quieter than that French sardine can," Jan said.

Smart. Once we were on bikes, we'd blend back into the crowd, no longer the strange couple in the old car who shot Pieter Faber. I pulled off my scarf and shook out my hair. I was sweating with the summer heat and remnants of fear.

"How long ago did you plan this?"

"Few days ago."

"Why didn't you tell me?"

"I thought you'd be less nervous this way."

I wanted to protest but knew he was right.

"Honestly," he continued, "I wasn't sure if you'd do it right on the spot like that." He smiled. "But you did." He stood close and tilted my chin up toward him. "Of course you did." He leaned down as if to kiss me, then stopped, looking into my eyes.

He nodded again. We were so close I could see the cadence of his heartbeat in the hollow at the base of his throat. He let out a long, slow exhale, the first and only indication he'd been worried at all. I rose to my tiptoes and planted a kiss on his mouth. He laughed and we kissed through the laughter, the relief of having completed our terrible mission successfully, the danger forgotten. He wrapped his arms around me and crushed my body against his, and for a moment I flashed back to the murderous hug I'd given Faber, his belly against mine. I shivered, then drove it out of my mind by clinging to Jan even harder, burying myself in the stubble on his skin, the warmth of his sweat and breath, pure as rainwater and wind.

"I love you." The words seemed to announce themselves from my heart directly, without calculation or forethought.

"I love you, too, Hannie," he reciprocated immediately, kissing me harder, as if to seal a vow. My hands crept up the back of his shirt to touch his skin and his did the same, delirious and lost in each other, the horror of what we'd just done to Faber transfigured into pure life force, our hearts pounding with righteousness and love. Yes, love. For the first time. I knew I'd never felt anything like it before.

"We can't stay here," Jan murmured between kisses.

"Not for too long, no," I said, unbuttoning the top button of his shirt. He sighed and kissed me again, his hands tangled in my hair. I undid the second button.

"Hannie," he said, "wait."

"Nobody's coming for us," I whispered, surprised by his hesitancy.

"But, Hannie . . ."

"Yes?"

"Hannie." His tone changed. Still affectionate, but with new gravity. "There's something I need to tell you."

I tried to read his expression but got nothing.

"Hannie," he whispered, almost a sigh. He looked at me expectantly, as if he were about to bend down on one knee and propose.

"Oh, Jan, come on," I said with a little laugh.

"Hannie, I'm married."

I laughed again. "Stop it."

"And I have a child, too. A daughter. She's two years old."

I stayed standing, somehow. I stared at him, unable to comprehend. Barely breathing.

"I do love you," he said. He reached for my hand and kissed it, holding it against his mouth and pulling me closer. "I love you, Hannie. I do."

The world paused. I felt as mute and thoughtless as the shovels and rakes stacked up against the wall, dumb witnesses to the storm of emotions churning all around us.

The air was hot, dusty, and a rivulet of perspiration trickled down my rib cage. Barely breathing. *Keep breathing.*

"I'm sorry," Jan said, his voice husky with feeling. "I wanted to tell you before."

"It's OK," I said. "It's OK." Hearing the words, it began to feel OK, too. I took a deep swallow of air and exhaled. My mind was clearing. "It's OK," I repeated. "I know."

Jan's brow furrowed. "You do?"

No, I didn't. Yet, at the same time, I knew. I already suspected there was something else in Jan's world, understood that I and the RVV were only getting half his life while he spent the other half . . . somewhere important. I'd told myself he was busy with other jobs, other Resistance groups, but on some level, I knew.

I nodded.

Jan narrowed his eyes, trying to decipher me. "How?"

"I just did," I said, my voice breaking on the last word. I quickly coughed and cleared my throat to cover it. I loved Jan and not even this thunderclap of disappointment could touch that. What did it mean that he was married, had a child? I had no idea, just that I didn't want to think about it right now. I couldn't. The moment I allowed my thoughts to settle, more questions arose: Who is she? Where is she? Do you love her? Does she love you? Does she know?

"It's OK," I repeated.

"All right," he said gently. "But what does that mean?"

He stood before me, blue eyes wide, his sweet boyish face open, those broad rough hands I loved to feel against my skin now resting at his sides, posture open and defenseless before me. My fellow soldier and partner. My friend, my teacher. My deadly accomplice. My first and only love.

Nothing else mattered.

"I love you, Jan," I said, relishing each word and the privilege of saying them, of having somebody to feel this way about. Overwhelmed, I closed my eyes and kissed him. This, kissing him now, was the only thing that made sense.

After a minute Jan started to say something, but I knew more conversation would just muddle things up, so I placed my fingertip on his lips to shush him.

"Woman," he muttered, his eyes sparkling.

"Shut up, Jan," I whispered into his ear, then kissed him again. "Nothing else matters."

Chapter 24

FOR THE FIRST few days after the Faber attack, we waited for news of Nazi reprisals, but nothing happened. I knew I should visit my parents and Philine, but I dreaded the prospect of sitting in cramped rooms worrying about Sonja together, so I put it off.

"Hannie." A knock on the door of the bedroom I used at the RVV apartment. It was Hendrik. The door cracked open and his handsome face peered in. "Jan made coffee," he said. "Join us." It was early morning, but the room was already washed with summer sunlight. Sometimes it amazed me, the way the earth kept spinning and the sun kept rising no matter what. I stretched and admired the play of light on the plaster walls.

"Hannie!" Hendrik peered in again. "Are you coming?"

"You didn't say it was an emergency." I went out to the round table, where he and Jan stood next to a scattering of the latest newspapers, including the Nazi-controlled Haarlem newspaper, the *Haarlemsche Courant*, which Jan now held aloft, his eyes alight.

"'Verwildering!'" Jan exclaimed brightly when he saw me. Savagery.

"Pardon?" I said.

"'De wilde vrouw,'" said Hendrik, a bemused smile on his face. The wild woman. "You're suddenly notorious."

Jan beamed. "Hannie, you're part of the Nazi propaganda machine now." He scanned the article, reading highlights aloud. "'A member of the Dutch Fascist Party was killed the other night.... Made worse by the fact that it was a woman who committed this crime against life. . . A young woman with red hair.'" He winked at me. "'The brutal singularity of this desperado and her crime will burden our nation for a long time to come.'"

"Let me see that."

I was embarrassed by the attention but also secretly thrilled. *Desperado!* The article took up the entire left side of the paper, and I pictured it sitting on Nazi-loving tabletops all over Haarlem in the coming hours. I wondered how many of my fellow citizens would suspect that little Hannie Schaft was the "savage" redhead in question. None of them. A lump formed in my throat. I knew Sonja would be proud of me.

"Remember what I said in Heemstede?" Jan said, giving me a friendly nudge. "About the 'Girl with Red Hair'?"

"Well, they don't call me that here."

"They may as well," said Hendrik, "since that's what they're calling you everywhere else. In any case, they describe your hair. It's time, Hannie." He pointed to my head.

"Ugh," I said. "Do I have to go to a hairdresser?" I'd never been; my mother had always trimmed my hair. Then Sonja had taken over. At this point, it hadn't been cut in months. And it had never been colored or bleached.

"No," said Hendrik, "too expensive. You'll have to do it yourself."

"I could shave it for you," Jan said with a grin. "Keeps the lice away."

"I'll manage it."

"All right, desperado," said Jan. "But really, it's good news. The Fascist Baker of Heemstede is dead!" He turned to Hendrik. "Who's next?"

"Nobody," said Hendrik. "Not until she gets a disguise."

Jan wheeled around, fixing me with a glare. "Woman, go fix your hair."

AN HOUR LATER I let myself into my parents' house and nearly knocked over Philine. It took us a moment to apprehend each other; I was wearing a silky scarf over my braids and spectacles with scratched lenses, and Philine was downstairs, where she must never be.

"Hannie!" She recognized me and threw her skinny arms around my neck, hugging me. I pushed her toward the stairs.

"Are you insane? You have to get back up to the room, Philine."

"It's fine, it's fine," she said, bolting the door—though it would be easy for a suspicious German to kick it in, bolt or no bolt.

"You're doing this now? Answering the door? Chatting with the neighbors?"

"No," she said. "Not talking to the neighbors. But yes, occasionally I open the door, only when I know it's your parents coming home. No one else ever comes over, anyway. I spotted you through the window on the stairs, even with this silly disguise." She sighed. "Don't look at me like that. Your parents approve."

"They do?"

"Well"—she shrugged—"they tolerate it. But I really was going crazy locked up in that room."

I pulled off the scarf and glasses, feeling like a child playing dress-up. "You can't do it anymore," I said. "It's getting worse."

She laughed. "Worse? What about the Americans, in France?" The Allies had landed on the beaches of Normandy a few days earlier and it had raised hopes. Not mine or anyone in the RVV's, but normal people's. "Can you believe it?" Philine went on. "Oh, I hope they get to Holland soon."

According to whispers in the Resistance, they wouldn't be here for a while. "I wouldn't get your hopes up," I said. Philine's smile vanished. "Sorry," I quickly added. "They'll get here. But for now, you need to be even more careful." I glanced around. "Are my parents here?"

She shook her head. I looked at her more closely. Every item of clothing on her body, from the pale green cotton summer dress to the white lace-cuffed socks with the embroidered roses, had once belonged to me. Philine looked down, shy, and plucked at the dress. "Your mother said it would be OK." She looked back up, worried. "Sorry."

"No, it's fine," I said. She had the human-hanger look of a 1920s flapper now, chic but only a few pounds from alarming. Her cheeks were flushed from the excitement, and the green dress highlighted her amber eyes. "They look good on you," I said. I was just as close to the edge of malnutrition as she was. As we all were. I had fine lines and wrinkles at the corners of my eyes that hadn't been there six months earlier. We were all in bad shape.

"Come on," I said, "let's go upstairs. I need your help."

Everything of Sonja's was gone from the bedroom now except a small makeup pouch and the old movie magazines, which were stacked on the floor next to the bed, their bright, garish covers now faded and soft as old cotton. I hadn't seen a current one on the newsstands for ages now.

"I wish Sonja were here," I said.

"Have you heard anything?"

I considered telling her all the possible ways Sonja might be alive somewhere and unable to communicate with us, but it was exhausting just thinking about it. And Philine knew as much as I did. "No," I said.

Philine nodded.

"Philine," I said, "I need you to dye my hair."

"Oof," said Philine, looking skeptical. "Now I really wish Sonja were here." I set the scarf and spectacles down on the bureau, and she laughed. "I didn't want to say it before, but . . . you really do need help with your disguise. You look hideous." I gave her a friendly punch in the arm.

Hendrik had procured what he swore was hair dye, bottled in an amber jar and reeking of petrochemicals, and thrust it at me that morning as if coloring my hair were just another "special responsibility" God had given me, as a woman. Surely I knew what to do with it?

We did our best. The kitchen sink would have been the obvious place to attempt it, but even with the blackout curtains, there were too many windows (and neighbors) for Philine to spend too much time in there. The bathroom was too small for the two of us, so we ended up back in the bedroom, where I lay across the bed, my wet head hanging over the side, water and chemicals dripping into a zinc tub on the floor. Philine sat on a stool next to the bed, massaging the tar-like substance into each strand of my hair.

"Well, if nothing else, my hands are now dyed black," Philine said, "so maybe it's working on your hair, too."

"Just hurry," I said, "I'm getting cold."

"I'm trying."

I had an odd view of Philine from my upside-down vantage point, my eyes at the same level as her chin. I watched the corners of her mouth twist and wrinkle as she worked on my hair, the taut skin along her jawline, her pale neck. I knew her face intimately, and it was comforting to be this close to her. She smelled of my house now, like milk and bread and warm dust. Like my mother. I stared at the soft hollow at the hinge of her jaw. I spotted the barest speck of a pinprick in her earlobe. "Are your ears pierced?" I asked, surprised.

Philine smiled. "I did it myself when I was thirteen, but I let them grow back in. I got in so much trouble."

"Naughty girl," I said.

She chuckled. "Can you imagine? My father was absolutely horrified. It seemed like the end of the world, at the time."

"But it wasn't," I said softly.

"No."

We let the moment hang there, enjoying it. The way things used to be, when something as silly as a pierced earlobe was a scandal. When getting a subpar grade on an exam could ruin a whole day. We were children then.

"You should pierce them again," I said.

"Ha!" Philine laughed. "Maybe I will."

"Thanks for doing this, Philine."

"You're welcome," she said. As unpleasant as the process was, I could tell she was happy to have something useful to do. "Did you have to choose black? It's so harsh."

"I didn't choose it. It's all they had."

"Mmm." She began to squeeze out the water from the roots to the ends. "You may have noticed that I haven't asked why you're doing this," she said, using her fingers to gently untangle the wet strands.

"Thank you," I said.

"I know we all have secrets to keep."

I nodded, and blackish water splattered from my hanging hair. "Stop that!" said Philine, grabbing it in a wet ponytail. She laughed and held her index finger under her nose in the universally recognized caricature of Adolf Hitler: "Heil!"

"Never!" I said.

"Ve know about the boy," she continued in her exaggerated accent. "Tell us everything."

I sighed.

"Hannie?" The real Philine was back. And genuinely curious. "Are you still seeing him?"

I nodded upside down again, and she laughed.

"You're in love with him."

"I think I am," I said, then felt like a traitor for hedging. "Yes. We're in love."

"You're in love!" she said, clapping her hands softly. "What is it about him?" she asked. "You never liked any of the boys at school."

This was true. "Well, he's not like the boys at school," I said. "Not at all. He's handsome and he's very courageous . . ." Philine raised an eyebrow, worried for me. She handed me a towel and I wrapped my hair in it, then sat up on the bed. "He makes me feel like somebody new. Better."

"Well," she said in a soft voice, "you do seem different now. You're so . . ." She waved her hands like a magician. "Not just the hair either. You used to be so shy," she said, "but now you're so bold. Like a soldier."

I laughed, embarrassed, and began combing out my hair. It looked like a mop soaked in molasses.

"I'm serious," she said. "I'm proud of you. And happy for you. That you're in love."

My chest tightened and my eyes got wet. Sonja was gone and here was Philine, wasting away, heartbroken and lonely, in my childhood bedroom. Had I been able to transport them out of the country, I might have felt heroic. But not now. Philine still wasn't safe, and Sonja . . . no, they were the courageous ones. And my parents. Just having Philine here made them criminals. I composed myself. "He's taught me a lot."

"I'll bet."

"Philine!" We both laughed. I needed someone to talk to. And, looking at the color in her normally sallow cheeks, so did she.

"There is something," I said.

"What do you mean?"

"He has . . ." I searched for the best way to say it, the least shocking phrase, but finally just kept it simple, as he had. "He's married. And he has a daughter. I only found out recently."

"Oh." Philine's face remained poised in an expression of curiosity, but I could see her mind working. Should I admit that I was going ahead with it? Would it change how she felt about me? Would she even—

"Hannie," she said with a sigh, "we're in a war." She shrugged.

"Yes," I said, hopeful.

She looked around the little bedroom and its single blacked-out window. "Before all this, I might have reacted differently. But now . . ." She sighed. "Does it really matter?"

Her equanimity startled me. Philine normally saw things in black and white. But the war had changed her, too. It changed everything.

"Well . . ." I stalled.

"All I know," she said, picking at a thread in the quilt beneath her, "is if I could feel the way you do . . . about anyone . . ." She wiped her eyes with her sleeve. "I would do it. I don't believe being lonely is noble or good. If you have a chance at love . . ." She wiped her eyes again.

"Oh, Philine." I sat beside her and hugged her. Her thin, birdlike bones began to tremble under my touch, and I cried, too, for the first time since Sonja's disappearance, and we held on to each other like drowning people clinging to a life preserver. The crying was dangerous, like an ocean wave. Once you got caught up in it, it might drag you under forever.

"Girls?" With a light tap on the doorframe, my mother announced herself. She looked as if she'd just smelled something rotting. "What happened to your hair?"

"Philine dyed it for me," I said, getting up to kiss her on the cheek. "Hi, Mama."

She looked at me with worried eyes. "Hmm." She spun me around to see the new look from all sides, and shook her head and sighed. "If you think this is best."

"It is," I said.

"All right, then." She patted my arm. "Any word from Sonja?" she asked.

"No."

She walked over to us and sat down on the bed next to Philine, putting her arm around her. I almost cried again at the tenderness of the moment. Gratitude filled my heart and I felt it blossom, like the delicious ache of the first stretch in bed in the early morning. I would never be able to thank my parents enough for what they were doing for Philine. And Sonja. And me.

"I know it's difficult," my mother said, "but we have to believe Sonja's safe. There's no reason to think she's not." There was every reason, but I didn't say it. "You're only worried because you love her, and she loves you, too. That hasn't changed."

"I know," I said, trying to stop my tears and separate my horror about Sonja's fate from the chaos of emotions I felt about everything else in my strange new life: Jan, the war, the work we were doing.

My mother handed Philine a handkerchief, and she blew her nose. "Now, what do you think of Philine's ensemble?" she said. "We were really running out of clothes."

"They look better on Philine," I said sincerely.

"Maybe we'll become fashion models when this is over." Philine laughed, sniffling.

"Not me. I plan to eat everything I can once this war ends," I said. "I may become the fat lady at the carnival."

"Now you sound like the girls I know," said my mother. "Come on, now, gather yourselves. There's laundry to be done."

"What's this?" My father loomed in the doorway, tall and sturdy as an oak, a bemused smile on his face. I glanced in the mirror on the bureau and caught my new reflection, my face framed by a pink-and-black hairline, the skin irritated and shiny. My scalp burned and I looked insane. But I was no longer the Girl with Red Hair. "Mijn kleine vos is weg," he said. My little fox is gone.

"Hi, Papa." I gave him a kiss on the cheek.

His nose wrinkled at the scent of the hair dye. "Hello, sweetheart. Having a nice time?"

I nodded.

"You heard about the Americans coming ashore in France?" he asked, still staring at my hair.

"Yes," I said. I knew they were all waiting to see if I had some inside information about the long-awaited Allied landing on the continent, but I didn't. Nor did I want to give anyone false hope, myself included. "I haven't heard anything."

My father nodded.

"Well, I should get going," I said awkwardly, gathering my things. "And for God's sake, don't let Philine answer the door anymore." My mother gave me a look for taking the Lord's name in vain. If she only knew.

"I didn't answer the door!" Philine protested.

"Don't worry about us," said my father. He lifted his hand but declined to actually ruffle my newly dyed hair. "Waar is mijn kleine vos?" he asked. Where is my little fox?

"Ik ben er nog, Papa." Still here.

My mother turned away, her head lowered.

"Here," said Philine. She handed me the scarf and spectacles. "Don't forget."

"I won't," I said.

She walked me downstairs and we said goodbye. I heard the oak door bolt shut with a thunk and familiar squeak of brass hinges; then I heard another sound: Philine's sneeze, soft as a mouse. My eyes rimmed with tears. Years before, in that same small brick house, my father sitting at my twelve-year-old sister's bedside, stroking her birdlike back as she hacked and coughed. Diphtheria. My father kissed Annie's shaking shoulders and whispered: "Vier dingen laten zich niet verbergen: vuur, schurft, hoest, en liefde." Four things cannot be hidden: fire, scabies, coughing, and love.

"I don't have scabies," Annie said.

"No," my father said. "But you always cough. And I love you."

I wiped my face and left them behind.

I rode down little Van Dortstraat, my damp hair catching the breeze. The yellow-brick houses, the slow canal, all of it the same since childhood. I slowed at the end of the street to let an old woman cross. She glanced at me and then turned for a second look: it was Mrs. Oosterdijk, who had lived two doors down from me since I was born. She stared at my black hair and my spectacles, looked me up and down, frowned, then kept walking. She didn't know me anymore.

Chapter 25

WHO'S THIS, MATA Hari?" Jan laughed, holding open the door at the RVV. He stroked a strand of my now-black hair as I walked in.

"Mata Hari was framed," I said with a laugh. I spun around so he could see the whole look. "What do you think? Philine dyed it for me."

"Very pretty," Jan said, nodding. "You look French. But I miss your red hair."

"Oh, thank God," said Hendrik, spotting me from the kitchen. "And I agree, you look like a Parisienne."

"I don't want to be a Parisienne," I said. I'd been thinking about Sonja the whole ride back. "I want to get back to work."

"That's our girl," said Hendrik with a smile.

"So, it's Ragut, then," said Jan. He meant Zaandam's chief of police, Willem Ragut, one of the deadliest collaborators in the Netherlands. He'd sent scores of Dutch Jews to Westerbork, some of whom were his own neighbors. The Germans adored him. We'd hated him for a long time, and Freddie had spent days and days tracking his movements and learning when he was most likely to be alone. "Freddie said he's got a schedule you could set your watch to."

"He's been a target for a long time," said Hendrik. "Nobody's managed it yet."

"She's ready," Jan said, gazing at me. Hendrik had told me Jan had never worked well with anyone else.

Hendrik looked somber. "I'm not saying this to stop you," he said. "But there was another Silbertanne massacre last night. Over a dozen Resistance members were executed in Amsterdam yesterday, outside a safe house near the Oude Kerk."

I knew of one of the safe houses near the Oude Kerk—Old Church— in the oldest neighborhood in Amsterdam, where the houses were built into the deep walls of the canal itself. They had been very useful recently for hiding Jews.

Jan let out a low whistle. "All the more reason."

"The Germans seem to be getting more determined," Hendrik said. "And more effective. Silbertanne is extending its reach, cell by cell."

"So?" said Jan. He stretched his fingers in and out of fists. "We're not calling it off."

"There's also a rumor that some unknown hero tried to assassinate Hitler himself yesterday on the Eastern Front. Didn't succeed, apparently. But it might be fueling this new wave of retributions."

Jan set his jaw, silent. He hated being told what to do.

"Perhaps you'd like to discuss this with your partner?" Hendrik said.

Jan looked at me. "We're doing it."

I looked to Hendrik.

"Also," Hendrik said, clearing his throat, "I think we now know who that couple was in the Haarlemmerhout. Brasser had some information about that, too."

"The man was in the SS," I said, stating the obvious.

"Yes," said Hendrik, and Jan stared at me, astonished.

"What?" I said to Jan. "Truus figured it out."

"Oh," he said.

"Brasser said one of his guys was supposed to meet them and bring them underground."

"The SS corpse?" Jan interrupted.

Hendrik held up his palm. "If I may?" Jan shut up. "The gentleman in question was an SS member named Bakker. The woman was one of us. She'd managed to flip Bakker, who was giving them all kinds of intelligence on Silbertanne. Apparently, they were intercepted by the Germans before they got to the meeting point."

"Oh," I said. The scenario hadn't occurred to me because it didn't seem possible that an SS member would defect. I'd never heard of it. Then again, the Nazi propaganda newspapers would never report it if they did.

"It was a Silbertanne job, too," said Hendrik.

"What was her name?" I asked.

"Irma," he said. "But that wasn't her real name."

Irma had been doing my job, or at least a version of it. Seducing a member of the SS on behalf of the Resistance. Or maybe she was really in love with him? That was difficult to believe. "Why leave them in the woods?" I asked. "Don't they prefer to string up defectors on the lampposts or something? To scare the others?"

"They used to," said Jan, "at the beginning of the war." He looked at Hendrik with a new thought. "Now they're hiding them . . . because there's too many defectors."

Hendrik nodded. "Bad for morale."

"That's a good sign," I said. "They're losing faith in the mission."

"Fuck all of them," Jan said, but his voice was less bitter now, more swaggering in tone. My theory may have cheered him up a bit. "Hannie, you still want to do it?"

Hendrik's note of hesitation worried me. There would almost certainly be devastating reprisals for Ragut's assassination . . . but I believed in the end we would save more lives than we lost. Removing this evil man might actually make a difference to the Resistance effort, and really, if any killing was justified, it was this one. We could talk ourselves out of every job if we tried hard enough because there would always be innocent victims. Just as we would invariably make mistakes. I hoped I wouldn't be the one making them. "Yes," I said, "let's do it."

"Tomorrow, then," said Jan.

I nodded.

Hendrik stared at us for a minute, trying to read our faces. "Fine, go ahead. It may indeed be a surprise, coming so soon after the Oude Kerk executions. But you will need to be extra cautious. As chief of police, Ragut will be carrying a gun, and he might have extra security with him, so watch for that."

"We know what to do," said Jan, already at the front door. "Come on, Hannie."

"All right," said Hendrik. He winked at me. "Here's to the Girl with Black Hair."

I AWOKE BEFORE Jan the next morning. He lay beside me in the narrow bed, dead asleep, naked and warm. I watched his chest rise and fall, blond fuzz there catching the cool light of morning with each inhale. My hand reached out to touch him, but I stopped. Sometimes I just wanted to gaze at him, to imagine the way things might be for us if there were no war, no Resistance. Would we ever do normal things like seeing a movie or a day at the beach? It was difficult to imagine.

"What are you looking at?" said Jan, feigning irritation. He pulled me toward him, and we kissed. He wasn't the type to worry about his breath in the morning or whether he'd combed his hair. He didn't really agonize about anything. I knew he didn't waste his time fretting about whether we were just a wartime thing. I slipped out of bed and began dressing. "In a rush?" he asked, disappointed.

"Sort of," I said. "We have a lot to do today."

"Yeah," he said, yawning. "I suppose we do."

It was an hour's bike ride to Zaandam, and I used the time to go over our plan again in my mind. I didn't know the town as well as Jan did, but he'd drawn maps for me. The old, slow-churning windmills of Zaandam appeared miles before we got to the edge of the city, crowding the river-bank. Though the sails of the windmills still turned, the grain mills they powered were empty, even in the heart of summer. War was bad for crops.

Jan steered into a quiet residential street on the edge of Zaandam and I pulled up alongside him. It was early afternoon and already heating up.

"Pretty," he said. "Your cheeks are pink."

"Yours, too."

"So, this will be like before," he said, ignoring the compliment. "You go first. I'll follow. Don't look back, don't turn back, and don't stop. I'll be right behind you, just like the Faber job."

"And like when we did Hendrik."

He smiled. "Just like that. But no vomiting, please."

"Right." I nodded. "Let's go."

"Hannie," Jan said. "Don't go too fast today. We can't make mistakes. And we have time." He glanced at the sun in the sky. "A little."

"I'm not rushing," I said. "Do I look all right?" I wore a scarf over my hair, even though it was now black, and the spectacles felt weird on my face.

"Like a killer," he said, "a cute one." He leaned over and kissed me on the cheek, and an old woman passing by tsk-tsked us, so he kissed me harder. "All right, my little aanvalshond," he said, once she had passed. "Time to let you off your leash."

Attack dog. In my mind I saw German shepherds pacing bent-legged back and forth in front of Euterpestraat 99. I wanted to take one on.

———

By now I knew both ways to assassinate a Nazi: alone in the dark of night or on a bright street filled with people at midday. As the first shooter today, it was up to me to call off the attack should I notice anything amiss. I was in control of that. But it was Jan who'd created the original plan, from the escape route to the timing of the attack itself. I hadn't been invited. As I turned onto a busier street, I braked so hard Jan nearly smashed into me.

"Verdomme, Hannie. What's wrong?"

I yanked the glasses off my face, my hands shaking. "I can't see," I said. "They're dirty." I reached for the hem of my skirt to wipe the lenses.

"Give me those," Jan said. He held them up to the sunlight and then, with two quick jabs of his thumbs, popped the lenses out completely, then handed them back. "How's that? Now you can see."

"OK," I said, too nervous to chat. I put the glasses on, a little annoyed that they were so much improved. By the time Ragut noticed the lenses were missing, he'd be dead.

"Don't worry so much, Hannie, we know what we're doing."

"Stop saying my name," I hissed.

He laughed. "Get on your bike, woman. We could have been done by now."

I started riding again, with Jan's wooden tires clacking along right behind.

As chief of police, Ragut was constantly surrounded by his minions, and even at his home there were always guards around. After consulting with Freddie, Jan decided to make an asset of a busy daytime street, where the chaos of the crowd would mask some of the mayhem we were

bringing. Ragut would be exiting an office building in the center of town
where he had a regular afternoon meeting. We knew the address.

But the little streets of Zaandam were so much narrower than I'd
imagined. We were soon threading ourselves into the center of a tight
maze, two- and three-story buildings rising like walls on either side, with
few alleyways or side streets to offer last-minute escape routes. As we got
deeper into the town center, the city was busier than I'd expected, with
sullen clusters of German soldiers sloping around wherever I looked.
They must have installed a new base nearby. I wondered if Jan had
planned for that.

I swerved my bicycle through the soldiers and shoppers like a needle
through silk and found myself arriving at the target zone too quickly. I
dropped my feet to the pavement and stopped. The exact spot where Ragut was supposed to appear was two short blocks ahead, but both sides of
the choked little street were crowded with municipal offices, shops, and
an old wooden church that was squeezed in like an old memory amid the
newer construction.

"Hey." Jan's bike tire brushed against mine as he pulled up behind me
"It's just ahead." At least he was whispering now.

"I know," I said. "It's so crowded, I thought I should wait for you."

"You can't do that."

A corkscrew of messy blond hair fell across Jan's forehead, his skin
tanned now from the summer sun. Occasionally the light and an expression on his face came together in a vision that forced me to pause.

"You hear me, Hannie? Don't wait for me. The plan doesn't work
that way."

"I know," I said, "I won't."

"Good."

One last time I considered asking him: *Are you sure? Should we do this
today?* But I had no good reason, just a feeling. We needed to be at our
target destination in the next four or five minutes if we wanted to cross

paths with Ragut. Even through the crowds I could make out the spot near the curb where we could pull close to the sidewalk and take our shots, then keep riding down the busy street. I took a deep breath. I stepped onto the pedal with my right foot.

Jan grabbed my shoulder. "What's that?"

"What?"

It was a sound.

All around us, the shoppers and hawkers and students and families were doing the same thing we were, heads whipping around to find the source. At first it was a high whine, like the buzzing of an electric wire or a bad radio frequency. But as it grew louder the sound dropped lower, to a rumble. Then a roar.

"Bombers," Jan whispered. Everyone had the same thought, and fear rippled through the crowd like a stone dropped in a pond. True panic was about to set in.

"Come on," he said, pulling me toward the middle of the street. Everyone else was fleeing to the sides. The path down the middle was clear as a racetrack.

"Jan, no," I said, but he grabbed me by my upper arm, cinching it like a steel manacle. It hurt. It got my attention.

"Keep going," he said, and looked into my eyes as if seeking something there: Was I still in this?

"We're still following the plan?" I asked, shocked.

"Go!" he hissed, and pushed me forward. So I went. For a moment, I felt as exposed as an actor onstage, riding down the center of the downtown street, alone. But Jan was behind me. I couldn't see him, but I knew he was there. And now I saw he was right in continuing. Despite the lack of cover, we rode like ghosts, invisible among the screaming citizens who were only concerned with diving for cover under fruit stands, inside shops, and anywhere else they could get away from the sound, which was louder and louder now, no longer a waking lion but a steam engine churning above the clouds—we still couldn't see them—the impossible yet familiar sound of the heaviest thing in the world floating through air and screaming destruction.

I felt something sharp in my stomach and I wondered if I'd been shot, somehow, and then realized it was just a cramp. Pure fear. I forced my eyes to the preordained spot, and then it occurred to me: Ragut wouldn't come out now. No one would. Yet just as I turned my head to yell to Jan, something silvery flashed in my peripheral vision.

It was Ragut. Chief of Police Willem Ragut stepped out to the street in his police uniform to protect the public. I felt a smidge of respect for him before remembering all the Jews he'd already sent to their deaths, all the resisters, too. Fuck Ragut.

He was tall with a barrel of a belly, cinched tight in his dark blue wool uniform with its absurd cross-shoulder sash like some sort of puffed-up petty dictator. Well, he was that. He looked up as I rode toward him and our eyes met. Dutch blue eyes, blue as Jan's, blue as my father's. A girl riding toward him, her eyes Dutch blue, too. The corner of his mouth curved as if to smile, even in the chaos and the screaming engines that now droned so close I felt they might scrape us with their great steel bellies, and I smiled back, pulled my pistol from my right coat pocket, dipped my handlebar down to swoop right up against him, smelling his shaving cream, cigar smoke, observing a pearl of butter on his lapel where he'd been careless at breakfast, the pomade in his hair, and the scent of wool. My knuckles brushed against his uniform as I jabbed the gun into his gut and squeezed the trigger: BOOM-BOOM. The double tap, like Jan. Two shots and gone.

I leaned over my handlebars and yanked the gun back, afraid he might grab for it, and kept riding, the bomber planes still screaming above, people all around us screaming below. Would I even hear Jan's follow-up shots amid the noise? But then I heard another blast and then another, and I was able to exhale. Jan had gotten there just behind me. I knew I couldn't wait for him, but I yearned to at least turn and look back. *No, stick to the plan.* I kept my eyes locked on the escape route ahead. When I finally turned onto a small side street, the roar of the bombers began to fade. Had they actually dropped any bombs? I hadn't seen a blast or smelled smoke.

I kept pedaling, occasionally catching the eye of someone crouching behind a house window, wondering who the crazy woman in the scarf and glasses was, out riding in a bombing raid. The longer I rode, the quieter the planes got, until it became clear they weren't bombing us at all. They roared off over the North Sea and then they were gone. I didn't even know whose planes they were: Germans? Americans at last? The British returning home? I asked myself questions to stay focused. I kept riding. So far, everything had gone perfectly. The bomber planes had actually helped.

Within ten minutes, right on schedule, I was at the rural outskirts of Zaandam and out of the fray. I could see the rickety shed at the edge of a farm that was our designated meeting spot after the attack. There was no sign of Jan behind me yet, but that was OK. We had more than one option for escape routes. I'd been able to follow the fastest one, but because Jan was bringing up the rear and more likely to be followed, he'd probably taken one of the less obvious routes, his preferred kind, full of sharp turns and more difficult riding.

I opened the wooden door to the shed. It was dark inside, but I found a shuttered window, and when I opened it, the blazing light of the summer afternoon bored into the darkness, blinding me. As my eyes adjusted, I made out a couple of milking stools, a jumble of farm tools, and equipment in various states of repair. It was a stuffy little cave, but I wouldn't be here long. I sat down against the wall with a thud, suddenly aware of my exhaustion.

A clanking sound of metal came down the dirt lane. I held my breath and peeked through a knothole in the door. It was the dairy farmer who owned the place. I was to make no contact with the farmer or his family. So I watched. I liked seeing who these people were, these silent resisters who risked everything to give us shelter. Looking at him, you'd never suspect he was any kind of rebel. Just another tired old man carrying a patched-up tin pail in his gnarled hand. I silently thanked him. He opened the gate to the pasture beyond and kept walking with a limp, maybe from the previous war.

I'd been so worried about Jan following me that I hadn't given any thought to whether anyone else was. Had no one seen us? Was that even possible? Had they not heard the gunshots? The bomber planes—I shook my head at the memory. We could never have planned a better or louder distraction. I looked forward to telling the story to Hendrik when we got back. And Truus, though I hadn't seen her in a while. I closed my eyes and allowed myself something even harder to come by than sugar cubes: a moment of satisfaction. I could hear Jan's scratchy voice in my ear, whispering it the way he sometimes did when he knew I was feeling down: *Well done, Professor.* I wouldn't even punch him for saying it.

Ragut is gone. No one followed you. You're safe in this shed. Jan will be here soon.

Soon.

Chapter 26

H E SHOULD HAVE been ten minutes behind me. I waited another thirty. Then an hour. By now it was late afternoon and the inside of the shed was hot as a woodstove. I leapt to my feet. I should find him. He was probably waiting for me somewhere, worried about me. I wheeled my bicycle to the shed doors, then stopped.

The only person I was supposed to communicate with for the next twenty-four hours was Jan, unless Hendrik somehow made contact. That was the plan. Stick to the plan. It was so much easier to keep running than it was to sit still. Waiting. But it was intolerable, I wasn't going to just do nothing, and . . . I looked around the dusty dairy shed, smaller than a truck's cargo space, barely big enough to stretch out and lie down. This had been Philine and Sonja's life for over a year. Caged, trapped, with nothing to do but wait. And all the other men, women, and children hiding themselves away, day after soul-crushing day in cupboards and closets and spaces even more cramped than this. I had told Philine it took guts to sit and wait, and it turned out I wasn't strong enough. And where the hell was Jan? I told myself I'd give him five more minutes. Then I heard it.

The soft crunch of bike wheels through weeds, then a soft tap-tapping on the shed's wobbly door. I exhaled. *At last. You bastard.* I wanted to kill him and kiss him, simultaneously.

"Finally," I said, trying to mask my worry with sarcasm as I cracked open the door.

"Hannie."

It was a voice I hadn't heard in a while. Truus. Her smile, if you could call it that, was a tight press of the lips.

"Hey," she said.

"How did you find me?" I asked.

"Hannie . . ." She stayed in the doorway, a slim silhouette in the after-noon light. "I'm so sorry."

"What? Why?"

She walked in, letting a wash of fresh air into the shed. "I don't know how to say this . . ." I searched her expression for clues. She looked angry.

"Jan was shot, Hannie. By Ragut."

"Ragut?" I smiled at the absurdity. "No, Truus. We got him."

"Yes, but he got one shot off at Jan before he . . ."

I stared at her. Truus was not supposed to be here. She wasn't part of the plan. She couldn't possibly know what was going on. "No, that's not what happened," I said. I was there. She wasn't. But inside I felt some-thing crumble. I hadn't actually seen any of it happen. But still, I knew what we'd done. "We shot him," I said again.

"Hannie . . ." Her voice trailed off. "You didn't hear any other shots?"

"I did, but that was Jan," I said, trying to replay it in my mind. But she was right: I'd heard two shots. I assumed the second one hit Ragut.

"How did you find me?" I asked again.

"I was the one who told Jan about this place."

Of course she was. Truus was the invisible fixer of the RVV, always providing one last detail to make the plan work. Truus knew everything. "Tell me what you heard," I said.

She nodded. "Someone from the Zaandam RVV got in touch with

Hendrik about an hour ago and told us what happened. Hendrik went looking for Jan and I went looking for you." She told me the story, fitted together from sympathetic bystanders and a network of emergency whispers in the Resistance. After the bomber planes passed, people looked around for signs of destruction and saw two men, one a police officer, lying on their backs on the curb. The people flocked to them, calling for medical help. Jan, who was the other man on the ground, came back to consciousness, saw the commotion, and ran away from the crowd.

Her version explained every single sound I'd heard as I rode away. One gunshot, then another right after. I'd assumed they were both Jan's shots. But as Truus told it, the first one came from Ragut. I was already away, so he shot Jan. Jan shot back. But he missed. An accident. It could happen to anybody. Even Jan.

"Where is he now?" I could already feel the answer's impact, an approaching tidal wave.

"He was hurt," she said. "It's serious."

My legs buckled and Truus grabbed me. "I'm fine. I'm fine." I steadied myself against the wall. "Where is he?"

"I don't know."

"So, he could be alive?"

Truus frowned. "It's possible. But . . ."

Not probable. Just like Sonja. Simultaneously dead and alive, depending on how optimistic you felt that day.

"He was hurt badly," Truus said. "And if the Germans find him, it'll be worse."

"But he's been shot. He needs a doctor. Where is he?"

"He hasn't made contact with any of the Resistance medics," Truus said. "Hendrik was checking the hospitals when I left."

I took a deep breath, trying to calm down. We had to find him.

"OK," I said. "Let's go."

———

WHEN WE ARRIVED at the RVV apartment in Haarlem, it was empty. I'd allowed myself to hope Jan might be there by now. But even Hendrik was gone.

"Wait," said Truus. In the center of the dining room table, an old kitchen cleaver had been thwacked down, pinning a note beneath its nicked, rusty blade. There, in Hendrik's elegant handwriting, was a simple note:

> *Wilhelmina Hospital—Amsterdam*

I knew the hospital; it was just a few blocks from the university. I'd picked up a few things there for Nurse Dekker when I was still a student. That seemed like another life. I swallowed a lump down my throat.

"Don't worry, Hannie," said Truus. "We don't know what's happened yet."

"It's not that." But it was.

"Come on, we'll take the next train."

Truus handed me a handkerchief and pushed me back outside and somehow got us to the train station. Every so often, I felt my cheeks get wet, not even realizing I was crying. Truus squeezed my hand tight. On the short ride to Amsterdam, I began to collect myself. "I know how to get to the hospital," I said.

Chapter 27

I DON'T REMEMBER MUCH else about the train ride. I do remember that every time I heard a sharp noise—the punching of a ticket or the shutting of a window—it sounded like gunshots: pop-pop-pop. I came back to life as we found our way through the busy streets of Amsterdam, Truus leading me by the hand like a child.

It was almost the longest day of the year, so the slanted, fading sunlight lasted longer than it seemed it should. Neither bright nor dark, the twilight settled over the city like a hangover. I hadn't been in Amsterdam since the last time Jan and I had looked for Sonja, at least a month ago. Not much had changed. *Voor Joden Verboden* signs still hung from the park gates and shop windows, and nobody met anyone else's eyes in the street. No tramcars ran because there was no fuel and now no tracks—people had dug up the wooden rail ties for firewood the previous winter, along with the elegant hundred-year-old elm trees that used to line the canals. The streets were relatively busy because of the midsummer holiday. The fact that the Allies had made it to southern Holland had given people a bit of hope, and through the open windows of apartment buildings you could occasionally hear the sounds of families enjoying each other's company. How novel. Mounds of stinking trash rose at the edge of the street every block or so. Amsterdam. Beautiful Amsterdam.

We had no bikes, so we jogged. After about twenty minutes, I no longer knew if I was tired. When we got close to the hospital, we slowed to a walking pace. Reaching the corner of Eerst Helmersstraat, I stepped off the curb, but Truus jerked me back onto the sidewalk.

"Wait," she said, glancing around the intersection. "We can't just walk up to the front desk and ask for him."

Thank goodness one of us was thinking clearly.

"Come on," she said, still holding my hand, and we crossed the street to a café with a window facing the hospital.

"I don't have any money," I said.

"I do." We sat down and I fanned myself with my hand.

"One coffee, please," said Truus.

The waiter looked at her and then at me. "Two?"

"Just one," I said.

"These tables are for customers only, miss." He cleared his throat. He reminded me of Philine's father, slightly nervous, very orderly. The last we'd heard of Mr. Polak, he was moving into a different apartment and promised to write. Philine hadn't heard from him for weeks.

"I'll have a glass of water," I said.

He cleared his throat. "Paying customers."

Truus fixed her gaze on him with a look of contempt I'd never seen before. She rummaged in her pocket, turning it inside out to make sure she got everything. No one in the RVV came from wealth, but Truus and Freddie were by far the poorest. She managed to fish out a few cents and palmed them on the tabletop with a metallic slap. "A coffee and whatever this will buy," she said.

He paused.

"Please," she said. Her voice broke a little. "It would mean a lot."

I looked up, my eyes red behind my spectacles, which Truus had insisted I wear when we left the shed, along with the headscarf. I knew I looked half crazy. The waiter sighed. He scraped the coins off the table and went back inside.

Truus exhaled. "Verdomme." She cursed under her breath at everything around us, from the soldiers to the exhausted-looking passersby. We had a good view of the hospital and its ancient vaulted entryway. A Nazi flag flew there, of course. "Let's wait here a bit," she said.

I nodded. We had no plan. So we sat and watched as people entered and exited the hospital across the street, nurses in uniform and everyday citizens going about their business or visiting someone inside. Thinking of Jan, I felt my heart twist in pain. *Please let him live.*

"It's like a fortress," Truus said, trying to imagine a way to slip inside the huge stone building without detection. It looked impossible.

"They built it during the medieval plagues," I said. Nurse Dekker told me that.

"The hospital?"

I nodded.

"A plague sounds relaxing."

"Ha-ha."

The waiter returned and set down two coffees.

"For me?" I asked.

His annoyed expression thawed a bit. "Het ga je goed," he said gruffly. Be well.

"Bedankt," I thanked him, nearly dissolving into tears. I sniffled. He smiled and left us alone. Good people were still out there.

We drank our coffees as slowly as possible. A few times, Truus looked as if she was about to say something to me, but then stopped and stayed quiet. I had only questions and I knew Truus had no answers, so I stayed silent, too.

"Look," she said at last, and we both heard the wail of a makeshift ambulance—an old police wagon—coming from the opposite direction, headed for the hospital entrance. As it slowed to make its turn, I strained to draw any information I could from the moving vehicle, but it passed in a blur through the arched entryway and disappeared into the interior courtyard. We couldn't make out the driver, much less the patient in the back.

"Truus," I asked, "who told Hendrik that Jan was here?"

"Brasser or one of the other Zaandam guys, probably. Somebody in the RVV."

"How did he know?"

Truus sighed. "You know how it is. All rumors. But it could be true."

"Why bring him all the way to Amsterdam? Why not just go to the hospital in Zaandam or Haarlem?"

"If he's in the hands of the police, they'll want to interrogate him, if possible. And all the top SS officers are in Amsterdam."

"What do you mean, 'if possible'?"

Truus just looked at me.

"Right." They couldn't interrogate a dead man. I put the thought away. We sipped at our drinks and then chewed on the hard nubs of chicory at the bottoms of our cups. The waiter didn't bother us again. The longer we sat at the café, the more predictable the scene in front of the hospital became: people coming and going, an occasional ambulance entering or exiting, and nothing at all learned about the fate of Jan or whether we were even looking in the right place.

"We can't stay here all night," I said. "This café will be closing soon, for curfew."

"I know," Truus said. "But I don't know what else to do." She ran her fingertip over the rime at the lip of her cup and licked the last bit of flavor from it. "I guess we could go back to Haarlem and see if there's any news there."

"No," I blurted. Leaving Amsterdam would feel like a surrender, as if we were giving up hope. "Would it be so terrible if we did walk up to the main entrance and just asked? I could pose as his . . . sister." Not wife.

"You can't be seen anywhere. Not even in that scarf. It's too risky."

"I dyed my hair," I said, frustrated.

"Yes, and it was that black-haired girl who shot Ragut, remember? They'll probably just add her to the 'Girl with Red Hair' bulletin at Gestapo headquarters."

"Ugh," I grunted, "I'm not the only woman out here. What about you?"

"Yeah, well, I'm not the one who shot the chief of police today."

"It could work," I insisted.

"Just be patient." She gave me a kindly kick under the table and I grudgingly kicked back. We looked back at the hospital. The building itself was so huge that it took up nearly the entire block, and most of it lay behind an ancient six-foot stone wall. A gate was attached to the end of it. No guards.

"Look," I said. "See that little black gate off to the side there? I've seen nurses going through it. It must be a side entrance."

"I did notice the delivery area down the street," she said, nodding toward a wider gap in the wall where service trucks drove through. "Maybe we should try down there. Less busy."

"I don't think so," I said. "I mean, which do we resemble more, delivery drivers or nurses?"

She looked at me and smiled. "Right now, you look like some kind of mad Russian babushka in that outfit."

"Come on," I said. "I can't stand sitting here any longer."

"Fine." We gathered our things. A few steps from the table, Truus found a twenty-five-cent coin on the sidewalk. A treasure. I was about to tell her it was a good omen, but she had already turned, jogged back, and set the coin down on the saucer next to her coffee cup, to pay for mine. She saw me watching.

"Blijf altijd menselijk," she said by way of explanation. "That's what my mother always says."

Blijf altijd menselijk. Stay human.

We lapped the block across the street from the hospital a couple of times, looking for anything that might cause us trouble. A group of people, some nurses in uniform, some in street clothes, approached the black gate. Truus and I didn't have to speak. We both ran across the street at the same time and joined the tail end of their group. It was easy. Once inside, the rest of the group continued walking across the courtyard while Truus and I lagged behind and then pressed ourselves against a shallow recess in the old stone wall. It was a start. We could finally see the whole hospital building, the three stories of lighted windows, some with offices inside and some the rooms of patients.

"We have to get in there," I whispered.

Truus sighed. "Then what? This place is enormous." The structure directly across from us was lit extra brightly, the receiving area of the hospital. As Truus spoke, a phalanx of Wehrmacht soldiers marched down the ground-floor hallway, their rounded green helmets rippling like reptile scales. Acid remnants of the coffee churned in my stomach.

"He must be in there," I whispered. "Look how many soldiers are here." The name Jan Bonekamp was well-known to the Germans, but they'd never had a good physical description of him. Capturing him alive would be a huge victory for Aktion Silbertanne and the SS in general. They would keep him heavily guarded.

"There's soldiers all over this city," Truus said. This was also true.

We waited another minute. Everything seemed routine. Peaceful. No more soldiers in sight.

"I'll go to the front desk and ask for a random name," Truus whispered. "While they're looking it up, I'll try to get a sense of anything unusual happening in there. See if the SS is around or any more soldiers. You stay here and keep watching that window." She pointed to where the soldiers had passed. "If it looks safe enough for you to come in, I'll walk to the window and clasp my hands together like a prayer. That's the sign for you to join me. OK? But not unless I give the sign."

I ached to go inside with her. But I trusted Truus more than anyone.

Truus began walking across the bricked plaza and across the inlaid mosaic in the middle, an icon of the ancient Dutch Lion. I dug my fingers into the crevices of the stone wall behind me, holding myself back from joining her.

Truus arrived at the building and reached for the brass handle of the great oak door.

A harsh male voice rasped from a few feet to her right:

"Stop! Stop! It's a trap!"

Truus spun toward the voice.

"Get out of here! Run!" the man screamed now. Still shouting, he ran toward Truus, she reared back, the people in the courtyard scattered, and I froze in place, recognizing the screaming man. It was Hendrik, racing across the bricks in his three-piece brown suit, forelock flapping, bellowing at Truus as loud as he could, this man who never raised his voice even when I tried to shoot him.

Truus didn't hesitate. She whirled around and ran back toward me, her eyes wide and terrified. Then, from within the thick old walls of the hospital came a thundering of boots on the shiny tiled floors: the same soldiers who'd just marched by were now running back.

If she'd seen the soldiers, I couldn't tell.

"Go, go, go!" she screamed at me, grabbing me by the sleeve and dragging me with her to the wall at the perimeter of the courtyard. There was no exit that I could see, but it was overgrown with ivy, and we flattened ourselves into it for cover.

Back in the center of the courtyard, Hendrik slowed, then turned around to face the mob of helmeted soldiers who were still pouring through the door with their rifles and handguns drawn. Truus grabbed me by the wrist, pulling me to the gate. As we ran through, I let myself look back once, hoping to see Hendrik right behind us. He wasn't. I pulled Truus to a halt.

Hendrik was standing still, holding his ground in the dead center of the courtyard, a small, dull black pistol in each hand. The soldiers in the front of the pack slowed down, confused that he wasn't trying to flee, creating a traffic jam of excited soldiers crushing each other in a domino fall. One of the soldiers barked at Hendrik in guttural, hysterical German, his voice so wild with fury I couldn't make out the words.

Then I heard Hendrik's unmistakably smooth voice rising above it all, that special elegance that he maintained even now, in this moment of terror. "Gentlemen, gentlemen," he crooned. "Come on, you . . . fucking pigs."

The mob roared but stayed put, yoked to an absent chain of command. Hendrik stood like a gunslinger with his long legs spread wide, both guns pointed at the soldiers, cocked and ready to fire. I'd never heard him swear before, never seen him violent. He was so brave. It was a standoff. Truus and I watched, holding each other.

The two sides stared each other down, five seconds at most. Then, finally, the heavy oak door swung open again, and a trio of older, long-coated Nazis with shiny helmets ran into the courtyard. But not to the front of the pack. To the side, sheltered from Hendrik's line of fire by their own men.

Hendrik saw them and smiled his beautiful smile. "Cowards," he said calmly, now that the noise had died down. The courtyard was quiet except for the sounds of the soldiers' shuffling feet. The three officers conferred quickly; then one called out, "Ergebt euch—" He stopped and cleared his throat, then spit a ball of mucus on the bricks. "Ergebt euch friedlich," he continued, in a slightly deeper voice. "Surrender peacefully, and we will let you live."

"I can't hear you from all the way over there," said Hendrik.

The thready-voiced Nazi spoke again. "We will let you speak with your comrade if you surrender now."

Hendrik scoffed. "Tell me the name of the comrade first."

The three Nazis leaned together again. Then a second one spoke, his voice low and monotone. "Jan Bonekamp."

I stopped breathing. Truus held me against her, and somehow, I stayed upright.

"So, you allow me to come in and talk to him," said Hendrik. "And then what?" As he finished saying it, he took one significant step to his left in an attempt to capture the senior commanders in the line of fire of at least one of his guns. When he did, the cluster of soldiers and officers flinched as one, like a school of fish.

"Hold your fire," the officer barked. He made sure not to expose himself to Hendrik's sight line, but craned his neck to try to get a look. "Bonekamp has been very helpful," he said. "Perhaps you are one of the comrades he told us about?"

"Must not be him, then," said Hendrik. "He would never talk."

"Ja?" the officer turned back to his colleagues and shared a smile, then looked back at Hendrik. "Jeder redet." Everybody talks.

My spine turned to ice.

A ripple of murmurs ran through the soldiers and their commanders. Hendrik remained standing tall, but his shoulders seemed to sag slightly, like a windup toy on its way back down.

Back in the shadows at the edge of the walled courtyard, Truus turned to me. For a moment, I wondered if she could even see me; I felt ghostly. My head floated and my ears rang like they did after shooting practice. Truus had a look of horror on her face. I knew I did, too.

"You going to make me shoot through your own men to get at you?" Hendrik shouted, his voice more tired now.

"Please, my friend," said the officer, "let us help each other."

Hendrik shook his head in amazement. "Come over here and say it again."

The officer sighed. "I cannot do—"

"Because you are a fucking . . ." He searched for the word in German so all the soldiers would understand. "Ein Feigling!" A coward. Hendrik smiled.

The soldiers' eyes widened, and Hendrik gestured at them with his other gun, making them jump. The officer turned to the soldiers, uttered a silent command, and the men jostled into formation, the front line on their stomachs, commando-style, those behind them on their knees, and the rest standing, rifles pointed over the heads of those in front, until they were a solid wall of steel muzzles. Hendrik continued taunting them.

"These poor dummies know, too, eh, boys? Come on out here, Kommandant, and at least kill me like a man. This hundred-to-one business is pathetic, you have to—"

With every gun in the formation pointed at slim, two-fisted Hendrik, who was still shouting, the entire company fired their guns at once, a tidal wave to snuff a single lit match.

Hendrik's body twisted in a grotesque pirouette, arms flailing, his slender torso rippling with the impact of the shots, until he fell to the bricks of the courtyard in a heap, twitching. An eager young rifleman broke from the middle of the pack and ran toward Hendrik, pulling him up by the lapels as if showing off a record-breaking fish. He looked back at his confederates with a grin and a predatory sheen in his eyes: *Got him.* The soldier hoisted Hendrik's body, pulling his arms around his neck as if donning a backpack. As he did, I saw a flash of Hendrik's little penknife, its thin silver blade dragging across the soldier's neck. The soldier's face paled as a brilliant red geyser of gore spilled into the warm summer air. He shrieked and clutched at his gushing throat. Hendrik collapsed, falling to the stones like a heavy, blood-soaked blanket, the knife still clutched in his fist.

The soldiers went berserk.

Flooding the courtyard, they ran at Hendrik. Truus dragged me out the little black gate and onto the street beyond. We heard shouting and gunshots as we ran. Just like on the first night with Officer Kohl in the alley, Truus and I tore through the streets tethered to each other by mortal terror. We ran toward the train station, our only route out of the city. We had to get out. As we ran, I saw Truus glance back to see if we were being followed. I didn't trust myself to look backward anymore. I kept my eyes focused on the blue of her jacket and my mind on trying not to trip. We slowed when we got to the station, for fear of attracting attention. Truus once again took me by the hand, and we walked as fast as we could to the platform and stood there panting, not talking, not thinking. Just breathing.

When the train arrived a few minutes later, the car was mostly empty, and we found seats facing each other on the side closest to the city. As the train began to heave itself down the tracks, we stared at each other. There was too much to say and we couldn't talk here, anyway. The few flickering lights of Amsterdam receded behind us. My thoughts alternated between mayhem and blankness. I closed my eyes. A few minutes went by.

"Hey," Truus said, tapping my leg. "You awake?'

I nodded, eyes closed.

"It's just . . ."

I opened one eye and looked at her. "What."

"If they know your name," she whispered.

My eyes blinked all the way open. She didn't have to say it; I could read it in her face. "They'll go to my house," I said.

"Your parents."

"And Philine."

I searched the blackness outside, looking for landmarks and urging the train to go faster. "We have to get there first." Truus squeezed my hand. I began to silently calculate all the consequences of the SS discovering my name. "He could have given them yours, too. And Freddie's," I said.

Truus nodded, her expression grim. "When we get to Haarlem, I'll go to my mother's and you go to your parents'. We can meet after, at the safe house near the markets downtown."

"OK." The weariness I'd felt had turned to burning electricity in my veins. My knee bounced, fingers tapped, desperate to get to our stop. I saw a vision of a blood-soaked Hendrik, dead. I tucked it away. *Go. Go. Go.*

"Don't do anything stupid." Truus gave me a stern look. "I expect you to be at the safe house well before dawn."

"OK," I said again, barely listening. I knew the house she meant.

"Wait for me two blocks west," she said, "just in case."

I looked at her, confused.

"Who knows what else he told them?" said Truus with a shrug. I shook my head, disgusted.

"I can't stand to leave Hendrik there." She wiped her eyes and I put my arm around her wordlessly.

A moment passed. We were both thinking the same thing.

"Jan could still be alive," Truus said. "In the hospital."

"I know," I said. "And still fucking talking."

Chapter 28

THE TRAIN HAD not yet stopped when Truus and I jumped onto the platform and headed in opposite directions. My parents' house was a ten-minute ride if you went directly, but I forced myself to take a safer, wider loop and approach the house through back alleys and yards. I climbed a fence, then hopped onto someone's roof, hoping to get a view of my street. Although it was evening, the midsummer night was still alight, and I'd have to be careful to not be spotted.

I flattened myself onto the scratchy weave of the thatch roof. At first I saw nothing suspicious. No sirens, no flashing lights. I hopped to the ground and started jogging through the back alleys, making a zigzag pattern to my house. The three of them had to get out of the house as quickly and quietly as possible. They could stay at the safe house with Truus and me, at least for the night. Then we could work out something else.

I scooted through gaps between houses and found the hidden path that led from the Dubbelmans' house to the greenhouse in Mrs. Snel's backyard, right next door to my parents. I peeked through the clouded glass and over the fence, where I could see their kitchen window. Some small creature skittered across my foot in the greenhouse and I jumped.

Be careful. I peered out again. The familiar quiet of my sleepy little neighborhood, which I'd been listening to since I was born.

Then I heard thunder.

From several blocks away at first, then closer, a serpentine file of heavy military trucks rumbled along the big boulevard, then turned, sickeningly, onto my little street. There were no sirens or horns or shouting. Not yet. The trucks rolled on, and when two of them made a right turn onto the street perpendicular to mine, I slipped out of the greenhouse and made for Mrs. Snel's garden gate, then into my own backyard. The trucks were minutes away. I ran to the kitchen door, and just as I touched the doorknob, I heard shouting inside. I pressed my body against the exterior of the house and crept to the kitchen window.

My mother stood with her back to me in the kitchen doorway, watching the front door. I tapped my fingernail on the kitchen window to get her attention. She heard it and glanced around, her long blond and silver hair swinging. She only ever let it down like this at nighttime, to brush it through. She looked like a younger woman. I saw my sister Annie in her now.

I tapped again. She turned to the kitchen and the window over the sink. *I'm here, Mama. I'm here.* I knew I couldn't call out to her, though I wanted to. *Over here.* TAP-TAP. *Please.* She tugged on my father's sleeve and then something banged hard against the front door and the whole house shook. He clutched my mother to his body and held her close.

"Aufmachen!" a German voice barked from outside the front door. Open at once.

Don't open it. Don't open it. The soldiers would break the door down if they didn't, but it would give me a few more seconds to come up with a scenario for getting my parents to safety. I could run into the house and throw myself in front of them, like Hendrik; I could run around the side of the house and maybe shoot one or two before being shot myself; I could create a distraction in the backyard; I could . . . damn it. None of these plans ended with my parents escaping.

"Aufmachen!" the voice came again, then a burst of German shouting, orders being given.

My mother and father stood together a few feet from the front door, clutching each other.

"Just a moment, just a moment," my father said as he and my mother inched backward. "Just a moment."

Yes, walk backward to the kitchen and run out with me. Please.

I was reaching for the back doorknob when I saw the front door splinter apart, shattering into ragged planks of wood as a long black battering ram bashed through it; then the soldiers rushed through the smashed door and spread throughout the room, their dark helmets shining like a streaming swarm of insects of the Einsatzgruppen, the lightning bolts of the SS insignia gleaming on their gray-green uniforms. They clustered around my parents, smothering them in bodies and shouts and weapons, and I heard a high-pitched shriek. My mother. A noise I'd never heard before.

The helmets crashed against each other and into every stick of old furniture in the house as they separated my father from my mother, dragging them in different directions, four soldiers on each one. The mirror in the foyer crashed and tinkled to floor, crushed under boots stamped-ing inside, machine guns sweeping across every surface, sending plates and doilies and glasses and books across the room.

A tall Nazi officer with a gas mask hanging from his belt stood in the front door, surveying the chaos. He reached over, took my father by the biceps, and shouted at him, then ordered his men upstairs.

Not upstairs.

Philine.

With my hand on the knob to the back door, I stopped. The whole house was shaking with the pounding boots of the soldiers, and the air was filled with their barking shouts, spittle arcing through the lamplight as they fought each other for proximity to the prisoners, table legs screeching, snapping, the men snarling in a delirium of destruction, their movements jerky and agitated, probably dosed with the little white pills the Germans used to help them kill faster.

Through the window I caught a brief glimpse of my mother, her long hair in tangles and sticking to her face, seated on the sofa, head in her hands, crying, the soldiers keeping her there with cocked rifles while my father was surrounded in the entryway, still shouting about human rights but mostly just shouting. "Aafje! Aafje!" If my mother heard him, I couldn't tell.

More soldiers flooded the house and front yard and moved around the side of the house, over two dozen of them, armed and excited. I could go in, but I'd never get out. I heard the thunder of boots on the stairs and the bedroom doors banging open, shouts, then more soldiers coming back down. I couldn't see Philine. I stood on the back porch, frozen to the spot. I caught snatches of my father's angry red face, the worn hem of my mother's white cotton nightgown grazing the floor, then a black leather boot catching its edge and tearing the soft, old fabric beneath its sole. My stomach turned in on itself and my throat went dry.

Branches and a garden trellis crashed from the side of the house: the soldiers were coming toward the back. With one last look through the kitchen window, I scrambled back over the fence into Mrs. Snel's yard and then ran, right and left and through the neighborhood and back to my bicycle. The shouts and commotion of the goings-on at Van Dortstraat 60 faded behind me as I rode, lights still flaring against the darkened houses on the street. Then the sirens began. The Germans wanted the whole neighborhood to wake up, to see what happened to the families of traitors like Hannie Schaft.

———

I WAS MORE than two blocks west of the safe house when I stopped. Something wasn't right. I ditched my bike and crept nearer on foot. The street was quiet, no sign of soldiers. But the sidewalk in front of the apartment building was cluttered with junk: heaps of clothing, broken furniture, shattered crockery. I slipped into the shadows and waited, not wanting to go any closer. It was about five minutes before I heard anything. Then the soft rattle of metal against metal sounded down the block and I knew. It was Truus. The rack on the back of her bicycle was always coming loose; I knew the sound as well as I knew the music of my father's keys jangling from his key chain when he came home from work and set them on the oak hutch next to the front door.

"Hey," I called out softly. Truus thrust her hand into her pocket where she kept her gun. "It's me," I said, unable to think of anything better. I stepped into the dim light so she could see me. She ran over.

"How are your parents?" she whispered.

"The SS got there first."

She waited for me to say more.

"I don't know if they're just going to arrest them, or . . ." I gulped back a sob, unable to say the words.

"I'm sorry, Hannie." Truus put her arm around my shoulders. I didn't say anything.

"What happened at the safe house?" she asked, looking at the mess on the sidewalk.

"No idea. I just got here."

"They must have raided it." She exhaled audibly and said what we were both thinking: "Silbertanne." She paused. "What about your friend Philine?"

I shook my head. "I don't know. I never saw her."

"Maybe she escaped before they got there."

"Maybe," I said. I was trying to believe it. First Sonja disappeared, now Philine? I felt an ache in my chest, a painful tightness. It was difficult to breathe.

"If they'd found her there, it would have been worse for your parents. She probably got out first."

"I hope so," I whispered.

"Breathe, Hannie." Black spots bounced through my vision, so I rested my hands on my knees, closed my eyes, and tried to restore myself. Truus stroked my back and I tried to slow my thoughts. Only then did it occur to me.

"Oh, Truus," I said. "What about your mother? And Freddie?"

"They're fine," Truus said. "We should go there."

"We can't," I said. "They'll find out where your mother lives, eventually."

"I doubt it," Truus said with conviction. "If they go looking for her address, they'll find an empty mooring. My mother lives on a houseboat. She picked up her anchor earlier today and floated downstream. She got advance warning from the network."

The strategic importance of living on a houseboat had never occurred to me, and I was Dutch. The Germans would have no idea where to look.

"We can't stay here," Truus said. We started running through the city, following the meandering route through the darkest, most desolate streets to avoid being seen. I followed Truus and tried to clear my mind of everything I'd seen in the past few hours. Hendrik, dear, elegant, courageous Hendrik, was dead. But my parents and Philine were still alive, I told myself. Truus and Freddie and their mother were still alive. I was still alive, though I felt mostly dead. And I hoped Jan was still alive in the hospital, too.

Because I wanted to kill him myself.

Chapter 29

THE OVERSTEEGENS' HOUSEBOAT had been poled into a backwater industrial zone at the edge of Haarlem where all the broken things wash up. The long, sagging vessel could have passed for abandoned, riding low as a crocodile in the murky water, its black paint chipped and dull. No status-seeking Nazi official would ever requisition this humble barge. We would be safe here.

Truus helped me across the narrow gangplank to the top deck, in the dark. "Here," she said, pointing out a bench that lined the edge of the boat. The moment I sat down, I broke down. My body began to shake, every single muscle and bone.

Jan.

My teeth chattered.

Hendrik. My mother and father.

I braced myself on the bench with both hands, trying to push every thought from my mind. It was too painful.

"Oh, God," I whispered, and a great, choking sob rose from my chest. Where was Philine? And sweet Sonja? Tears welled and burst, my nose ran, my entire face was melting from the horror of it. I held tight to the bench, the only stable thing.

Truus sat beside me, rubbing my heaving back but not saying

anything, which was the best thing she could have done. I leaned into her, and she absorbed my shuddering body with her own, holding me and saying nothing. We rocked back and forth. Eventually she managed to pry me off the bench and took me below deck, where she tucked me into a bunk and then crawled in beside me, as if I were a baby who might roll off the bed if left unattended.

I couldn't stop crying, my lungs gasping, nose sniffling, burying my face into the musty pillow and silently screaming. The tears, over time, dried up, until I could only moan softly. Exhaustion began to fold itself around me like soft, downy wings. What bliss: oblivion. The big nothing, no thoughts of the dead, no images of the blood, the guns, the pounding, pounding, pounding of black leather boots. I wasn't asleep yet, just floating. Truus stroked my back slowly, coaxing my breathing back to normal.

I felt nothing. I was barely there. And then I was gone.

WHEN I AWOKE the next day, I was alone. I lay in the snug, warm cabin, staring at the varnished paneling just a foot above me on the bunk, following the whorls of wood grain as if they held an answer to be found. Above us I heard the clunking footsteps of people on the top deck and the low music of their muffled voices. I closed my eyes. Everyone I'd tried to protect had vanished overnight. Crushing sadness took my breath away.

The sisters slid in and out of my consciousness that day. Freddie with a glass of water that she left on the shelf for me, Truus gently smoothing my tangled hair from my eyes. I slept, my thoughts occasionally startling me with a jolt of fear, then subsiding like the tide.

ON THE SECOND day, I woke up to Truus sitting beside me on the bed.

"Hey," she said.

"Hey," I rasped, the first time I'd used my voice.

Truus helped me get up, helped me bathe with a metal tub and a tea-kettle, and dressed me in clean clothes of her own. She and Freddie somehow found an egg and boiled it for me, the first nutrition I'd had in days. Truus's mother, Trijntje, orbited us occasionally, her face concerned but, like my own mother's, focused on practical things. She hung laundry on the deck to dry in the sun, and I spent an hour watching my own blouse and skirt flap and flutter in the breeze, as if it were me hanging there. After a while, Truus helped me downstairs and back into bed, the only place I wanted to be. A thousand hours of sleep, that's all I wanted. That and a void into which I could disappear forever. When I heard Truus come in sometime later that night, her voice lifted me out of the nothingness. I rested on my elbows, squinting.

She touched my hand. In her other one, she held a cigarette at arm's length, keeping the smoke away from me. "Not really supposed to smoke down here," she said with a shrug, and continued smoking. "You OK?"

"I think so," I croaked.

"Mother says tomorrow we've got to get you up and back to work. She thinks, and I agree, that it's the only thing that will make it better."

"Ha." A pathetic sigh of a laugh. "Work?" I said. Better? What did that even mean? I wasn't sure I was strong enough to hold a teacup.

Truus stroked my hair. "I know how you're feeling," she said.

Her family was intact. A jolt of anger flooded my senses: What about my family? The moment passed. I couldn't stay angry at Truus. I expected her to launch into another one of her pragmatic pep talks, but she didn't. She stretched out her legs beside me, observing.

"What?" I said.

"That was rough, Hannie." The way she said it in the past tense, as if the bad part were over now. Didn't she realize it had only just begun? "I'm sorry."

I nodded. I was too weak to marshal an argument. Definitely too feeble to get back to work. Maybe I would never work again. I closed my eyes.

Without a prompt, Truus began to speak. "Hendrik told me he had a job for me," she said in a calm, soft voice. "But it would involve children."

I opened them.

"They always try to get me or Freddie to do the stuff with kids," Truus continued. "It's easier for the children to deal with a woman, maybe. Looks less suspicious. In any case, the assignment was all planned out, a joint action with a cell in Amsterdam and another in Dordrecht, which was where I would be headed, about fifty kilometers from the Belgian border. This was an emergency. Twelve Jewish kids needed to be evacuated from Amsterdam immediately. And there was no one else to do the job. They said there'd be another person there to help me from another RVV cell. So I said yes."

She lit a fresh cigarette with the end of the old one and took a deep breath. "They said I should dress like a German nurse, pretend I'm taking a dozen sick city kids to a hospital in the country. Gave me a real nurse's uniform with the white cap and all. Even gave me a Nazi handkerchief with a swastika. Which I blew my nose on, first thing."

I smiled slightly, trying to imagine Truus as a German nurse. She kept talking.

"I met them at the Amsterdam Centraal station. Twelve kids. The youngest was a little girl, maybe three years old, with brown curls and big brown eyes. A baby, really, but big enough to walk around on her own and therefore dangerous. She held the hand of an older girl with one long brown braid hanging down between her thin shoulders named Louise. To be honest, I didn't have much experience with children. I still don't. So I put Louise in charge of Rosie, the baby.

"The children believed I was a Nazi. I could tell by the way they looked at me. You know how kids look now, like sad little adults?"

I nodded. We all saw it. Young people who had seen and felt too much.

"Anyway," said Truus. "I got the kids on the train by shouting at them like I imagined a Nazi nurse would. The train started rolling, but Rosie was crying, and we couldn't have that. Couldn't afford to annoy anybody or attract attention. I almost shouted at her again, but then I saw Louise take her own little handkerchief to fashion a kind of doll, tying a string around the neck and dancing it on Rosie's lap to distract her."

"Were they orphans?" I asked. "Where were their parents?"

"I had no idea," said Truus. "When had they last seen their own families? How long had they been in hiding? Where did they think we were going? I didn't know and nobody ever told me. I wouldn't even know who to ask."

"Did anybody question you, stop you?"

"We had a couple close calls, but we got lucky. We made it to a little village next to the Rhine River. We had to cross it, and someone would take the children on the other side. All I had was a map of this village we were in near Dordrecht, with a path drawn through a field to the riverbank. On the map, the field was dotted with circles. Those were land mines. I told the kids to follow me exactly. I didn't mention the mines.

"I found the opening some local resister had made for us in the fence. It was wide enough for the children, but I was bleeding on my arms and legs by the time I got through. I couldn't feel anything. I was too scared of what lay ahead."

It was the first time she'd ever mentioned fear. She went on.

"I lay flat on the ground in the field with the children and gave them their orders: 'No talking. No laughing. No coughing. No noise at all. And follow my lead exactly.' Fog came off the river and floated over the field, so whenever a searchlight passed, it was all lit up. It wasn't easy going through the stubble of old grass, rocks, and the stinging nettles, but the children were incredible. Every inch forward I braced myself for a metallic ticking or an explosion. But I stuck to the map and somehow we made it through.

"I belly-crawled down to the river to see if it was low enough yet. To be honest, I didn't really know what to look for. So I made the decision to go. I was supposed to wait for the sign of a blinking light from a lamp on the other side. When it did, the searchlights were supposed to turn off in our section for five minutes, allowing me to put the children in the boats and get across.

"That's when I realized there were two boats. For two fake German nurses and twelve children. But of course there was only one fake nurse: me. Even the oldest boy wasn't big enough to handle the other boat on his own.

"Then I noticed we'd gotten there at the wrong time. The water wasn't as low as it should have been. And in all the time we'd been hiding there, I had yet to spot a lantern—our contact—on the other side. I was minutes away from losing whatever control I had over the kids. If they talked or stood up, we'd be spotted in moments and taken prisoner, or gunned down right there on the beach. We had to try."

"My God, Truus," I said. I put my hand on her shoulder, but she took no notice of it and kept talking, as if she were in a trance.

"'Get in the boat,' I told the kids, and I started lifting them up and over the low sides of the boat. The oldest boy, though, hung back.

"'We can't all fit,' he said. 'We should take two boats.'

"'We can only take one,' I said. 'Hurry up.'

"He lagged behind, staring at the other boat as if considering taking it alone. If he had, I wouldn't have stopped him. I couldn't have. In the end, he helped a smaller boy in, helped me push our boat into deeper waters, and grabbed the second set of oars. Once we were all in, the boat was completely overloaded and water began washing over the sides. We hadn't even launched into the current yet.

"The boy just gripped the oars and stared across the river, waiting for another searchlight like a dog waiting to be kicked. The children huddled together in a cluster on the bottom of the boat as the older boy and

I began to row. With our very first strokes, the oars screeched in their locks, a loud, piercing sound. This was supposed to be a secret crossing. I looked back and saw the boy wrapping his oar with his scarf to try to muffle the sound. Brilliant. I wrapped the swastika handkerchief around one and then looked for something else, anything.

"'Give it to me,' I said.

"Louise looked at me. 'What?' She had Rosie in her lap as if she were her own baby, and in turn, Rosie cradled the little handkerchief doll Louise had made.

"'The doll.'

"She didn't want to do it, but she knew we had to. 'Hey, Rosie,' Louise sang to her. She plucked the doll from her chubby fingers, made it do a little dance in the air for her, then tossed it to me.

"'Baby!' Rosie said. It was first word I'd heard from her. She started to cry.

"I tore the doll apart to wrap it around the oar. We were already drifting away from our target beach on the other side, and water kept sloshing into the boat. The older boy and I started rowing again and the muffling cloth helped, for about six strokes. Then, when we were halfway across the river, the wrappings slid out of place and the screeching returned. Rosie was sobbing, and the other kids started crying, too. We were in deep water now, the current moving faster and faster, and we were speeding downstream, way past our destination. A new searchlight blazed on and started its sweep.

"'Get down!' I shouted and we all ducked. I couldn't tell if we'd been seen, but I immediately popped up and started rowing again. The boy did, too. The current was too strong. But what could I do? Frigid water splashed in, and two little brothers in the center of the boat wailed. 'Be quiet!' I said. But they couldn't stop."

I grabbed Truus's hand. I pictured Truus in the uniform and the children in the boat, soaking wet and screaming.

"Then everything lit up. Every searchlight on the bank swept toward us. We were a perfect target in the middle of the river. The light was blinding and the children were terrified.

"'Get down, get down!' I shouted. I pulled at the oars again, putting the obvious problem out of my mind: we were rowing toward the searchlights. What would happen when we reached that shore? We'd never make it back across now. We had to stick to the plan.

"I looked behind me. The older boy on the oars stood up. He was wearing what must have been his father's suit because it was falling off him. He had the oars still gripped in both hands and he faced the lights. The children screamed. He stood there like a little Jewish saint, haloed in the light. Then he shouted at them. I couldn't believe it."

"What did he say?"

Truus smiled a little bit. "'Shoot, you goddamned Huns!'" She paused. "For a moment, nothing happened. Then, with a sound like tiny whips, ZIP-ZIP, his thin body zigzagged as the bullets just tore through him. He arched backward just like a fish on a line and disappeared into the river.

"I shouted, but I couldn't reach for him without upsetting the boat. It didn't matter. All the children were screaming now, and the bullets kept coming. After a few seconds, the boat flipped over and we were all underwater.

"When I came up, I saw the heads and legs and arms of children floating away from me downstream. If they were still screaming, I couldn't hear them.

"When my head went underwater, I could hear bullets passing by me even there. I tried to swim toward the children, any of them, but the first girl I grabbed was already dead, a perfect little hole in her temple. Her eyes were rolled back in her head. I let go and she drifted away. I assumed I'd been shot, but I couldn't feel anything. I was drifting. A few minutes later I found myself near the side of the river we'd started from. I stood up, looked around, and waded back out in the water, trying to save someone, anyone.

"I heard a voice. 'Mama! Mama!' screamed a girl. I think it may have been Louise. But she was too far down the river for me to reach her, so I just listened to the voice get quieter and then disappear. I grabbed a boy's leg that floated by and dragged him to the bank. He was dead. Drowned. One of the older boys. I walked into the river and tried again. I heard a gurgle and saw a flash of something bright, reached for it, and found I had the collar of a little sweater in my hand. I tried to keep my head above water as I swam back and deposited the child on the beach. It was Rosie. She made a gurgling sound in the back of her throat, so I dragged her to the edge of the minefield, where we had a small amount of cover, then began pumping her arms and pressing her little stomach, trying to get the water out. There were motorboats and lights and shouting in German behind me. If there were any more children in the river, it was too late. I couldn't go back. As soon as I saw Rosie was still alive, I swung her onto my back and crawled back into the minefield the way we came, or so I hoped, scrambling through the field in my freezing clothes, trying to stay on the path. If we hit a mine, well . . . honestly, I sort of hoped we would."

I looked at Truus, but she was staring into space, far beyond me.

"I just wanted it to end." She took a deep breath. "Somehow we made it through the field. I pushed Rosie through the barbed wire. She was limp, but by some miracle she seemed otherwise untouched. I kept checking her body for bullet holes. I ran down the road carrying her in my arms. No idea what to do, I saw a house and ran to it. *Please be friendly,* I thought. *Please don't be collaborators.* I fell against the door and a farmer inside peeked out to look at us. I intended to just leave Rosie on the doorstep. But then I passed out."

"Oh, Truus." I held her hand.

"Fortunately, the farmer and his wife were on our side. They were the

ones who'd cut the hole in the fence. They were scared—we weren't supposed to be in their house—but they helped us. I stayed for a day or two,
recovering. And they promised to find a safe home for Rosie. Then I left."

"And?" I said, waiting for the resolution.

"Rosie?" Truus shook her head. "I don't know what happened to her."
She had the unconvinced smile of a philosopher. "I do think about her
sometimes," she said. "I asked the farmer's wife for a handkerchief and I
made her a new doll before I left."

Truus dragged on her cigarette, her face blank. "So I decided to quit
Resistance work," she said. "I figured I'd be fired anyway. I'd failed at the
task, only saving one of twelve kids. I hadn't completed the job. Obviously, I wasn't any good at it. But when I got back to Haarlem, I didn't get
fired. I told Hendrik what happened and he was just . . . sad. Still, I offered
to quit. He laughed at me."

"My God, Truus," I asked. "When was this?"

"A while back. 'Forty-one, I think."

Three years ago.

"I told him I was done. But Hendrik refused to hear it. He gave me
and Freddie some easier jobs, just to keep us working." She stared at the
butt end of the cigarette, waiting for it to burn her fingertips. When it did,
she flipped it through the porthole and into the canal outside. "So I kept
going. Because what else was there to do?" She laughed. "The Germans
hadn't quit. The war was still going. Everything was still shit. A dozen
other Jewish kids probably died while I was trying to deliver my own
group. So, yes, I kept going.

"I discovered something. After that night, nothing could touch me.
Anytime I wanted to give up or I got scared, I just thought of the boat
and the water. Because nothing could really be worse, but I survived."
She stretched, emerging from her reverie. "And so did Rosie. And so
did you."

I was quiet for several minutes after that, not knowing what to say. I didn't think it was possible to admire Truus more . . . but I did. She was so stoic, so mild in her everyday ways, but beneath that was a warrior.

"I'm so sorry, Truus," I said, putting my hand on hers.

She gave mine an affectionate squeeze and then shrugged.

"I try not to think about it. It happened. And I didn't stop. And you shouldn't either." She looked over with her calm, half-lidded blue eyes that never missed a thing. "So? Have I convinced you?"

I was quiet. Nothing felt adequate.

"Hannie," she said, "what Jan did to all of us was terrible. It was wrong. But you're not the only one who's gone through"—she searched for the phrase—"the worst thing that can happen. You stay in this work long enough, and the worst thing will eventually happen. Now it has, for you. So you can't stop. You know what Hendrik says—said—don't you?"

I shook my head.

"'There is no winning in the Resistance,'" she said, imitating Hendrik's smooth radio-presenter voice. "Not in this war, anyway. It's not a fair fight. Then again, there's only one way you're certain to lose, and unlike every other bastard thing in this war, it's something you can control."

I stared at her, baffled.

"Give them nothing."

She stayed quiet, waiting for a response. It took me another few moments.

"Jan talked," I said.

"That's right."

I thought of Philine and Sonja and my sweet parents who'd trusted me, wherever they were. Goddamn Jan Bonekamp.

"OK," I said. "I won't stop."

"Nope."

I sighed. "And I'll give them nothing."

Truus smiled, this time with true warmth. "Good." She stretched her arms and cracked her neck and sighed. "We'll start again tomorrow."

Part Three

The
Hunger
Winter

1944–1945
Haarlem

Chapter 30

Summer 1944

W E SLEPT BELOW deck on the houseboat, the sound of water lapping at the hull all night. Whenever I awoke, the memories flashed past like the blur of the landscape outside a train. The burst of cracking gunshots behind me as I rode away from my parents' house. The hours of waiting for Jan. My parents, dragged apart by SS thugs. The end of everything. The slithering line of gray-green trucks. Failure. The bystanders. Hopelessness. Philine. Jan Bonekamp. It got worse when I closed my eyes. Sonja. Worse when I tried to think about anything else. Betrayal. Goddamn Jan Bonekamp. Then I'd try to go back to sleep.

We got the news through the whisper network the morning after: Jan was dead. So was Chief Ragut. Jan's shot killed Ragut, but Jan had been shot in his side. He fell off his bike and tried to run. Apparently, he took a chance on a random house, seeking refuge, but the two old sisters who lived there called the cops. The SS arrived, too. No hiding under the kitchen floorboards this time. They transported Jan by ambulance to Wilhelmina Hospital in Amsterdam to be questioned by the higher-ups, just as Truus suspected. The rumor-passers claimed Jan was tortured there, that the Nazis refused to give him painkillers, that they made his wounds worse to try to get him to talk. They said at first he refused. Then they said someone gave him what they claimed was "truth serum" and had a nurse pretend to be a fellow resister. Then a senior SS official, Officer Rühl, came in. Whatever this Rühl did worked. Jan told him everything: about the RVV, Hendrik's name, my name, possibly the Oversteegens', too. All the names, all the hits, all he knew. And then he died. That's what they said.

I didn't let myself believe it. Torture? A treacherous nurse? Truth serum? That was something out of a comic book. After a few more days of ruminating, though, my attitude changed. It didn't matter if the details were accurate; the consequences were the same. My family was gone.

I was the reason they were gone.

Jan played his part, but none of it would have happened if I hadn't put everyone around me in danger first. I had to find them. If I lost all five of them, Annie, my parents, Philine, and Sonja . . . I would lose everything. A corner of my heart wanted to add a sixth name to the list because I'd lost him, too. But that tender corner of my heart needed to toughen up.

I lay staring at the ceiling, listening to the slap of canal waters against the sides of the boat. Betrayal is difficult to fully comprehend. It's an acknowledgment of the absurd, this Thing That Cannot Happen . . . that then happens. It's like watching someone take off a mask to reveal the same person you always knew, just slightly uglier. Suddenly alien. Perhaps you laugh at first, but soon panic sets in.

I'd believed I was prepared for something like this. Since the day the Nazis invaded, the whole country had to reckon with betrayal. The Dutch royal family escaped to England to wait out the war. A good percentage of our elected leaders chose to work with the Nazis. Friendships with neighbors began to chip away as some started to turn each other in. And when the person you love betrays you, your faith in the species starts to crumble. As for my faith in love . . . I still loved Philine, Sonja, my parents. And yes, I still loved Jan, but now there was nothing to do about it, no way to express it. He didn't belong to me. I stayed under the blankets as long as I could.

Around nine a.m., Truus knocked on my cabin door and then let herself in. "Time to get up."

I pretended to be asleep.

She wasn't fooled. "You're lucky," she said. "My mother was just about to come in here and roust you herself, but I told her I'd do it. I'm a lot gentler than my mother."

I said nothing, hoping she would go away. Moments passed. She didn't.

"Hannie. There's work to be done."

"Did Jan rat out you and Freddie?" I knew she heard all the rumors from her mother.

"No, not as far as I know," she said. "But if it makes you feel any better, he gave them his . . ." She paused. "He told them everything."

"You mean his wife." Saying the words produced actual physical pain, my heart suspended in my chest, heavy as a brick.

"You knew." She raised an eyebrow.

"He told me," I said.

Her eyes widened. This was a shock.

"I don't know, Truus," I said, shaking my head. The memory of Philine's words buoyed me. "We're in a war."

Truus nodded.

I let out a sigh.

She sat down on the bed next to me. "They tortured him. And he talked about all of it. Not just you."

"I know," I said, trying to sound undaunted.

"He loved you," Truus said softly. "I've known Jan for a long time. I saw it in him, he was different with you." She smiled.

Then it faded.

"And . . ." She paused, her complexion paling behind her freckles. "Well. Hannie, according to my mother's source, he called your name at the hospital." She took a deep breath and waited for my reaction.

"What?" My heart slammed in my chest, comprehending what it meant before I did. "He called my name?" I tried to think, to breathe. *He called my name at the hospital!* And then: *Oh, God. He called my name at the hospital.* My name. Now the Nazis knew my name. I took a deep gulp of air, trying to steady myself. "He did?" I asked again, stupidly, my resolve buckling as I tried to hold back a wave of grief and terror rising from my gut. *He called my name.*

"He did it because he loved you, Hannie. He was in terrible pain. And they brought in a nurse and told her to pretend to be his girlfriend. And it worked. When he talked, he thought he was talking to you."

I stopped breathing momentarily, stunned all over again.

"He was dying, Hannie. They injected him with something and he just . . ." Truus sighed. "They said they gave him truth serum. I'm not excusing it. But he thought you were there and he was talking to you. That's what they said."

"He knew better," I said, trying not to sob. I allowed myself to imagine the terrible moment: Could he have done anything different, in such pain? But it was too much. I buried my head in the quilt, weeping. *Oh God, poor Jan.*

And *oh God, fuck Jan.*

You never talk to them. Tell them nothing. It's the only rule. That's what he'd always said to me.

"I know," said Truus in a soft voice. I didn't have to say it aloud; she understood everything. And I didn't have to explain the sorrow, either. More than anyone else, she knew.

"It doesn't matter," I said. "It doesn't matter now." I shook my head, trying to untangle the knot of lies I'd been living with for the past year. Jan had been living with them, too. For a flashing moment I allowed myself to imagine his wife and daughter—did they even know he was dead yet?—but it was too overwhelming. I put my head in my hands and wept again. It was too much. Truus stroked my shoulder and kissed the top of my head. I paused in my crying, taking a deep breath and trying to return to the present moment. Here, now, on this boat. I was alive; he wasn't. Yes, I still loved him. And I knew he had loved me, too.

"I'm all right," I said. Truus nodded.

The door rattled. We looked up to see an older version of Truus, freckled and steely-eyed, smiling and tough. I wiped my eyes and blew my nose, hoping I didn't appear too pathetic.

"All cried out, then? Good." Her eyes twinkled with tenderness. "Get up, girl. Time to air these sheets." I could see both of her daughters in her. The no-nonsense personality, the pragmatism. She threw the blankets back, exposing me like a bug under a flipped rock. Like the bug, I tried to crawl back under.

"No, no," she said, taking me by the bony elbow and pulling me up. "It's the middle of summer. Go outside and get some fresh air." Her touch made me miss my mother.

"Yes, Mrs. Oversteegen," I said.

At this, she and Truus both laughed.

"I'm not your school principal," she said. "Call me Trijntje."

"Sorry," I said. "Trijntje." She was so vibrant with competency I would have followed any order she gave. She rested her hands on her hips. "Freddie's up on deck, waiting for you two," she said. She whacked me on the bottom with a soft feather pillow. "Now get out of here. Take in the sunshine." I shuffled into the living area. Just as I was about to ascend the ladder to the top deck, I felt Trijntje's hand on my arm.

"I'm sorry about your family and your friends, Hannie," she said in a gentle voice. "Very sorry."

A tidal wave began to roll inside me, and I knew if I spoke, I would weep. I nodded.

"Remember," Trijntje said, her eyes twinkling with hard-lived tenacity, "waar de wanhoop eindigt, begint de tactiek."

Where despair ends, tactics begin.

ON DECK I sat down between Truus and Freddie, in a daze. "Waar de wanhoop eindigt, begint de tactiek," I said.

Both sisters chuckled. "You've been talking to our mother," Truus said.

I smiled.

"She has a thousand little sayings," said Freddie.

"But they're all really the same thing," said Truus. She and Freddie looked at each other as if silently confirming what that was. "Keep going," said Truus.

Freddie considered it, then nodded. "That's basically it. Just keep going, no matter what."

"Hold on," I said. "I thought she said, 'Stay human.'"

"Yes," Freddie explained, "but that's the same thing." Her voice was so clear, so childlike. She was only seventeen. I was glad to see Freddie with us. I knew Hendrik had respected her; the background work she'd performed as scout and intelligence gatherer had been crucial to all our jobs. Freddie was a soldier. And here she sat in the summer sunlight, blond hair loose and drying in the sun, arching her back like a harmless kitten. Maybe that was how young and fresh I looked to people when I started in the RVV. I didn't look like that now.

Truus pushed a bread board toward us, arrayed with the usual unappetizing collection of whatever was available at the distribution center the previous day: thin gray toast tasting of wood pulp, spread with fake butter made of beetroot paste, with a chipped mug of watery beige tea to drink. At least it was hot. I sat on the bench and offered my pale face up to the sun, like Freddie. The flare behind my eyelids scoured my thoughts clean. Each time a wave of despair rolled through me, the sunlight blasted it away. And that's all I really craved: blankness.

"Your hair looks nice, Hannie," said Freddie sweetly.

"No, it doesn't," I said flatly, and we all laughed. I looked like a witch. "For God's sake, can I just drink my tea?" I said with mock irritation.

"Actually, it's just warm canal water," Freddie said, laughing again. I pretended to spit it out.

"Did you look at my bike yet?" Truus asked her sister.

"Yeah, it's fine. Just a loose bolt in the frame. I fixed yours while you were resting," Freddie said to me. "Repaired the wood on the front tire and realigned your brakes."

Was there nothing these Oversteegen women couldn't do? Just then Trijntje emerged from below deck and walked over to us, a bemused smile on her face. She was happy to have her daughters home. "Sunbathing, ladies?" Trijntje never sat down. Even as she paused on deck, her hands were at work, reaching to tauten the line of laundry flapping like sails across the deck. "You three can rest today, but soon it's back to the job, eh?"

I assumed the three of us were all thinking the same thing: Hendrik was dead; our cell was effectively dead, too. Who would provide us with missions now? Trijntje reached into the bosom of her blouse and pulled out a slip of paper, then handed it to Truus.

"That's her address," she said with a smile on her face.

"Whose?" asked Truus.

"Madame Sieval."

I looked to Truus and Freddie, but their faces were blank.

"It will take a while to get to her," said Trijntje, busying herself with the clothesline, "so you'd better start soon. In the meantime, you can make yourselves useful making some deliveries for me. There's plenty to be done."

Truus and Freddie smiled knowingly. *Where despair ends, tactics begin.*

Chapter 31

SHE NEVER LEAVES the house," Freddie said, shaking her head and slumping onto the chair across from me in the low-ceilinged below-deck kitchen. Truus and I had been waiting for Freddie to return from her final surveillance post for the notorious Madame Sieval, a Frenchwoman who had lived in Haarlem for years and was known for turning in neighbors and anyone else she suspected of being Jewish or harboring a Jew. She lived alone, as far as we knew, staying mostly indoors, and when she did go out, it was at irregular times and impossible to predict. "I think we should find a new target," said Freddie, shaking her blond braids.

In a poetic reversal, I was now a sort of onderduiker in the Oversteegens' home, though I refused to stay caged up on the houseboat. The three of us stole extra ration cards from an empty administrative building one night and distributed them to families in need, mostly to people hiding their Jewish friends and neighbors. Compared to what we'd been doing in the RVV, it wasn't the most exciting work, but Trijntje wouldn't listen to us whine about being bored. "This is resistance, too," she said, "and it's the way most people do it. You don't need guns and bombs to be a revolutionary. Caring for people is the most revolutionary work anyone can do."

IT WAS PROBABLY a good thing we were forced to scale back. The shock of losing Jan and my parents and Philine all at once had left me numb. I assumed that would make our violent work easier, a straightforward path of vengeance fueled by rage instead of fear. War made sense when it was a simple case of an eye for an eye.

But as pure as my vision for Resistance work was, my mind was heavy with sorrow. The only family I had now was Truus and Freddie, and I found myself following them around in a daze, depressed and numb. Truus was beginning to worry.

"What do you think, Hannie?" Truus was doing this more and more, prodding me to participate in my own life. "Should we give up on Sieval?"

"OK," I said, not quite tracking the conversation. I preferred to let Truus make the decisions these days, and just follow her lead. I didn't have the energy to imagine anything but the next step: get my satchel, check my gun, hide the gun in the satchel, ride my bike wherever Truus said. I was that kind of soldier now. Cannon fodder.

"Hannie!" she said, clapping her hands in front of my face as I stared into the middle distance.

"What?" I flinched.

"Come on, now, this is serious. What do you think of Freddie's assessment?"

"I'm not saying you have to give up on Sieval," said Freddie, who deferred to Truus in terms of managing me, "but I don't know how you're going to do it without breaking into her house. And if you do, I don't know what you'll find there."

"Maybe," said Truus. "Let's go by there today and see for ourselves. All right, Hannie?"

"Sure," I said. "Anybody have a smoke?"

"You should eat something," said Truus, who had been bugging me about my lack of appetite but gave me one anyway.

"I'm fine," I said, lighting up and coughing like a barking seal. I pounded my chest and shook it off. "I get all the vitamins I need from cigarettes." I laughed, but nobody joined in. I watched the smile slide off Truus's face. "What?" I asked, then followed her gaze to Trijntje, who was standing at the top of the stairs with a letter in her hand. I recognized the common stationery of the Resistance network: thrice-used scrap paper smuggled out of administrative offices, the only writing paper still available. The crinkles at the corners of Trijntje's blue eyes relaxed, no longer smiling.

"News, Hannie," she said, holding up the note, "from Brasser."

My feet were two anchors fixing me to the spot. If it were good news, she would have just burst out with it. I stayed still. "What is it?"

Trijntje smiled now, but it was a bloodless replica of her usual easy grin. "Your parents are alive, Hannie." I heard the words but held their meaning at a distance, waiting for the rest of it. I felt the eyes of all three women resting on me, looking for my reaction.

"And?" I asked. There had to be an *and*. Or a *but*.

"But they're being held in Herzogenbusch," she said calmly, "until you turn yourself in."

"Hannie!" Freddie ran toward me. I had no idea why until the next moment when I felt her small frame supporting me. My legs rippled like ribbons into a heap beneath me. "Hannie!" Freddie said, searching my eyes.

"I'm OK," I said in a high, thready voice. My ears rang and filled with static, as if I'd been standing too near a gun. Or been shot by one. My parents were alive . . . in Herzogenbusch, a Nazi concentration camp one hundred kilometers south of Haarlem, near the Dutch city of Vught. I sat where I'd fallen, grateful for the solidity of the wooden planking beneath me, until I began to sense the subtle shifting of the houseboat as it bobbed in the water . . . Nothing in this world was fixed or stable. My parents weren't dead and that was good news. But they were being held for ransom.

"I'm the ransom," I said softly, shaking my head. In four years of nightmares, I'd never envisioned this scenario. All the possible outcomes spooled out in my mind like fine silk threads, raveling into knots and fraying at the ends.

"Hannie?" said Truus. All three women now clustered around me, their faces tight with concern. "Let's go downstairs. We can take on Madame Sieval another day."

At the sound of her voice, my focus returned. Like a flashlight in the darkness, the name Madame Sieval illuminated the path forward. So, my parents were in a concentration camp? There was only one thing to do: keep going. The clarity of it was the closest thing I'd felt to joy in months. "No, we do it today," I said, looking Truus in the eye, my voice clear.

"Are you sure?" she asked, eyebrows raised. "If you need time—"

"I don't," I said, feeling the warm return of color to my cheeks and the shakiness of my joints evaporating. I clambered to my feet, helped again by Freddie. Everything was clear to me now. "If I turn myself in to the Germans," I said, looking to Trijntje for confirmation, "there's no guarantee it would help my parents." Trijntje nodded. "They might be dead already," I said. "Who knows exactly when Brasser wrote that note or how solid the information was?" She closed her eyes and nodded again. So that was it, then. There was nothing to do but keep going. No matter what.

MADAME SIEVAL LIVED on Twijnderslaan, a small street in between the Frederikspark and the Spaarne River in a relatively busy part of town.

Her house, like my parents', was made of brick and connected to the houses on either side. This made it difficult to approach without being seen. "Park your bikes here," said Freddie, who had spent entire days on the street, observing. We followed her into a skinny alleyway between two buildings on the corner. From there, we had a view of Sieval's front door. "I hope you brought a book, because it gets very boring around here," Freddie said.

"Got it," said Truus.

"You're welcome for all the priceless information, by the way," Freddie said.

"Thanks, kid," said Truus flippantly, and Freddie punched her in the shoulder. The ice in my heart melted a little bit, watching them.

"Hey, I know this street," Truus said, looking out from our hiding place. "Remember they used to have an ice house down there, Freddie?"

"Yeah," said Freddie, "I remember they used to chop up those huge blocks of ice out in front, for the big hotels," she said, smiling. "The ice chips would go flying and we'd run over there and gather them up and suck on them like candy." I could picture it, too. The shop was closed up now, but I remembered the purveyors with their wagons full of ice, insulated with hay, and the huge iron tongs they used to pick up each big block. I'd liked those ice chips, especially on a hot day.

"My God, Hannie," said Freddie, "you're smiling."

"Are we getting the old Hannie back?" Truus asked, a tender smile on her own face. She was worried about me, I knew.

I shrugged. The old Hannie was a naïve girl who was overconfident and believed she had some control over what happened in her life and the lives of others. The new Hannie understood that control was itself an illusion.

"Hannie?"

I didn't realize I'd scoffed out loud. "Sorry," I said.

Truus was still waiting for an answer.

"The old Hannie?" I repeated. I didn't want to argue with her. Too exhausting. "Sure," I said, gazing at the peeling paint on the ice store's sign, the wood curving with age. "I think the debris of the old Hannie is still lying around somewhere."

"We could use her," said Truus.

Useful was the last thing I felt at this point. But I was willing to show up and I knew she was trying to be nice. "I'm fine, Truus." I nodded toward Sieval's house. "Look." All three of us watched as a middle-aged man approached Sieval's front door and knocked. He wore normal street clothes, no military or police uniform. "It's not Fake Krist, is it?"

Fake Krist was a local policeman and a fanatical fascist even before war broke out. He'd been on our list at the RVV for months as a key target. Krist was named head of the Kriminalpolizei, or Kripo, as they were known, the Nazi SS Criminal Police, as soon as the occupation began. They were essentially the Nazi detective force. Krist was excellent at his job, known for his mass arrests of Jews and those sympathetic to them—as many as twenty-five ambushes in one evening. He arrested courageous rabbis and sympathetic pastors; he arrested terrified mothers and children. All were sent to Westerbork. He'd been a scourge since the war began, and citizen volunteers like Madame Sieval made his work possible. My fingers tightened around my pistol, already transferred to my pocket. Krist would be a very satisfying name to cross off our list.

"That's not Fake Krist," said Freddie flatly. "I've seen Krist—he's been by before, surrounded by security—and this is not him."

"Maybe he's an undercover cop?" I said, gripping my pistol again, hopefully.

"Relax, killer," Truus said, frowning at me. "We don't shoot anyone we can't identify."

"Yeah, yeah," I said. I was starting to feel awake for the first time in weeks.

"I think he's delivering something," said Freddie. The front door opened a sliver, and the man slipped an envelope through. The door shut and the man walked back down the street. "That's probably all the excitement we'll get today," said Freddie, "based on the past few weeks. I'm telling you, this woman knows she's being watched."

"We're all being watched," I said. "She's not special."

"Ha," said Truus. "There she is: old Hannie!"

I didn't argue. We made ourselves as comfortable as possible in the alley, leaning against the walls and smoking. This went on for the next few hours. The three of us took turns walking around the neighborhood, scouting for anything interesting. Nothing. So much of Resistance work was like this, seemingly pointless.

"I'm going to walk around the alley behind Sieval's," I said, finally. "She might not even be home." The girls nodded, and I took the long way around the block. Madame Sieval's backyard was entirely walled off, no way to spy on her unless I snuck through the back gate, a move ill-advised in broad daylight. I walked farther down the alley and came back out to Twijnderslaan a few houses up from Sieval's. By now it was mid-afternoon, and I was hungry, discouraged, and ready to leave. I glanced across the street to try to catch Truus's eye.

Just then the door to No. 46 rattled on its hinges. I backed up against the house next door and cocked my gun inside my pocket. I looked over at the sisters again: Truus and Freddie had heard it, too, and they crouched in the alleyway across the street, staring at me. I held my finger to my lips as we heard Madame Sieval's doorknob clunk and begin to turn. Truus steadied herself against the brick wall beside her and held her pistol pointed toward No. 46 from across the street. But I was just a few meters from the doorway; I would have the clear shot. Jan had always emphasized in my training that assassination was a job best performed at point-blank range. I wasn't a trained sniper, and our battered guns were not always accurate. But I was close enough. Truus and I locked eyes. She understood.

This was the first time I'd held my gun with the intention to use it since the day Jan and I shot Ragut. I'd wondered what this moment would be like—would I lose my nerve?—but I already felt energized in a way I hadn't since Ragut. I didn't need more food or more rest. I needed something fierce to do. Everything slipped away, the weeks of malaise and blankness. I found my focus. I pressed my back against the cool bricks of the building and held my pistol against my side, hidden from anyone who might walk by on the street. But there was nobody around. Conditions were perfect, as Jan used to say. Damn him.

We heard it at the same time: the brass thunk of a heavy lock being turned in the door of No. 46. Then the door started to move. Across the street Truus steadied herself, Freddie perched behind her. She had a gun, too, but in general Truus encouraged her little sister to stick to less violent actions, unless necessary. Jan had told me approvingly that Freddie had killed a Nazi when she was only fifteen.

The door began to inch open, creaking on its hinges. Truus raised her gun, looking down the sight as I did the same. We'd be firing from two different angles, each of us at one point of a triangle with Madame Sieval at the third. It was nice to not have to shoot from the seat of a moving bicycle. I felt steady, calm, prepared to complete the task.

I saw a hand on the doorknob. A woman's hand, the arm and wrist obscured by what looked like a fur coat—not something one saw on the streets every day. I forced myself to wait until more of her body was exposed, for a better target. And to make sure she wasn't surrounded by Kripo security officers. It would be suicide to try to attack them all.

In another moment, the upper part of Madame Sieval's body emerged from the doorway, her well-coiffed head swiveling, scanning the quiet street for danger. She looked to be in her early thirties, with a thin face and high, arched black eyebrows, her cheeks pale with powder. My center of gravity shifted as I leaned onto my front foot, locking my right arm for stability and bracing it with my left. *Wait, wait...* I made myself pause while the rest of her torso revealed itself: a bigger target. The door squeaked on its hinges as it opened a tiny bit wider, and I burst from my hiding place, running straight at her, arm and pistol outstretched. She was an easy shot in her ridiculous fur coat, this traitorous bitch who'd sent dozens of families to their almost certain death, and—and—she held a little girl by the hand.

I took two bounding steps and then reared back like a horse shying from a firecracker, whipping my head around to find Truus, who was also several steps into her charge across Twijnderslaan—but I wasn't sure she could see the little girl from her angle. Somehow in the final moments before we both squeezed our triggers, our gazes met and locked on each other, communicating something fundamental and profound. Something beyond language. We both whirled around, running in opposite directions, leaving Madame Sieval and her young charge standing in the doorway, breathless.

I ran blindly, trying to distance myself from the near disaster, skidding as the bricks slipped beneath the thin leather soles of my school shoes, sliding to the street and catching myself with one hand before rising again, still running. A little girl? Freddie had never mentioned children. I tore down the bustling boulevard of Kleine Houtweg at the intersection and wove myself into the crowd of shoppers gathered on the main street, jogging for blocks until I was sure no one was following me. Spotting the bridge at the Spaarne River, I headed for the towpath along the water and disappeared underneath the bridge, sinking to the muddy riverbank to breathe. A truck rumbled by overhead and the Spaarne splashed and my lungs rasped, terror running off my body in freezing perspiration. God. A little girl. I could still see her chubby pink hand as

Madame Sieval held it. I sank to my knees in the mud and wept, my body shaking with sobs, nose running, stomach muscles cramping as I doubled over, racked. A teenage boy walked by at one point, his face worried, but he left me alone and I was grateful. I wasn't the only one breaking into tears in public these days.

"Hey." I looked up at the sound of the soft voice. It was Freddie. A second later, Truus rolled up behind her.

"You OK?" I asked.

They nodded and Truus handed me a handkerchief.

"Thanks." Freddie patted me on the shoulder, and Truus helped me to my feet, and we stood there for a moment while I composed myself.

"Well, you gave Madame Sieval quite a scare," said Truus with a wan smile. "But it's fine. Nobody saw us." She looked me in the eyes.

"Who was the little girl?" I asked.

"I don't know," said Freddie, desperation in her voice as if afraid we wouldn't believe her. "I never saw her before."

"It's all right," I said, smoothing one of her braids aside to place my hand on her shoulder. She was, arguably, still a little girl herself. Truus handed me a cigarette without being asked, and I took it gratefully, then shared it with her. She took a drag and handed it to Freddie. We stood watching the Spaarne roll by until the cigarette was gone.

"Well," said Truus, "so much for Madame Sieval." I nodded. There was no hope of taking her by surprise again anytime soon. It was too bad; the thought of eliminating her had cheered me up. I sighed. "What?" she asked.

"I may not be a 'good' person," I said, "but at least I managed not to shoot a kid."

Truus smiled in understanding. "We're not Nazis."

"I guess that's something," I said, toasting her with her own handkerchief as I handed it back to her. "Thanks." She took it from me with a funny look on her face, thinking. Standing there, she smoothed it flat against her thigh, then folded it, dug around in her pocket, wrapped some string around it, and handed it back. "You keep it. A gift."

Two of the corners had been knotted to form hands and a length of twine was wrapped to form a head. It was a homemade doll. I'd never known Truus to take time for anything more frivolous than a cigarette. It took me a moment to understand. Tears wobbled at the edges of my eyelashes as I cradled the doll in my palm. *Stay human.*

Chapter 32

Late 1944

YOU'RE GUERRILLAS NOW," Trijntje informed us. Truus, Freddie, and I still thought of ourselves as RVV, but we weren't really a cell anymore. We briefly considered making contact with another Resistance group before deciding that we'd rather keep working on our own. Trijntje was aware of plenty of actions in need of our support, and she brought us information on potential targets. We operated as unofficial members of the official Resistance.

"Besides, we're girls," Freddie said one evening as we sat by the woodstove on the houseboat together, sorting through her mother's store of old clothing to see if anything could be salvaged or used to patch something else. "If we joined another group, they'd probably make us wash dishes or knit sweaters." None of us were willing to take that risk.

"This is better," Truus said. "We don't take orders from anybody. We choose our own missions. We stay out of sight."

"We don't rat out our friends," I said. At this point, I only trusted women named Oversteegen.

I was starting to feel more engaged with the world as the weeks passed. We all secretly hoped the Allies would liberate us by Christmas.

They'd arrived on the border of Belgium in September, and for a brief moment, the whole country unfurled its orange banners and actually danced in the streets . . . but it was just a rumor of peace and the Nazis shut it down the following day. Dolle Dinsdag, we called it. Crazy Tuesday. The Allied soldiers stopped at the Rhine and hadn't moved since. We all felt a little crazy after that.

It hadn't occurred to anyone that only half the country would be liberated. Those of us in the occupied zone felt even more isolated as we watched the Germans around us fortify their defenses.

Starvation anxiety began to spread through the population like an infection, turning once-generous neighbors into hoarders. As the weather grew colder, we saw fewer people on the streets. They were hibernating in their houses and apartments, living on rations and trying not to expend energy they didn't have. One night, Trijntje surprised us with three cookies she'd found somewhere, and the four of us split the cookies and a boiled potato for dinner. For me, going to bed hungry every night was its own kind of fuel. I couldn't personally import more food to our little country, but I could keep killing Nazis. I didn't mind saying it that way now. As Hendrik used to point out, every Nazi we took out saved a dozen Dutchmen. Even if it was just one, it was enough for me to feel good about it.

"You finally have some pink in your cheeks," Trijntje said one morning as I helped her fold laundry. "You're coming back to life."

"There's even more to do now," I said, "since the soldiers are taking the winter off." After intense fighting on the beaches of Normandy in June, a thrilling crush of Allied forces had been slowly, brutally grinding their way northward to Germany throughout the autumn. They called their grinding route through northern France, Belgium, and into south Holland Hell's Highway. But just as winter set in, the highway ended. A mere one hundred kilometers south of Amsterdam, they were stopped by the German army at Arnhem Bridge. The Allied soldiers were dug in for the winter, huddled and miserable, sniping at the Germans at every opportunity. Just like the rest of us.

Trijntje was more compassionate. "Who can fight in this cold?" It was an unusually bitter winter already. She shook her head. "The Germans will make it harder for us."

"Everyone knows the Krauts have terrible morale; they almost assassinated Hitler last summer." The prospect excited me. "Maybe they'll back down if we make them miserable enough."

Trijntje looked at me with a combination of motherly love and a lifelong radical's understanding of the way things really were. "Yes, I remember," she said. Only the Resistance newspapers ran the story, and we'd hoarded every scrap of information we could find about the assassination attempt. The bomb had gone off, but somehow Hitler was unhurt. According to official Nazi Party news, it never happened. "Yes, well," she said, "did you also hear that a few days ago the Nazi high command executed five thousand civilians as retribution?"

"No," I said. Five thousand was . . . insane. How did you murder five thousand people? All I could imagine was an earthquake or a tidal wave. A force of nature, not man.

"Mmm," said Trijntje, eyes focused on folding her dish towel, "five thousand. They were just waiting for an excuse, eh?" Her mouth twisted in disgust. "You think the animals who did that are going to just surrender and hope for the best? They'll try to kill every last Dutchman before they leave this country. You watch."

Trijntje rarely allowed her emotional temperature to rise above a light simmer, so her harsh comments worried me. None of us talked about it, but I, at least, was constantly wondering: What had happened to my parents and Philine? To Sonja? And if the Germans were growing more vicious, how would it affect them? Had it already?

"You all right, Hannie?" Trijntje smiled at me, searching my face. "Go on and find the girls and do something useful. It will make you feel better."

———

"You should do Hertz first," Freddie said. "He's awful. And I don't think he has any idea he's a target." As we walked down an empty street near the old RVV apartment, she grabbed for a strip of a Nazi propaganda poster on the brick wall and tore off a long ribbon. The poster sagged and then dropped to the pavement. An act of resistance.

"Let's do it tonight," I said, looking to Truus.

"What, you think some other Resistance group is going to get to him first?" She laughed.

"Maybe," I said.

"If they do, so what? One less Nazi."

"But we could do it right now." Just the thought of it got me excited.

"How about we do it right?" Truus was getting annoyed by my fervor for the fight, not to mention my appetite for violence. "You're not the only one fighting this war, you know." She looked troubled. It was the same lecture Hendrik used to give Jan: *Slow down.*

"I'll scout it tomorrow," Freddie said.

"Fine," we both said.

After a week of Freddie's spying, Truus finally relented. "We'll go tonight," she said. "Be ready by five." I was thrilled.

An hour before we were to leave, I began constructing my costume for the evening. The Germans were still looking for the Girl with Red Hair, but fortunately my hair was holding its black dye. I was more careful about my disguise when I was out in public now, making sure not only my hair was right but also my outfit and makeup, taking the time to darken my eyebrows and lashes with the satin pouch of makeup Sonja had left behind. I enjoyed the transformation now, from the powder puff to the red lipstick. The blue dress still fit loosely, so I wore that and found a pair of outmoded patent leather heels from Trijntje's trunk of castoffs that looked as if they'd been there since the 1920s. Peering at my reflection, I noticed faded bloodstains on the bodice and skirt, but they passed for everyday filth. Nobody actually looked nice anymore, and all our clothing was worn to threads. Even with its disquieting brown blotches, it remained my prettiest dress.

"Jesus, Hannie, are you ready yet?" Truus slung herself around the doorway and watched me make myself up. It was nearly five o'clock. She approved of me wearing a disguise—she demanded it—but she had a low tolerance for vanity. I knew it and I didn't care. Vanity made me feel strong. I thought of the phrase I'd seen once in a children's book about cowboys and Indians: *war paint*.

"Almost," I said, stroking the delicate wand of mascara out to the tips of my strawberry-blond eyelashes.

"We're going to be late. And if we're too late, we'll have to—"

"Truus!" My hand wobbled and I tried not to blink. I was still an amateur at this. "Give me a minute."

She grunted. "You're procrastinating."

"No, I'm not. This is probably the most difficult thing I'll do all night."

"Yeah," she said, laughing, "I can tell. Come on."

I admired Truus's pragmatism, but sometimes it drove me crazy; everything was black and white. "Look, Truus, we could die out there tonight, yes? So just give me one more second to do this right," I said. I didn't want to try to explain to her what I was doing because she wouldn't understand. I finished my right eye and pushed the lashes up with my fingertips to give them some curl, something I'd learned from watching Sonja, back in her Amsterdam bedroom.

"You look fine," she said.

"Just fine?" I teased, swiveling around to reveal the glory of my handiwork. "If I have to die tonight, Truus, I'm going to die beautiful." I winked, and the wet mascara sealed my eye shut. "Damn it."

"Ha!" Truus laughed at me. "Don't die now; we're leaving in five minutes."

TRUUS AND FREDDIE and I rode our bikes the roundabout way to avoid checkpoints and arrived down the street from Officer Hertz's house just before curfew. It was already dark outside, and our breath was white in the damp, freezing air. We were cold all the time now, but at least the piles of trash on every corner didn't smell so bad.

Hertz's life was boring and predictable. We knew all his moves; they were always the same. He came straight home after work and went back in the morning. The only potential complication was his Dutch girl-friend. Sometimes she was at his house and sometimes she wasn't. Truus and I took about five minutes to discuss it before deciding we'd shoot her, too, if necessary. Another backstabber.

Truus looked across the street and gave a sharp nod. "It's clear. Fred-die just gave the signal." I looked for Freddie, but she was invisible. Our secret weapon. Truus and I began walking down the block toward the gabled brick house Hertz had stolen from some unfortunate Haarlem family. We made a point of talking softly to each other like normal young ladies, friends just out to get some fresh air before curfew.

"That's it," Truus said. Solid and stout like all the other houses on the block, this one radiated something menacing now that we knew who was in it.

"You do the talking," Truus said, "now that you did all this." She ges-tured at my painted face. "You look pretty. He'll like that."

"How do you know?" I said.

"Don't all men?"

She had a point.

I knocked on the door. This was not a stealth operation, and that was part of its strength. Nobody expected an assassin to politely knock on the door. I heard the deep voice of a man and then the higher register of a woman's voice. Someone peered through the little window first, then unlocked it, and a woman poked her head out.

"Wie bent u?" Who are you?

The sound of her Dutch voice gave me chills. She was attractive in a bombshell way: blond hair, blue eyes, big bosom. She couldn't have been more than a few years older than me, I realized. Our childhoods couldn't have been that different. Same town, same country. She might have gone to the same school I did. Was she thrilled to see Hitler take over the country, or had she just made a series of small decisions that led up to cohabitating with a Nazi? I realized I didn't care, because it didn't matter. Here she was.

"Wat wilt u?" she asked again. What do you want?

She looked conspicuously well-fed. Flushed, plump cheeks. Full breasts pushing against her soft, clean sweater with no moth holes or burn marks or unraveling sleeves. Any residual smidge of sympathy I may have had now melted into air.

"Ja, hello," I said in a bright, brisk voice. "We were sent with a message for Officer Hertz. It's regarding the food transports from Friesland." This was a line we used a lot in the RVV. Hendrik said it was specific enough to sound legitimate but vague enough to pass off as a misunderstanding. I waited for a response.

The blonde paused, and I felt a tingle of suspense down my spine. She glanced at Truus and then gave me a thorough looking over, lingering finally on my face. It wasn't a look of recognition. It was, *Who is this dressed-up woman asking after my boyfriend?*

She sniffed. "Een momentje," she said and then shut the door.

Truus elbowed me, excited. So far, so good. We heard the two voices again, now speaking in German.

"What's he saying?" Truus asked.

"Something about not wanting to be bothered after work, I think."

We were about to find out.

Thudding heavy footsteps came toward the door. It opened again. A large man, about six feet tall, with the jowly face of a mastiff. His expression changed from irritation to obnoxious curiosity at the sight of us. I wondered if his girlfriend was still in the hallway.

The door opened inward, and he had to step back to accommodate something I hadn't seen for a long time: a big, round belly. The brass glint of his belt buckle was barely visible under his ballooning gut. He was actually wiping a morsel of food from his lips as he began to speak. Our food. Anything they were eating in here was stolen from the Dutch people. My mouth watered, despite myself. I gripped my pistol, still tucked in my coat pocket.

"Ja?" he said, his voice gruff, if teasing. A man used to getting his way. "What is this message that's so important I have to miss my supper?"

I registered the slightest movement from Truus, and in an instant our two pistols were in his face. Just as I squeezed my trigger, I saw a spark of recognition in his watery eyes: *So this is how.*

We fired in tandem, both of us aiming for the head. BLAM. BLAM.

I spun and ducked to avoid the spray and ran to my bike. Truus ran to hers. Everything was calm for a moment and then I heard a shriek.

"Help! Somebody!" she screamed. Truus and I took off in opposite directions. The woman's voice disappeared behind us.

Ten minutes later, we stood at the edge of the nearby Spaarne River. It was smooth as black silk in the evening darkness and so quiet, all I could hear was the pounding of my heart. I felt dizzy, but that happened a lot these days.

"You all right?" Freddie popped her head out from behind a tree. We nodded. "Good," Freddie said, and dropped herself onto the damp grass. She pointed at Truus's sweater, where dark splotches mottled the weave on her shoulder. Freddie gestured to her to wipe it off, but she ignored it, staring at me instead. Was I one of those people who had a terrible injury but didn't realize it? I'd seen a man like that once in Amsterdam, just walking down the sidewalk, calm as anything, while the left side of his scalp, including his ear, drooped toward his shoulder like a wet rag. He appeared to be unaware. Truus stepped toward me, licked the pad of her thumb, and pressed it in the hollow just above my lip and under my nose, smearing something away in a gesture that was somehow rough and tender at the same time.

"Blood mustache," she said. "It's ruining your makeup." A smile curled at the edge of her mouth. "Now you're cute again."

"Thanks," I said, checking my lipstick in a cracked compact mirror. "Truus?" I asked.

"Yes?"

"Am I imagining it, or did you say 'Murderer!' when we, you know…" *Shot him.*

"I figured it was a courtesy." She looked out at the canal and her smile dissolved. "I wanted him to know why."

"He knew," said Freddie.

"Well, now his girlfriend does, too," said Truus.

I wouldn't say the three of us were happy at that moment, exactly. But we were content. We stood in silence, watching the water slide by. All the trees that once lined the banks had been cut for firewood and now the procession of stumps looked like a series of stepping-stones, leading to the sea. The frozen landscape was beautiful but bleak.

Freddie spoke. "Hannie?"

"Yes?"

"I can see your roots. I meant to tell you earlier today."

"OK," I said. I rarely looked in the mirror, so I appreciated the information. "I'll take care of it." We stood there, thinking, smoking.

"What do you think will happen," Freddie said, still staring out at the water, "after the war?"

"Parades?" said Truus. "And hopefully some food."

"No, I mean to us? What will happen to us?"

Truus looked at her little sister. "What do you mean?"

"Well, will we just go back to our normal lives? School and all that?" It was so easy to forget that Freddie hadn't even finished high school yet.

"I don't think it will be normal," Truus said. "But it will be good. You'll get a medal. For bravery and loyalty to your country." She touched Freddie's shoulder. "You'll be the youngest to receive one, I bet."

"If I get one, the two of you will get them for sure," said Freddie. "They'll have a parade for all three of us. The Girls of the RVV."

"We'll stand up there next to the queen," said Truus with a little laugh. "Wearing our medals, waving to our adoring fans." Freddie laughed at that. "What do you think, Hannie?" Truus looked at me.

The conversation made me uncomfortable. I didn't know what to say. I didn't trust myself to speak.

"The Girl with Red Hair!" Freddie roared in a whispered mock cheer. "You'll be a hero for sure."

I shook my head.

"Don't tell me you're going to go back and become a boring lawyer after all this?" Freddie asked.

I smiled. "No, I don't think so," I said. I had an answer for them, but I didn't want to scare Freddie. "A stuffy old lawyer? That probably isn't possible anymore," I said. They laughed.

I didn't tell them that when I tried to envision life after the war, I saw the flags and the fanfare, I saw the queen, and I even saw Truus and Freddie. But I wasn't with them.

Chapter 33

Winter 1944

T RIJNTJE'S KITCHEN HAD two stoves. One was the traditional cast-iron stove that used to stay warm all day, heating the house and cooking food for meals. That one was now relegated to once-daily use to warm the living quarters, as coal and wood were in such scarce supply. We waited until frost grew on the insides of the windows before burning any of our precious fuel, bits of lumber scavenged from demolished buildings or washed up on the banks of the canal and left to dry on deck in the thin winter sun. For cooking, we used a kind of camp stove rigged up by the resourceful Freddie, just a large tin can that could be heated with cooking fuel, if available, but more commonly by a hoard of old ledger books she'd discovered at an abandoned office building, years of handwritten numbers and equations dissolving into smoke to warm our sparse meals.

"Mmm, hot chocolate," said Truus, inhaling the vapor of the steaming, plain hot water in her cup. Freddie closed her eyes and imagined it, too. "I'd like a bit more whipped cream in mine, thanks," she said with a smile on her drawn face. With her heart-shaped face and almond eyes, Freddie had always resembled a little wood nymph, but even more now since her chin was pointed, her cheekbones severe, the curve of her girlish cheeks flattened by malnutrition. Fantasizing about what we'd rather be eating took up a large part of our free time.

"Poffertjes," said Truus. "God, I could eat a whole pan of them." We all licked our lips thinking of the puffy little buckwheat pancakes that were typically available from street vendors all over the city this time of year and served with sugar and jam . . . but not this year. "Pannenkoeken," I offered, "with apples and syrup," and the sisters nodded vigorously, imagining the thin, delicate crepes. "Yum," Freddie said, then erupted into a coughing fit. Truus and I shared a look over her bowed head: Freddie coughed all the time now. Then again, most people did.

Trijntje stood by the sink, preparing sugar beets for the evening's meal, a long process of slicing, shredding, boiling, sometimes fermenting the tough white root into a pulpy substance that could, with the help of an onion and some spices, be considered food. "Hunger sweetens even raw beans," she said. My mother used to say the same thing. "It could be worse," she continued. "These could be tulip bulbs."

"Come on," said Truus, but she was serious.

"No, it's true," she said. "Mrs. Hondius says she made a stew of them the other night and they were quite good with a bit of curry. But she advised against crocuses. Too fibrous." She shook her head at the thought and slipped her thumb into her mouth to cram a clove into the molar that had been giving her pain for weeks. Even finding a clove was a struggle these days.

Truus and Freddie and I looked at each other, and Freddie shrugged, wiping her mouth after the coughing fit. "I saw a boy chewing on grass yesterday by the canal," she offered.

"Don't do that," said Trijntje. "Gives you a stomachache."

"Don't worry, I'll never be that hungry."

"Come on, now," I said, trying to do my part for the group's morale, lifting my steaming cup as if proposing a toast. "What are we doing next?"

Truus propped her feet up on a chair and looked in no hurry to move on. "Maybe we should wait to see if they do the Christmas raids first."

The Christmas raids. All sorts of rumors had been passing through the Resistance network, plots we heard about through Trijntje. It was all Aktion Silbertanne stuff: roundups of "troublemakers" (transients, Gypsies, homosexuals, anybody they didn't like the look of), increased harassment at checkpoints, talk about mass arrests of onderduikers sometime during the winter holidays. But how was it really different from any other moment in the past four years? I'd always appreciated Truus's sense of caution, but I was finding it difficult to care as much as she did about Silbertanne's threats. So they would meet our violence with their violence? That was nothing new. Having a mission—someone to track and take down, even a package of ration stamps to deliver to a waiting family—helped distract me from the endless, aching, thudding monotony of chronic hunger.

TRUUS SHOOK ME awake the next morning before the sun was up. "Come on," she said.

It was unlike her, or any of us, to wake up early these days. We stayed in bed as long as possible both to stay warm and to reserve our energy. "Where are we going?"

"Just get up," she said. "I'll give you a ride."

I climbed on the back of her bicycle and wrapped my arms around her body, resting my head against her back.

"This better be worth it," I said, trying to clear the cobwebs from my head in the morning winter gloom. Mornings were dark in winter. Everything was, except the white snow.

We rode for ten minutes before she stopped.

"Over there," she said. "Stay on the bike."

We'd arrived in a typical residential Haarlem neighborhood, mostly apartments and single homes for young families. It was around six in the morning and the streets were empty. The Germans only allowed two hours of gas for heating per day now, so people were indoors waiting for the day to get warmer before venturing out. Yet across the street, a crush of two dozen people bunched in family groups and shivered, wrapped in coats and blankets, outside a row of eight small houses. Some of the people were barefoot. Wehrmacht soldiers herded them together, their long guns at attention.

"What's going on?"

"Freddie heard there might be some kind of payback this morning. Silbertanne."

I felt my hands start to tingle and held Truus harder, telling myself it was just to stay warm. We all knew about the retributions. But I'd never seen it with my own eyes. Vague panic buzzed in my brain, a novelty these days. But there was nothing to do.

Guttural shouts pierced the quiet morning air. A group of German soldiers marched toward the eight little houses and their evicted tenants. The soldiers' rifles were flattened against their backs; they'd swapped them for flaming torches and cans of kerosene. In a matter of seconds, each tiny house was ablaze, orange flames leaping into the gray morning air and shimmering waves of heat coming off the structures as the soldiers doused the rear of the houses with more fuel.

The huddled people gathered closer together, some of them sobbing. Children wailed. A commander shouted and the crying quieted. I watched as a neighbor down the street peeked out his front door to see what was happening. As soon as he saw the soldiers, he ducked back inside, but they had seen him, too, and marched to his door, dragging him outside in his socks to witness the spectacle.

"Fuckers," said Truus.

"Why these poor people?" I said.

"No reason. Totally random. They just want to make someone pay."

Truus spit on the ground, and her body vibrated with tension beside me. These people were paying for what we did. Or tried to do. And had been doing for the past two years.

Another bystander turned onto the street and stopped when he saw the commotion. The soldiers rushed to him, too, standing him next to the neighbor in socks. Making as many people witness it as possible. Using their rifles, the soldiers separated the men from the women. Then the children from their mothers. At this, the women began to shriek and fight, and the soldiers descended on the mothers with batons and fists. The men strained to help their wives and children, but soldiers held them at gunpoint.

"Put the women in the van," said the Kommandant, and the soldiers wrestled the women into the back of one of their infamous transport vans, pushing the doors shut behind the women and locking them in. From the two small windows in the back, women's faces pressed against the glass, still screaming. The sides of the van thundered with their pounding.

"Bring him out," said the Kommandant, gesturing at a brown-haired man in a flannel dressing gown. He looked about thirty. The Kommandant turned to the group of children, ranging in age from toddlers to teenagers. "Which of these are yours?"

The man began shaking and his face went slack. "No," he said.

"Tell me or I'll shoot them all," the Kommandant said in a reasonable voice.

"No," the man said again.

The banging inside the van grew louder, like timpani in an orchestra. "No."

"Very well," said the Kommandant, and raised his pistol with a straight arm, squinting one eye.

"Wait!" the man said, struggling to get free of the soldiers holding him back. "Daniel! Maria!" he screamed, the terrible sound of a helpless parent.

Two children were pushed out of the group by a soldier. Daniel was a scrawny boy of perhaps thirteen. Maria looked a few years younger. Both were shaking, their teeth chattering in the freezing air, eyes bright with fear. "Go to your father," the Kommandant said, and the children rushed to the man's side, weeping. The soldiers let go of him, and he took the children in his arms, kneeling down on the sidewalk to hold them close.

As he did, the soldiers began backing away. The heat coming off the burning houses blew toward them, lifting the threesome's thin clothes and their hair like a summer breeze. When the soldiers were a few feet away, the Kommandant spoke again.

"Fire."

The soldiers raised their guns and shot at the father and his two children, reducing them to a pile of bloody corpses in seconds.

Rage rocked the van on its wheels. The group of men on the sidewalk fought to break free, and I saw a soldier beat one of the husbands with the butt of his rifle until his face was dripping red. The remaining children screamed and sobbed.

"Next," the Kommandant said, and a soldier pushed another man forward. As each man approached, he struggled, trying to decide what to do. Name his children? Name someone else's? The sounds from inside the van were like something from the lowest depths of hell. It didn't matter what the men did; everyone was getting shot one way or another. Finally there was only one man and two children left, a boy about seven, a girl a few years older. Brother and sister. They stood frozen in place, not even crying anymore. Stunned. The Kommandant walked toward them.

"Is that your father?" he asked in a mild voice.

The older girl nodded.

"Bring him over."

The man rushed to his children but kept an eye on the Kommandant and the soldiers the whole time, terrified, placing his body in between the guns and his children.

"Shh," the Kommandant said as the little boy began to whimper. "Don't cry, little one. I need you to do a very special job. Can you do that for me?"

The boy shivered. The inside legs of his pants darkened with urine.

"I need you to tell your father and your mother—and your sister, this big girl here—that they must work to protect this country, eh? To keep it free of vermin, Gypsies, Jews, Jew-lovers, resisters, and anyone who would stand in the way of progress. That's not so difficult to do, is it?"

The boy was silent. Everyone was. Even the mothers in the van.

The Kommandant looked up. "That's our message, eh?" He looked at the two latecomers on the sidewalk who'd been selected as witnesses. Their faces were tear-streaked and red with rage.

"Tell your friends," the Kommandant said to the two men. "We didn't kill these people. The Jews hiding in your closets did. The Jew-lovers who think these vermin deserve more than you upstanding Dutchmen. The Resistance, cowards in the shadows, they did this to you. We are merely trying to keep the peace."

He turned on his heel toward the man and his children. They flinched.

"Easy, easy," he said. He reached into the breast pocket of his uniform and pulled out two cellophane-wrapped candies, tossing them to the boy and the girl, who let the candies fall at their feet. "Sorry, Papa," he said to the father. "Only for the children." He nodded to his soldiers, and they returned to formation, neat lines of three.

"Auf Wiedersehen," he called out as he got into the front of the van, where the pounding resumed. He shot his arm out in salute. "Heil Hitler."

"Heil Hitler," the soldiers shouted.

The van with the women inside rumbled away, swaying on its chassis with the trauma of the anguished women trapped inside. The two witnesses ran to the man and his children, still kneeling on the sidewalk.

When the van rounded the corner, the boy and girl reached for their candies and shoved them in their mouths. They were starving.

"Hold the bike," Truus said. I caught the handlebars, and she ran to the side of the building, puking into a pile of trash on the sidewalk. She stood bent in half, her elbows on her knees, dry-heaving. Not enough food in her to come back up. She wiped her mouth on her sleeve and looked back at me, as if expecting me to join her.

But I just stood holding the handlebars with my shaking hands, feeling blank as a bank of snow. Did I regret the attack on Hertz? No. I still hated that criminal. Hertz, Faber, and Kohl? No, I did not. Did I feel guilty for doing work that caused the deaths of innocent people like the ones suffering before me? No. And, sometimes, yes. It was evil and senseless.

But so was everything else.

I watched the houses burn. The street must have once been a pretty, elm-lined neighborhood. Now not only was every towering shade tree chopped down to its roots for firewood, so were quite a few of the houses. Jews had lived there, probably, and now that they were gone, not only their furniture but also every floorboard, beam, joist, and banister had been stripped for fuel. Like the rest of us, these houses wouldn't last the winter. The city itself was dying.

"Maybe we shouldn't have come," Truus said.

"No," I said. "It's good we came." The words slipped from my lips like a confession. "We're the audience they hoped for."

"Fuck them," said Truus, maneuvering the bike out of the alcove.

"Stop," I said. "Listen."

Around the corner where the van had disappeared, we now heard it again. Coming back. We pressed ourselves into the hiding place. The van stopped in front of the man and his children and a woman was pushed out. She ran to join them, sobbing. Grabbing the hands of her children, she started running down the street and away from the fire, her husband following right behind.

The Kommandant stepped out of the front of the van, planted his legs wide, and took aim at the staggering quartet with the calmness of target practice. BLAM. The mother dropped to the sidewalk. Her children collapsed on top of her, wailing and trying to revive her. The father, too. BLAM. The Kommandant braced his pistol with both hands. BLAM. BLAM. BLAM. All movement stopped. The inside of the van was silent. The Kommandant nodded to the soldier, got back in the van, and drove away. The two witnesses sagged against each other, watching it go.

Truus stood with her hand over her mouth. "Hannie," she said.

My fingers curled tight around the handkerchief doll she'd given me, flattened into my palm. "Truus."

Her face was pale as ice. Tears began to roll down her freckled cheeks.

"We can't stop, Truus," I said, reaching for her hand. "They won't."

Chapter 34

21 March 1945

THE AKTION SILBERTANNE massacre hung over us like a lead quilt, weighing on us as intended. Freddie brought me a wormy crab apple to cheer me up, carving out the disgusting bits. I wasn't sad, exactly. Just numb. Even the German soldiers, who were surviving on food stolen from Allied airdrops, seemed to have lost some of their ferocity. Did I still wonder about my parents, Philine, Sonja? Of course. But I was so tired.

There was good news in other parts of Europe, Allied soldiers marching into Dutch cities and villages to the south of us, driving the Nazis out in prison trucks. But not here. Here, every day the air grew colder, the rations smaller, and the killings and kidnappings of citizens more numerous than the day before. We called it the Hunger Winter.

Many thought the occupation would end any day now. But what would the end of war even mean? Food, maybe? I didn't have the energy to imagine it.

Freddie and Truus gave me another talking-to, telling me I needed to stay active, keep myself distracted.

"Fine," I said. "I'll do anything. Who's the target?"

"No target," Truus said. She didn't trust me with one of our regular jobs, not in my state. "Deliver some papers, why don't you?"

"Sure." So the next afternoon I got on my bike and rode to the drop-off point to find the stack of underground newspapers to deliver. Good old *De Waarheid. The Truth.* I shoved the papers in my satchel and continued on my way. I'd done these deliveries a thousand times and Truus was right; it was good work to do. I gulped a few lungfuls of fresh air. Deliveries. Just like in the old days, working for Nurse Dekker. What seemed like a century ago was less than three years.

OUTSIDE IT WAS chilly, but a teasing hint of springtime gave the afternoon a welcome freshness. The angled rays of sunlight zigzagging through the buildings alongside the canal felt warmer, more powerful today than the day before. Swallows knifed through the air, skimming the surface of the water and looping up again in joyful arcs. It was a relief to see that not every living thing was miserable. I walked my bike instead of riding it, just to watch them fly.

The Jan Gijzen canal was wide and flat. A few boats rippled past, but it was otherwise placid. The rumblings of military trucks in the distance. Seagulls.

Then a dog barked. You didn't see many around these days. I followed the sound and saw a small black-and-white mutt, shaggy as a mop, standing on the roof of a houseboat moored near the foot of the Jan Gijzen Bridge. The dog, like the birds, didn't know he was at war.

"Koest, koest," a woman's voice said. Hush. The cabin door creaked open, and a woman my mother's age pushed the door wide and emerged backward, pulling something outside with her. A wizened older woman—her own mother, presumably—wrapped in homemade quilts and seated on a cane chair like a bundle of kindling. The daughter gave the chair one last heave, and it popped out of the narrow cabin doorway, and the two women almost ended up in a pile together on the deck of the boat, but somehow the daughter righted the rickety chair at the last moment and they were fine, wobbling and laughing at themselves. The older woman lifted her face to the waning sunlight as if emerging from a long hibernation, an old gray bear. The daughter arranged her mother, facing her into the sun. The dog jumped from the roof of the cabin down to the deck, then into to the lap of the mother, who cuddled him like a baby doll. He squirmed, his tail wagged. He licked her face. "Oh, Ralf!" she said, laughing.

I laughed. The sound of it startled me.

I was walking parallel to the houseboat now and, hearing me, the daughter and mother waved hello. The little dog barked at me, and we all laughed. I waved back. Ralf barked again. The daughter disappeared back into the cabin. The mother leaned back in her wicker throne. I couldn't stop watching them, fascinated by this exotic normalcy.

The daughter emerged from the cabin again, this time holding two cups of tea. Was it always just the three of them, a daughter, a mother, and a dog, or was there once a husband, a father, a son? How had they survived the dwindling food, the freezing winter, the leaks in the boat?

"Excuse me, miss, are you . . . ?"

I was staring so intently at the two women I'd steered my bike into the sandbags on the edge of the ramp leading to the bridge.

"Sorry," I said to the line of people already queued, waiting to pass through the checkpoint. There was one on every bridge now. I backed my bike up and walked it around to the end of the line, behind a dozen others. It was a slow process as the soldiers at the front demanded paperwork, pretended to inspect it, offered some kind of obligatory rude remark, then moved on to the next citizen. I pushed my fake glasses up my nose and pulled my scarf down tighter around my head. *Sigh.* I still hated waiting in line.

The dog barked again, and those of us at the back of the line watched as the daughter found a stick and then threw it into the canal. The little dog ran to the roof of the cabin and launched himself into the water, swimming back with the stick in his teeth, a wide, fanged grin. Everyone in the line laughed and the guard at the front looked our way.

The game of fetch continued, the dog delighted to dive into the frigid water, the mother and daughter praising him each time he returned, then laughing and shooing him away every time he shook his coat off at their feet."

"Was ist los?" The guard stepped away from his station and walked down the line to get a view of the canal. On the boat, the women, oblivious, continued throwing the stick. Those of us in line went silent. I heard the splash of the dog jumping into the water again.

Then we saw the guard signaling to three soldiers loitering on the bridge. The guard shouted orders at them. The soldiers walked to the middle of the bridge and positioned themselves along the side closest to the houseboat and the mother and daughter and the dog. The soldiers knelt down simultaneously and rested the barrels of their rifles on the low stone walls at the side. I heard the gasps of people behind me before I realized what was happening.

BLAM BLAM BLAM.

Then laughter from the soldiers.

They were shooting at the dog in the water.

BLAM BLAM BLAM.

Sounds of anger and disgust erupted around me as we all watched the soldiers try to hit the little dog as he swam, bullets hissing by his wet head poking above the surface, eyes white with fear. The beginnings of shouts formed in our throats and were promptly swallowed, the fury folded in on itself and absorbed back into the body. I could feel it in the pit of my stomach. Acid.

I saw the faces of the people around me twist with disgust, then resolve into masks of muted rage. Finally, a little boy standing behind me burst into gulping sobs. The crowd channeled our emotions into him even as his mother tried to muffle the sounds, wrapping the boy in her coat so the Germans wouldn't get irritated. They'd shoot at anything.

Two men and a boy at the other end of the line made a break for it, leaving their place in line and running away from the bridge and back the way they came. Better to cross somewhere else or give up on crossing at all today. Leaving the line was tricky, as it made you look suspicious; the soldiers sometimes ran after you. But they ignored the men and the boy. Deep breaths moved up and down the queue, a breeze of relief.

As I stood there, I was finding it more and more difficult to breathe. Five years in, Nazi occupation had succeeded in taking control of every aspect of our lives, from the food we ate to the newspapers we read to the educations we abandoned. Yet what I saw in this queue was the beginning of the end. Because if the Nazis succeeded at controlling our inner lives, dictating our feelings, our human responses to cruelty, injustice, and greed . . . even if they lost the war, they would win. Look at the way we were all standing here pretending it was normal for three grown men to shoot at a harmless little dog.

It was not normal. It shouldn't be.

The mother and daughter on the boat were still screaming at the soldiers to stop, furious, their faces bright with anger. The guard in charge walked to the edge and the women went quiet. The dog was still paddling, his splashing paws and high-pitched whine the loudest sounds now. We all stared at the soldiers. Surely they were finished with this exercise. But the guard nodded, and they fired again. A bright dog-yelp pierced the air, and we all looked down to see the dog still paddling, but slower now, and in circles.

"Stop," I heard myself say.

The people standing near me nodded and murmured affirmatively even as they instinctively moved away from me: *She's not with us.*

The soldiers stopped shooting and the guard frowned. The rest of the people filed back into an orderly line. But not me. I was stuck to the spot, a few footsteps outside the queue, watching the daughter run to the shore, wade into the black water, and pull the little black-and-white dog out. He was shaking, dripping wet, and looked like a mink, slick and skinny. A trickle of red blood ran down the front of the woman's shirt where she had him pressed against her, and the little dog yelped and licked her face, his entire body wiggling. He was jostled as the woman and her son behind me tugged me toward the line. I was going to lose my place. I looked up, and that's when I saw her there, across the street, on my side of the bridge. Truus.

Our eyes met, and she waved frantically, as if she'd been trying to get my attention for some time. I raised my hand to acknowledge her and held up a finger to let her know it would take me a minute to get to her; then I started to turn my bike around. They hadn't stopped the two men and the boy.

"Fräulein?"

It was the guard in charge. He walked toward me, his features delineating as he approached. A cleft in his chin made it harder to shave there. Stubble. Eyes the color of a dirty puddle. Thin, his shoulders pointed inward. I'd assumed he was old, but he was perhaps twenty-four. My age.

"Entschuldigen Sie, bitte," I said, making the extra effort to be polite in German. Excuse me, please.

A hand on my bike. "Warten Sie, bitte." Stop, please. He was polite, too.

I glanced at Truus, still waiting for me across the street. Her eyes narrowed; she looked troubled, her hands on her hips.

"It's OK, I'm going back," I said. I gave him a smile to grease the wheels.

"Fräulein."

I faced him again. "Yes?"

"Papers, please."

Chapter 35

I WONDERED HOW LONG Truus had been standing there, watching me. And why.

The guard held the black sticklike rifle all the German soldiers had been carrying lately, so crude it looked like a child's drawing of a weapon, cheap but deadly, especially at this range. The officers were strutting around by the kiosk as if they thought they were winning the war just by standing there. But the soldiers knew better. As miserable as we all were, we had also all heard the rumors. The Allies were coming. Finally. In the past week and a half, I'd passed over the Jan Gijzen Bridge with barely a glance as the soldiers were busy exchanging gossip with each other.

Not that evening.

"Guten Abend," I said again. Greeting them in German usually smoothed the interaction, but the skinny guard wasn't charmed. He made a sweeping gesture with the long gun, directing me to turn so he could see my face from all angles. He turned, too. Knifing cheekbones and dark eyes and the expression of an old man who'd seen some things. What did he see in my face? Fear? Fury? Hunger? I hoped he saw hatred, too.

"Ihre Ausweis, Fräulein," he said, his voice flat.

I reached into my coat pocket for my ID. Reminded myself to glance at the name before handing it over just in case they quizzed me. I burned my real ID card two years ago, the day I joined the RVV.

But when I felt for the card in my coat pocket, it wasn't there.

"Mach schon," he said, shifting his feet in pinching boots. Hurry up.

This got the attention of the next soldier, a man with a hank of greasy, dark hair slicked across his skull like a wound. He strolled over to take a look.

"Was ist los?" he said.

What was going on was me searching all my pockets and still finding nothing.

"Warten Sie, bitte," I said. Wait.

Slick raised an eyebrow.

"You're not German," he said.

"No," I said.

But I've been practicing my language skills on you bastards for the past four years.

"I'll get it," I said, reaching for the leather satchel looped around my body.

"Halt!" Slick raised his pistol. Cheekbones saw it and jerked his gun up, too.

I raised my hands, remaining calm. A thing that starts badly doesn't always have to end badly.

"Just getting my ID, like he asked," I said.

Cheekbones nodded for me to go ahead, but as I raised the flap of my satchel, Slick grabbed my wrist, hard.

"You look in the bag," he said to Cheekbones.

The air rushed out of my body. I swallowed, my knees locked.

I felt as if I were watching the scene unfold from somewhere far above, floating over myself like a cloud. There was a gun in my bag. If I had my gun on me, I usually avoided checkpoints. But they'd let me through so many times, and this was the risk we always took when we carried guns. As Jan—damn him—once said to me, "The gun only works if you have one." He had carried his pistol on his person every day and slept with it under his pillow. Oh, fuck Jan.

Slick reached for my hands and placed each one on the handlebar of my bike. "Don't move," he said.

I wouldn't. I leaned on the handles for support and stared at the ground. I couldn't see what they saw, only feel my body jerked back and forth from Cheekbones' efforts. He flipped the top flap open and stuck his hand in, rummaged around.

I couldn't breathe. But I tried. Was Truus watching all this?

"Are you a student?" Slick asked me while Cheekbones kept digging.

I shook my head.

"Married?" he asked.

I shook my head again. Truus loved to tease me about how chatty I could be with the soldiers when I was trying to pry information. But not now. I felt like I might vomit. I took a quick glance behind me. Everyone in line behind had me had miraculously dissolved back into the city once the soldiers were distracted. I would have done the same thing. Thank God it was just me and not Truus, too. Once again, the distance of a few meters made all the difference. Truus was safe. I took a deep breath. I looked up at Slick from under my mascaraed lashes and licked my chapped lips. I'd probably never looked uglier in my life. Witchy, like Truus said. Oh, well.

"Wie heißen Sie?" I asked him. My voice quavered. What's your name?

"Hält die Klappe!" he hissed and took a step toward me, and I flinched.

Yes. I'll shut up. I resumed staring at the ground. God, I hated them.

"Look, newspapers," Cheekbones said, and I thought I heard a note of relief in his voice. Just newspapers.

"Give them to me," Slick said. His voice was calm now. A smile drew a line across the V of his face. Cheekbones relaxed for the first time since this began. He stood up straighter.

"*De Waarheid*," Slick said, reading the name of the newspaper.

It meant the same thing in German as in Dutch: *The Truth*. He said it like a one-word joke.

I was silent as icicles of sweat crept down my belly and back. Shivering now. I kept my mouth shut. *Don't make a scene*, I told myself. Too late. I was the scene.

Slick took ahold of my coat collar and pulled me so close I could see the deep furrow each tooth of the comb had made through his pomaded hair that morning. I recognized the sweet, rancid scent of my high school chemistry lab: formaldehyde. He cleared his throat like a big man.

"Fucking. Communist. Resistance. Scum." He hissed it, pulling me closer with every word. There was something rotten in his mouth. A warm spray of saliva hit my cheek, and I couldn't wipe it off. He'd been waiting to say this to someone, so he said it again: "Resistance. Scum."

"Resistance?" someone said. It was a new voice, less aggressive. "Mal sehen," the voice said. Let's see. An SS officer walked toward us from the far side of the bridge. Another narrow face, this time dwarfed by a ridiculously oversized officer's cap.

"Guten Abend," Big Hat said, peering at my eyes, my face, my hair. Not too closely, I hoped. The cheap hair dye was just beginning to fade, and the red would soon start to show through. But only if you were really looking for it. Freddie had been doing it for me ever since Philine vanished; she'd offered to do it a few days earlier, but I put her off, dreading the cold, wet procedure.

"What's your name, miss?"

I took a breath and heard it rattle through my pneumonic chest. "Johanna Elderkamp," I said in a calm voice. *Please, God, let me be carrying only the Elderkamp ID and not an envelope full of incriminating fake documents.* I was usually careful about checking for these things, but my mind was foggier lately and I couldn't raise the energy to care as much about precautions.

Big Hat took a step back to get a better look at me. "So, what's all this, then?" I'd worn my disguise, but whatever natural charms I'd once possessed were now long gone. My skirt drooped from my hip bones, held up by a length of twine, and I hadn't bathed in a week. My dyed hair was greasy and scraped back in a ponytail. I was wearing ugly, fake glasses.

I shrugged, smiled. "A misunderstanding," I said.

"She's Resistance, sir," said Slick. "I'm placing her under arrest."

Big Hat pressed his thin lips together. He looked concerned. Not unfriendly.

"You searched her?" he asked.

"She was carrying these," Slick said, nodding to the copy of *De Waarheid* now lying on the ground. Big Hat nodded. Distributing *De Waarheid* was a serious offense. But it was nothing compared to being caught with a gun. And they still hadn't found the gun. They could still let me go.

"Anything else?" he asked.

No. Please. I couldn't breathe.

"Nichts Besonderes," Cheekbones said. Nothing much.

Big Hat nodded at him, and Cheekbones shoved his hand back in my bag, pulling out more items one by one and dropping them on the ground. He listed them as he went: "Handkerchief, more newspapers, mirror . . ."

At the very bottom of the bag was a blue-and-white wool scarf my mother had knitted for me. And wrapped inside that scarf was the little black pistol Jan had given me way back when. It was loaded, of course.

"Bitte, Offizier . . ." I said to him. *Please.*

"SS-Sturmbahnführer Lages," he said, gifting me with his name. "Willy Lages."

I'd heard it before. Willy Lages was notorious, a leader in Aktion Silbertanne. I wanted to wrap my hands around his skinny neck, hurt him.

Instead, I gave him a look that was meant to say: *Come on, friend, we both know this is ridiculous. Come on. Please.*

"Where will you take her?" he asked the soldier.

So I was being arrested. Was Truus watching it all unfold? I knew she was and felt worse. I knew the agony of helplessness.

"Van Gijzen station, sir."

"Take her to Ripperdastraat," he said. "Wait for me for questioning."

"But if she's Resistance—"

"Freuler," Lages said quietly.

"Sir." The muscles in Slick/Freuler's jaw twitched.

"Freuler," he said again.

Freuler's eyes went wide. "Sir?"

"Take her to Ripperdastraat."

"Yes, sir." Freuler stood erect and shot his hand up in an enthusiastic Heil Hitler. Cheekbones quickly did the same. Ripperdastraat. The Nazis had taken over the three-story department store on Ripperdastraat to house the Haarlem headquarters of the Sicherheitsdienst: the SD. Thus, Aktion Silbertanne. That was their work.

But it could have been worse. At least they weren't taking me to Amsterdam. I might still find a way out if I got to Ripperdastraat. I was pretty sure they didn't even have a real jail there. The tension in my neck and shoulders melted momentarily.

"Vielen Dank," I said in German to Lages, trying to convey my gratitude.

He glanced my way, his face unreadable. To Freuler: "Wait for me."

"Yes, sir."

Cheekbones clamped his grip on my upper arm, his fingers encircling it completely. A black van was already waiting at the edge of the canal. Those fucking vans. He walked me over, pushed me inside, and the steel doors sank into place with a crashing clank. I scrambled to my feet to look out the slit of a window, but I could see only a slice of the action outside. Soldiers walked back and forth, trying to look busy, and officers conferred with each other. Cheekbones bragged about catching a resister. Everyone was excited. A gust of wind off the canal caught the edges of a tossed copy of *De Waarheid*, and the pages rose and separated and floated up through the darkening air.

"Fang es!" Lages barked, and the soldiers ran, chasing the leaves of drifting paper like children after balloons at a party, desperate but entertained.

"Christ." One tripped over something on the ground and nearly fell into the canal.

My bag.

He kicked it toward the water. I exhaled. *Kick it into the canal*, I urged him silently. I'd seen German soldiers throw lots of things into our canals: stolen bikes, students' backpacks, each other. *Kick it into the canal.* They could shoot you for carrying Resistance newspapers, I knew. But a gun was much worse.

Of course they could shoot you for anything. For nothing at all.

Stop.

What's worse than getting shot? My stomach turned, and I forced the question away. In the RVV we didn't talk about torture much. But we talked enough to know.

Kick the bag into the canal. Kick it.

The engine of the van rumbled to life and the steel walls shuddered.

Kick it into the canal. Please please please.

The tips of my fingers clung to the sharp edge of the window, the narrow rectangle of vision sliding away as we moved. The van stopped and I saw Lages walking back to his post. Good. *Go back to your normal level of terror, you prick.*

Then Lages stopped and looked at the soldier who'd tripped.

"Was ist das?" he asked.

"Sir?"

Lages nodded at the bag at his feet. "Take that, too," he said as the soldier picked up my bag. "Put it in the van."

The soldier ran out of my line of vision, and I heard the front passenger door of the van open and slam shut again. The engine ground into gear and we were moving forward.

That's when I spotted her, finally. She was standing against a building a block away from the bridge, watching the whole scene. Truus. Her exhausted, freckled face wore the dispassionate mask of the Resistance, but by now I knew that face better than my own. Her expression confirmed what I already suspected. I sank to the bare floor of the van, clinging to a buckled seam in the metal wall as we bounced over cobblestones, bricks, and more bridges on our way to the interrogation. This was really happening. I'd spent the past years imagining being caught in the act, ratted out, or arrested, and I'd imagined thousands of ways to deny charges, divert attention, and make my escape. But I never thought I'd be seized for something so . . . small. Carrying *De Waarheid* through an everyday checkpoint? So stupid. I made myself take deep breaths, close my eyes, reduce myself to zero. Focus. In the rest of Europe, the Germans were retreating, desperate. It wouldn't be long until that happened here. I could hold on.

I'D MADE A mistake. I walked up to a checkpoint as if I knew how things would play out. Strolling up cocky, distracted, just like Jan. Well, fuck Jan and fuck me.

I'd been caught. It had always been a possibility. And I knew why.

"*De Waarheid*," I whispered to no one.

The Truth.

Part Four

The
Dunes

March–April 1945
Haarlem, Amsterdam,
Bloemendaal

Chapter 36

I'VE BEEN SITTING in this small room for an hour, two hours, maybe just ten minutes. At least I'm no longer in the van. We must be in the basement near the furnace room because I hear a distant hissing and banging somewhere nearby. I hope it's a furnace.

Three soldiers walked me down here, sat me in this plain metal chair facing a bare wooden desk with my hands shackled behind me. Then two of them left, and the other is still standing by the door, one of those long guns resting against his shoulder. He's smoking a hand-rolled cigarette and I'm following the curls of smoke as they rise and disappear.

I wonder if Truus knows where I am. She might assume I'm in Amsterdam, at SS headquarters. Freddie will find out. They'll learn where I am and . . . that's about it. Realistically, they're not going to smuggle me out. That never happens.

On the other hand, the Allies have already reached Cologne—they're in Germany, for God's sake. Postwar plans are being made. If I were German, I'd be more worried about that than about the Dutch Resistance. But I no longer try to get inside their heads.

"Heil Hitler," the soldier says, dropping his cigarette to the floor and saluting as the door opens and the SS officer from the bridge walks in, carrying a thick stack of paperwork and manila file folders. Big Hat. Willy Lages.

"Heil Hitler," he says and glances at the cigarette still smoldering on the green linoleum floor. He nods, and the soldier picks it up and resumes smoking. He turns to me and smiles.

"Heil Hitler," he says to me.

I say nothing.

"OK, OK," he says, setting the papers on top of the desk and sitting himself down next to them, looking at me with curiosity. He's relaxed, almost friendly. I decide to mirror his mood.

"Could you help me with these?" I say, indicating the handcuffs behind my back.

He pauses and I read his face. Surprise, distrust, puzzlement. He nods to the soldier, who walks over and unlocks the shackles.

"Thanks," I say. Casual. I rearrange myself in the chair with a ladylike cross of the legs and try to imagine I look cute, though I know I don't. I can still act cute, though. Half of my mind is racing with panic, and half is slowed way down, trying to make logical decisions.

He takes off his big hat and sets it on the desk, smooths his hand over his balding head. He's in his forties. Dark hair still covers some of his scalp, and his eyebrows are dark, too. Even his eyes are dark, like black buttons. His nose ends in a downward point; his teeth are crooked. He wasn't hired for his good looks.

"I am SS-Sturmbahnführer Lages," he says, in case I forgot. They love to tell you their long, stupid titles. He leans over and touches my cheek. His cold finger gently guides my chin up to look at him. "We can be friends, can't we? You can call me Willy."

I want to bite his hand, break his arm, stomp him to death. I stay quiet.

"I need to ask you some questions. And once we're done with those and as long as you tell the truth, we can go on being friends. Maybe even work together, eh?"

"OK," I say.

Go to hell, I think.

"Good," he says, and he looks genuinely happy for a moment. "So," he says. "We looked through your bag. And we found your ID." He holds it up now.

I shrug. Maybe a low-ranking grunt searched the bag and hasn't told Lages about the gun yet. This would be going very differently if he knew.

"Your photo looks a little different than you look now."

I know it. I'd never had the chance to get a new photo taken with my black hair. Despite the fact that the photo is black and white, it's possible the shades of gray might suggest something else. He pulls out a silver cigarette case from the inner pocket of his wool uniform and taps a cigarette on it, then gestures to the soldier for a light. He takes a long drag and leans back against the desk, relaxed, just looking at me. "Come on, now, Schatz," he says. Oh, now I'm his sweetheart. "What's your real name?"

I smile. My real name? That doesn't have much to do with this. But I'll let him keep calling me sweetheart. I stay quiet.

"What's funny?" he says.

I say nothing. The soldier in the corner clears his throat. My silence embarrasses them.

"Just tell us your name, dear," Lages says, his voice cooler now. "That's all we're after."

"Johanna Elderkamp," I say.

"No!" he shouts and slams his hand on the desk. I jump. So does the soldier. "We know who you are," he says, rising to his feet and walking the three steps it takes to reach me. He bends over so his face is right next to mine, cheek to freshly shaved cheek. He washed up before he came to see me.

"We don't pick up too many Resistance girls these days," he says.

"Not anymore. They're home taking care of babies, tending to mother and father. But not you, eh?"

I stay quiet. I stare at my hands on my lap, my fingers laced through each other like the game Annie and I used to play as little girls: *Here's the church, here's the steeple, open the doors and there's all the—*

"Tell me your name." He shouts into my face, gripping my shoulders. I turn away. How many times will I be spit upon today by these assholes? He leaves me with a shake and walks to the other side of the room to compose himself. The soldier lights a new cigarette for him, and he takes two deep drags before turning to face me again. I'm not charming him. But he hasn't gotten any information from me either.

That's my only goal now: Say nothing. Give them nothing. Not even my name.

"Would you like something to drink?" he asks me, his voice smooth again. "Coffee? Tea? A glass of water?"

I say nothing.

"Anton, two coffees," he says to the soldier, who nods and steps outside.

"Now." Officer Lages sits before me again, leaning against the desk. The handcuffs are next to him, unlocked. I wonder. I sit up in my chair but make no sudden movements. He seems to trust me, for no good reason. I cross my legs the other way. It's just the two of us in here. My fingertips are itching, and I grip the seat of my chair, waiting before I make any move. I need to be smart.

"Alone at last," he says. As disgusting as he is, Lages is not nearly as awful as many of the other Kraut officers I've encountered. I doubt he'll try to put his hand up my skirt, for instance. He genuinely seems to think we have some kind of connection, that I'm somehow grateful for his interest in me. "It's been a long war, you know? I thought I'd be back in Braunschweig by now. So did my wife." He looks up at me. "Yes, I am married. Surprised?"

Why would I be surprised? Every horrible man finds some foolish woman to marry, as far as I can tell. I say nothing.

"I was a police officer before the war," he says, as if I want to know more about his life. "My three brothers, they still work in the trades like my father did. Hard work. They're builders. Not me." He taps the side of his shiny skull. "I had a brain for it. Came first in the police exams. They made me an officer and then they brought me here."

"You like it here?" I say.

He nods. When I talk, it makes him happy. Like he's getting somewhere. "It's good. I miss my home, of course. My wife."

"Kids?" I say.

His dark eyebrows drop. "We have not been blessed with children. Not yet."

I imagine his home life, alone with Mrs. Lages. I see a cramped, silent room.

"But you never know," he says. When he smiles, he's even uglier.

"Yes," I say. *Please, God, don't bring any children into that horrible room.*

"What about you?" He turns back to me. "Not married? No children?"

I almost chuckle. Me, a mother? I haven't gotten my period in a year. I shake my head.

"Why not?" he asks.

Because I've been too busy trying to shoot all you bastards in the head, that's why. Because when you spend all your time hating things and cursing people and plotting assassinations, you don't think about ways to create life. You stay focused on ways to end it. Because I've never had a real boyfriend, not in twenty-four years. Not even Jan Bonekamp.

I shake my head, stare at the floor. "The war," I say. "You know."

"Ja, ja." He nods. "But no wartime romances? A young girl like you?" Maybe he thinks I'm still a teenager. People often do.

I shake my head. As if I would share a single detail of my real life with him.

The door opens, and Anton walks in carrying a metal tray. He sets it on the desk.

"I take two sugars and cream," Lages says. It's like a line in a movie; it has nothing to do with reality. There is no sugar and cream anymore. "You?" he says.

"Three sugars and cream," I say, as if asking for my diamond tiara. Then I watch in shock as Anton turns to the tray and its decanters to prepare our demitasse cups with sugar cubes and a generous pour of what does appear to be cream, or at least milk. Amazing. Saliva fills my mouth, like a slathering dog. Lages hands it to me, and when I sip the sweet, creamy coffee, I feel as if I've been injected with some kind of miracle drug. Pleasure ripples through my body at the tastes and textures. Real coffee, real sugar, real cream. Maybe they didn't give Jan "truth serum." Maybe it was just coffee and cream.

But it could be poisoned. I stop drinking.

Lages drinks his and nothing happens. I gulp mine down, too. I haven't been poisoned; Lages still needs something from me.

"These small pleasures, eh? Even down here." He gestures to the four bare walls around us. Looking at them seems to remind him of the task at hand. "So. I know you are a Resistance girl, delivering these criminal newspapers."

I say nothing.

"No matter," he continues. "My point is, we know a few things about each other now. So let me explain something to you. What is it, March? Nearly springtime. I'm a busy man, I can't spend hours interrogating every pretty girl we bring in. What's the point? We have terrorists to worry about. But sometimes a girl like you can help us with the real criminals. Anton knows—" He looks over to Anton, who nods.

"This can be a helpful arrangement for us both," he continues. "A girl like you provides us with a little bit of information about the things you know, names, addresses, perhaps a few plans you might have heard about, even rumors. We accept rumors. You help us with these, and I help you get out of here. None of your little Resistance friends will ever know we talked. You return to your world, I to mine. And together we help rid this little country of its native criminal element, eh? Together."

I say nothing. But I'm relieved he's getting to the point. The small talk was driving me insane.

"Anton?" He nods, and Anton leaves the room. All my muscles tense. I long ago prepared myself for the possibility of rape. But Anton's only gone a moment, and when he returns, he's holding my bag. It's obvious there's still a few things inside. He sets it on the table and it makes a muffled clunk. So much for these bastards being thorough. The combination of coffee, sugar, and the knowledge that my trusty pistol is just a few inches away revives me. A thrill of possibility runs down my spine, like a wild animal plotting to escape my cage. My fingers ache to touch my gun.

"Anton knows how we do it," Lages continues. "Not so many questions, just a few, and we're on our way. Can we agree on that, Schatz?" He smiles at me.

Sure, sweetheart. I look at him with a neutral gaze. Not hostile, just blank. If Anton leaves the room one more time, I can do this. Get the gun, shoot Lages, shoot my way out of this building. I know I can.

"Done with your coffee?"

"Thank you," I say. And as I hand him my delicate china cup and saucer, he grabs my wrist and twists it, the chinaware flying and smashing to the floor with a glassy tinkle. Anton is still as a statue. He's seen this before.

Lages leans in and whispers in my ear. "We found the gun."

Damn it.

He stands up, reaches into the bag, and pulls it out. My gun. The clatter of its hard metal grip clanking against the wood table is the first familiar sound I've heard in hours. So small and banged up it looks like a child's toy. Doesn't matter. This gun has killed half a dozen Nazis. It can kill more.

"Your. Name," Lages says, nearly tearing the thin skin of my wrist with his grip. His voice is no longer friendly or calm. It's a low, flat directive.

I don't respond.

"Tell-me-your-fucking-name."

His face is so close to mine I turn away to avoid my lips brushing his face. His cheek presses against mine, and he twists my wrist harder. I feel a soft cord of muscle in my left arm unravel and snap like an electric shock under his hand, and my fingers start to tingle. I lock my jaw, close my eyes. Say nothing. My eyes water.

"Anton," he says. And Anton takes my tender wrist from him and thrusts it behind me, shackling it to the other one. Then they jam both underneath me so I'm sitting on my cuffed hands and have to hunch over so as not to dislocate my arms. Though I suspect it's too late for my left arm already.

They both stand above me. "Hold her there," Lages says. Anton places his hands on my shoulders, holding me down on the chair from behind, and then Lages grabs me by the ear, forcing me to look up into his dark eyes.

"Tell me your fucking name."

"Elderkamp," I say through gritted teeth. He slaps me across the face. It's the first thing that's made sense since I entered this room. This is the way things are supposed to go, just as I've imagined them: I defy him, and he hits me. That I understand.

He grabs me by a fistful of hair, preparing to hit me again. Then he pauses.

"Look at me," he says.

I stare up at him sideways. I'm not afraid to look him in his weasel eyes. *Fuck you.*

With a sweaty thumb he drags his finger across my cheek, coming away with a smear of mascara. He rubs his thumb against my eye, and I shut it, his finger crushing my eyelid. "Look at this," he says to Anton, holding his black-stained thumb in the air.

"Die Hure," Anton says. Whore.

"Yes," Lages says. "But it's not just the makeup. Look."

With Anton still holding me in place, I feel Lages's long fingers grip my skull, and for a moment I'm amused. Does he think he can crush it with his bare hands, the idiot?

But that's not what he's doing.

"Look at that," he says, forcing my head down to my knees so I'm staring at the linoleum, his fingers parting my hair and combing through it like a rough schoolmistress checking for lice. He keeps going, pulling hanks of my hair aside, separating the strands. "It's dyed," he says. "Black dye."

"Die Hure," Anton says again.

Men like you need whores.

"More than that," Lages says, his voice higher now, almost giddy. "She's in disguise. And look." With a quick jerk he yanks a tuft of my hair from my hairline and I shudder, imagining the scrap of bloody flesh that went with it. My scalp throbs, somehow sickeningly wet and on fire at once.

"You see this? You see it?" Lages steps back, holding his trophy into the light.

Anton and I both follow his gaze, mystified.

Officer Lages holds the hair up to the light, using his fingernail to flake off bits of the cheap black hair dye. The look on his face is beatific, enlightened. He walks over to his paperwork, sets the hank of hair down on the desk, and flips through pages of bureaucratic notes, sharp black swastikas positioned at the top of each page like an army of spiders. He's reading something, then looks back at me as if checking something, then keeps reading. Anton holds me down by the shoulders. Finally, Lages picks the lock of hair up again. He strokes it, combing it with his bony fingers, smiling.

"You know who we have here, Anton?" he says, his smirk turning to a delighted, gray-toothed smile. "This, I believe, is das Mädchen mit den roten Haaren."

The Girl with Red Hair.

"Lieber Gott!" Anton's shock is sincere.

Lages laughs, too, and claps Anton on the back. "You just served coffee to the Girl with Red Hair, mein Lieber Junge!" Then he looks down at me as if I'm the prize sow he's raised for the fair, holding the hank of hair like a blue ribbon. He seems almost grateful. Happy.

"You know it was Herr Führer himself who put the bulletin out for you," he says, beaming. As if I should be honored. And I am honored to have played any part in making one of Hitler's cursed days a little more annoying. "He tells us you are a bad example to women everywhere."

I smile.

"So, Girl with Red Hair," he says. "Tell me your name."

I feel a trickle of something cold above my eyebrow. Blood.

"Johanna Elderkamp," I say.

I expect a smack in the face, but Lages just laughs.

"No, my little Whore of the Resistance," he says. "Your name is Hannie Schaft."

I have only one thought: *Fuck you, Jan Bonekamp.* All the times I've imagined this interrogation, rehearsed it in my mind, I've said nothing, revealed no names. And that's what I will do. Goddamn it. Yes, my name is Hannie Schaft. But I can deny them that.

"This is . . . this is . . ." He seems genuinely overcome with delight. I can't be the first prize he's caught. But it seems like it. "This is a great day for the Reich," he says, and glances at his minion. "And you, Anton. I'll name you in the report."

"Sir," Anton says, smiling.

I hold Lages's gaze, trying to find the bottom of the darkness in his eyes, failing. "We won't forget this one, eh, Hannie Schaft?" He leans closer to me and I feel his thin lips pucker against my cheek. I slam my skull against his, and he staggers back on his heels, eyes watering, laughing.

"Never been kissed, eh?" He looks at me with pity. "Not surprised. She's not as pretty as they made her out to be, is she?"

Anton laughs.

"Don't be sad, dear," Lages continues. "We're all a little uglier these days."

I spit at him, but it's pathetic; my mouth is dry as dust. He laughs and returns to the paperwork and writes a few notes on a form, signing his name with a flourish. Then turns back to me. "Anton will accompany you." He looks at his watch and shakes his head. "I look forward to speaking with you tomorrow, Schatz. Maybe then I can get that kiss."

"Varken," I say. Pig. He might not be familiar with the Dutch word.

He frowns. My gun sits on the table. I lunge toward it and Anton grabs me by the collar of my blouse, throwing me down to the floor and pinning me there with his knee in my back.

"Take her," he says to Anton. "Keep her handcuffed, don't do anything stupid."

"Ja," Anton says. "Third floor?"

"No," says Lages, straightening all the paperwork and slipping it back into a brown paper envelope with yet another black swastika stamped on it, and handing it to Anton, too.

"Amstelveenseweg," he says. "Amsterdam."

Chapter 37

I'VE NEVER BELIEVED in destiny, yet the feeling I have now in the back of this van feels like gravity pulling me toward my fate. Somehow, I knew I'd end up at Amstelveenseweg prison in the end.

We all know it. Amstelveenseweg prison is a house of horrors, or so we—resisters, Jews, everyday citizens—hear. Torture rooms. Interrogators trained in extracting information from us with methods too hideous to contemplate. I've contemplated them, of course. Bodies contorted for hours or days, until blood circulation stops. Beatings. Burning cigarettes. And every medieval torture device one can imagine.

I wonder what Truus is doing. Does she know where I am? Do they think I'll talk?

I won't.

The van finally stops. It's the middle of the night now. The van idles at some kind of checkpoint. I hear the muffled voices of the driver and someone outside, but I can't tell what they're saying. Then the van makes a U-turn and we drive a few blocks more. The van stops again. The night is pitch black except for a lone lamp overhanging a door in front of me as I'm pulled out of the van, still shackled. The building is much bigger than I expected.

"Move," Anton says, shoving me toward the light. We reach a soldier at the metal doors. It looks like a medieval fortress with its high, gray stone walls.

"This is her?" A soldier looks me up and down. "But her hair's black," he says, disappointed.

"It's dyed," Anton says coolly, as if he's the one who figured it out. "Whore in disguise."

"She's so small," he says.

Anton shrugs. "She had a gun."

As far as I know, my little pistol is still sitting on that wooden table back in the Haarlem interrogation room. I feel as if I've left a limb behind.

"The guards will take her," the soldier says, and Anton pushes me forward into the hands of two new soldiers. Before they take me away, Anton taps me on the shoulder.

"Just one kiss, Mädchen mit den roten Haar?" he says with a smile.

"Fuck you." All the soldiers laugh.

THEY WALK ME through a maze of cold hallways and upstairs, around corners, more stairs, and finally a kind of catwalk facing a gaping darkness that must be the central atrium of the prison. I wait for the guard to open my cell, his key chain clanging in the quiet of night. But I wouldn't call it peaceful. A damp draft wafts up from the central darkness and I shiver. I can't remember the last time I ate. The guards grip me harder, as if I'm trying to escape. I'm not. There's no point.

"Flashlight," the guard with the keys says, and one of the others hands it to him. He switches it on, and a small pool of light illuminates the four of us in the gloom. Thick gray-black stone walls on one side, a steel railing on the other. The prison cell is not barred, but walled in with the same massive stone blocks. A metal door is the only way in or out. A window high up in the door above my head is the only way to see inside. He points the flashlight at the outside of the door, and I see something else. A child's school chalkboard hanging from a hook on the door. On it is scrawled one word in the medieval German black-letter script they use for the *No Jews Allowed* signs: *Mörderin.*

Murderess.

It makes me proud. They've been waiting for me.

They shove me inside the cell and take another several minutes to unlock my handcuffs. The room is about the size of the back of the van. No windows except the one facing the corridor. A metal cot with a moth-chewed wool blanket and a metal bucket in one corner. This cell is just a place to die.

The guards have all gone quiet. This place is too grim for the usual bullshitting that keeps them from going crazy here. They leave me in the middle of the cell and bolt the door quickly behind them, without a word.

I stay standing, waiting for my eyes to adjust to this blackness. In the meantime, my ears take over, scanning my surroundings for sounds. I can hear everything. A drip of water in the corridor. The scuffling of mice or rats against the stones. The bellows of my own lungs, breathing. A woman's voice.

"The Girl with Red Hair?"

I stay silent, wondering if I imagined the whisper. Then I hear it again. Louder.

"Is that you?"

"Who's there?" I whisper back.

"A friend," she says. "Verzet."

Resistance.

I walk toward the door.

"No," she says, hearing my footsteps. "Over here. On the floor by the wall. Just listen to my voice."

I do, and I follow it to the metal cot. I pull it aside and feel a draft of air near the floor where a rectangular gap about the size of a pack of cigarettes provides an airway between cells. It's a drain. But I can hear her now. "I'm here," I say, wishing I had a cigarette.

"We saw the sign on your door," she says, her voice soft but excited. "Then people started talking. Is it really you? Hannie Schaft?"

After three years in the Resistance, I'm still amazed by the power of rumor, the unstoppable force of gossip and the way it seeps through anything, even prison walls. It's only been a few hours since Lages plucked out my red hair in Haarlem, but that's how fast rumor travels. It arrived here before I did. I don't know who this woman is, and there's a good chance she may be a spy, a fake fellow prisoner who wants to get me talking. But it doesn't matter.

I'm not talking to anyone. I've planned for this. How to subtract yourself until there's nothing to peel away. I started doing it on the bridge, and I'm doing it now. I'm not the Girl with Red Hair or Hannie Schaft or even Johanna Elderkamp anymore. I'm just another Mörderin, here to face my fate with the rest of the so-called murderesses.

"Are you?" she says again.

"Why are you in here?" I whisper. The only way to give nothing of myself away is to give nothing of myself away. Even to this anonymous prisoner.

"I'm a doctor," she says. Then: "I treated Jews."

"Oh."

"Did they hurt you?" she says. "Torture you?"

"I'm OK," I say. I try to swing my left arm and wince at the pain running from my shoulder to my wrist. I tuck my hand into the waistband of my skirt to keep it from moving. It still hurts. My wrists are bloodied from the handcuffs and the pressure of sitting on them.

"What did they do?"

"Nothing," I say. "Just asked me some questions."

"They didn't torture you?"

I don't want to talk about it. "They pulled my arm pretty hard and made me sit on my hands. I wouldn't call it torture." If I don't acknowledge it as torture or fear it as such, it will just be something obnoxious to endure.

"Oh!" A gasp from the other cell. "They must be worried about you."

"What do you mean?"

"That's why they do it," she says. "So if you escape, they can give the seat cushion to the bloodhounds, to smell."

I sink to the cot and twist my wrist to stretch it. I don't want to think about what I smell like. I close my eyes and focus on calming my thoughts. I'm not going to escape. "Oh," I say.

"Tania," she says. "I'm Tania Rusman."

"You can call me M."

"Just M?" she says.

"Mörderin." I smile to myself. Even in the basement interrogation room of the SD headquarters in Haarlem, they were worried about my escape. Even here in this stone fortress, I make them nervous. Good. Coming here has made it much clearer to me than it ever was before. I squeeze Truus's handkerchief doll buried in my pocket, my little good-luck charm.

They're afraid of me.

Chapter 38

I'VE BEEN IN this cell for a few days. I can see the sunlight passing over the stone wall opposite the window in my door, so even though it's always dark inside, I know if it's day or night.

I'm surprised. I thought they'd be in a hurry to interrogate me, given the speed at which this war is wrapping up. But here all the guards still seem to believe Germany is stronger than ever. Hitler's Reich Broadcasting Corporation doesn't report on Allied victories.

I TALKED TO my neighbor, Tania the doctor, about it the second day I was here.

"They've already lost, you know."

"Who?" she said.

"The Germans. The Allies have reached Germany."

She was quiet for a moment. "Then why are we still here?"

"I guess they're waiting for it to become official. Treaties to be signed."

"Does everybody know this?"

It was a good question. The heartbreak of the false Allied liberation last September still lives inside every Dutch person. We didn't want to set ourselves up for that kind of crushing blow again. Yet the news from Radio Oranje, from every Resistance source, was a steady stream of German defeats and retreating soldiers. "The Red Army is marching toward Berlin," I told Tania. "Churchill, Roosevelt, and Stalin have already decided how they'll divide Europe once this is all over."

"Really?"

"Yes," I said. Normally I tried not to raise anybody's hopes about the war effort, especially my own. But I wanted to offer something to this suffering woman. "How long have you been here?" I whispered.

"Over a year."

I tried to imagine that. I couldn't.

"The end is coming," I said, trying to believe it. Hope might be of use in here. "The question is when."

"Well, no one knows it in here," she said. "In this place, everything keeps getting worse."

Aside from the lack of light in my cell, the space itself is filthy. It smells of human sweat and excrement, and the floor and walls are covered in a grainy film that always feels slightly damp. The cough I had when I got arrested is getting worse. Each time I breathe, I know I'm inhaling the poison of this place. I try not to scratch myself on anything rusty. The sounds of other prisoners hacking and sneezing let me know I'm not alone in illness. So this is my strategy: stall and stall and stall, eat the time away until it's too late, the Allies arrive, and the country and the city and this fucking prison are liberated. Any day now. Just don't let me die of consumption before they end this war.

Chapter 39

I HAVEN'T WALKED MORE than a few consecutive steps since they dragged me into my cell four days ago, so I find walking to the interrogation room challenging, even with the help of a guard on each side. But it's my first chance to see the prison in daylight, and as I make my way through, I try to take in everything in sight.

That's when the whispers begin. The turning heads and shuffling feet. *Hannie. Hannie.*

The eyes of hundreds of women, studying me from all angles. I can feel their collective gaze upon me like walking through a pool of sunlight on a winter day.

Hannie. Het meisje met het rode haar.

The Girl with Red Hair.

The withered brunette in the cell lifts her fist.

"Verzet."

I intend to.

IT'S A RELIEF to be deposited on a hard wooden chair in this unpleasant little room. Anything is a nice change from my dark cell. We're in an office with a desk, a bookshelf, and a few framed things on the walls. Some kind of Nazi proclamation stamped with a golden Reichsadler, the Nazi eagle. A sentimental painting of an alpine scene with mountains, fir trees, and snow. A family portrait: husband, wife, one young son, all staring at the camera with no idea of what the future holds. None of us ever knows.

"Heil Hitler," a voice says behind me.

The two soldiers standing next to me salute.

The man walks around to get a look at me.

"Huh." He leans against the desk and visually examines me from head to foot, the way my mother might inspect a fish at the market before buying it. "Not what I expected."

I almost laugh. He's in his mid-thirties, blond hair and blue eyes and a strong jawline that gives him the look of a bland businessman in an advertisement for briefcases.

"My name is Emil Rühl, officer of the Sicherheitsdienst," he says. He's German. "And you are?"

I stare at the floor.

"Hannie Schaft, yes?" He smiles as if reuniting with an old friend. "You heard them out there—they all know."

I'm silent.

"Come now, Hannie. There's no need to play this game anymore. It's over. You can relax. And I'm sure you need the rest because you've been very busy." He paused. "At least, that's what your boyfriend, Jan Bonekamp, told me."

A surge of nausea destroys my composure and I fold in half—to vomit. I don't want them to see me react to anything, but this is beyond my power to stop. My stomach is empty so I cough, gagging, and use the opportunity to spit on their floor.

Rühl grimaces and takes a step backward, then continues. "I suppose it's more accurate to say that he talked to the nurse. You heard about that, yes? Bonekamp didn't want to talk to us, not until we brought a nurse in who pretended to be you."

I swallow hard.

"She didn't look much like you—it's not easy to find a redheaded nurse on short notice—but it didn't seem to matter to Bonekamp. Maybe he couldn't see so well by that point. It's possible; he was very badly hurt. But once you—she—started asking him questions, he told us everything." He peered down at me. "Did you know that?"

I grit my teeth. It hurts twice as much, hearing it from Rühl.

"OK, that's OK. It can't be easy to hear." He leans forward. "Pardon me," he says, "but I have to see this for myself." My hands are cuffed behind me, and I sit still while he inspects my hairline and plucks out a few hairs. Gently, not like Lages did. He holds them up to the light.

"Turn on another light," he says to the two soldiers who stand beside me.

"That's all the lights, sir."

He leans down toward the small desk lamp to try to see better. "Damn it. Whose shit office is this, anyway?"

"Sir?"

"Take her outside."

The soldiers lift me by the arms and frog-march me out to the catwalk, within sight of the cells. Every prisoner's head turns to watch. The central atrium is covered by a windowed dome, so natural light pours through. The guards lean me out over the railing to catch the sunlight in an awkward maneuver, and Rühl attempts to examine my scalp while maintaining a sense of dignity. I kick my feet and shake my head to make their job harder, and the women prisoners start laughing. First, just a few, and then the sound spreads like lightning until the entire prison is filled with the dark, wild sound of bitter laughter. Women's laughter.

Rühl's face goes dark red. I know because it's right next to mine. He glares at me, then rears back and straightens himself up. The guards hoist me back over the railing. The women cheer.

"Wash her," he says to the guards. "Get that dye out of her hair. Then bring her back to me." He turns on his heel and disappears into the inner hallway as the women continue screaming at him. When he's gone, their cheer changes.

They're chanting my name now.

Hannie.

Hannie.

Hannie.

As exhausted as I am, a surge of joy darts through my body. I've finally arrived at the one place where resisters outnumber the Nazis and their miserable collaborators.

I love these women. And I feel their love for me.

Chapter 40

THE LAST FEW days have been difficult.

They washed my hair, which meant leading me to a large tiled shower area. Here, there were women workers. They regarded me with suspicion, even fear, whispering as I walked by. But they left me alone to undress and wash myself. I stood under the freezing-cold water and let it soak me, shivering, watching the nits get swept down the drain. They gave me some kind of paint thinner to put on my hair, and it stripped the black out and burned my skin, leaving my hairline, scalp, and shoulders with red welts. But the dye washed out and I was relieved. I never felt like myself with that hair.

They took me back to a different cell. Solitary confinement in a quieter part of the prison. It is just as disgusting. One tiny slit of an inner window, otherwise total blackness. At first I didn't care; I was so exhausted I just slept. No idea for how long. I woke up shaking with cold and banged on the door for a blanket. No one came. No Tania to talk to.

Then someone showed up, threw a blanket in, and told me they'd be back for me in an hour for the next interrogation.

Another day passed.

Food is shoved inside twice a day: some kind of watery potato soup and bread so mealy it dissolves into crumbs when I touch it. I eat every-thing. I'll need my strength.

Someone came and said they'd be back in six hours to take me to the interrogation. Then they returned ten minutes later and said we were go-ing right then.

If they think misleading me about time will break me, they can keep waiting.

THIS TIME THEY take me to a new room, not the cozy office. This is a big storeroom of a space down in the basement, with bare floors and walls and a table and a few bare chairs. Caged lightbulbs hang from the ceiling beams. At the center of the room, the floor slopes slightly, down to a gi-ant drain.

Emil Rühl waits for me at the table, smiling.

"Much better with the red hair," he says, walking up to me. I stand with my hands cuffed behind me. He walks up just a few inches from my face. "Now. Let's start with your name."

I'm silent.

Rühl smiles. He turns to the guards in the room as if to make a joke, then whirls back and slaps me across the face. He's wearing leather gloves.

"Name, please."

I'm quiet. He slaps me again. Other cheek.

"Name."

Silence.

"You realize we know your name because your lover, Jan Bonekamp, told us, yes? Still, we need you to say it."

I say nothing.

SLAP.

"Name."

Silence.

SLAP.

He does this enough that my face goes numb. I taste blood in my mouth. It almost tastes like food. I savor it.

Irritated, he walks to the wall and slams his hand against it. "Here," he says to the guards, "bring her here." They walk me over and he pushes my face against the spot on the wall he's picked, which is a few inches below my nose. I bend my knees slightly to make contact with it.

"There," he says. He turns to the guards. "Make her stay right there, touching the wall, until she tells you her name. And when she does, come get me." He slams the door behind him as he leaves.

As soon as he does, I straighten up and try to stretch my back. A guard shoves me back down, forcing my knees to buckle. "You heard," he says. "Stay there."

So I stand there, or try to, for hours. The muscles in my thighs begin to burn and then cramp. I experiment with resting on one foot, then the other. My feet go numb. The muscles in my back begin to spasm. And it's just so fucking stupid. Sticking my nose against the wall like a naughty little schoolgirl. This anger gets me through another hour or so. The guards are bored, although they're relieved by new guards every so often. At one point I wake up, having fainted to the floor. They pull me up and push me back into place. Finally, after what feels like days, though it must be hours, they drag me back to my solitary cell.

I give them credit for finding a method of torture that leaves no visible scars. It will get worse.

Chapter 41

April 1945

Today I had visitors.

The guards left me alone for one night. I lay on the pallet on the floor and massaged my legs and tried to stretch all the muscles in my back and neck. My body felt like it had been twisted in a vise. Eventually the door opened, and two guards arrived and yanked me off the floor.

"I can walk," I said, throwing off their hands. They flinched, surprised. I hadn't spoken in days. And they let me walk unassisted through the prison.

The same thing happened, just as it had before. As soon as I appeared from my cell, the whispers trickled through the prison like water finding its way downhill. Within minutes, the atrium was flooded with voices shouting: *Hannie. Hannie. Hannie.* The women banged cups and any other metal objects they could find against the bars of their cells. It was so loud I wanted to cover my ears. But I just smiled and stayed silent. It made the women scream louder. A fleeting whiff of joy, imagining how the Germans must hate it.

They walked me into a dark room with a row of tables at the back. Three young women stood against the wall facing the tables, looking scared and miserable. When they saw me, something flickered in their eyes. They looked at each other and without speaking seemed to affirm my identity. As the guards pushed me into line next to them, they smiled and scooted over to make room for me. We were all about the same height. Two of the girls had light brown hair, and one was a blonde. They're prisoners, I can tell, because of their gauntness and filth. The brunette next to me twiddled her fingers out and touched mine. Solidarity.

Then the door opened again and a woman walked in, escorted by two guards. A civilian. She stood out not just because she was a busty blonde, but because she looked clean and smelled nice. She was from the outside. I've only been in here a couple of weeks, but already everything beyond the prison wall seems like another planet. Her side of the room was so dark I couldn't make out her features.

"If you see the woman who shot your fiancée, just point to her," said a voice that I recognized as Emil Rühl's.

The woman stood behind the table. She set her purse down and rested her hands on the tabletop, peering over it at us. "That's her," she said, her voice shaky and brittle. "Right there."

"Which one, miss?"

As she leaned into the glow of the lamp, I recognized her. It was the blonde, Hertz's Dutch girlfriend, the woman who wouldn't stop shrieking after Truus and I shot him in his doorway. I smiled inside, remembering Truus wiping off my bloody mustache afterward. Seemed like a lifetime ago. The girlfriend's face was powdered, her nails painted. As she got closer, cowardice radiated off her like heat. I watched as one of her hands unconsciously picked at the other one, peeling the skin of her scabbed cuticles. She leaned in close until she was almost touching me, and I could smell the scent of her powder and see the way it clumped in the creases around her mouth and eyes.

"This one," she said. Her breath smelled of sour milk and made my mouth water. "But her hair looked different."

"It was dyed black," said Rühl, pleased with the way this was going.

"Oh," she said. She stood back and looked at the other three girls in the lineup. "Is her friend here?"

"Why, you see her, too?" said Rühl.

"No," she said. She pointed at me again. "Just her." It took everything I had not to bite the tip of her finger off. I licked my lips, and she snatched herself back, her doughy white hands fluttering.

Rühl guided her back to the table. I sensed a swell of relief coming off the other three girls in line. I glanced over at them, and all three looked at me, their eyes communicating conflicting emotions, trying to support me even as they thanked fate for sparing them this time. I smiled and they beamed back. Most were missing at least one tooth.

"Quiet!" Rühl shouted, seeing us. But we hadn't spoken. The girls started giggling.

"Shut them up!" Rühl said, and the soldiers took a step toward us. The girls went quiet again.

"Did she confess?" asked the blonde.

Rühl cleared his throat and began shuffling paperwork. "She will, she will. And now that you've made an identification," he said to the blonde, "I'll need to you to sign this paperwork."

"She hasn't confessed?" The blonde looked upset. "What has she told you?"

"Don't worry about that, Fräulein," said Rühl. "If you could just fill this out."

"Who does she think she is?" said the blonde, her voice rising. She looked back at me. "Why don't you tell them what you did? You seemed nice when I opened the door and then—"

"You're lucky to be alive, you Nazi-loving bitch." I hadn't intended to say it. It just popped out.

"What?" The girlfriend looked as if I'd slapped her. She looked to Rühl. "Is she talking to me?"

"Say again?" said Rühl, daring me.

I just smiled. The three girls next to me started giggling.

"Shut up!" he said.

"You can't let her talk to me like that," said the blonde. I looked at her, and all I could see were the dozens of Jewish families and resisters her boyfriend had sent away to be killed. Everything she wore, from her patent leather pumps to the perfume, was paid for with money earned by hunting Jews like Sonja and Philine.

"Fuck you," I said. The girls snorted.

She gasped, turning to Rühl the way collaborators always turned to Nazis for help. "She can't say that."

Rühl marched over and grabbed my chin in his hand. "Shut. Up." He flung my head back, and it banged against the wall behind me. The girls gasped. I felt a lump forming on the back of my skull. It ached. But I was gratified. The expression on his face gave me everything I craved. He'd gotten nothing from me. I made him feel like a fool in front of these women. That was good enough for now.

"Take them back to the office," he said to the guards. "And put her"— he pointed to me but, I noticed, still refrained from calling me by name—"back in isolation." As the guards walked me out of the room, I made eye contact with the blonde. Her eyes flared with anger at my insolence. I winked. She threw her purse at me, but I ducked and it hit the guard, who scrambled to pick it up off the grimy floor.

"Get her out of here," said Rühl.

When I walked out to the catwalk with the guards, the prison once again erupted in cheers.

Chapter 42

I SPENT MORE THAN a week in isolation after that. Some days they neglected to feed me, though it can be hard to be certain when it's always dark. I thought I heard someone last night and then realized it was my own voice I was hearing, whispering aloud the thoughts going through my mind. I try to limit those thoughts to the basics: food and water. To pass the time, I imagine the feast I'll enjoy when this is all over. Roast pheasant, baked potatoes, cherry compote, red wine, loaves of white bread. A pitcher of fresh white milk, yellow butter dripping off a warm iced bun. Ice cream. Chocolate. A cigarette.

It hurts to sit or lie down on this hard mat since I've lost almost all the fat on my body. My hips hurt if I sit on my butt; my shoulder blades and elbows ache when I lie down. But standing requires energy.

"Get up, Hannie. Get up, darling." It's Hendrik.

"I'm trying to sleep," I say.

"Get up—get up—get up," he says in his singsong voice.

"Ugh," I say, pushing myself to a seated position.

"Come on," he says. "Almost there."

Using the wall for support, I raise myself to standing, my knees wobbly. "Happy?"

"Happy," he says. Then disappears. Hendrik has been visiting me like this for the past few days, an elegant angel trying to keep me alert. The only way I know he's not really here is because if he were, he'd give me a cigarette. But he can't because he's dead.

I'd love a cigarette.

"CIGARETTE?" THE DOOR to my cell is wedged open and a guard stands in the space, the glowing cherry of his lit cigarette the first sign of light I've seen in days.

I try to stand and the guard walks over and hands it to me, but my hands are shaking so badly I can't hold it. He plucks the lit cigarette from his own mouth and puts it against mine for a drag. I inhale, momentarily ecstatic, then start coughing so hard I have to sit down again.

"They're coming in a few minutes," the guard says. As he closes the door, I see they've transferred my chalkboard sign over to this cell now. It still says the same thing: *Murderess.*

They don't come in a few minutes, of course. It's twelve hours, maybe a day before the door opens again and two guards arrive to pull me out.

"Ugh," one of them says. I know I smell terrible, even though I can't smell myself anymore. I haven't used the bucket much since I've eaten almost nothing, but my small, stuffy cell must reek anyway.

We go through the same routine, the procession through the prison, the women cheering, the guards getting irritated. Right before they take me down to the basement again, I catch the eye of a passing prisoner. The look on her face reveals how shocking my appearance must be. I know it is, even if I haven't seen a mirror in a month. I can feel my body caving in on itself. A downy fuzz has appeared on my cheeks the last few days, something I've seen on starving people. The body's last attempt to keep itself warm.

———

BACK IN THE basement room again. Emil Rühl is there along with three other members of the SD—not prison guards.

"Here's our leading lady," says Rühl. He looks at me as if I'm going to introduce myself. I've already decided to say nothing. No wisecracks this time, no nothing. It's the simplest way through and I'm too deranged with exhaustion to do anything else. As soon as I sit down, I feel my eyelids droop. I could actually fall asleep right here. I want to.

"No, no," Rühl says, lifting my chin. "Gentlemen, this is Hannie Schaft. By the end of your time together, she will have admitted that and much more." Rühl turns back to me. "I'm leaving you in their hands, dear. These boys have special training in verschärfte Vernehmung, eh?"

Sharpened interrogation. I've never heard that one before. The "boys"—men in their mid-twenties—nod but do not smile.

"Be a good girl, Hannie. The sooner you cooperate, the sooner this will all be over, and we can be friends." Rühl walks to the door. "Heil Hitler," he says, and salutes.

"Heil Hitler," the soldiers and guards reply.

Rühl leaves. Two guards stand beside me. The three SD guys stand on the other side of the table.

"You can go," says one of the SD men. "Wait outside."

"Should we cuff her?" a guard asks. I'm sitting in the chair untied. I don't have the energy to stand up, much less run.

"No, just leave her," the man says. The guards give each other a look and then walk outside. The door locks behind them.

"What is your name?" says one of the SD men. He's tall, with shiny black hair and eyebrows like slashes of black paint.

I say nothing.

Black nods, and one of the men, the youngest-looking of the three, comes around the table to me.

"Give me your hand," he says.

I do nothing.

He leans down to see my face. "I'm talking to you. Place your hand on the table." I raise my eyes to look at him and freeze. We both do. I know this man. This boy.

"Tom," I whisper.

His eyes widen and he takes a step backward.

"What did she say?" says Black.

"Nothing," says Tom.

I keep staring at him. Could it really be him? Tom. I never even knew his last name, this first boy I kissed. An awkward, awful kiss.

"Hello, Tom," I whisper. I can't speak any louder, or I would. *You collaborating piece of shit.*

"What's she saying?" Black is getting annoyed.

"Nothing," says Tom, and grabs my right hand and places it on the surface of the square metal table. It looks like a skeleton's hand, articulated and white.

"You know her?" says Black. An accusation.

"She's crazy," says Tom. "I'm ready."

The third SD man walks around the table to me. Tom holds my arm and presses my hand flat on the tabletop. He nods at the third man, a shorter, fatter man with freckles.

Freckles places a small leather case on the table, about the length and width of a man's forearm. He unzips it and folds open the case, which appears to be some kind of surgical kit. In my peripheral vision, I see an array of shining silver instruments: scalpels, tweezers, a magnifying glass, scissors, needles.

I'm like a rabbit, twitching and nervy. No longer exhausted, I look at the three men and wonder if I could possibly take them down somehow. But of course I can't, and there are the two guards outside. Still, I don't have to make this easy for them, whatever this is.

I try to get up from my chair, but with his arm already on mine, Tom pushes me down easily. This gives him confidence, and he smiles, proud.

"Shackle her to the chair," he says.

"Come on, Tommy," I say, panting from my brief exertion. "You know me."

Freckles looks at him, confused.

"Do it," says Tom, still pinning my arm to the table. I'm barely resisting. I don't have the energy. Freckles shrugs and takes a few shining silver implements out of the case. Laying them down on the tabletop—scissors, tweezers, and a scalpel—he looks to Black for a sign. Black nods.

The three of us watch as Freckles places a long, narrow, pointed pick at the top of my index finger's fingernail. It's like a miniature ice pick, but sharpened to a tactical point. Then, using a similarly minute silver mallet, he starts tapping the point under my fingernail. Tap, tap, tap.

The pain is shocking. I hear myself gasp, feel myself losing breath as every cell in my body is suddenly focused on my finger and the excruciating sensation of soft flesh being ravaged by sharp steel. It must stop, immediately. But it doesn't stop. Tap, tap, tap. It gets worse, my fingernail splitting lengthwise and blood erupting from the soft pink nail bed. If I look at it, it's worse. I turn my head.

Tap, tap, tap.

He taps it three more times, and the nail splits in half completely, opening like a door. Freckles looks up at Tom and Black.

Tom's face is the bluish white of Delft china. Drops of perspiration bubble on his upper lip. I look at him, but he averts his eyes. Black nods at Freckles, who puts down the mallet and spike and reaches for the tweezers.

"What's your name?" says Black.

"You know," I whisper.

Freckles pinches half of my fingernail with the tweezers and pulls. I scream—I can't help it. My finger pours blood. The half a fingernail lies next to my hand on the table. Tom looks like he might faint.

"What is it?" Black says again.

I shake my head, and Freckles rips off the other half. I scream again, writhing in my seat, held down by Freckles and Tom.

"Just tell us your name and we'll stop," says Freckles, as if I've simply misunderstood the question.

"Tommy," I whisper. He doesn't remember me or my name. He probably kissed a lot of people at dances in college. I didn't.

"Tom," I whisper again.

"What's going on?" says Black, leaning over the table and looking at Tom. "Do you know each other?"

"No, she's crazy," he says.

"Tommy," I whisper again.

Black leans back. "If you do know her, you can verify her name. Is this Hannie Schaft?"

Tom looks around for help. "I don't know," he says. "How should I know?" He looks at Freckles. "Do the next one."

Gratifying. Tom has decided it's worse to admit he knows the Murderess than to be useful and identify her. They're still scared of me. Freckles looks at Black, who nods. And they do the next finger. And the next.

I continue screaming until I faint. They slap me awake. In between fingers, I try to get at Tom. Why didn't I ask his surname, at least? I don't know how long it goes on. Minutes? Hours? Eventually, they shackle both my hands to the chair and Freckles packs up his case, wiping each tool with a snowy white linen handkerchief before putting it in its place. They walk out without saying anything.

"Bye, Tommy," I whisper. He ignores me.

The guards come inside and stop once they cross the threshold. The room is illuminated by one lamp on the table, fixing me and the tabletop within its tight circle of light. I'm slumped on the chair, my chin on my chest. I'm barely conscious, but awake enough to feel the pulse of my heartbeat through the tips of the four fingers of my right hand. Each heartbeat is agony, a rush of sensation to the raw ends of my fingers. I can hear the soft drip of blood falling to the cement floor.

And on the table, lit up like an actor in the spotlight, are eight ragged pieces of fingernail, like the horns of some tiny animal, pulpy and red at the ends where they were connected to the flesh. A sticky pool of black blood seeps out beneath them.

It's funny that something so small could hurt so much, I think.

Maybe it wasn't Tom, I think.

Then darkness. At last.

Chapter 43

LATER THAT DAY they do the fingernails on the left hand. This time I faint before they get to the pinky.

Chapter 44

I WAKE UP IN a new cell. Actually, my old one. Even before I open my eyes, I can sense people nearby. Even through the foot-thick stone walls, I can sense the murmuring of women's voices.

"Tania?" I say.

"Oh, Hannie," she says, as if she's been waiting all this time to hear me speak again. "Are you all right?"

I try to speak, but nothing comes. My mouth is as dry as sand. I fling my arm out to see if a jug of water has been left in my cell, and as I do, the searing pain of my bloodied fingertips rushes in, jolting me into full consciousness. "Ow."

"What did they do to you?" Tania says.

I need a few moments to gather myself before I can speak. It gives me time to think about my answer. Whatever I say to Tania will get repeated down the line, through the whispers.

"I'm fine," I say. "I haven't given them anything."

I hear what sounds like the soft clapping of hands. "Hannie, we love you," Tania whispers, then stops, coughing hard. She collects herself. "Stay strong."

"I love you, too." My voice is barely audible. "Vuur, schurft, hoest, en liefde," I say.

"What's that?" whispers Tania.

Fire, scabies, coughing, and love.

SOMETIME LATER IN the day, the door to my cell opens and guards drag me out again. They drop me on the floor of the infirmary, the same place I showered weeks earlier. "Clean her up," says one of the guards.

The women attendants gather around me and lift me to a canvas cot. I pass in and out of consciousness as I feel them touch me, prod me, bathe me with sponges and cloths. It seems too gentle to be real. When I awake, the pleasantness stops.

"That's good, let's go." With one arm over each of their necks, the guards drag me outside.

OUTSIDE. FOR THE first time in a month, maybe. I wince in the sunlight, its warmth almost painful. As we enter the central courtyard, I hear the ambient talking and other noises go quiet. Through my watering eyes, I can see a space has been cleared against a brick wall. The guards drag me toward it. On each side, dozens of women prisoners stand, watching. They're filthy and skinny as sticks, and they hold hands and whisper to each other as I pass. I hear the name "Hannie Schaft" here and there. And the occasional hissed "Verzet."

Resist, resist. I intend to. It's still my only plan. Give them nothing.

"Stand there, against the wall," says the guard, pushing me. I know what this is because I've seen it in films. An execution. A firing line. The red bricks are warm against my back. I raise my hand to wipe the hair from my eyes and the entire courtyard goes quiet. My hand. The infirmary attendants have wrapped my fingertips in gauze, but the blood has already soaked through and my entire right palm is streaked with red blood running down my forearm and staining the sleeve of my formerly white blouse. I put my hand down and once again feel the pulsing beat of my heart in my fingertips, aching. I pull the handkerchief out of my skirt pocket and press my right hand into a fist, trying to stop the throbbing. It's not just a handkerchief, though. It's the doll. Flattened and creased and grimy and stained, but it's the little handkerchief doll Truus gave me. The guards let me keep it when I got checked in; after all, it's just an old hanky. The knots are gone from the corners, the twine around the neck, too. It appears to be nothing but a tattered pocket square. But that's not what it really is. It's Truus, Freddie, Hendrik, even Jan. It's my parents, Philine, Sonja. It's Rosie. Truus made her a doll, and she survived. Truus made me a doll . . . and I'm still here. I'm not letting go. The handkerchief has already turned from dirty white to bright, bloody red.

"Stand up!" the guard says again, and I straighten my spine. Acclimated to the afternoon sunlight now, I see the prisoners standing behind the guards, their faces anxious, emotional. And right in front of me, I see a half dozen Wehrmacht soldiers in uniform, standing at attention in a semicircle with their rifles at their sides.

"Achtung!" a voice says. It's Rühl. The soldiers click their heels. "Heil Hitler," he says.

"Heil Hitler," the soldiers repeat with a salute.

"Hannie Schaft," Rühl says, his voice booming across the courtyard. "We've given you several opportunities. Now is your last chance. We know you are a criminal, trying to destroy the hopes and dreams of hardworking people of the Netherlands. Hurting—killing!—innocent people. Some of them her fellow Dutchmen. Yes, it's true." He looks around the courtyard, nodding, as if expecting the prisoners to take his side. They're silent.

"All we want is for you to admit who you are and what you have done. It's not much. You see, this is what we must do if we are to serve the cause of justice. We must ensure we don't blame the wrong person for a crime. That would be unjust. The Third Reich is a regime of laws, Miss Schaft. No one is above the law."

"Emil," I say. "Sounds French."

Rühl looks at me, infuriated by my insolence.

"What's that, Miss Schaft?"

I don't have the energy to say it again.

"Well, have you anything else to say? This is your last opportunity."

I lift my head. The soldiers look straight through me, not at me. Their faces are nothing but flesh masks. They look constipated more than anything else. This makes me smile.

"That's it," Rühl says. He directs his voice to the soldiers. "Achtung!"

They click their heels.

"Aim!"

The soldiers lift their rifles to their shoulders, all pointed at me. My empty bowels churn. If I wasn't so dehydrated, I'd pee my pants. The women prisoners hold hands over mouths, eyes, ears. I hear the sound of someone crying. I remind myself to breathe. I can't manage more than a shallow sip of air, but it's enough to remind me that I'm still alive. That I've given them nothing. Not even my name.

"Alfred?" Rühl says.

CLICK.

Silence.

Scuffling of feet. Gasps.

I open my eyes. In the middle of the firing line stands a man with a large portrait camera. CLICK. He takes another shot of me.

"For our files," Rühl says, staring at me with a sick smile. I stare back. "Next time we shoot with guns."

I smile. I squeeze Rosie's doll. Drops of blood fall to the stones at my feet.

The women cheer.

Chapter 45

15 April 1945

I HAVE NO IDEA what time or even what day it is. I hug the dirty hand-kerchief doll to my breast and listen to the sounds that drift in from outside my window; sometimes I hear the jarring, familiar jingle of a bi-cycle bell from the street. Just a hundred yards away, on the other side of the wall, people are walking free. It's a matter of inches, of a few feet. Still, I know I'm on the right side.

The door opens and the guards set a tray of food down. "Eat fast, we're taking you out."

I stuff something brown and slimy in my mouth, and they walk me through the prison again. The prisoners cheer. I'm too tired to acknowl-edge them. Soon I'm in the hushed interior of the building, so removed from the prisoners we could almost be in a normal office building if it weren't for the bars on the windows. My old friend Emil Rühl sits across a wide teak desk. They sit me down in a cushioned chair on the other side. It's the softest thing I've felt in a long time. Maybe ever. I'm not used to anything feeling good.

"Look at you," he says, shaking his head. He seems genuinely sad. "Wait," he says, and leans over and rummages in a desk drawer. There are two guards in here with me, but none of them are worried about my jumping up and attacking Rühl. I barely have the energy to imagine it.

"Here," he says, and hands me a handheld round mirror with an ebony frame and handle. I take it from him awkwardly with my bandaged fingers—I see him recoil at the sight of them—and I hold the mirror up to my face.

It takes a moment.

Then I recognize her. An image looks back at me from the glass. A human, that's the first thing I think when I see my reflection. Starvation has erased not only soft features and personality, but even my sex. I could be male or female. I could be young or old. I'm a face on a body, and I'm still alive to look at myself. I'm proud of that.

"What's the date?" I say, my voice a rasp. I try to smooth my matted hair.

Rühl nearly jumps out of his chair. He hasn't heard me speak more than a few words, ever. "What did you say?"

"Date." I'm too tired.

He glances at his desk calendar, one of the thousands of bespoke items in this room embossed with a screaming swastika. They always catch my eye. "April fifteenth," he says, finger lingering on the square on the page as if waiting for me to challenge him. But I'm no longer thinking about Emil Rühl. If it's April fifteenth, then I've been here over a month.

Why isn't the war over? Where are the Allies? They're somewhere out there, lost like my parents and Sonja and Philine.

I crane my neck to look out the window to the Amsterdam street below, but it's the wrong angle. All I can see is the sky. The sky is blue. A bird flies past the window—a sparrow—and is gone. The sparrow in the hall. I did a presentation on it in year nine. A sparrow flies out of dark storm and into a king's great hall, filled with light and warmth, and then flies back into the darkness and cold. And that's what man's life is like, a brief period of light between the darkness of death and nonexistence. That's what I wrote, anyway.

"... of special concern to you?" Rühl says. I missed the first part. Mind wandering.

"What?"

Rühl snorts. I've offended him. Whatever we can see from the limited perspective of our brief time on earth, flying through the lighted hall, reveals nothing about what comes after or before.

"What are you talking about?" Rühl looks at me with brows furrowed.

"Nothing." I hadn't realized I was talking out loud. In the blue sky, I try to imagine a fleet of RAF planes tearing through the air, announcing the end of all this. *Just bomb us,* I think. *Flatten this prison. Bomb me.* But there are no planes in the sky. Just birds.

"I was there with Jan Bonekamp, you know," Rühl says. "At the hospital."

I stare at him. I want him to say more, but I refuse to ask.

He can't stop himself. "I was there for his final moments. His last words." He pauses to gauge my reaction. If I'm having one, there's nothing I can do to hide it. But I find I'm too exhausted to express emotion anymore.

"They weren't about you." Rühl smiles like the proud owner of a winning racehorse.

"Fuck you," I say.

One of the soldiers coughs and Rühl's face goes scarlet.

"Listen, you little bitch, I could have had you killed weeks ago. Many here would have preferred that. I assumed we could work together. Help each other. But you haven't helped me at all."

I just watch him talk. My mind wanders back to the sparrow, the freedom of flight. Then to Jan. They think I'm surprised? I don't know what reaction I'm supposed to have. Honored? Horrified? Heartbroken? I've already survived all that.

"You have the next day to think about it. This is your last chance, Hannie. Don't break your parents' hearts, eh?" I look up. "Oh, yes, they're still alive. For now." My heart thuds in my chest so hard it hurts. My parents are alive? What about Philine? I want to ask, but it's useless.

"It's not too late to do the right thing. Like your darling Bonekamp did."

My darling Bonekamp. I did love him. I was in love with him—is that the same thing? I believe he loved me. The way he loved many things. Carelessly.

"What is it?" Rühl stares back at me.

I haven't spoken aloud, I don't think. *Don't break your parents' hearts. They're alive. Maybe. Maybe if I . . . no. Don't be stupid, Hannie. He's lying.*

Just before darkness comes, I see the blue sky behind Rühl, and I hope to see the sparrow again.

"HANNIE, HANNIE, ARE you there?"

It's so dark it must be nighttime. Perhaps days have passed, perhaps hours. I don't know. Tania's voice seeps through the drain so softly I barely hear it. "Hannie?"

"Tania," I whisper.

"Are you all right?"

Today they took me to the basement room, kept my hands shackled behind me, attached the handcuffs to a rope threaded through a hook in the ceiling; then someone began pulling on the rope from behind me, raising my arms higher and higher until my shoulders dislocated; then my elbows broke.

Back in my cell now, I remember a flash of roaring pain when somebody pushed the bones back into their sockets. My shoulders are swollen and black with bruises. All my fingers are wrapped in gauze except my thumbs. I see them, pink and healthy at the end of my arms, and it amazes me how one part of my body can continue to function so well, while inches away another part, my fingertips, putrefies and withers. I gave them nothing. Not even my name.

"I'm fine," I say to Tania. "I'm fine."

Chapter 46

17 April 1945

COME ON." GUARDS are pulling me to my feet. I stagger through the prison, drooping off their arms like moss off a tree. The sound of the prisoners this morning is terrifying. What starts as shouts—*Hannie!*—dissolves into whispers and angry yelling and jeers, booing the guards, throwing things at them as we pass by. They think I'm dead. I can't remember the last time I ate or drank anything. But I'm not dead. I'm still alive.

Then a young woman leans through the bars of her cell just ahead of me. She reaches out and touches the edge of my sleeve, and as her nails catch in the fabric, our eyes meet.

"Hannie Schaft?" she asks.

The guards are pulling me away, but I twist around to see her. "Shh," I say.

She screams as loud as she can: "Lang leve Hannie Schaft!"

Long live Hannie Schaft.

The prisoners go berserk. The cheer races through the prison like a flood, drowning everything else.

Lang leve Hannie Schaft.

Lang leve Hannie Schaft.

Lang leve Hannie Schaft.

The whole stone fortress echoes with the sounds of women wailing and screaming and hating these Nazi bastards and hanging on to life, and I love them. And as I'm dragged outside, I throw my head back and I scream. No words, just sounds so primal they scare me. Like a wounded animal, which is what I am. They scream back. I love them.

I'm tossed into the back of a van, panting. My old friend, the black van. They love throwing women in these. Through the porthole window, I see a blond driver get in behind the wheel, along with another anonymous guard. Emil Rühl walks out. Of course Rühl is here. He wouldn't miss this. Behind him walks a tall, gangly man with a puckered face like a mole: it's my other old friend, SS-Sturmbahnführer Willy Lages, from the Jan Gijzen Bridge. He and Rühl Heil-Hitler each other, talk for a moment, salute again, and then Lages gets in the van. Rühl stays behind. The motor rumbles, the wheels turn, and I see the gray stone walls of Amstelveenseweg prison grow small in the tiny window. Then I faint.

I wake up in the middle of a city. I can see tall buildings through the window and hear people talking outside. The passenger door of the cab opens and a new man is joining us. Behind him I see the red-and-white painted sign of the Bakkerij Vink Haarlem. I used to get apple tarts there. Why are we in Haarlem? They can't be taking me home.

Are they taking me home?

Truus. What is Truus doing right now?

Why are we in Haarlem?

Then the rear doors of the van swing open and the new man looks inside, sees me slumped against the wall of the cargo area, and throws something in next to me on the right. The doors close and slam into their locks with a crash of steel.

It's a shovel.

THEY'RE NOT TAKING me home.

Between Amsterdam and Haarlem, I slept. I'd fall down if I tried to run anywhere, but my mind is alive and awake for the first time in weeks. The van drives on, the noise of the engine and the tires on the rutted road cloaking everything in a blank roar. Good for thinking.

They're not taking me home.

We're not in town anymore. The van stops only rarely, rolling through intersections. There's little outside noise. I pull myself up to the window and see fields outside, some planted, some fallow. It reminds me of picnics with Truus and Freddie.

Truus and Freddie and Trijntje. The Oversteegen women are alive.

My parents? Alive, I decide to hope.

Philine and Sonja? Alive, I decide to hope.

Hendrik is dead. Heroically.

Jan is dead. Jan . . . I close my eyes when I think of Jan and my heart flickers. It always does, remembering the way he made me feel. I welcome the pain of missing him; it's all I have left. The only thing worse than this heartbreak would have been never to feel it at all.

I will soon be dead.

Maybe little Rosie is alive. She's still so young. I feel so old . . . Is twenty-four old? Maybe not, but I'm no longer young.

The blue sky out the window is the same blue as the blue sky outside Rühl's window. Because it's the same sky. I can see the prison. Hear Tania's voice in the drain. Feel, in my bones, the roaring cheers of the prisoners. Register the fabric of my sleeve ripping as the young woman leans out. *Hannie?*

For the first time since it happened, I think about the first time I killed. Officer Kohl, in the alley. I'd been afraid to revisit it. Now I want to. We all die. But I was useful that night.

I can still be useful.

I can still resist.

The van rattles and I slide to the grooved metal floor and the back doors open.

"Get out." Someone grabs the shovel.

I crawl out of the van. At first, all I can see are tall spiny bushes surrounding us, taller than me. The other two men come around the van. SS-Sturmbahnführer Lages nods at the man with the shovel.

"Come on," says the new man, pulling my elbow. I flinch at the touch and hop ahead of him. He lets me lead. I have no idea where we are or where we're going.

And then I do. My feet are bare and I step out of the bushes onto a sandy path. There's sand everywhere, sun-warmed and soft. I came here with Jan once. We're at the giant sand dunes at the edge of the North Sea. I long for my gun. I stumble and Lages yells at me.

"Keep walking," he says. "Follow the path."

I follow it. It's not easy. The sand is slippery and I'm weak. The glorious warmth of the sun and the ocean breeze are overwhelming, like a drug. I could overdose at any moment.

I fall.

"Get up."

I get up. Take a few steps. Fall again. I laugh.

"Shut up and walk."

I try, but I can't stop laughing, an airy, hollow laugh that's more wind than sound. I see Annie watching all this and laughing, too. It's absurd. How did I get here, in the dunes, starving, defiant? How did she?

"Annie?" I say.

"Hallo, Jopie." My sister's beautiful smile. She's still twelve. I'm no age at all. Time is unraveling itself around me. I can feel it. Time is slowing down, dragging, then skipping ahead, jumping. Not an arrow. A whirlpool.

Then I hear something, maybe an insect or even a sparrow, buzz past my ear. A distant BOOM. I've fallen again. I try to push myself up and feel something on my ear and touch it. Hot, sticky. I get to my feet and stare at my hand, painted red. I see it running down my left shoulder. Red blood. I reach for the doll in my pocket. Guns are raised as I pull it out.

"It's nothing, just a handkerchief," one of them says. I press it against my bloody head. Truus is still here, somehow. Helping me, like she always has. Helping me stay human.

The shovel man is lowering his gun. He looks scared. Of what?

Oh. The blood. My hand is red and dripping. He's not a very good shot.

Annie and I laugh. They're not taking me home, are they? Annie smiles at me. She always had the most beautiful smile. Everyone said so after she died. She looked like my mother.

I turn to look at the three of them standing there behind me, lined up in a row like little boys playing with guns. Why am I sitting in the sand? *Resist.* I push myself to standing, swaying in space. These silly men with their guns. They're terrified of something.

"I can shoot better than you," I say. It's true.

Lages snarls and raises his gun, saliva spraying from his mouth. He's shouting something. I can't hear his voice. His fingers twitches on the trigger.

I'm not scared. I'm defiant. I gave them nothing. Not even my name.

A huge sound, like thunder.

BOOM.

The bloodstained doll flutters to the sand.

Two sparrows, wheeling. A bee.

I gave them nothing.

Ocean, pounding.

Sky.

Not even my name.

Afterword

HANNIE SCHAFT WAS taken from Amstelveenseweg prison on 17 April 1945 and driven to the sand dunes near Bloemendaal, about twelve miles from Amsterdam. According to her captors, she was forced to walk in front of them as they marched her deep into the dunes. She was then shot from behind by German soldier Mattheus Schmitz. The bullet grazed her head and knocked her to the sand. She stood up, turned to face her executioners, and shouted, "I can shoot better than you!" At that point, Dutch collaborator and policeman Maarten Kuiper raised his machine gun and shot her to death. (Most of what we know of Hannie's last moments comes from Kuiper, who was interviewed after the war.) They buried Hannie Schaft in a shallow grave in the dunes, where many resisters were left in unmarked sites in the hope they would be forgotten.

Thirteen days later, on 30 April 1945, Adolf Hitler died by suicide in Germany, and a week after that the German Third Reich surrendered unconditionally to the Allied Powers. The Netherlands was finally liberated on 5 May 1945. In the months after, hundreds of bodies of murdered Resistance fighters were recovered from the dunes. Hannie was buried in a flag-draped coffin in the National Cemetery of Honor in a ceremony on 27 November 1945 attended by Queen Wilhelmina of the Netherlands and a crowd of hundreds. Among the 422 Resistance fighters found in the dunes, Hannie Schaft was the only woman.

In addition to her six confirmed assassinations of Nazi German officers and Dutch collaborators, Hannie (and Truus and Freddie) performed scores of dangerous weapons transports around the country, mostly by bicycle. Along with Jan Bonekamp, Hannie broke into the Krommenie city hall, confiscating documents useful to the Resistance, as well as raiding a significant chemical facility in Amsterdam. In 1944, Hannie, posing as Johanna Elderkamp, successfully infiltrated a highly restricted complex of German V-1 and V-2 rocket facilities on the Dutch coastline whose attacks had been devastating southern England. Hannie drew detailed maps that were passed on to the British Royal Air Force (RAF), which used them to send three hundred RAF aerial bombers on successful bombing missions in 1944, destroying the Germans' rocket-launching capabilities on the coast. Not long before her capture, Hannie and Truus declined to bomb a busy Amsterdam department store, arguing that too many civilians would be hurt. Hannie and Truus were also offered the opportunity to kidnap Reichskommissar Arthur Seyss-Inquart's children, an assignment they both refused. "We are not like the Nazis," Hannie said at the time. "We of the Resistance do not kill children." Neither plan was ever carried out.

After her death, Hannie Schaft was initially celebrated as the "Symbol of the Resistance" by Queen Wilhelmina and was posthumously awarded the Dutch Cross of Resistance. Supreme Allied Commander General Dwight D. Eisenhower awarded Schaft a posthumous American Medal of Freedom. But by the beginning of the Cold War, Hannie's connection to the nominally Communist RVV led the Dutch government to ban any memorials in her name. In 1951, the government turned ten thousand mourners away from her grave site with the help of armed forces and tanks. After the Soviet Union fell in the early 1990s, her reputation was gradually restored.

Today, Hannie Schaft's gravestone in the Cemetery of Heroes reads:

JANNETJE JOHANNA SCHAFT
16 Sept. 1920–17 April 1945
Zij diende
[She served]

Hannie's parents, **Aafje Talea (Vrijer) Schaft** and **Pieter Schaft**, were held in the Herzogenbusch concentration camp near the city of Vught in the Netherlands until nearly the end of the war, when they were allowed to return to their home in Haarlem. When peace was declared on 5 May 1945, Hannie's parents assumed she would be released from prison. On 21 May, they were informed that their daughter had been executed, despite the Germans' agreement with the Allies to cancel all executions weeks earlier. The Schafts continued living in Haarlem after the war.

Philine Rosa Polak Lachman (1921–2018) survived the war, thanks to the help of her family friend **Marie Korts**, a German woman who had immigrated to the Netherlands after World War I and worked as a house-keeper for the Polak family throughout Philine's childhood. (Philine's mother never fully recovered from the 1919 Spanish influenza outbreak and succumbed to tuberculosis in 1923, when Philine was two.) Marie hated the Nazi regime and made contact with Philine via the Resistance network, which showed up to rescue her at the Schaft home the night Hannie's parents were arrested. (This begs the question: Why did the Schafts remain? Perhaps they remained in their home afterward because they believed they were safe, now that they were no longer hiding onder-duikers, but it's difficult to say for sure.) Philine was taken back to Amsterdam, where she spent the Hunger Winter trying to survive in a safe house built in 1667 with no electricity or heat. "I thought of jumping in the canal," she said later. "Death was living with us all the time; there was no future. It didn't exist." Marie Korts, now working in the home of an SS officer, once again came to the rescue, hiding Philine overnight in the SS officer's kitchen and waiting there with her silently all night, knowing they would both be shot if discovered. The next morning, the Resistance found a new hiding place, and Philine escaped again.

By the day of liberation on 5 May, Philine was so frail she could barely celebrate. "We were very hungry and weak and exhausted. I can't say that I felt much emotion; I was too far gone. Most people were." She was also nervous about seeing her old neighbors again, those who were not Jewish. "I thought they'd say: 'Here are these damn Jews again. Why weren't they all killed?' I thought they might think that way," she recalled. "Because after you're told so many times that you are an Untermensch [in German, 'subhuman'], some of it sinks in." Wearing her missing father's oversized pants and shirts, as her own clothes had finally worn out, Philine ventured out into public life again for the first time in three years. On Dam Square the swastika flag had been removed and "there were Allied troops, Canadian troops in the square. The first Allied soldier I saw, I asked for an autograph on my ID and he was from Winnipeg. I'd never seen an Allied soldier before and we received the Allies with great joy."

Philine's joy vanished when she attempted to reunite with Hannie, after finally making contact with Truus. (Hannie told her dear friends about one another before she died, and Truus and Freddie and Philine remained in contact throughout their lives through their support of the Dutch National Hannie Schaft Foundation.) "Truus and I spent the first free day after the war standing in front of the prison in Amsterdam with red flowers," she recalled, "waiting to receive her when she came out. But she wasn't there to come out."

Shortly afterward Philine also learned that her father, **David Polak** (1885–1943), had been killed at the Sobibor concentration camp in Poland not long after Philine left home to live with the Schafts. Twelve other members of the extended Polak family were also killed in concentration camps.

Philine resolved to immigrate to the United States to reunite with her brother, Jaap Polak (later known as Jack Vanderpol), at Walter Reed General Hospital in Washington, DC. He had escaped the Netherlands before the war, joined the US Army, and sustained serious injuries in the Battle of the Bulge. In Washington, Philine met a fellow Holocaust survivor, Erwin J. Lachman, formerly of Berlin, Germany, and they married and had two children.

Philine remained committed to the ideals of human rights and justice she and Hannie shared. She went on to work for the International Monetary Fund as Assistant General Counsel, where she rose to become the highest-ranking woman in the IMF. Through Philine's efforts, Marie Korts was recognized by Israel's Yad Vashem World Holocaust Memorial as Righteous Among the Nations in 1992. Marie remained in Amsterdam after the war, and Philine visited her there many times throughout their lives.

Although she did not talk about her wartime experience much as a young woman, in later years Philine began to feel it was important to share what had happened, especially in response to those who denied the reality of the Holocaust. "Before the war I wasn't political," she told an interviewer, "because my father [wasn't]. After the war I discovered I can't afford to not be political because politics is what killed us." Philine contributed extensive oral history interviews to the Shoah Foundation, and she spoke at the sixtieth anniversary commemoration of Hannie Schaft's death in Haarlem in 2005. In later life, on her birthday, Philine liked to say, "They tried so hard to kill me, but I'm still here!"

In 2017, at the age of ninety-six, Philine reflected on her life. "The way I tried to live my life is 'Tikkun Olam,'" she wrote. "That means make the world better. It is the only Hebrew I know! For me it has meant to try never to say things that could grieve the other person, or that would harm him mentally or materially." Even in her nineties, Philine's personal experience of the war remained vivid and visceral: "I had of course to wear a yellow star," she recalled. "That is something you put on, but you can never take it off."

Philine R. Lachman died in Maryland in 2018 in the loving care of her children and grandchildren at the age of ninety-seven.

Sonja Antoinette Frenk (1920–1943) did not escape to America. She was discovered and betrayed in Lyon, France, where she was captured and sent to the Auschwitz concentration camp in occupied Poland. She was murdered on 23 November 1943. Soon after Sonja left Amsterdam with Hannie Schaft, Sonja's father, Willem Frenk (1891–1943), was killed in the Sobibor concentration camp, just as Philine's father was. Sonja's mother, Esther Engelina Blok Frenk (1891–1980), survived the war and eventually remarried.

After seeing Hannie get arrested at the Jan Gijzen Bridge on 21 March 1945, **Truus Menger-Oversteegen** (1923–2016) held out hope that Hannie was still alive. Sources in the Resistance pointed her to Amsterdam's Amstelveenseweg prison. Truus went to the prison, once again dressed as a German nurse, asking to visit Hannie Schaft. Checking her roster, the guard showed Truus that the name "J. Schaft" had been crossed out, indicating an execution. Truus fainted when she heard the news, fell to the floor—and two revolvers slid out of her pockets. Fortunately, she regained consciousness quickly and no one discovered her weapons. Hoping perhaps Hannie had merely been taken to another location, Truus continued to believe she was still alive. Like Philine, Truus remembered the day they went to look for her at Amstelveenseweg prison, after the liberation. They watched every prisoner emerge and meet their families until no one else came out. She and Philine gave the bouquet of red tulips to the last woman to leave the prison.

Truus married Pieter Menger, a fellow resister she met during the war when they were assigned to blow up a dam. They married after the war and had four children, naming their firstborn daughter Hannie. Truus became an internationally recognized artist, sculptor, and human rights activist, working to fight racism, sexism, and all forms of injustice. She became involved in the anti-apartheid movement in the 1980s and worked closely with the African National Congress (ANC) and its leaders, Nelson Mandela and Oliver Tambo, and she founded an orphanage in Soweto for children with disabilities. In 1967, Truus was recognized by Israel's Yad Vashem as Righteous Among the Nations. On her seventy-fifth birthday she was invested by the Netherlands' Queen Beatrix as an officer of the Order of Orange-Nassau for her chivalry.

Truus's wartime experiences defined the rest of her life; both she and Freddie suffered from nightmares and depression in the decades that followed. "I'm a traumatized person," she told an interviewer. But she found ways to keep going: through her art, through her activism, and by visiting hundreds of schools over the years to talk to children about the dangers of intolerance. "I ask the children what they would have done themselves," she said. "The answers are often heartwarming." At one school she was asked if, after everything she'd seen, she could still believe in God. "I was not brought up religious, so you might ask whether I believe in humanity," she answered. "I believe in the goodness of man." Truus established the Hannie Schaft Foundation in 1996 and remained an activist against fascism and injustice until her death in 2016 at the age of ninety-two.

Freddie Nanda Dekker-Oversteegen (6 September 1925–5 September 2018) married Jan Dekker and had three children and returned to civilian life after the war. Like her sister, Freddie was haunted by memories of the Resistance, which left them both with lifelong psychological trauma. Seventy years after the end of the war, the Oversteegen sisters were finally awarded the Mobilization War Cross for their service in the Resistance. In interviews later in life, Freddie was asked how many

Nazis she had killed. She refused to say. "I won't tell you the number of people I shot," she said. "I was a soldier. A child soldier, but a soldier, nevertheless. You should never ask a soldier how many people he shot." Freddie served on the board of the Hannie Schaft Foundation and remained committed to anti-fascist causes until her death in 2018.

Johannes (Jan) Lambertus Bonekamp (19 May 1914–21 June 1944) was remembered by his Resistance comrades, including Hannie, Truus, and Freddie, as a great hero. He first emerged as a Resistance fighter after organizing a strike at the Hoogovens steel factory where he worked in 1943. Bonekamp was renowned among his peers for dedication to the Resistance cause as well as his courage and daring. Jan would perform assassinations, sabotage, and any other job asked of him, including a valiant but doomed attempt to liberate political prisoners from Amsterdam's notorious Weteringschans prison, where Anne Frank and her family were later incarcerated. After being shot during the Ragut assassination with Hannie, Jan was taken to a hospital in German custody. According to Nazi Kriminalsekretär Emil Rühl, who interrogated him, as Jan lay dying and in excruciating pain, the Nazis assured Jan that they were fellow Resistance members and would pass along a message to his comrades, which was when Jan gave up the name and address of Hannie Schaft, among others. Jan was survived by his wife and young daughter.

Jan's remains were recovered after the war and the Oversteegen sisters requested that he be buried in the National Cemetery of Honor along with Hannie, but instead the Bonekamps chose to bury him in a family plot in Westerbegraafplaats cemetery in his hometown of IJmuiden, where it is the site of an annual remembrance ceremony by the Jan Bonekamp Society. Two monuments, one each for Jan and Hannie, were erected in downtown Zaandam at the site of the Ragut attack. Over the years, Truus and Freddie regularly paid tribute to Jan's bravery on the annual fifth of May celebration of Dutch liberation.

Hannie was devastated by Jan's death. "I will try to save some of the debris of my old self. But that probably isn't possible anymore," she wrote in a letter in the months afterward. "Don't think poorly of my friend [Jan]; he behaved beautifully. You can only hope for more people like him. He was one of the finest men I ever met. Remember this."

Willy Paul Franz Lages (1901–1971) was the German chief (SS-Sturmbahnführer) of the Sicherheitsdienst (SD) in Amsterdam during World War II. He was also the head of the occupying government's Zentralstelle für jüdische Auswanderung (Central Bureau for Jewish Emigration), the Nazi department responsible for deporting Dutch Jews to concentration camps outside the Netherlands. In this role, he authorized the deportation and killing of tens of thousands of Dutch Jews, including Anne Frank and her family.

Willy Lages was arrested after the war and accused of crimes against humanity, which included the murder of hundreds of Dutch citizens. He was tried at Nuremberg and sentenced to life in prison. In 1966, he was released on humanitarian grounds, due to illness, and allowed to return to West Germany. Once there, he received medical treatment and died in 1971.

Emil Rühl (1904–unknown) was the Kriminalsekretär (senior criminal secretary) in the occupying Nazi regime's Amsterdam secret police, or Gestapo. Rühl was tried and convicted for his participation in illegal executions, the murders committed as part of the anti-Resistance Aktion Silbertanne, which he directed, as well as the mistreatment of prisoners in his care and the torture of Dutch Jews; he was also known to have waterboarded French prisoners. Rühl was sentenced to eighteen years in prison but was released after serving seven, in 1956.

Maarten Kuiper (1898–1948), the man who fatally shot Hannie Schaft, was a Dutch police officer who was a member of the fascist Dutch National Socialist Party (NSB) before the Nazi occupation. Under the Nazi regime he joined the Sicherheitsdienst (SD) and became a notorious "Jew-hunter," receiving eight guilders (about twenty dollars at the time) in exchange for every Jewish person he turned over to the Nazis. Kuiper participated in Aktion Silbertanne and, like Willy Lages, was also involved in the arrest and deportation of Anne Frank and her family in Amsterdam in 1944. Kuiper was arrested and tried for murder and crimes against humanity. He was found guilty of sending hundreds of Dutch Jews to their deaths in concentration camps as well as the direct murder of seventeen Jews and members of the Resistance. He was executed on 30 August 1948 in Fort Bijlmer, the Netherlands.

Before Adolf Hitler died by suicide in April 1945, he elevated **Arthur Seyss-Inquart** to Reichsminister of Foreign Affairs, replacing Joachim von Ribbentrop. Seyss-Inquart attempted to escape justice by fleeing from the Netherlands as the war ended, most likely headed for South America like many of his Nazi colleagues. But he only made it to Hamburg, Germany, before being stopped on 7 May 1945.

It was an Allied soldier named **Norman Miller**, a young Royal Welch Fusilier infantryman assigned to that day's traffic duty, who recognized the newly appointed minister of the Third Reich during a routine traffic stop. Miller (birth name: Norbert Müller) was a German Jew, born in Nuremberg in 1924, who had been sent to England for safety as part of the British Kindertransport program (through which ten thousand Jewish children were evacuated from Nazi-occupied Europe). Miller was an orphan; his entire family—father, Sebald, mother, Laura, and sister, Susanne—were killed in the Jungfernhof concentration camp in Latvia on 26 March 1942. Once he recognized Seyss-Inquart, Norman Miller arrested the high-ranking Nazi on the spot, ensuring he would face justice for his crimes at the postwar International Military Tribunal.

Arthur Seyss-Inquart faced that tribunal in Nuremberg in 1946 and was charged with conspiracy to commit crimes against peace; planning, initiating, and waging wars of aggression; war crimes; and crimes against humanity. Throughout the trial, Seyss-Inquart insisted that his "conscience was untroubled," despite the genocide and famine he had inflicted on the people of the Netherlands. He deeply resented being forced to surrender.

As early as December 1944 Supreme Commander Dwight D. Eisenhower and the Allied Expeditionary Force (SHAEF) were deeply worried about the "starving Dutch," who were subsisting on less than 1,000 calories a day. Commander Eisenhower warned Seyss-Inquart that, to avoid "deaths through famine on a considerable scale ... for sheer humanitarian reasons something must be done at once." Yet the Reichsminister stalled. As he did, large portions of his army began to flee back to Germany and they enacted a scorched-earth policy, stealing and destroying Dutch food resources in their retreat, and this went on for months.

On 23 April 1945 Eisenhower sent a message to the German military that they were "directly responsible" for "the starving people in Holland . . . and if [Seyss-Inquart] fails in this respect to meet his clear obligations and his humanitarian duty, he and each responsible member of his command will be considered by me as violators of the laws of war who must face the certain consequences of their acts." By this date, historians now estimate that approximately twenty thousand Dutch civilians had died as a result of starvation during the Hunger Winter.

Still, Seyss-Inquart stalled.

Finally, on the day of Adolf Hitler's suicide, 30 April 1945, SHAEF Chief of Staff Lieutenant General Walter Bedell Smith met with Seyss-Inquart, furious at being forced to negotiate emergency food distribution with "one of the worst war criminals." Reminding the Reichsminister the war would soon be over, he spoke bluntly. We "cannot accept the liberation of corpses," he warned.

Reluctantly, Seyss-Inquart agreed to open a few supply lines to allow food into occupied Holland.

"Well, in any case," said a disgusted Smith, "you are going to be shot."

"That leaves me cold," Seyss-Inquart replied.

"It will," agreed Smith.

Arthur Seyss-Inquart was found guilty of war crimes and crimes against humanity and hanged to death in Nuremberg prison on 16 October 1946, at the age of fifty-four.

Author's Note

Although Hannie Schaft died before the end of the war, many of her fellow Resistance fighters survived. They ensured her legacy would not be forgotten, writing their own memoirs and giving court testimony and interviews throughout their lives. There is, however, one gap in the record: the voice of Hannie Schaft herself. She wrote only a few letters and gave no interviews because protecting her identity was crucial for her Resistance work. What remains of Hannie's voice are the remembered conversations she had with friends and family and a dozen or so photographs, as well as the memories of her Nazi captors, who were the last to see her alive.

For this reason, I have chosen to tell this true story using some of the tools of fiction in recreating conversations and inner monologues that bring the humanity of her story to life. Some names have been changed, and some of the characters and scenes in the novel are composites, based on more than one real person or story. All of the prominent characters in *To Die Beautiful* are inspired by real individuals, with the exception of Nurse Bettine Dekker and Hendrik Oostdijk. The character of Nurse Dekker was modeled on the countless women of the Dutch nursing and childcare sectors whose compassion, strategic planning, and sheer courage saved the lives of thousands of Jewish people, particularly children, during the Second World War. The character of Hendrik Oostdijk was inspired by the many brave Dutch men who left their families and their professional careers, sacrificing their lives to fight against the Nazis for their countrymen. The name of the commander of the real Haarlem RVV cell was Frans van der Wiel, and it was he who recruited Truus and Freddie as Resistance fighters when they were just sixteen and fourteen (he got their mother Trijntje's permission). Frans van der Wiel survived the war.

I'm grateful for the staff and resources of the following Dutch institutions for their help as I researched this book: Nationaal Archief (National Archives) of the Netherlands; NIOD Institute for War, Holocaust and Genocide Studies; Anne Frank House & Museum; Verzetsmuseum (Museum of Resistance); Hollandsche Schouwburg National Holocaust Memorial; Jewish Historical Museum of Amsterdam; and Museum of Haarlem.

Further research materials were accessed at the National Archives (United Kingdom), the Imperial War Museum London, the Royal Welch Fusiliers Archive at the Wrexham Museum (Wales), the Nuremberg Trials Collection at Yale Law School, the USC Shoah Foundation Visual Archive, the United States Holocaust Memorial Museum, and the Yad Vashem World Holocaust Remembrance Center (Israel).

For those interested in deeper reading on the Dutch experience in World War II, there are many excellent firsthand accounts. Truus Menger-Oversteegen wrote a wonderful autobiography entitled *Not Then Not Now Not Ever*, which was invaluable for my research. *The Diary of a Young Girl* by Anne Frank is well-known, but other important memoirs include Etty Hillesum's *An Interrupted Life: The Diaries: 1941–1943* and *Letters from Westerbork*; Edith Velmans's *Edith's Book: The True Story of How One Young Girl Survived the War*; and *Steal a Pencil for Me: Love Letters from Camp Bergen-Belsen and Westerbork* by Jaap Polak (no relation to Philine) and Ina Soep—all moving personal memoirs of daily Dutch life under Nazi occupation. J. J. Boolen's *Five Years of Occupation: The Resistance of the Dutch Against Hitler Terrorism and Nazi Robbery* was published on a Resistance printing press before the war ended and provides detailed reporting on Nazi atrocities. For more reading recommendations about the history of the Netherlands in World War II, please visit buzzyjackson.com.

I was very fortunate to be welcomed by the families of Truus and Freddie Oversteegen, the family of Philine Polak Lachman, and the relatives of other World War II Dutch survivors in Haarlem and the United States. I am deeply grateful to them for entrusting their memories to me, and I hope I have managed to capture in these pages some of the extraordinary strength, bravery, and resolute moral integrity of Hannie, Philine, Sonja, Truus, Freddie, and Trijntje that first inspired me to share their story. They are my heroes.

Acknowledgments

SCHOOLS, STREETS, AND awards are named after Hannie Schaft in the Netherlands, but until I visited Amsterdam's Verzetsmuseum (Museum of Resistance) in the winter of 2016, I had never heard of her. Since then, many colleagues and friends have helped me understand Hannie's life and the broader story of the Netherlands' experience during World War II, and I am grateful for their wisdom and generosity.

I'd like to thank the following people in Amsterdam, Haarlem, and Zaandam for their help as I researched Hannie's story: first, Dawn Skorczsewski, who introduced me to Hannie and the history of the Dutch Holocaust, as well as Jan-Erik Dubbelman, Erik Gerritsma, Dienke G. Hondius, Katinka Kenter, Lewis Kirshner, Diederik Oostdijk, Greet and Luuk Plekker, Esther Shaya, Bettine Siertsema, Frances Walker, Matt and Emma and Lucy Lynch, and Star.

I was fortunate to write part of this book at The Mount (Lenox, MA) thanks to its Edith Wharton Writers-in-Residence Program. I'm always grateful to Jackson Kirshner, Ruth Baum Jackson Hall, Jon A. Jackson, Devin Jackson, Keith Hall, Ben Kirshner, Delight and Paul Dodyk, the Kiryks, the Schulzes, the Kirshners, the Mescherys, the Lewons, Gary Morris, Michelle Theall, Amy Thompson, Hannah Nordhaus, Radha

Marcum, Haven Iverson, Rachel Odell Walker, Rachel Weaver, Teri Carlson, Dianna Chiow, Heather Havrilesky, Stephanie Kelsey, Sarah Sentilles, and Edith and Hester Velmans, as well as Gav Bell and Drea Knufken for their support for this book from the very beginning.

This book would not exist without the vision of the extraordinary women of the Friedrich Agency: benevolent forces of nature Molly Friedrich and Lucy Carson, along with Hannah Brattesani, Heather Carr, and Marin Takikawa. Additional gratitude goes to sage advisers Hilary Zaitz Michael and Nicole Weinroth of William Morris Endeavor.

To my Team Hannie comrades at Dutton, Michael Joseph, and the extended Penguin Random House universe: Jason Booher, Claire Bowron, Lexy Cassola, Patricia Clark, Mary Beth Constant, Alice Dalrymple, Caspian Dennis, Feico Deutekom, Maxine Hitchcock, Kaitlin Kall, Chris Lin, John Parsley, Emily Van Blanken, Amanda Walker, and, most of all, my brilliant, bighearted editors Jillian Taylor and Maya Ziv: I'm so grateful for your belief in Hannie and your astoundingly gracious support. Thank you for being the secret army behind this book.

To Benjamin Whitmer, my adviser on all things artistic and ballistic: thanks for the firebox and shovel.

Finally, a sincere thank-you to Tessa Lachman, Katinka Kenter, and the families of Truus and Freddie Oversteegen and Philine Polak Lachman. I am humbled to bear witness to their extraordinary lives. In that spirit, I'd like to give the indomitable Trijntje Oversteegen, mother of Truus and Freddie, the final word:

Blijf menselijk.

Stay human.

xo Buzzy Jackson

Notes

Epigraphs

vii **"I spent five years sitting next to her in class":** Cornelius Mol interview by Ton Kors, File 248-A2452—Schaft, Hannie, NIOD Institute for War, Holocaust and Genocide Studies, Amsterdam.

vii **"I have a lot of respect for pacifists":** Hannie Schaft, "People I Admire," File 248-A2452—Schaft, Hannie, NIOD Institute for War, Holocaust, and Genocide Studies, Amsterdam, 1935.

vii **"We would be starting a kind of secret army":** Freddie Oversteegen in Noor Spanjer, "This 90-Year-Old Lady Seduced and Killed Nazis as a Teenager," Vice, May 11, 2016, https://www.vice.com/en/article /dp5a8y/teenager-nazi-armed-resistance-netherlands-876.

Chapter 24

248 **"A member of the Dutch Fascist Party":** "Savagery," *Haarlemsche Courant*, June 15, 1944, 2, held at North Holland Archives, the Netherlands, https://nha.courant.nu/issue/HC/1944-06-15/edition/2 /page/2?query=.

Afterword

410 **"I can shoot better than you!":** Ton Kors interviews and notes, File 248-A2452—Schaft, Hannie, NIOD Institute for War, Holocaust and Genocide Studies, Amsterdam.

411   **"We are not like the Nazis":** Hannie Schaft in Truus Menger, *Not Then Not Now Not Ever,* trans. Rita Gircour (Amsterdam: Nederland Tolerant—Max Drukker Foundation, 1998), 178.

412   **"I thought of jumping in the canal":** Philine Lachman quotations throughout from "Oral History Interview with Philine Lachman-Polak," conducted January 22, 1995, accession number 1995.A.0577, RG number RG-50.179.0001, The Jeff and Toby Herr Oral History Archive, USC Shoah Archive, and United States Holocaust Memorial Museum, Washington, DC, https://collections.ushmm.org/search/catalog /irn512184.

416   **"I'm a traumatized person":** Truus Menger-Oversteegen, interview by Natascha van Weezel and Anet Bleich, "Interview Truus Menger," August 7, 2013, *Natascha's Wondere Wereld,* https://nataschavanweezel.blogspot .com/search?q=truus.

416   **"I won't tell you the number of people I shot":** Freddie (Oversteegen) Dekker in Sophie Poldermans, "The Remarkable Story of Three Teenage Girls Who Seduced and Killed Traitors During WW II," *Bust* magazine, Summer 2021, https://bust.com/feminism/198335-teenage-nazi-killers .html.

417   **"I will try to save some of the debris of my old self":** Hannie Schaft in Sophie Poldermans, *Seducing and Killing Nazis: Hannie, Truus and Freddie: Dutch Resistance Heroines of WWII,* trans. Gallagher Translations (SWW Press, 2019), 72.

419   **It was an Allied soldier named Norman Miller:** "'Sixth' Men on the Air," *The Flash* (Anglesey and Caernarvon, Wales), issue 3, December 10, 1945, The Royal Welch Fusiliers.

420   **to avoid "deaths through famine on a considerable scale":** Dwight D. Eisenhower, Walter Bedell Smith, and Arthur Seyss-Inquart quoted in Harry L. Coles and Albert K. Weinberg, "Piecemeal Liberation of the Netherlands Amid Serious Civilian Distress," in *Civil Affairs: Soldiers Become Governors* (Washington, DC: Center of Military History United States Army, 1964), 831–834.

About the Author

Buzzy Jackson is the award-winning author of three books of nonfiction and has a PhD in history from UC Berkeley. A recent fellow at the Edith Wharton Writers-in-Residence, she is also a member of the National Book Critics Circle. She lives in Colorado.